I0525599

A SPORTING AFFAIR

THE CORINTHIANS BOOK ONE

PAULLETT GOLDEN

This is a work of fiction. Names, characters, places, and incidents either are the product of the author's imagination or are used fictitiously, and any resemblance to actual persons, living or dead, business establishments, events or locales is entirely coincidental.

The scanning, uploading, and distributing of this book via the internet or via any other means without the permission of the copyright owner is illegal and punishable by law. Please purchase only authorized copies, and do not participate in or encourage piracy of copyrighted materials. Your support of the author's rights is appreciated.

Copyright © 2025 by Paullett Golden

All rights reserved.

Cover Design by Fiona Jayde Media
Interior Design by The Deliberate Page

Also by Paullett Golden

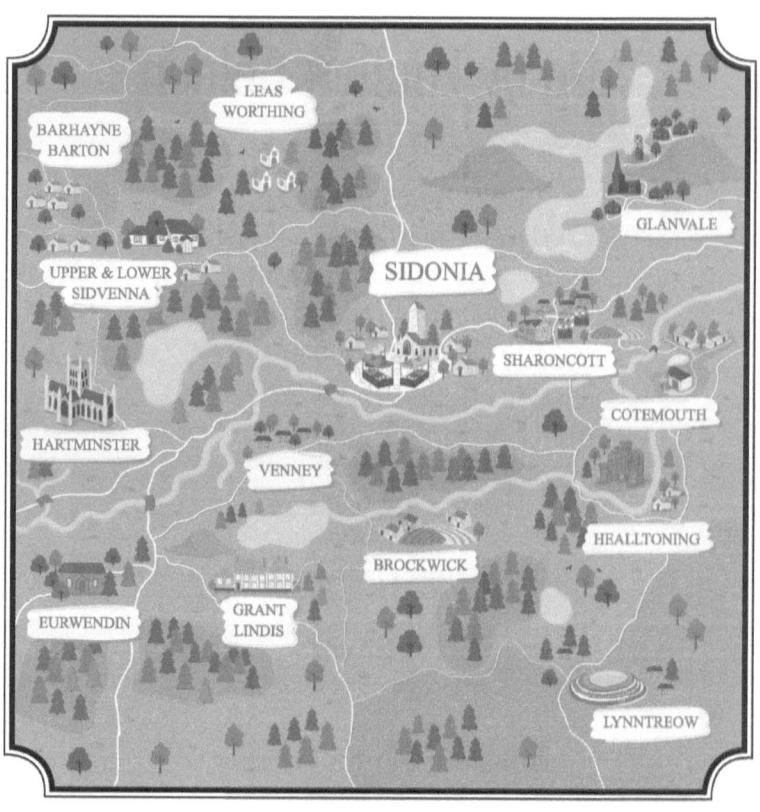

This book is dedicated to all who fight silent battles, determined to overcome the darkest days.

Praise for Golden's Books

"An amazing book by an author that has honed her craft to perfection, this story had me gasping with laughter and moping my eyes as the tears rolled down my face."

— *Goodreads Reader*

"Paullett Golden isn't afraid to weave complex family matters into her historical romance... The author's strong points are her ability to reveal the vulnerability of her characters while showing you how they work through their differences."

— *Readers' Favorites Reviewer*

"There are rare occasions when a plot, characters, dialogue, and backdrop align to make an inspiring book. This is one of those times. This book was a tumultuous, all-encompassing love story. I fell in love with every aspect of this book... The author created a world that I want to visit again and again."

— Jenna of *Reading Rebel Reviews*

"The author Paullett Golden has a gift for creating memorable characters that have depth."

— Paige Lovitt of *Reader Views*

"Character development is wonderful, and it is interesting to follow two young people as they defy the odds to be together. Paullett Golden's novel is compelling and a stellar work that is skillfully crafted."

—Sheri Hoyte of *Reader Views*

"It's thoughtfulness about issues of social class, birth-rights, gender disparities, and city versus country concerns add provocative emotional layers. Strong, complex characterizations, nuanced family dynamics, insightful social commentary, and a vibrant sense of time and place both geographically and emotionally make this a poignant read."

—Cardyn Brooks of *InD'tale Magazine*

"The author adds a few extra ingredients to the romantic formula, with pleasing results. An engaging and unconventional love story."

—*Kirkus Reviews*

"The well-written prose is a delight, the author's voice compelling readers and drawing them into the story with an endearing, captivating plot and genuine, authentic settings. From the uncompromising social conventions of the era to the permissible attitudes and behaviors within each class, it's a first-class journey back in time."

—*Reader Views*

"[The Enchantresses] by Paullett Golden easily ranks as one of the best historical romances I have read in some time and I highly recommend it to fans of romance, history, and the regency era. Fabulous reading!"

— *Sheri Hoyte*

"What I loved about the author was her knowledge of the era! Her descriptions are fresh and rich. Her writing is strong and emotionally driven. An author to follow."

— *It Was Only a Kiss* author Shannon Gilmore

"I enjoy the way Golden smartly sprinkles wit and satire throughout her story to highlight the absurdity of the British comedy of manners."

— *Goodreads Reader*

"With complex characters and a backstory with amazing depth, the story … is fantastic from start to finish."

— *Rebirth* author Ravin Tija Maurice

"Paullett Golden specializes in creating charmingly flawed characters and she did not disappoint in this latest enchantress novel."

— *Dream Come Review*

"I thoroughly enjoyed meeting and getting to know all of the characters. Each character was fully developed, robust and very relatable."

— *Flippin' Pages Book Reviews*

"This is one of the best books I've read EVER! It made me smile, it made me laugh, it made me angry and then it made me very happy."

— *FH Denny Reviews*

"One of the best historical romances I have ever read. Everything about this book is empowering and heart touching."

— *SR.EE Vine Voice*

Prologue

June 1813
Devonshire

The open window invited entry, a siren-song for his intentions. Moonlight cast a midnight glow on the curtains hanging heavy in the still air. Not so much as a candle shone, the house dark, the residents abed.

With the back of his hand, Rafe wiped a bead of sweat from his brow.

Perfect. A grin tugged at the corners of his lips. He held the element of surprise. To see her expression would be worth the effort.

Inhaling the scent of evening's dew, he drew in courage to enact his plan.

Eyes darting from the window casement to the adjacent garden wall and back, he shrugged off his top three layers: caped greatcoat, frockcoat, then waistcoat. Tossing each onto the wall's capstone was the work of a moment, but he paused five breaths longer to prepare for the climb.

Rafe gained purchase of the rough-hewn stone, one boot tip nestled in a toehold, fingertips perched over jagged fissures. Spying his next quarry, he reached up to clasp a jutting stone edge, then shimmied his boot to propel himself closer to his goal.

After heaving a grunt and rubbing his forehead against his shirtsleeve, he renewed his grin at the grand scheme. This surprise would have tongues wagging for at least a week. His best scheme yet.

Grasping the smooth stone at the top of the wall, he pulled himself up to meet his awaiting coats. Secure on the wall cap, Rafe beheld his destination— the window. Whoever had thought to build a garden wall within reach of the casement window had forever won Rafe's favor; mischief made easy.

He took advantage of the silent night to listen for hints of life beyond the window. All remained still.

With an impatient swipe to his boots, he knocked away dust, grabbed his coats, then stood. In five strides atop the wall, he reached the open window. One article at a time, he flung his coats over the windowsill, hearing the satisfying *swish* of them landing on the rug within. Clasping the casement frame with both hands, he used two footholds on the house's stone façade to hoist himself up and hook a leg over the sill.

Almost there. Almost inside.

Wearing little more than buckskins, boots, shirt, and a victorious smile, he angled into the bedchamber and arched his foot, toes reaching for the familiar canework seat of the settee that would grant him smooth and silent entry.

He arched. He stretched. He tapped.

Where was it…

As it dawned that there was no settee beneath the window, Rafe slipped over the sill.

With a strangled cry, he crashed into the room with a rolling tumble. Knocking into a washstand with the force of his weight, he grunted, his shoulder smarting at the contact. To his dismay, a water pitcher toppled off the stand. He shrieked as it narrowly missed him on its collision course to the floor, dousing the side of the four-poster bed along the way.

So much for the element of surprise. Rafe groaned.

To stand, he clasped the saber leg of a desk, which turned out not to be a desk. Rafe squeezed his eyes closed as whatever he had grabbed crashed against the wall with an unholy *crack*.

Lunging to his feet, he had exactly five seconds to consider the stomp of footsteps along the corridor outside the bedchamber before a scream rent the air.

His heart palpitating, palms perspiring, and body coiling, he jerked his attention to the bed. A sliver of moonlight slanted across the figure of a young woman. Bedlinen clutched to her chest, she stared back at him.

Ignoring the pounding against the bedchamber door, he stuttered, "Wh-who the devil are you?"

Chapter 1

H is voice, assured and confident, thundered in the cramped quarters. "May it please your honor, I appear for the Crown. My learned friend appears for the defendant." A careless hand swept the air from beneath the voluminous sleeve of his banyan. "The Crown will prove beyond any reasonable doubt the defendant in the dock is guilty." With a glance at his notes, he prepared for the examination in chief of the first witness for the prosecution.

The case was straight-forward. Why had he not challenged himself, chosen a case that required more skill, especially during re-examination? Sifting through his papers, he tossed aside that case and grabbed another. Yes, this would do.

Clearing his throat, he said, "Mr. Pendergast, during your testimony, you told the court you were walking along High Street, your destination Mr. Waters' house. Is this correct?" He paused to savor his wine. "For clarification, this was before you witnessed the crime, correct?" Another sip. "I request exhibit three be brought forward."

He eyed his glass. Empty.

Cursing under his breath, he traded his papers for the bottle. Also empty. He gave it a wistful swish. Definitely empty. With a shake of his head to dispel drowsiness, he turned in search of another bottle. The cabinet held only disappointment. Grumbling, he glanced down. If he were to retrieve a bottle from downstairs, he would need to exchange his slippers for shoes. His fingers reached up to comb through his hair, catching the night cap instead. Ah, happy tidings he had not ventured out of his apartments in his cap. He would never have heard the end of it.

Blinking, he eyed the mantel clock. The numbers blurred.

Whatever the time, Mr. Rafe Fitz-Stephens decided it was too late for another bottle, and he was too beyond his faculties to practice another case. Tomorrow would arrive far earlier than he wanted, and so long a journey would require ample sleep. Narrowing his gaze at the stack of notes on his desk, he sighed. There would be little time to study once he reached home. His family would demand his attention. The village competition would devour more than a week of his stay. His friends needed attending to, as well. No time for studies.

What if he received his Call to the Bar while he was away?

Reconsidering, he shuffled the papers into a tidy enough stack. He might find a minute or two to study if he applied himself. Best bring these along. There were at least three cases he had hoped to question his father about, although his father only ever presided over civil cases, never criminal. Nevertheless, he would value his father's insight from a magistrate's perspective.

Tucking the material in his bag, he trundled to his bed.

In a few days, he would be enjoying the comfort of his old bed. The quarters at Gray's Inn of the Inns of Court were not uncomfortable but…. Shrugging off his banyan, he tipped onto the lumpy bedding. What he would not give for a feathered mattress.

Rafe had not *lied* to his family. Not exactly. Not unless one considered an omission of a change of plans a lie. He could make a case for it in court, if he were prosecuting, but then, he could also make a convincing defense for himself if needed.

Shifting in his saddle after several days on the road, Rafe formulated his defense. "I call the defendant, Rafe Fitz-Stephens, to the stand." His voice rose above the growling of his stomach.

There was a tavern some short distance ahead. His horse was as eager as he for food and rest. He patted Alfgar's neck, receiving a snort for the effort.

His parents had anticipated his arrival for a month. Rafe had never missed the annual Fracas Frolic, a week-long racing competition between his village of Grant Lindis against the nearby village of Eurwendin. But without a nod from the barristers he dined with at Gray's Inn in London, he did not dare leave. His summons was imminent, and he worried an untimely holiday would sabotage his progress. At length, he had written to his parents with his apologies. This year, he had explained to them, he would not be returning home for the competition.

But then, everything changed. He *did* receive a nod. Although he had grabbed paper and quill, ready to share the news with his family, he thought this too good an opportunity — he could surprise them with his arrival. It did not leave much time to prepare for the competition, but surprising his family would be worth the trip. His mother's expression, alone, would be worth it.

After a week on the road, and the passing of familiar landscape as he journeyed from London to Devonshire, he would soon appear on their doorstep, the learned son returned. Unencumbered by trunks, he carried only what his saddlebags could hold, enough for the requisite overnight stops along the way. All he needed awaited him in his old abode. He hoped he had not outgrown his waistcoats — the most important element of his barrister training, after all, was dining. So many dinners. And among the best he had ever tasted, although he would only confess that to the family cook under duress, perhaps not even then.

His stomach grumbled again.

On second thought, why stop at the tavern?

He was ahead in time, by all accounts, and at this rate, even with a stop at the tavern, he would arrive home far too early to be assured anyone would be there. His timing should be later, more towards dusk, when he knew with certainty his parents and brothers would all be home, likely gathered around the card table.

If he continued past the tavern without stopping, he could reach Axminster in a couple of hours, and then, instead, take his rest at Rupert Headley's home in Glanvale. There, he could enjoy a good meal and conversation, never a more perfect way to pass the time.

As though Rafe had spoken his thoughts aloud, his horse snorted in protest.

"Am I to understand, Alfie," he asked his horse, "you would prefer we stop at the tavern *and* in Glanvale? I'm uncertain we have time for both." After a nicker in response, Rafe said, "You're correct, I suppose. We *should* catch them at supper, or better still, tea after supper. They'll be in the drawing room, then, the perfect place for a surprise appearance by yours truly. Right. We'll make both stops. A bite at the tavern, and then on to Headley's!"

Alfgar had the right of it, as horses usually did. There was ample time. With a house full of boys, save for Rafe's mother, evenings extended well into the night. Today would be no exception. Yes, there was ample time for both. In case he was mistaken, he picked up the pace to reach the tavern sooner.

Chapter 2

Rafe angled his beaver hat to reduce the glare of the setting sun. The stopover at the tavern had taken longer than anticipated, as had the remaining jaunt into Devonshire and through Axminster. Still time for an unexpected visit to Mr. Rupert Headley's humble country manor, he wagered. One welcome hour or two but no more than three. Best to keep to two hours, for he had a generous hour ride from Headley's to home.

He cringed at that remaining hour. The need to dismount and stretch was imperative. The bumping and jostling had done him in. His legs were sore. His back was sore. His derriere was sore. Despite the meal at the tavern, his stomach growled again. Poor Alfgar was sweating beneath the saddle more than Rafe would like, and for that matter, Rafe himself was far sweatier than he would like, certainly if he wanted his surprise arrival with family to be a welcome one.

He leaned forward and sniffed. "Is that you, Alfie, or me?"

After the harshest winter of Rafe's memory, one that extended into May, no less, the weather had no right to turn this balmy.

Calling on Headley would be just the thing. He could wash, change, and eat, while Alfgar received much the same treatment, and then they could both arrive home fresh as daisies. On his best dressed days, he would not consider himself a dandy, but his acquaintances would, even on his worst dressed days, which said a great deal about his discomfort with road grime.

Squinting against the sun, he spied ahead the rising terrain of the hill that marked the threshold of the Hartminster deanery. Just over the crest, he would arrive at Glanvale, a small but wealthy village nestled in the valley within Devonshire's natural landscape.

The scenery was one to admire with lush meadows and bubbling brooks. Rafe was too hot and tired to admire anything except the proximity of his destination. Handling the reins with one hand, he retrieved his handkerchief from his coat pocket and dabbed his forehead. How had it not rained since he left London? A blessing while riding, but must it follow that without rain, the heat should be oppressive? He was certain this time last year he was still wearing an extra layer for warmth, summer month or not.

At the first bridge, he veered right to cross over the river. The path widened into a well-kept drive. Two miles west, and in the shadow of twin hills, Headley's family home welcomed Rafe. Only a modest hall, but it was a sight to behold for this weary traveler.

Alfgar champed at his bit, and Rafe's lips curved into a broad smile as he heard the pack of dogs herald his approach. No baying hounds sounded off behind those great double doors. Oh no. The barks ranged from howls to yips, a pack representative of every misfit and stray Headley's mother could adopt, save for the wolfhound belonging to Headley himself, and the pug belonging to Headley's younger sister, Miss Diana.

Before he was past the gatehouse, the front door opened, releasing the little demons. Alfgar snorted his displeasure.

"So distracted by the beasties," Rafe said to his horse, "I wager you've not noticed the grooms heading our way, eager to pamper you. You'll be so fussed over, you'll not want to leave. Well, I don't fancy walking home, Alfie, so don't become too comfortable."

Before the last word left Rafe's lips, Rupert Headley stepped into the courtyard, commanding the dogs to heel, or trying to.

Careful of the smaller dogs, Rafe drew Alfgar to a stop and dismounted. He would need to retrieve a few items from his saddlebags before they took the horse around to the stables, but first things first.

With hand outstretched and smile wide, he made for his old friend. "How did you know it was me?"

Headley clasped Rafe's hand. "Diana saw you from the parlor window." He stepped back to take in his guest's state. "You look like a glorified Londoner, Fitz-Stephens. You smell like one, too."

"I resemble that — er — resent that remark, Headley."

"What the devil are you doing on my doorstep unannounced?"

Rafe doffed his hat to the relief of his flattened hair. "Change of plans. Here for the Fracas Frolic after all. With any luck, I'll receive the Call while on holiday. Couldn't resist seeing your ugly mug before heading home."

"Staying for the evening, then?" Headley patted his leg for the dogs to follow as he waved Rafe inside.

"Not this evening, no. A drink, a washbasin... a bite to eat wouldn't be declined, if I could beg a few scraps. I only have an hour, two at most. I want the timing to be perfect to surprise the family."

As they stepped into the entry hall, Rafe pivoted, remembering his gear in the saddlebags.

"Leave it," Headley said, anticipating Rafe's intentions. "They'll bring the bags to your suite. Need a valet?" Before Rafe could respond, Headley added, "I would give my left arm to see your mother's expression when you arrive on the doorstep. Game for a wager rather she swoons with happiness or beats you over the head with her fan for not telling her?"

They lingered in the entry only briefly, the dogs making conversation difficult, their whines and barks echoing. While he was still unwashed, Rafe took the opportunity to greet each one he had known for years, along with a few new ones he had not yet met. After the butler nodded to Headley, Rafe was shown to his usual guest suite to make himself more presentable.

A light breeze wafted through the billiard room by way of the open windows. With the sun having set, the air had cooled considerably, almost to the point of carrying a chill. Rafe made no complaints. He looked into his glass and gave the amber liquid a swirl.

"I'm surprised," Mr. Rupert Headley was saying, "you didn't plan the journey better, at least early enough to stop in Sidonia for shopping. You'll be passing through town regardless."

Rafe waved off the observation. "I did not wish to arrive home to find the family paying calls. Evening is best. They'll be around the table with cards or at billiards. Besides, they would wonder what I was up to if I arrived laden with gifts. Not usually my style."

He shared a chuckle with his friend, who was lounging in a leather chair opposite, ankles crossed, cup balanced on his waistcoat. Headley was less imposing when seated. Although a gentle giant, he was a full head taller than Rafe and a shoulder wider, clearly muddled breeding and hardly an English gentleman at that stature, or so Rafe had teased throughout their formative years when Headley began to outgrow his friends.

Rafe closed his eyes. The hour ride loomed. Had he not been so determined, he would beg a room for the night. Even his bones ached. He had also missed dinner, having to settle for a light supper in the billiard room.

In the distance, a voice buzzed. Rafe swatted the air.

"It'll be a winning wager," the voice said, "if I accept."

Finding his family playing cards? Was that the wager? "*Ita vero*," Rafe affirmed in Latin with a soft snore.

Something kicked his foot none too gently. Jerking awake, Rafe blinked at Headley's raised eyebrows. Had Rafe drifted? Intolerably rude of him. He patted his cheek, then tossed back a burning gulp of his drink before setting it on the end table.

Headley asked, his tone languid, "Is my racing that aristocratic tosspot in Healltoning not entertaining enough for you?"

"A duel would have made a better story."

With a scoff, Headley sat up to top off their drinks. "Last one for you, mate. Instead of invigorating you, it's putting you to sleep. You will need your wits about you for the ride. Would you like me to send a groom to light the way?"

Rafe shook his head. "Almost a full moon. Ample light. I wouldn't turn down a lantern, but no need for company." Retrieving his refilled glass, he inhaled the sharp aroma before taking a drink. "More pressing, what can I do to convince you to compete with me against Eurwendin? And no excuses about this not being your battle since you don't live in Grant Lindis. Anything to wipe the smug smile from their faces after winning last year. Come now. Bribery? A challenge? Flattery? What'll it take?"

"Agree to join me for the day when I call on Selwyn Relish."

"Selwyn!" Rafe brightened. "I had hoped to call on him. Hardly a favor for a favor when I'm eager to see the new members of the Vitruvian Society. Met any since I've been in London?"

"I've not. Remiss of me. I haven't the excuse of distance, either."

"Been too wrapped up in curricle racing to engage in *real* sport? I see I can't leave you unguarded for too long. Who is the tosspot now?"

Headley smirked. "You'll rescind that remark if I win the competition for your village."

"It's *team* racing, Headley. There are no champions."

"If that were true, you wouldn't have invited me."

Rafe raised his glass. The retort on the tip of his tongue turned into a curse when he glimpsed the table clock. "By Jupiter! How have we whiled away the hours? If I'm not off in the next half hour, they'll have retired before I arrive, and that would *not* be a welcome surprise. Some host, you are. How did you allow me to stay so long? This is sabotage!"

Headley set aside his cup and rose from the chair. "Unintentional, I assure you. The room for the evening is on offer. You could leave at dawn."

"And surprise them in the morning room? Not likely. Father enjoys an early morning ride, rarely breaking his fast with the family. Mother prefers a long morning toilette in her dressing room. And my brothers will sleep until noon — unquestionably. They'll be gaming into the wee hours, so my timing is perfect this evening, but I dare not dally."

Arms crossed, foot tapping, Headley questioned, "Then why are you still seated? I'll ring for your horse to be brought around."

Chapter 3

After traveling south past Glanvale, he hesitated at the crossroads in Sharoncott. Usually, he would take the south route, then loop around to the west, but given the late hour and that he was, moonlight and lantern aside, traveling in the dark of night, he felt the safest choice would be west through Sidonia to stay on the turnpike as long as possible. It meant paying tolls and extending the ride by several miles. Not ideal.

Rafe eyed the narrow, desolate path leading south. No tolls. Fewer miles. But…

Caution won. He guided Alfgar west towards the market town.

The road was well maintained, wide, and typically rife with traffic, but he doubted he would see many, if any, travelers this late at night. At one time, Hartminster had been the heart of the deanery with its impressive abbey, wherein both the dean and his lay chair resided and worked, regular visits from the deacon, and a thriving market. When the market moved to Sidonia, the town doubled in size within a year. Now, Sidonia was the heart of the deanery, even if the dean remained in Hartminster.

At this time of night, it would not be a thriving town. Likely, the only establishments open would be the coaching inns. He would not be stopping at any, not unless a strong coffee was in order by the time he reached the edge of town. Renewed by the fresh air and determination to reach home in good time, he did not suspect he would need coffee.

Having the road to himself, he was tempted to hum, sing, or carry on a lively one-sided conversation with Alfgar. He did none of these. Instead, he kept his wits about him. His ears listened for unnatural sounds. His eyes combed the road and surrounding land for signs of anything untoward, be they wild animals, highwaymen, poachers, or otherwise. The closer he came to town, the more uneasy his supper sat. Call it what one willed, uneasiness replaced joviality. The plan to surprise his family had sounded grand until he realized the reality of riding under the cloak of darkness. Oh, sure, the moonlight was bright enough. He had no trouble seeing the path. And yet there was a queerness about being so exposed at night. He felt vulnerable.

There was no fear or worry he could not hold his own. Should he come across a bandit lying in wait, Rafe would be the one to ride away unscathed. He was confident in that regard. But he would rather avoid confrontation. The whole of being set on by brigands made him downright queasy. After all, he had donned his smartest riding attire in anticipation of arriving home, complete with perfumed linen. A gentleman did not scuffle in fashionable riding raiment.

Much to his relief, the outskirts of Sidonia surrounded him before he realized he had traveled so far.

From earth to cobblestones, the road narrowed. Alfgar's gait slowed to a friendly *clip-clop* across the stones. All was quiet, so different from the London that never slept.

They hoofed their way straight down the main without stopping. As cobblestone turned back to earth, mud replaced the hard-packed road they had been traveling. So, this was where all the rain had been that Rafe had bemoaned only hours prior. Thankfully, it was not currently raining. The rutted road sloshed and slurped beneath Alfgar's hooves. Rafe did his poor best to avoid the deepest puddles.

They crossed over the first stone bridge without incident. The farther they wended their way from town, the higher Rafe's spirits, his attention turning more towards the surprise to come than worries of bandits. Should he sneak around to a servant's entrance and pop into the drawing room from one of the jib doors? Mother's fan would go flying from her shock. If they were in the games room, that would spoil his plan. Best enter the front door and have the butler discreetly point the way. But then, how to get the butler's attention at the front door without knocking and alerting them all? Hmm. If he walked in without knocking, the exclamations from any nearby footmen would give away the game.

As he worked through another possible scenario, Alfgar shimmied nervously, hesitated, then continued forward.

Rafe's attention focused. His eyes darted. His ears strained.

Alfgar bobbed his head and blew angrily from his nostrils.

Rafe moved the reins to one hand, his free hand reaching beneath the folds of his overcoat, readying for battle.

As they approached the next bridge, Alfgar's *clip-clop* became a *clip-clump*, and with another hesitation and shy, the horse showed every sign of favoring one of his front legs.

Ah.

Exhaling his guard, Rafe pulled Alfie to a stop and dismounted. He took a moment to scratch Alfie beneath the chin, mostly an excuse to slow his own pounding heart. Tugging free the lantern, he moved to the troubled leg. A thorough perusal showed no injury or harm. He persuaded Alfie to lift the leg and show his hoof.

"Tell me you've not been walking shoeless for long."

Alfie admitted nothing.

Rafe looked back from whence they came. Somewhere, Alfgar had thrown a shoe. There were a few options, none of them ideal. Regardless, he would need to retrieve the shoe. For all he knew, it could be facing up with nails to the sky, waiting for some poor beggar or his horse to step on it. Safety aside, Rafe needed to retrieve it to see if there was a chance of reshoeing here and now, however temporary a fix it would be.

Guiding Alfie to turn around, they retraced their steps. Rafe held the lantern aloft, scouring the slush for signs of a horseshoe or nails. They ambled. They trudged. Alfie expressed his displeasure. Rafe slipped and muddied his freshly polished boots.

Nearly halfway to the first bridge, Rafe spied the offending shoe. He tugged it one way. The mud tugged it another. With a firm jerk, Rafe freed it from the sludge. He turned it over in his riding gloves. No noticeable damage or bend. It could be reshod for the ride home.

However good the plan, it only took leading Alfgar to the flattest and least muddy terrain for Rafe to realize the pebble in the works. The horse's sole had been bruised from loose rocks.

"Of all the pranks, Alfie, you chose this one." Rafe shook his head but stroked his horse's neck. There was no point in them both being glum.

Had the sole not been bruised, shoe or not, Rafe could have ridden Alfgar home. Alas, Rafe refused to exacerbate the bruising. He reattached the lantern and dug through his saddlebags for a strip of linen.

"If I were any other man, you would need to prove your resilience and take us both home, but we know I'm your humble servant. Now, lift your leg, Your Grace."

Before wrapping the hoof to protect the bruised sole from further damage, he gave everything a thorough feel to check for jagged edges or stuck nails. Riding gloves or not, Rafe bemoaned the state of his best riding suit. All his washing and the splash of perfume were for nought. He supposed the situation could be worse: the band of thieves he had fretted over could have leapt out from beneath the bridge.

Hoof wrapped, saddlebags secured, Rafe took the reins in hand and began the ginger walk home alongside his horse.

The walk to Grant Lindis would not have been too terrible if it had been Rafe alone. He could have quickened his pace for better time and made the most of the evening march, in all likelihood cutting cross-country rather than following the main road, but he had Alfgar to consider, as well as his gear, so they set a slow but steady pace. There was no way to know the hour. If he hazarded a guess, he would say the journey took two hours rather than one, but he could not say for certain.

As he reached Grant Lindis, the familiar sign above the blacksmith's shop greeted him. He slowed, then stopped in front of the shop door.

It was not that much further to Devington Priory. Once home, he could settle Alfgar into the stables for the evening. Alfgar disagreed. His limp had worsened over the past few miles. However near they were, there was still mileage between the village center and home, mileage he would rather not have his horse endure if limping. Hindsight had Rafe wondering if he should have backtracked into town rather than continuing forward, but he did not know the farriers in Sidonia and would prefer not to test them during a time of need. He swallowed his *should have* thoughts.

Rafe gazed at the darkened windows. He hated to wake them. Oh, he hated to do it. Chewing on the inside of his cheek, he waffled, indecisive.

His companion snorted.

Rafe knocked firmly on the door. He waited several minutes before trying again. It took three tries before the door swung open.

Candle in hand, nightcap adorned, the blacksmith's wife scowled at the intruder. Rafe blanched under her scrutiny.

Recognition dawned in her sleep-crusted eyes. The frown curved into a smile. "Young Master Fitz-Stephens! Here was I thinking you were off to be a barrister, only to be at my doorstep gone on mid-night. Mischievous as ever."

He chuckled, relieved she had not beat him over the head with a pot. "Only a brief return, here for the Fracas Frolic, then back to London."

"Ooh, we'll win with you here." She squinted at him, then took in his horse's hoof wrappings. "You didn't wake me about the races."

"'Fraid not, Mrs. Smith. Alfgar threw a shoe just outside Sidonia. We've walked the distance, and I'm not comfortable walking him the rest of the way home. He's limping fiercely. Think Mr. Smith could see to him? You know he's the only farrier I trust."

Unmoved by flattery, she spluttered, "*Now*?"

"'Pon my soul, no, Mrs. Smith. I'm already guilty as a gypsy for waking you."

Relief renewed her smile. "Bring him 'round."

Rafe spent the next half hour or longer helping settle Alfgar for the night, accepting a kindly offered drink, and making quick use of a washbasin before resuming his journey to Devington Priory.

Rafe held little hope his family remained awake, not at this hour, whatever hour that happened to be. Eager for the trip to be at an end, he jogged the remaining distance, his mind on a good night's sleep more than on the element of surprise.

Blast. He had left the saddlebags in the stall. His jog slowed, and he considered turning back. No, no, there was nothing in the bags he did not have at the house in his dressing room. Thinking clearly was proving more difficult by the minute. He had been awake since well before dawn, eager to be on the road and not waste daylight, especially given the frequency of stops for Alfgar to rest and eat. The evening, as with every evening since he had left London, had offered little in the way of sleep. Even with the most respectable inns, there was not much to be said about quality accommodations.

As he crossed onto the drive, he considered his choices of entry. If the front door were unlocked, he could sneak inside and up to his room unseen, assuming the household was, indeed, abed. If the door was locked, he could try any of the servant entrances. If they, too, were locked, which he doubted, he could try the windows. As warm as the evening, he could not imagine the windows being closed. Luck may be on his side. He did not think he could swing a morning surprise for all the reasons he had given Headley, but at the least he could pop in during his mother's morning toilette. It was mostly she who he hoped to shock. In all likelihood, she would send her tray of chocolate and toast flying as she shrieked with dramatic flair.

He was grinning by the time the Gothic-screened forecourt came into view. The stone archways emulated cloisters, one of the few surviving structures of the dismantled monastery. The framework of the west wing was all that remained of the monastery, the rest of the house a combination of architectural styles, a new addition with each century. The east wing had been built by his grandfather. His grin broadened into a smile to spy his bedroom window, open in hopes of a breeze. Oh, how he longed to prop his feet up, lay his head down, and slip into a dreamless sleep.

From the main approach, he could see the drawing room windows, as well as the main apartments. He could not see the games room. Of the windows he could set eyes on, not one hinted at a candle flicker. The house was as dark as the night around him. *Ita vero,* he had lost the element of surprise.

Tomorrow morning, he reassured himself. He could at least surprise his mother, and that was what mattered most.

His feet led him to the front door. Quiet as a thief, he tugged the iron handle. It made a soft *thunk* but resisted. Locked. If he knocked, he would wake more than the butler. He stepped back to survey the ground floor windows.

Ah! So giddy, he had to repress the impulse to laugh aloud. His gaze turned towards the jutting stones of the garden wall beneath his bedchamber window. A thorough wash and a jolly night's sleep were within reach. The years of collegiate training and professionalism stepped aside at the return of his playful boyhood. How many times in his youth had he climbed that wall? Rafe chafed his hands together, eager to grasp the sturdy stone.

Removing his layers to make climbing easier and protect the fabrics, he began the ascent. Next time he saw Headley, he would regale him with this bit of foolhardiness. Was he the only one of their old club to relive youthful mischief? Surely not.

Wall mounted, Rafe snatched his coats, dusted his boots, which were lamentably caked in more mud than dust, and walked to the open window. To his knowledge, his mother did not know he had *ever* made fond use of the garden wall for entry or departure. No need to change that. He doubted she would ask how he sneaked inside unseen. With a toss of his garments over the windowsill, he swung himself up and over to straddle the frame.

And then, everything that could go wrong went wrong.

The settee he always used as a stepping stool was not where it should have been. The washstand waged an assault on his person. The desk was not a desk. And the scream ringing in his ears did not belong in his bedchamber, much less his bed.

He tumbled into the room, grace personified, and rose to the peculiar awareness that reality was beyond his grasp.

In *his* house, in *his* bedchamber, and in *his* bed, sat a young lady clutching the bedlinen in fright, her mouth agape, and her hair in papillote curlers.

Caught between a chortle and a scream to match hers, he managed to sputter, "Wh-who the devil are you?"

Rather than answer, she whipped her attention to the door as it swung open. A gentleman in his dressing gown and cap stepped in, empty candlestick holder held as a weapon. Piling behind him, Rafe could see a woman, a young girl, and at least two servants, one of which had a lit candle.

Baffled, bristling, and bemused, he looked from the young lady in his bed to the strangers at the door. Had he not been certain the panic in his breast was real, he would wonder if he had fallen asleep at Headley's and dreamt the past several hours, his dream now reaching its pinnacle. If he could but awaken.

Everyone spoke at once. Simultaneous voices overlapped, the older gentleman with the candlestick blustering in anger, the woman behind him yipping like Miss Diana's pug, and the lady with her papillote curlers hugging Rafe's bedlinen screeching about being burgled.

This was an easy explanation on his part. He was climbing into *his* bedchamber. What was their excuse? He looked down at his state of undress. His coats lay in a heap beneath the window. With only boots, breeches, and shirtsleeves, he was as undressed as they were in their gowns and caps.

Snap to, old boy. You can't stand here with your head up your arse.

Raising staying hands for attention, he said with the firm, clear voice of authority, never mind the circumstances, "I beg a moment of silence."

The din quieted, all eyes on him.

"We have caught each other at a disadvantage. Let us remain calm and approach this rationally, one voice at a time." He looked at the gentleman in the doorway. "Pray, may I be the first to enquire, *who are you*?"

The overlapping voices rose in shock and fury again before the man could answer. Rafe maintained composure and locked eyes with the candlestick-caper.

Above the raucous noise, the man pointed the silver stick at Rafe, then at his daughter, then back at Rafe, eyeing the unexpected guest's state of undress, and screeched with umbrage, "A lover's tryst! An assignation with my daughter! Thought you could sneak out unnoticed, eh?"

A protest trumpeted from the bed occupant. No one paid her any heed, accusatory attention directed at Rafe only. Rafe took an unsteady step backwards.

The woman standing behind the father, whom Rafe presumed was the young lady's mother, was sobbing into the shoulder of one of the servants, muttering some nonsense about ruination.

Rafe held up his hands again. "Let us, please, clear the confusion rather than venture dark and untrodden paths. Introductions would — "

"I demand satisfaction!" shouted the man.

A hand over his heart, as though struck by a poisoned arrow, Rafe said, "I do beg your pardon, sir. If this were, as you say, a lover's tryst, I should hope my ladybird would do me the courtesy of not wearing her hair in curlers. Now, let us be sensible and introduce ourselves, each party explaining — "

"Lothario! Rogue! Philanderer! I demand satisfaction!"

Chapter 4

A herd of elephants trampled down the stairs, or so it sounded to Rafe, startling him awake the next morning — or rather, a few hours later. Guffaws followed the stomps on the steps, the clamor softening as the culprits descended to the first floor, then further down to the ground floor. Who knew all it took to rouse his brothers before noon was a scandal involving Rafe?

He covered his head with a pillow and groaned.

Returning to sleep would only delay the inevitable. With a slow, reluctant sweep of his hand, he tossed back the bedding and swung his legs over the edge. He flexed his feet, the soles tender from the evening's walk. London was softening him. For years, he had prized himself on his athleticism, and now a short jaunt across the deanery had left him sore. His thoughts briefly turned to Alfgar and how *his* sole must feel this morning. Mr. Smith would have him right as rain in no time.

Rafe took care dressing, being fastidious. His waistcoats still fit — thank heavens for small mercies. Forest green was the choice for the day. Forest green and gold. The first four cravats were tried and tossed, the fifth folding just right. He splashed a dash of perfume about his person. Admiring the reflection, one corner of his lips curled into a smirk. Before leaving, he puckered his lips to blow the flirty devil in the mirror a kiss — irresistibly dashing, if he did say so himself.

With the last, he followed in his brothers' wake to meet his family in the parlor. No morning room surprise over the breakfast table. Unlike the Priory, the dower house, where his grandmother resided, did not have a morning room.

When he opened the parlor door, all eyes turned his direction, and all conversation halted. His father stood by the empty fireplace. His grandmother lounged in her chaise. Two of his three brothers were present, standing near the harpsichord as though to talk privately, never mind the room was far too small for unheard conversation. His mother had been pacing in front of the windows.

As soon as he closed the door behind him, conversation resumed, everyone arguing about "the incident" but no one listening to anyone except themselves. Rafe accepted the fauteuil chair across from his grandmother, Mrs. Edwina Fitz-Stephens.

Speaking over the hubbub, Rafe said, "I'm for the Priory. Don't believe I could eat until I've spoken with Mr. Slade. I propose we meet here afterwards."

His mother, Mrs. Marion Fitz-Stephens, flicked her fan closed with a *snap*. "That is most certainly not what will be done. *You* will eat a hearty breakfast while we rejoice in your return from London, which is precisely what we would have done when you arrived last evening had the situation been otherwise." She glared at her husband.

As soon as his father began to respond, Rafe's mother interrupted, her eyes trained on Mr. Anthony

Fitz-Stephens, but her words addressed Rafe. "Your *father* will go to the house and handle Mr. Slade. This is *his* fault, and he will make amends."

Rafe rose. "Rather than rehash the drama my arrival has caused both families, let us handle this rationally. *I* have caused the upset. *I* have been invited to discuss the matter with Mr. Slade."

His father shook his head. "I agree with your mother. I should be the one going to the house. Roland has been a good friend, and it's my responsibility to apologize for my son's mistake."

"His *mistake*?" Mother shrieked, flicking her fan open with a *click* and waving it so rapidly her curls swayed. "Rafe is above reproach. He is a *barrister*, a professional, a grown man, which is more than I—"

Rafe cleared his throat. "I've not yet been called to—"

"It was *your* grand plan," his mother continued, "to let the house to that, that, *those people* and relegate us to the dower house. There is nothing for which any of us should apologize. Go to the house and show Mr. Slade how imposing a squire can be when angered. *He* is the one who should apologize to our son."

His grandmother muttered to Rafe, "Your grandfather, God rest his soul, never would have allowed anyone except Fitz-Stephenses to live in the house. A disgrace to allow strangers to serve as master of one's own domain."

His father raised his voice to talk over Rafe's mother, while his grandmother began squabbling more loudly, wanting her displeasure known, and so Rafe inched towards the door. He cast an apologetic glance at his brothers, then slipped out of the parlor before anyone noticed his departure. Once outside, he took a deep breath. His shoulders shook with laughter. A stranger may think the family at odds. Not so. He suspected they were enjoying themselves. A day in the life of the Fitz-Stephens family, he mused. It was good to be home. Or specifically, in the bosom of his family, if not exactly *home*.

And that was the bone of contention.

He left the dower house to walk across estate grounds to the main house, not wanting to be late for his appointment with Mr. Slade. Nothing had been settled after "the incident," only the exchange of introductions which Rafe had requested *ad nauseum* until his wish was granted, at which time he was directed to the dower house with the insistence he return that morning to discuss his being found in a state of undress in Mr. Slade's eldest daughter's bedchamber.

Following "the incident," and in the mood for answers, not surprises, Rafe had knocked soundly at the dower house door. Ironically, he had not disturbed anyone, as all in the family, save Gran, had been in the drawing room gathered around the gaming table despite the late hour. It would have been a laughable moment had Rafe been in a laughable mood.

The situation was simple.

To fund his eldest brother Giles's latest expedition to Lord-knew-where, his father had let the house for the year. Understanding that Rafe would *not* be returning that year for the Fracas Frolic, they did not bother to inform him of the situation, it being a point of contention between Father and... everyone.

To maintain the trend of omitting information, Rafe thought it best not to mention he had climbed through the bedroom window, allowing them to believe of their own free will that he had marched through the front door, up the stairs, and through his bedchamber door like a civilized, mature man of four and twenty. He likewise omitted Mr. Slade's *demand for satisfaction*.

It was the last that plagued Rafe during his walk to the house. Did Mr. Slade truly intend to challenge him to a duel? Surely not. Had the gentleman been serious, he would have arranged his second to meet Rafe's second, not request Rafe come in person. Rafe found his breathing more shallow than usual, nonetheless. A simple misunderstanding. No need for bloodshed.

At least his brothers had found levity in the situation. Noel and Otis, fourteen and sixteen, respectively, had made the most sensible observation Rafe had heard all evening: "Only Rafe would complain about finding a girl in his bed."

Hand on handle, Rafe tugged at the iron to open the front door before releasing the ring in haste, as though singed by the metal. *Not* currently his house, he reminded himself.

Stepping back, he took a moment to steady his nerves. Reaching into his waistcoat pocket, he extracted a small, engraved box. A pop of the lid, a sift of the contents, and then a pinch, Rafe slipped the mint leaf between his lips. As he chewed, he tucked the box back into his pocket. Minty fresh breath.

Ready, he made use of the knocker.

Less than fifteen seconds passed before the door swung open, revealing a familiar face.

Rafe cracked a smile, genuinely relieved not everyone in his home was a stranger. "A sight for sore eyes, Peter!"

The footman maintained his composure, only the twitch at the corners of his lips betraying his pleasure. "Mr. Slade is in the study, sir."

"Right. Shall I see myself there, or…"

The footman stepped aside to allow Rafe into the wood paneled entrance hall.

Rafe removed his beaver hat, eyeing the corridor that would lead him to his father's — er — Mr. Slade's study. "I suppose you've heard about my grand entrance?"

Disguising his amusement with a cough, the footman nodded but said nothing. Rafe winked before following the servant down the hallway, his gait a confident swagger, his expression revealing nothing of the pounding in his breast or tremor of his nerves.

Demand satisfaction, Slade had said.

Circling his hat in his hands, he waited for Peter to knock, then announce the caller. A caller in his own home. He could understand how his grandmother and mother felt about his father's decision to lease the house, but then, he could also apprehend his father's plan. The Fitz-Stephenses were an old family, a wealthy family, but most of the wealth was in the estate, in their assets, not necessarily in ready money. If Giles needed blunt for another one of his adventures… well, Rafe could sympathize with his father's decision.

Mr. Slade invited Rafe to join him for port in front of the cold fireplace. Too early for a drink — Rafe had not yet broken his fast, for that matter — but it would not prove an auspicious beginning to the conversation if he refused. With a nod, Rafe accepted, taking the seat facing the windows. The curtains wafted in the breeze, the windows slanted open, a subtle reminder of last night's decision to scale a wall for fun. Then, no one knew *how* he had entered the room, did they? No one except the young lady in curlers.

"You claimed your presence in my daughter's bedroom was a misunderstanding," Mr. Slade began without preamble as he squeezed into the chair.

Rafe nodded, taking the man's measure. Surplus build — in girth, not height — and receding hairline, but laugh lines around his mouth and an intelligent gleam in his hazel eyes. Roland Slade was a cleverer man than his appearance credited, Rafe surmised. All the same, Rafe could take him, if it came to it, both in a duel and in an argument. But *would* he? From his understanding, the gentleman was an old Oxford friend of his father's, one who was letting the house as a favor, a way to fund a large sum of money while reaping the benefits of playing lord of the manor, however temporary. *Would* Rafe want to best the man, prove with a sleight of hand who was superior?

"While I do not wish to call you a fibber, Mr. Fitz-Stephens, you must understand my position as a father. I arrive at my eldest daughter's bedchamber to find a gentleman caller in his shirtsleeves. The evidence is clear. Following a midnight assignation, you thought to dress and sneak away, but were clumsy in the dark. I am impelled to believe what my eyes tell me, not what a rogue might say to save his skin, no thought to the young lady he's ruined."

"*Res ipsa loquitur*," Rafe muttered to himself in Latin.

"What was that?"

With a shake of his head, Rafe said, "The evidence speaks for itself from your perspective. Is there no opportunity for my defense?"

"You've already offered it, have you not? That you *did not know*. You plead ignorance. Not a convincing stance. Are you not studying to become a barrister? Since my residence at Devington Priory, your father has spoken highly of you, yet all I see before me is a young boy caught in bed with my daughter."

In a flash, Rafe saw where this was going. How he had not realized it sooner said more for his belief in human benevolence and the moral code of gentlemen than it did for his wit. All his worry about being challenged over a misunderstanding… He had not envisaged *this*. Not by any stretch of his imagination. The trap had already clinched his ankle. How could he be so unaware?

His fingers tightening around the glass, Rafe said, "That I've been in London, that I've never met your daughter, that I could not identify her in a crowd, that I was not told of the rental agreement—all of this is inadmissible, I comprehend, testimonial hearsay."

Mr. Slade offered the palms of his hands in a shrug. "I don't make society's rules, Mr. Fitz-Stephens. Whatever the circumstances, you have compromised my daughter. I've no wish for a scandal, and I will not see my daughter ruined by a rogue's maneuverings."

A rogue or a barrister-in-training? Ruined by a rogue yet matched with same-said rogue? Threats of a scandal when only family and two servants had witnessed the incident? Threats of ruining his *own* daughter? Accused of a tryst when a witness could verify his whereabouts prior? Rafe wanted to laugh at Mr. Slade's attempts at duress and slander, his empty threats, his sloppy *ad hominem*, the makings of a fallacious argument. If the man were as adroit as he thought himself, he could convince Rafe to do his bidding *ex gratia*, or in a moment of desperation he could throw in a little *quid pro quo*.

Rafe's fingers ached from clutching the glass in his hands. With a whip of words, he could metaphor-ically knock the leg of the chair Mr. Slade sat on, then return to the dower house, unaffected. The situation was clear, the man's machinations straight forward. This should be an easy extrication.

The problem? Rafe was a gentleman. Even knowing when he was being played a fool, he was a gentleman.

His sympathies went to Miss Slade. The young lady had not set a trap. She was a victim, unaware two gentlemen were deciding her fate, one a stranger. He had not had a good look at the young lady, had no way of knowing her disposition. Was there a reason her father was eager to catch the first passing fox, or was it that this was too prized a fox to release? Rafe had only himself to blame. It was Rafe who set his own trap by behaving like a devil-may-care juvenile.

The options were limited: puncture Mr. Slade's plans with a few well-placed darts; not waste his breath, just leave; play the game to extricate himself later. There were few situations he could not extricate himself from should he wish, but at what cost and at whose expense?

There were detriments to being a gentleman. This moment proved one of them.

Rafe sighed and set aside his glass. He would not allow Mr. Slade to defeat him. This was *his* decision as a gentleman. The onus was on *him* to rectify the situation caused by his own carelessness.

Standing, Rafe said, "If you will grant me permission, and if she would consider accepting, I wish to ask for your eldest daughter's hand in marriage."

As what Rafe could only describe as smug victory deepened Mr. Slade's laugh lines, there was but one thought: *I don't even know her name.*

Chapter 5

R afe held himself to a more exacting moral code than most. As did all barristers, and especially students of law aiming to be Called to the Bar. In addition to keeping terms within an Inn — in Rafe's case within Gray's Inn — by the end of his pupillage, a pupil must prove himself worthy to approach the Bar with more than his intellectual prowess and social inclinations when dining with senior barristers. He must have proven himself physically fit and morally stalwart. Any blemish in behavior would deny a pupil his Call, just as it would disbar a barrister.

These were Rafe's meditations as he stared out the window a few minutes after declaring his intentions to Mr. Slade. The latter had requested Miss Slade be brought to the study. Rafe focused on spying the dower house chimneys in the distance while reprimanding his cursedly impulsive behavior. A foolish action, one that not only landed him in this situation, dragging an innocent woman with him, but one that could ruin his professional aspirations. And to think, he had been so pleased with his gaiety that he had wished to regale Headley, reminiscent of their youthful exploits.

He *almost* chuckled to himself recalling the time Headley had been staying at the house, and Rafe had convinced him of the fun they would have by climbing out the window and down the garden wall to sneak over to Lindstow Manor, the private girls' academy neighboring Fitz-Stephens land. Then, it was not *a* time, rather the *many* times. Rafe *almost* chuckled, but then reminded himself he was repenting bad behavior.

The study door opened. Haltingly, Rafe turned around, his jaw clenched, and his fingers laced tightly behind his back.

First to enter was Mrs. Louisa Slade, that hysterical woman who had reminded him in voice and figure of Miss Diana's pug. He could still hear her racking sobs as she wailed about ruination. Now, she swept into the study with her chin raised, her eyebrows arched, and her lips pursed in expectation.

Following her, entered his intended. He would *not* have recognized her in the street, not without her paper curlers. He would, however, have taken notice of her. With her eyes downcast, he held the advantage. She was taller when vertical – he tucked away the memory of her being horizontal when last they met... and in his bed – taller than he expected, but it became her silhouette, which reminded him of the most celebrated dancers in London. The more he regarded her person, the more he relaxed. Her face was as comely as her figure, a tear-drop shaped visage framed by curls – and oh, what curls. There was an abundance of chestnut curls, on the frizzy side, truth be told, being tamed by a bandeau and jeweled hairpins that glittered when caught by the morning rays.

Was he smirking? He schooled his features, hoping not, and just in time, too, for she raised her gaze as she lowered herself into one of the chairs Mr. Slade had arranged in the snug near the hearth. Grey eyes, the shade of morning mist, locked with his.

He involuntarily shivered. Her stare pierced him with one accusatory word: *rogue*.

Chilled, his admiration of her figure forgotten, Rafe joined them, accepting the seat across from Miss Slade and next to her father.

Mr. Slade said, "I am the bearer of happy news. Mr. Fitz-Stephens, a true gentleman, has offered to restore our daughter's virtue."

Rafe flinched.

The once-more-virtuous daughter stiffened, her gaze searching her companion's for an explanation.

"Be a good girl," said Mr. Slade, "and hear what Mr. Fitz-Stephens has to say. Come, Louisa."

And without saying more, the Slades left the room.

The skin around his ankle itched as the trap tightened. Not normally of a nervous nature, Rafe rose, reached for his forgotten beaver hat, and circled it in his hands for something to do, something to hold, something tactile to help him focus.

He met her gaze and fought the desire to look away. Her eyes were lethal. They seemed to accuse: you *did this*. You *ruined me*. You *trapped me, intentionally, and I'll never forgive you*.

Rafe cleared his throat, swishing the brim of the hat against his palm. "My apologies. We've not been introduced, and it does not appear we will be."

She stared, unblinking.

"May I introduce myself?"

The unbreakable stare continued. He did not think she would respond. Had he only moments before admired her hair? Those abundant curls, so inviting, so teasing… they resembled Medusa's venomous snakes now, coiled to strike.

Then, in a silken voice, strong but smooth, she said, "If you must."

He hesitated, then said, "Rafe Fitz-Stephens. Second son to Mr. and Mrs. Fitz-Stephens. Three brothers. Pupil at Gray's Inn. I fancy long walks and climbing garden walls in hopes of meeting young ladies."

When her eyes narrowed, he knew his attempt to sound droll made him appear lecherous instead. Rather than exacerbate the situation, he opted for inviting silence.

She made no attempt to disguise her malice or her thorough perusal of his person. "Miss Genevieve Slade," was all she said.

Miss Slade remained seated, making no curtsy and offering no nod.

"A name well suited, fair and pure," he said, building his way to a compliment before she interrupted.

"Is there something you wish to say to me?" Her tone implied more than her words: the expectation of an apology, a curiosity of why they had been left alone, a plea for him to say his piece then leave, an exasperation to be in a room with him.

"Yes, actually. I'm here to offer you marriage. Will you do me the honor?"

Her expression flickered inscrutably. Horror? Shock? Amusement?

"I don't know you," she said. This time, her tone said what her expression had not: *me vexat pede*. She found him… a nuisance, a bother, a pebble in her shoe.

Rafe exhaled, inexplicably more deflated than relieved. "That is immaterial under the circumstances. I have unwittingly compromised you, and I am here as a gentleman to offer you marriage."

"Preposterous. You were in my room no more than five minutes, my parents present for the whole debacle. No one knows but them, one of my sisters, and two servants."

"Yes, Miss Slade, I know all too well the circumstances. Be that as it may, I am here to rectify my wrongdoings, salve any embarrassed my poor behavior has caused, and offer myself as your husband, should you wish to accept me."

Her head tilted slightly. With another sweep of her gaze, she took his measure once more. "Noble, I suppose, but unnecessary, and also impossible. I'm already betrothed."

Rafe squeezed the edge of his hat, taken aback.

Before he could respond, the study door opened for Mr. and Mrs. Slade's return. Mrs. Slade was cooing, and Mr. Slade was grinning. They circled their daughter with accolades and began at once to discuss wedding plans.

Without raising his voice, affecting calm and confidence, Rafe said, "Miss Slade has rejected my proposal. I thank you for allowing me this chance. I've no desire to overstay my welcome. If you'll excuse me, I'll — "

Mrs. Slade wailed, and Mr. Slade blustered.

"Wha-wha-what is the meaning of this?" Mr. Slade looked in horror at his daughter.

Miss Slade did not bat an eyelash when she said, "However thoughtful of you to *restore my virtue*, I cannot accept Mr. Fitz-Stephens' proposal because, as I told him, I'm already promised to someone else."

"Poppycock! You are no such thing!" And then, Mr. Slade's gaze roamed from his daughter to Rafe and back, dawning startling his features. "Just how many suitors have you invited into your bedchamber? Clandestine meetings with Mr. Fitz-Stephens while promising yourself to someone else? I cannot assume these are isolated cases. How many gentlemen have you entertained under my roof?"

Mrs. Slade began to sob, her cries punctuated by yipping hiccups.

Conversely, Miss Slade paled at the accusations.

Rafe stepped back towards the window and tried to remold the brim of his hat after strangling it during his failed proposal. He did not care for Mr. Slade's game, and playing it was becoming tedious. More than ever, his sympathies were with Miss Genevieve Slade. Not only had *she* been trapped in this situation by her father's machinations and Rafe's carelessness, but her heart belonged elsewhere. A worse fate Rafe could not imagine — marriage to a stranger while estranged from one's true love.

They badgered Miss Slade to know her secrets until she admitted with a defiant chin but drooping posture, "Mr. Alan Thorpe and I have an understanding."

The name held no meaning for Rafe, but the Slades changed their tune faster than a troubadour.

"*That* useless article?" screeched Mrs. Slade, whose tears had miraculously dried.

Mr. Slade leaned in to exchange harsh but muttered words with his daughter, although Rafe could not hear what was said. After the brief tête-à-tête, Mr. Slade turned to Rafe. "Quickly settled, Mr. Fitz-Stephens. No need to concern yourself with my daughter's teasing. A right Beatrice, she is, would have inspired Shakespeare. Her answer is *yes*, she *will* marry you, and we could not be happier to ally our family with yours. We'll set a time this week to discuss the settlement details, shall we?"

Rafe eyed Miss Slade warily.

The young lady met his gaze only briefly with what Rafe thought might have been a pleading look, then deferred to her hands as she folded them in her lap. Submissive, diminutive, biddable—not words he would have used to describe her moments ago, but she appeared to shrink into herself, an obedient daughter, chastised for her recalcitrance.

Her head bobbed, and she said so quietly, the words could have been whispered by the breeze, "Thank you for honoring me with your proposal. I accept."

Curiously, her words brought a sensation of relief. Not for him, exactly, as he was not eager to marry someone who stared daggers into him, had not planned to marry at so pivotal a time in his professional life, and did not readily wish to consider Mr. and Mrs. Slade in-laws after his brief acquaintance with them so far. Nonetheless, he felt relieved all was settled for Miss Slade. She needed him. She needed Rafe to rescue her from being bartered off by her father and from being separated from her true love.

Mea culpa, Miss Slade. Somehow, he would exculpate himself by righting these wrongs.

Chapter 6

The Fitz-Stephenses gathered in the parlor to hear the glorifying tale of Rafe's set down of Mr. Slade, that house-stealing blackguard who had the audacity to request an apology from Marion's angelic son. In contrast, the chaos resulting from Rafe's accounting of what *actually* happened in the Devington Priory study could be heard through the corridors of the dower house and beyond the baize doors.

Slouched in a chair, ankle propped on his opposite knee, chin cradled in his palm, Rafe brooded.

Around him, the family deliberated the proceedings.

Anthony Fitz-Stephens was defending, to anyone who would listen, "This is a *good* alliance, a dream come true, really. Considering how well-lined are Slade's pockets, the dowry is bound to impress. But that's only a perk. Slade is the best man I know. Had he not moved about so often, our families would have been closely tied all these years, our children brought up together."

"I can't trust a man with no sense of responsibility," Gran said in protest. "Three young girls, and he's raised them like gypsies. Any gentleman worth his salt would have purchased and settled, not moved from lease to lease. I care not a fig for what lines his pocket if he's no sense of what being a gentleman or a father means." She turned to her grandson. "You must put a stop to this, Rafe. There is no obligation on your part to proceed. No one would believe a word of that Banbury tale of you sneaking into her room, and it would ruin *their* daughter to tell it. Besides, your father, despite his questionable loyalties and poor decisions, is squire and magistrate—he is well versed in dealing with blackguards and upstarts."

Rafe dropped his hand to sit up, wondering if he would be able to join the conversation this time. In half an hour, he had not yet been invited.

Mother fluttered her fan to cool her ire. "It is distasteful enough they are living in *my* home, sitting on *my* furniture, ordering *my* servants, inviting us to dine weekly as though I was a guest in *my* home. Now they want *my* son? I'll not stand for this, Anthony."

Rafe leaned back in the chair and returned his chin to his palm.

Gran said, "Mark my words. This is a well-orchestrated trap. They want to secure connections with the Fitz-Stephens name and with the house, doubtless a ploy to continue living in the house beyond the lease."

"Rafe, darling," his mother said, "this will *ruin* your plans. You are to be invited to the King's Counsel one day, make your mark in London as a top barrister. How is this to be done if you're saddled with *those people*?"

"A dirty trick," Gran continued. "It's the mothers of spinsters about whom one must usually worry, not respectable fathers. They've taken advantage of your being a gentleman and abused you cruelly."

His mother added, "You can't allow them to force you into marriage, Rafe. Stand your ground."

Gran insisted, "Anthony, I demand you terminate their lease immediately. You were a fool to let the house. And for what purpose? So that spoiled son of yours can squander his inheritance before he's earned it? Gallivanting around the world, no better than these Slades. You don't see it, son, because you're blinded by his 'golden boy' wiles." Punctuating each word with a slap of her palm to the cushion of her chaise, she said, "He plays you like a fiddle." A shake of her head, then she muttered under her breath, "A travesty. That's what has befallen this family. Strangers living in the house, the heir voyaging seas he has no business sailing, compromising situations to trap our Rafe—what has become of us? My husband is rolling in his grave."

As Father crossed his arms with a "Now, listen here, Mother," Noel and Otis caught Rafe's attention for a hushed conversation of their own.

Rafe arched a brow.

Otis asked, "Is she an ogre?"

Noel pulled an ogrish face.

Rafe sat up and leaned forward, resting his forearms on his thighs. "That's your future sister-in-law you're talking about."

"*Nah*," they said in unison.

Too cheerily than the occasion warranted, Noel said, "Mum will make you cry off before the day ends."

"Make it seem as though they misunderstood—the Slades, not Mum," Otis advised. "You never *offered*, merely suggested you *might* offer. Convince them they misheard. That's what I would do."

"That's what Mum will have you do." Noel and Otis nodded to each other, pleased with their display of wisdom.

With a playful but warning look to both, Rafe rose to his feet. Patience personified, he waited. His parents and grandmama continued to bicker, talking over each other in teeth-achingly polite condescension, voices never raised. His father held his defense of Mr. Slade, supporting the match between Miss Slade and Rafe, the argument holding little weight with the pair of women set against the family and Mr. Slade's sly entrapment.

Not for long did Rafe have to wait before they realized he had risen from his chair. Their sentences trailed until all present held a collective breath.

Rafe flashed a smile before saying, "Now that we've cleared the air, we must no longer question *cui bono*? Your answers have pointed to Mr. Slade as the one to benefit, but I put to you an alternative. *I* am the one to benefit. I have proposed to Miss Slade, and Miss Slade has done me the great honor to accept. From this point forward, the Slade family will understand the meaning of *noblesse oblige*. They are beyond reproach and will know our respect. They will learn what it means to enter an alliance with the Fitz-Stephenses."

He paused to look from one family member to another before continuing.

"Contrary to appearances, this is not a story of parson's mousetrap. There is no evidence the betrothal is against my will or the will of Miss Slade—*actus me invito, non est meus actus*. This is a story of a boy who has fallen smitten with a girl at first sight. That girl, in turn, has agreed to make him the happiest of men. *This* is the account I posit, and I will brook no discrepancies. *Omnia praesumuntur contra proferentem.* Alternatives, inconsistencies, clauses, and exceptions to the account I have provided will be presumed erroneous and against the offeror. I request *pacta sunt servanda* — are we in agreement that we will do our best to fulfill the obligations set forth?"

He waited for lightning to strike.

His grandmother sneered but nodded. His mother looked at her fan but also nodded. His father grinned. His brothers each gave him a slow wink, as though to say either they suspected him of biding his time until he could escape the noose or that Miss Slade was the antithesis of an ogre.

Satisfied, Rafe said, "If there are no objections, I propose we adjourn to the dining room. I've not yet broken my fast and am a bit peckish." As he said the words, his stomach growled.

In truth, he was so famished, he could eat a horse.

Chapter 7

A copse of trees — one could almost call it a small forest — bordered the estate. Most of the grounds were parkland, superb for riding, but the patch of woodlands was an oasis when one wished to hide from family. At the edge of the almost-forest stood a folly — reminiscent of a ruined castle tower — overlooking the valley and the girls' school, Lindstow Manor.

In the month the Slade family had resided at Devington Priory, Genevieve had devoted her time to exploring the grounds. She frequented the folly. However well-meaning her parents, Genevieve could only tolerate so much of their good intentions, specifically when those intentions affected her future. She could not confide in her sisters about her frustrations. Cecilia was the closest at fifteen to Genevieve's nineteen years but could not sympathize with anything except which sash looked best with which gown. Nothing said to Theia, at eleven, could be expected to remain private.

Genevieve stroked Philomena, the mare she had chosen from the Priory's stables, before removing her riding gloves. She made herself comfortable on one of the stones scattered around the folly — the boulders clearly added for ruin authenticity — or as comfortable as one could be when sitting on cold stone, which she found infinitely more comfortable than any cushion in the drawing room given their proximity to her mother.

"I sound ungrateful, mopey even, Philly. I must rally or a fit of the dismals will be insuperable."

The horse ignored her, snuffling at the grass instead.

"Why I confess my woes to you is beyond my comprehension. When we move, which inevitably we will, you'll remain behind."

Adjusting the train of her riding habit, she drew her knees beneath her chin and hugged her shins.

"Truth is, you're my only friend." Uninvited, reality shivered through her. "Good heavens, Philly. I won't move, will I? If Papa is serious, and I believe he is, I'll marry a stranger, and then, at the end of the lease, they'll move without me. All I've ever wanted was stability of home, a friend or familiar face I could know beyond a dreaded year. Now that it might become a reality, I hardly know what to think."

Never had she been part of a village, part of a tradition, part of anything. Would she if she married this man? She did not think so. He had a life of his own and would resent her for being manipulated. Not only would he turn against her, so would all in the village, for no one in Grant Lindis would believe two strangers formed an instant attachment. If the villagers did not realize it themselves, *he* would ensure everyone knew he had been compelled to offer for her, sealing her fate as an outsider forever — the evil witch who had entrapped the Squire's son, one of the most beloved gentlemen in the village.

He had not seemed a resentful or gossiping type, but then, she had only spent ten minutes in his company yesterday, the most awkward ten minutes of her life. How could he *not* resent her? From what Papa had said during dinner, Mr. Rafe Fitz-Stephens was ambitious. A forced marriage on the cusp of his goal attainment could not possibly be welcomed. Why had he not fought harder? Refused to marry her? There was no scandal or ruin or compromise. He had not been ensnared, not really, regardless of Papa's bombast. It was Papa making the man *think* he had been caught.

"How dare he propose," she said aloud to the horse, who acknowledged her outburst this time with a friendly snort. "Did he not consider I might have other plans? A beau of my own? He did not consult me, ask me what I thought of Papa's daft advantage taking, *nothing*. If he had asked, I could have explained Papa is hot air, and if ignored long enough, will deflate before drifting to the next advantageous thing—be it person or place. But he did not ask me. He shouldered his way into the study and demanded Papa take advantage of him. Is he simple, or a glutton for punishment?"

Philly bobbed her head, then shook her mane, all as if to say, *he's a gentleman, Miss Slade.*

Genevieve harrumphed. "Whose side are you on?"

The crunch of underbrush sharpened her awareness. Planting her feet firmly on the ground and righting her skirt, she looked about her, concerned she had been overheard, disappointed to have solitude interrupted, and alarmed someone approached. She arched her back and craned her neck, searching. A slow, steady hoofbeat drew nearer.

"I wouldn't sit there if I were you," said a masculine voice behind her.

Startled, she leapt off the rock and spun around. Sitting atop a dappled Andalusian was Mr. Rafe Fitz-Stephens.

Genevieve clasped her hands at her waist. With recalcitrant chin and narrowed gaze, she said, "You don't own me. Yet."

Mr. Fitz-Stephens' brow furrowed in thought. Rather than reply, he studied her, his eyes never leaving hers. At length, he dismounted. His attention turned to his horse, his body inclined away from her.

In a casual tone, he said, "It rained this morning. The sediment runoff from the stone's erosion… stains."

The slow horror of his meaning sank in. While he was distracted by his horse, she tried to angle around to spy the back of her riding habit. A tug of the fabric, a feel of the gown, a glance down. She closed her eyes and groaned. Unmistakable wetness, with a thin layer of dirt, imprinted her skirt—in the shape of her derriere.

If she could have swung onto Philomena and darted for safety, she would have. Before she could decide how to react, what to say, or where to hide, Mr. Fitz-Stephens spoke again.

"May I introduce my companion?"

She looked behind him but did not immediately see anyone.

As he followed her gaze, he smiled, a simple action but one that left her short of breath. "My horse," he clarified. "This is Alfgar. Alfie, this is Miss Slade, the young lady I told you about on our walk here."

He winked at Genevieve, who could hardly be affronted that he was talking about her behind her back if it was to his horse.

When she did not speak or move, he continued, "If you hold out your hand, he'll be able to familiarize himself with your scent. Don't be alarmed if he licks your palm. I promise he won't bite."

"I know how to handle a horse," she retorted, but dropped her guard as she approached.

Holding her hand palm up, she invited Alfgar to take a whiff. Without hesitation, the horse stepped forward and shoved his muzzle into her palm, snorting and, indeed, licking. Had Mr. Fitz-Stephens not been watching her, she would have laughed. What gave her pause was not only that he studied her with such intensity but that even past the pungent aroma of the horse, he smelled divine, a delicious combination of citrus, rose water, and mint. Then, he *looked* divine, as well.

She averted her eyes to keep from staring, but she would not soon forget him. Lean and athletic, a strong jaw, full, almost pouty lips punctuated by a cleft chin, Nordic blue eyes, golden blond hair that, despite currently being capped with a hat, she knew was styled in soft waves, the sides short but the top full and lush. Why could he not be repulsively ugly? She would not mind him resenting her if he was ugly.

Stepping away from the pair, she swept her arms behind her to clasp her hands, self-conscious of the damp fabric.

"'Pon my soul," Mr. Fitz-Stephens said with astonishment. "You chose the mare. Did no one in the stables warn you away?"

With a few careful side-steps, she reached Philly's side without having to expose her back. "I won't allow you to speak abusively of her. She's my dearest friend."

He looked incredulously from the horse to her. "*She* bites."

"Only people she does not like."

"Touché." He reached into his pocket and pulled out his handkerchief. "May I see your hand?"

Genevieve took a further step back. "I beg your pardon."

"To clean your palm. Alfie may appear majestic, but he's, erm, a little on the snotty side, shall we say, and I'm not referring to arrogance."

It was the wet stone horror all over again. Genevieve paled. Unsure what else to do, she obeyed.

She need not have worried, for Mr. Fitz-Stephens was tender, methodical, and impersonal, making quick but thorough work to clean her hand with his handkerchief before folding the linen and tucking it back into his waistcoat pocket. He even returned to stand by his horse, giving her ample space. Appreciative of his thoughtfulness, she should thank him.

Instead, she scowled. "How did you find me? *Why* did you find me?"

"Mr. Smith brought Alfgar to the main house. I rushed from the dower house so I wouldn't miss him. And I thought — wait, let me take a few steps back. Alfgar threw a shoe on the way home from London. A pebble bruised his sole, and of course, I worried it had bruised the frog, but as it happens, no damage. To be certain, we'll entertain a leisure pace for the next week, and he'll be pampered aplenty in the stables, but he doesn't like being idle. Being at the main house presented the opportunity to call on you. I never made it that far, though. The grooms caught me in time to advise your whereabouts. And so, here I am."

"The grooms told you I was *here*? They couldn't possibly know." This was her secret place!

"You would be sorely mistaken if you were to think any stablehand employed by the Fitz-Stephenses would not know the whereabouts of a young lady under their watch, specifically a young lady riding alone."

She glanced around them, expecting to see spies hidden behind trees. Curiously, rather than feel her privacy violated, she felt safer knowing they were keeping a distant watch, not only that they *did* watch but that they maintained such great distance she had never been bothered. No one had shared her location with the family either. *That* would have been a violation. Then, they did tell Mr. Fitz-Stephens….

"Be assured, Miss Slade. No one is watching us now." Hastily, he added, "This has always been one of my favorite places. If you climb the steps to the top of the tower, you'll find an unimpeded view of Lindstow Manor."

"Is that not a school for young ladies?"

He waggled his eyebrows.

"Oh!" Genevieve bristled. "You, sir, are uncouth."

"*Au contraire, mademoiselle. J'incarne le bon ton.*" With a sweep of his hand, he doffed his hat and ran a hand through his waves. "I had hoped to make you laugh today. Break the ice, as they say. Neither of us knows each other, and I thought today could mark the beginning of our acquaintance."

To what end? They could not marry. They could *not*. Two strangers united over a mistake? All because her father refused to pass the chance at snaring her a husband? This was an impossible relationship. They shared nothing, and they would each hate the other for being forced.

"Papa will come to his senses," she said. "There's no need to change your plans on my account. He will come to his senses, and that will be the end of it."

His expression shifted from almost playful to sorrowful. "We're betrothed, Miss Slade. My only regret is that someone else has your heart. With time… perhaps…"

As his words trailed, Genevieve felt a stab of guilt in her breast.

No one has my heart, Mr. Fitz-Stephens.

She stared at the forest floor, unable to meet his eyes.

He said softly in Latin, "*Astra inclinant, sed non obligant.* The stars incline us, they do not bind us." After a moment's silence, he turned back to his horse and prepared to mount. "I'll leave you with your thoughts, Miss Slade."

Genevieve parted her lips to say something, but she did not know what to say. Press their need to break the betrothal? Invite him to call in a day or two? Thank him for his kindness? Rail at him for first choosing her room that fateful night, then for falling prey to her father? Admit she had no one and was infinitely lonely?

Instead, she watched him leave, her heart in her throat.

After changing out of her riding habit, she retired to the drawing room. As expected, Mama was there, reading her lady's magazine. Genevieve flopped unladylike on the sofa next to her mother and rested her head on the cushy shoulder.

"Papa *must* come to his senses," Genevieve said, outlining an embroidered flower on her mother's gown. "He'll listen to you." *If you've quite finished with the theatrics*, she thought but did not say aloud.

"Seems to me he *has* come to his senses. A perfect match and all."

"A perfect match? We'd never met!"

Her mother shrugged one shoulder before turning back to read the column.

Genevieve sat up and crossed her arms, on the verge of pouting with a petulance she had not exhibited for at least a decade. "A terrific beginning, as well, after he heard Papa accuse me of entertaining gentlemen callers. What was Papa *thinking*? I'm mortified by the whole of it. Something must be done."

"You're to blame after fibbing about the milksop."

"Mr. Thorpe is *not* a milksop. He is kind and caring and all the things Papa and you are not."

Her mother tittered. "He's a useless article, and you know it. Now, Mr. Fitz-Stephens, on the other hand…."

"You don't know him from Adam! None of us do."

Mama did not look away from her magazine, but her eyebrows rose in a far too telling manner. "Don't we?" was all she said.

Genevieve turned to face her mother better. "What are you not saying?"

Another shrug of a shoulder. "I haven't the faintest what you're implying."

"The two of you couldn't have planned this. That much I'm certain. You did not bribe him to sneak into my room and be caught. The mistake was genuine on his part. Pray, what are you not telling me?"

With a noncommittal hum, she said, "Your father knows what he's doing, always has. Trust him."

"Oh yes, because he has done so much to earn my trust recently."

"Ye of little faith."

Genevieve waved her hands in disbelief. She pouted. She sulked. She sighed. Mama only tittered at the dramatics.

Seeing this as a fruitless endeavor, Genevieve pecked her mother on the cheek, then left the drawing room for her bedchamber, an idea forming.

After shutting the door behind her, she sat at the escritoire and set about enacting a scheme that *could* free her of this haphazard betrothal. It also could complicate matters. She refused to think of that now.

Readying paper, quill, and ink, she began a letter to Mr. Alan Thorpe.

Chapter 8

When the next day's endless rain kept the Slade family indoors, the girls grew restless. Genevieve knew not a moment's peace. Cecilia and Theia begged her to escort them into the village at the first sign of sun, which did not peek from behind clouds until the day after.

Thursday morning began with an ominous, leaden sky, so dark, the girls whined in the morning room, then pouted in the drawing room, then hounded Genevieve to join them for a round of billiards. They made it halfway through the house on their way to the billiard room before the sun's rays filtered through the windows. A blessed sight.

And so, Genevieve upheld her promise and accompanied her sisters into the heart of Grant Lindis.

There was not much in the way of shopping. They would need to go north to Sidonia or west to Sidbury to browse. Grant Lindis did have a lovely tea garden, however, as well as a millinery, haberdashery, and draper.

However quaint, the village bustled with activity. The liveliness was not due to the shops, the girls soon discovered, but preparations for the Fracas Frolic. One might have thought this frolic was taking place this afternoon. Alas, not for another week and some days. What was the Fracas Frolic? What did this signify? Asking someone would brand *outsider* across her forehead, and so she feigned excitement.

Who she *should* ask was Mr. Fitz-Stephens. That would initiate conversation, however. The least desirable outcome was to become better acquainted with him. Rather than befriending him with questions and conversations, she needed to bide her time for Mr. Thorpe to receive her letter.

Not knowing did not dim the sisters' excitement, for the only topic to pass their lips on the walk home was this frolicking mystery.

When they arrived home, Papa must have heard them trampling about in the entrance hall. He greeted them directly. "I'm pleased to share that Mr. Rafe Fitz-Stephens will join us for dinner."

"Must he?" Genevieve asked.

When all eyes turned to her, she paled. Had she spoken her thoughts aloud?

"Yes, he must," Papa said. "Word of the betrothal must spread. Everyone will accept the match, seeing as how we are living in the Fitz-Stephens' house and I am a long-standing friend of Squire Fitz-Stephens. Soon we'll be invited to dinner by Quality. Let us see if Papa can find matches for all my girls, shall we?"

Cecilia and Theia protested.

Genevieve remained silent.

If he were already thinking of their marriages, did that mean he planned to settle at last? Somewhere near here? The girls were only children, after all, or as good as, too early to wed by Genevieve's estimation. But if he made connections now, that would open the door for good marriages when they were out…. Unless her father had gone mad and planned to marry them off this year, regardless of age.

Peevish, she said, "I refuse to believe you'll enforce this marriage. I don't even know him."

"All the more reason he should come to dinner. And often."

With a huff, she retreated to the safety of her bedchamber. She did *not* wish to become acquainted with him, however divine his perfume, sweet his smile, and kind his attempts at discourse.

Before she had a chance to change, sit, or meditate further, a soft knock interrupted.

Genevieve cracked open the door.

"May I?" Cecilia begged entry.

Widening the gap, she invited her sister in, then closed the door behind her. For sisters who only had each other, they ought to have been closer. That could not be further from the truth, however. Cecilia had made friends easily wherever they moved and never seemed the least disappointed to leave them behind, the game always to form new friendships rather than keep established ones. Theia was not bothered by friendships or otherwise, entertained by her music and art. Genevieve was the one who always felt alone. Friendships were not easy for her to form, especially knowing the acquaintance would end with the next move — there never seemed a point to form anything lasting.

Cecilia sat on the edge of the bed before bunching her skirt to draw her legs beneath her. "Well?"

"Well, what?" Genevieve stood with her back against the door, arms crossed.

"*Is* he your lover?"

With a strangled cry, Genevieve scolded, "That is *not* appropriate, Cecilia. How do you know that word? Stop staring at me like a mouse after the cheese. He *isn't*."

"Looked like it to me. I was there, remember. He was in his shirtsleeves, trying to dress in the dark!"

"No, he was *not*. That is not what happened. He mistook my room for his. In case you've forgotten, this *is* his house, and this *was* his bedchamber."

Cecilia gazed around the room as though searching for a piece of evidence to catch her eye, a stack of love letters, perhaps, or his hat left behind after one of their trysts. "If it was an honest mistake, why did he propose? Sounds like lover's guilt to me. Papa wouldn't have twisted his arm if it was an innocent misunderstanding."

"Yes, Papa would have because yes, Papa did. Mr. Fitz-Stephens agreed only because he's a gentleman, and that's what gentlemen do. They are true to their word, do all they can to protect a lady's reputation, and make the best of bad situations."

"Why should his mistake affect you? A simple apology would have sufficed."

She did not readily answer. She could not. She did not *know* the answer. Guilt could be a convincing influencer. Obligation to correct his mistake? But then, as Cecilia said, why should it affect *her* life? It was all grossly unfair.

"Because that's how things are done," Genevieve answered noncommittally.

"So… this works out for everyone. You will marry your *lover*, and I will move into this room. It's twice as large as mine."

"I'm not married yet, and he's not my... my... you know."

"Lover?" Cecilia enunciated with a gurgle of mirth.

"That isn't a word a lady should know, much less utter. And I will not marry him if I have any say about it. Marriage should be based on friendship, two people who rub well together. I can't build a friendship with him, not with marriage banns looming, and besides, why would I wish to befriend a Londoner with a penchant for sneaking into bedchambers?"

"Well, whatever you do, don't marry Mr. Thorpe." Cecilia wrinkled her nose.

"How did you..."

"Listened at the door, of course. I wouldn't have missed that conversation for the world!" Rising from the bed, she snatched a shawl hanging over the back of the chair. "May I borrow this? I want to wear it to church. It'll match my new bonnet." Without waiting for Genevieve's response, Cecilia waved her sister out of the way of the door and left with the shawl trailing behind her.

Chapter 9

With one leg crossed over the other, Rafe lounged in the garden room of Devington Priory, his gaze unwavering from Miss Slade — who pretended she did not notice, but judging from the rigidity of her posture, she most certainly did — while his attention remained on Mr. Slade.

The host was in new form, at least based on Rafe's brief experiences. Gone was the blustering, finger pointing Machiavellian, determined to matchmake his daughter by any means necessary. The man, instead, was all smiles and good humor, singing the praises of Rafe's father in their Oxford days.

Beyond the adjacent double doors, the dining table was being set. The scents wafting in had Rafe almost licking his lips. It would be the longest dinner engagement of the week, he suspected, the mischievous stranger dining with prospective in-laws and bride, but it marked one of the most important — his first real opportunity to observe Miss Slade and gauge her response to him.

The Slade family and Rafe enjoyed wine in the room with the best view, two sides of the room being three sets of French doors that opened onto the formal gardens to the back of the house.

"The Great Hall was once the dining room," Rafe found himself sharing after much prodding by Mrs. Slade. "Mother hated it. It echoed. It was drafty. It had no great view except the fireplace. Mother is nothing without her creature comforts."

Mrs. Slade tittered in agreement.

"She put her foot down, as she's wont to do. The saloon became the dining room. The stag parlor became this garden room. And both former designations relocated next to the billiard room, turning the west into the bachelor wing."

Mrs. Slade made some remark or another. Rafe did not hear her.

Instead, he lost himself to the memory. He had been all of ten when the great upheaval occurred. No one had slept until the rearrangement had been completed — a day in the life of the Fitz-Stephenses, he mused. His father had done little except mutter how much his mother would disapprove. Indeed, Gran had disapproved heartily. *The rooms were this way before you were born, Marion. How dare you upset the applecart for a* view. *Who wants a* view *while dining*?

Tangled in the fabric of memory, he was startled to realize he had lost the thread of conversation after it had moved forward. He listened to gain his bearings. Mr. Slade was sharing a tale of living in North Yorkshire. Good; Rafe had not missed anything significant. His eyes wandered back to Miss Slade's stiff profile.

He had been thinking periodically of their brief encounter by the folly. Queerly, what struck him most was her choice in Philomena. Of all the horses in the stables, she had chosen the mare no one would ride. At one point, the mare had been intended for his mother, but the two had butted heads too many times, and in the end, Philomena won the right to be the pampered lady no one bothered. Absently, he wondered if the choice of horse was a reflection of her own personality. Stubborn to a fault? A determined biter? He coughed to disguise his laugh.

"Will you sit with Genevieve at church?" Mr. Slade asked with an expectant stare.

Rafe's attention jerked back to his host. What had the man asked? After a speedy search through his peripheral memory, he turned to Miss Slade and raised his eyebrows in question, his expression asking for invitation or rejection before he answered. His delightfully conversational betrothed avoided his gaze.

"I would be *delighted*," Rafe said. "And speaking of delights. I am all eagerness to hear the vicar's sermon. I've missed his words of wisdom. No one has mastered doom and gloom quite like the Reverend Goodson."

Mrs. Slade, who sat across from her youngest two daughters, offered, "Then you've not heard. He has a young curate sermonizing now."

"Oh ho ho. That *is* a surprise," Rafe said. "As I live and breathe. Goodson allowing someone else at the pulpit?" He whistled low. "I'll have you know, our beloved vicar has not aged a day since my christening."

His immortality was undisputed, as no one could remember Goodson *not* being vicar. Not even Gran.

Mrs. Slade ventured, "The curate will be a welcome surprise for you, then, Mr. Fitz-Stephens. Young and affable. No doom and gloom there, I assure you.

Poor dear is curate for both Grant Lindis *and* Lynntreow. That is no short distance. The *poor dear*."

"Ah, I'm not surprised," Rafe said. "Lynntreow hasn't had a vicar in years. Baronet Lyttleparva is an exacting man, shall we say, and hasn't met anyone he likes well enough to recommend for the vicar's living. I had hoped the previous curate would win favor, but if our new curate is now taking Lynntreow in hand, in addition… well, there's a poor dear for you, the prior curate who not only was not offered the living but wasn't invited to remain as curate." He clucked his tongue.

Mr. Slade tilted his head, curiosity piqued. "Baronet Lyttleparva, you say?"

Rafe waited for his host to ask something specific about the baronet or hint to what he wished to know, but the man said no more, the wrinkles on his brow speaking for him. It was not difficult to surmise what Mr. Slade wanted, but Rafe could only guess as to why. To rub elbows with Quality seemed Mr. Slade's game. He wanted alliances with families like the Fitz-Stephenses. As to the end game, Rafe could not say. To find matches for his daughters? Or was there a more selfish intent at play? Perhaps there was not an end game. Perhaps Mr. Slade simply liked sharing his glass with those who afforded him a sense of importance.

"Mr. Fitz-Stephens," one of the younger sisters crooned, catching his attention away from Mrs. Slade's continued raptures about the young curate and Mr. Slade's lingering enquiry.

Miss Cecilia, he believed, was her name. She had been batting her eyelashes at him since his arrival.

However awkward that, given she was not only the sister of his betrothed but about the age of his younger brothers, he found himself more amused than anything, namely because with every batted eyelash, his oh-so-devoted betrothed responded with some subtle sign of reproach, be it flexing fingers or clenching her jaw. The theatrics of her disapproval had him chuckling to himself. It was just such insights of her for which he thirsted during this dinner engagement.

Turning his gaze to Miss Cecilia, he awarded her a winning smile. "Yes, Miss Cecilia. I am all agog."

She blushed, then darted a glance to her youngest sister before asking, "Do you like to read?"

"I've been known to turn a page now and then." He uncrossed his legs and leaned forward, watching Miss Slade in his periphery, even while he faced Miss Cecilia.

"Do you like…" she mouthed with silent exaggeration the words "*gothic novels.*"

Mrs. Slade yipped and plied her fan. "What have I *told* you! You're never to speak of those vile works in my presence!" She leaned back, looking pale and breathless.

"But I didn't, Mama! I *mouthed*, you see, which is altogether different…."

"In front of our guest!" Mrs. Slade protested, fumbling for her vinaigrette as she dropped her fan. "I am mortified!" With a sniff of her salts to restore her nerves, she moaned about the heathenness of her children.

Rafe cast an understanding smile to Mrs. Slade.

With giddy glances, Miss Cecilia and her sister pressed the conversation further.

Voices overlapping, Miss Theia said, "Radcliffe is my favorite," while Miss Cecilia said, "Mrs. Trowbridge is my favorite."

Shushing her sister with a quelling glance, Miss Cecilia said, "Trowbridge is bounds better than Radcliffe. You simply *must* read Trowbridge, Mr. Fitz-Stephens. The Count di Bianckino is *divine*!"

"He is *not*," argued Miss Theia. "He's a villain! A detestable blackguard!"

Sniffing with vexation, her sister defended, "And why should the villain not also be *divine*, hmm? Not all of us favor the twinkling-eyed hero."

As the two battled — Mrs. Slade suffering renewed vapors and waving her smelling salts, and Mr. Slade staring into his wine glass in hopes a pithy conversation was at the bottom of it — Rafe wondered where that left him in Miss Cecilia's estimation given the direction of the batting eyelashes: villain or hero?

More importantly, how did Miss Slade view him? Villain, without doubt.

He turned to Miss Slade, who feigned disinterest. "And you, Miss Slade? What do you enjoy reading?"

With a distracted and languid tone, she said airily, "I must beg your pardon. I wasn't listening. Did you say something?"

"Trowbridge or Radcliffe is the debate — where do you stand?"

"Unlike my sisters, Mr. Fitz-Stephens, I do not favor villains or villainous tales, least of all featuring Italian counts or *rogues*."

Just as dinner was announced, Rafe's lips curved into a grin to catch the deepening pink of Miss Slade's cheeks — her reply proved she had been listening to every word spoken.

The array of sumptuous decadence lining the dining table was fit for a king, not humble Rafe. Judging from the surprise flitting across Mr. Slade's brow as he surveyed the meal, this treat was courtesy of Cook rather than the host. After dinner, Rafe would slip into the kitchen to plant a kiss on Cook's cheek — *yes, Cook, I've missed you too.*

Accepting the chair next to his ever-affectionate bride-to-be, he catalogued the available foodstuffs, his mouth watering in anticipation. But first, his ladylove. He offered to plate her dinner. She pursed her lips, implying she was on the cusp of rejecting — and he suspected with what she thought would be a witty rejoinder about being of independent enough mind to plate for herself — but for whatever reason, she nodded acceptance. Small victory. He chose the best of the best for her, although he might have been a trifle too generous on portions. With a shrug, he began filling his plate with twice the amount. The dishes were some of his favorites, after all.

From the corners of his eyes, he observed her. Was she a finicky eater who poked at her food, or did she have a healthy appetite?

Without hesitation, she dug into the fare. Perhaps *dug* was discourteous. With ladylike gentility? Whatever the case, he grinned his satisfaction. She was not missish, then, at least not with appetite.

Mr. Slade asked, "Tell me, Mr. Fitz-Stephens, what parties does your family host in the autumn months?"

Rafe's cutlery hesitated. "Parties, sir?"

"You know," he waved his hand, as though the answer was obvious. "Foxhunting, shooting parties, and all." Without awaiting a reply, he continued, "I would benefit from the usual guest list and the name of the local huntsman, should I wish to host, that is."

Rafe weighed his response, choosing his words with care so as not to cause offense. "Can't say we're known for our hosting. More lawn than park, if you take my meaning. Mother enjoys hosting a retreat now and again. She would be happy to share her guest list with Mrs. Slade." She would ring his neck for offering. "The best foxhunt is in Lower Sidvenna. His Lordship's country estate is there, or one of them, rather. Exclusive guest list. Can't say I've ever been invited." To himself, he thought, *hence, Mr. Sycophant, I cannot make an introduction.*

Mr. Slade's disappointment was palpable but brief. His keen mind worked other possibilities. Undoubtedly, Rafe thought, Slade wished to chafe his elbows with the bluebloods. The man was not common, thankfully, however prone to histrionics he and his wife were, but his lineage, as far as Rafe knew, held no appeal, leastways for the nobs. Rafe could be wrong, but if Slade was of good family, why need an entrée into society? All the blunt in the world could not buy Slade recommended lineage.

But marriage could.

Rafe angled to admire Miss Slade, who looked most fetching in daffodil yellow today. Composed, austere, graceful. Except her hair. Libertine strands escaped the confines of their carefully wound curls, chestnut frizz haloing her coiffure. There was something enticing about the untamed curls. A glimpse of the real Genevieve?

Miss Cecilia, sitting opposite him, said, "Tell us about the Fracas Frolic. Genevieve took us into the village today, and *everyone* was talking about it. But *what* is it?"

To Miss Slade, he said, "I would be honored to escort you and your sisters on your next excursion to the village."

"Thank you, Mr. Fitz-Stephens," Miss Slade said. Firmly, but not impolitely, she added, "We do not require an escort so close to home. I'll keep your offer in mind should we wish to venture further afield."

"Ah, but you won't know all the best places in Grant Lindis without an escort in-the-know."

"What's there to know? A few shops and a tea garden."

"Tea garden? We don't have a tea garden." He glanced around the table for confirmation. "We have a tavern, rather."

"It would appear much has changed since your last return from London." A sneaky bit of smuggery curled the corners of Miss Slade's lips, or so it appeared to him.

Miss Cecilia, who huffed to have been forgotten, prompted, "The frolic?"

"Oh, yes!" Rafe set down his cutlery with a lingering look at his plate. "It's a century-long tradition between Grant Lindis and neighboring Eurwendin, this competition. For one week, we go head-to-head, a new event every day, each earning points."

Miss Slade's haughtiness slipped, her interest piqued. "What sort of competition?"

"Team racing, mostly. Let's see... there's the forest run, the regatta, the swim meet, and... whatever else they've chosen. Points are earned in the morning race. In the afternoon, it's fun on the green, three-legged races, and the like." Tapping the table next to Miss Slade's plate, he said, "There is always one event exclusive to the ladies. My mother will know what it is this year. Can I tempt you, Miss Slade?"

Her eyes flashed with something. Enticement? He could not read it, but he liked the fire behind that gaze, however brief the flicker.

"I couldn't say, Mr. Fitz-Stephens, not without knowing the event."

"I'll consider that a challenge to convince you," he teased with impishness.

And oh, how he loved a challenge. *Mulgere hircum.* To milk a male goat. In other words, to attempt the impossible—his specialty.

As conversation continued, Rafe's attention danced between Miss Slade, her family, and the beveled windowpanes. The sunny sky had darkened with an ominous cloud, and a light pitter-patter of rain glazed the glass. He had not intended to stay beyond dinner. Nothing to concern himself with yet, but the awareness of an incoming storm kept his eyes darting outside from time to time.

His primary concern was Miss Slade. Too soon to say what was to be done about their unusual situation. She was *not* amenable to the match. That much was certain. With care, he believed he could win her over. The pressing question: did he want to? She had expressed a promise to someone else, with someone, he assumed, she had fancied herself in love. Nothing about the match was particularly attractive to either of them. Well, except *her*. *She* was attractive. But he could not be guided by lust, least of all for someone who blamed him.

Once dinner ended, they returned to the garden room. The rain fell in a steady stream, although the sky had lightened, the dark cloud moving quickly past, of which Rafe was grateful. The rain would keep him longer than he wished, but less so than a storm.

The meal had been so satisfying, including not one, not two, but three of his favorite desserts, Rafe *almost* welcomed the delay in his departure. How he would be able to sup with his family this evening, he was unsure. Then, who was he fooling? Of course, he would be able to sup with his family. In fact, as satiated as Rafe was, if a tray were brought in now, he would willingly partake. One did not maintain an active life without ample sustenance, after all.

Folding his hands over his waistcoat, he looked to his hosts in anticipation of more conversation. They were an inquisitive lot. Far different company than his family, the Slades full of questions, and the Fitz-Stephenses full of answers.

"Tell me, Mr. Fitz-Stephens," began Mr. Slade, "about your London home. Fashionable, I suspect. In Mayfair? A home befitting my daughter?"

Miss Slade squeaked.

Mrs. Slade leaned forward in her chair with undisguised interest.

The sisters looked at each other and giggled.

Before he answered, Miss Theia, the youngest sister, said, "I've always wanted to see London. The country is *so boring*. Do you enjoy musical soirees? Do you attend the theatre? Have you been to the museum? A person could *live* in London! How *bored* you must be in Devonshire."

As she rattled on, he watched Miss Slade's reaction, which, unlike her mother, was of disguised interest. She tilted her head and leaned forward, poised to hear his reply, but she fidgeted with the embroidered sprig of her dinner gown, attention riveted on the thread, for all the world disinterested in whatever he had to say. Rafe tucked away the smile edging his lips.

"My apartments are at Gray's Inn, temporary bachelor lodging." He hesitated before continuing. How to word his answer without some reference to *marriage*?

When he married? Should he marry? If he married? After he married? *They* rather than *he*?

"My options are numerous," he said, settling on the obtuse. "I could choose a circuit, the Western circuit, for instance, to live near my family, and travel to the Quarter Sessions. I could choose London but agree to work the Assizes, as needed, for more time in the countryside. Alternatively, I could choose London as my permanent home, or within a reasonable distance, and take to the Old Bailey. Assuming, of course, I'm Called to the Bar. All have their advantages."

"London!" squealed the sisters.

Miss Cecilia added, "No sane person would choose the country."

"Are you so sure?" Rafe teased her with a daring grin. "I counter anyone who is bored in the country isn't trying. There's myriad entertainment available."

While he had intended to add the Fracas Frolic as an example, he saw from the widening of her eyes and the darting of her gaze between him and Miss Slade, that she was imagining far saucier entertainment than he had intended—sneaking into bedchambers being the primary source. Rather than clarify or dissuade, he simply resumed his smile, only directing it at Miss Slade.

"My *wife*," he continued with emphasis, "would be a driving force behind the decision. Raising children is not ideal in London, but she may have an interest in city life. I could be persuaded to take whichever route. The home, then, would depend on that choice."

He observed Miss Slade's agitated fingers picking at the innocent thread.

However much his answer aimed to tease her, what he described was not untrue, although it was more complicated. His plan had always been the Old Bailey. From there, he hoped for promotion to King's Counsel, potentially on to Parliament, or, alternatively, sitting as a Judge. He had never wished to become a circuit barrister. The circuit offered no opportunity for promotion, and less challenging cases, more misdemeanor than criminal, only a few shades darker than what his father saw as a magistrate. The circuit offered nothing beyond the humdrum dullness of traveling the circuit, an endless loop.

He *could* still fulfill his dream as a London barrister with a wife and family, but it would not prove easy. He had seen that already during his terms at Gray's Inn. Old Bailey barristers were married to the profession. The circuit barristers were the family men. It was not a matter of talent or respectability, only of life choices. Raising children in London did not appeal to him.

Rafe's eyes caught Miss Slade's and lingered. Were his as clouded as hers?

After fielding enough questions for the rain to subside, Rafe rose. "My thanks for dinner. I'm impelled to return while there's a part in the clouds."

"Please, stay longer," pleaded Mrs. Slade. "Don't let rain stop our fun."

Miss Theia suggested, "We could best you at billiards! We've been practicing."

With an apologetic bow, Rafe said, "I would be tempted by your offer had I not promised the remainder of the afternoon to my father. Actually, it is *he* who has promised the afternoon to *me*. I am not too humble to beg, you must know. After much pleading, he's agreed to confer with me about a selection of old cases I've been studying. Having a magistrate's insight will be advantageous. My hope is he'll amuse me enough to debate opposing perspectives, namely had I been a barrister on the case and chosen a different angle to argue."

As he rattled on about his scheme, he watched the Slades' attention waver. Their posture slackened, and their eyes wandered. All except Miss Slade, who listened with apparent curiosity.

Now that was interesting. While her family preferred talks of London, she perked at his plans to interrogate his father about law. He tucked that away to consider in more depth later. For now, he had Cook's cheek to kiss before making a mad dash back to the dower house before rain returned.

Chapter 10

The sun knew that today was its self-named day. After another full day clouded by rain, Sunday was, indeed, a sun-day. Genevieve spent most of church service catching glimpses of the rays through the diamond panes. Was Philly as eager to take advantage of the weather as she? Her feet tapped in anticipation of a ride.

The curate spoke of the upcoming competition, his sermon encouraging fellowship and community camaraderie. This would be his first competition. A simple statement but one that helped Genevieve feel not so alone in her outsiderness. She was not the only new face in Grant Lindis.

The Slades and the Fitz-Stephenses shared a pew, Genevieve and *the stranger* sitting between them. She had met the Fitz-Stephenses on several occasions prior to their second son's return, as Papa insisted they dine at the house once a week or more, something she could tell did not sit well with the Mmes. Fitz-Stephens but was a welcome invitation for the Squire and the two boys, who enjoyed teasing her sisters. Today, however, was the first time she had seen the family since the betrothal.

The father looked on her with approval. The brothers gave her a curious side eye. The Mmes.

Fitz-Stephens ignored her. And yet, so adroitly did
the mother and grandmother play their game, Genevieve did not *feel* slighted. There was neither a cut nor
apparent rudeness. With awe-inspiring grace, they
publicly accepted her into the fold without personally
acknowledging her. The whole of it had her gurgling
with silent laughter. They must think *she* had laid a
trap for Mr. Rafe Fitz-Stephens. A conniving, mar-
riage-minded woman who set out to ensnare him with
claims of compromise — who would not laugh at the
absurdity, least of all since she had spent every day
since the incident blaming him for much the same?

Her thoughts remained occupied as they rose for
the end of service and proceeded outside, so occupied
she did not pay her father any mind as he exchanged
pleasantries in the churchyard, not until her arms
prickled with gooseflesh. Donning her bonnet to
shield the glare and busy her hands, she glanced
around her. The hair on the back of her arms stood
on end. Gazes sought hers, each looking away just
as quickly — presumably no one wishing to be caught
staring or wishing to initiate conversation. The attention was, nonetheless, unsettling.

Both the Slades and the Fitz-Stephenses were busy
chatting with others, except her sisters, who amused
themselves, all oblivious to the stares. Casually, Genevieve stepped closer to her father, ears strained. He
was standing with a couple she did not know.

"I couldn't say more," came his voice, albeit with
practiced timidity, "but I anticipate a happy ending."

She could not hear the couple's soft reply.

Her father responded, his voice just loud enough
for others to overhear, "How does word of these

understandings spread, I'd like to know? As though the wind itself has a voice. They've sworn us to secrecy until…" he dropped his voice "…the banns." Papa's laugh was convincingly chagrined to have let his so-called secret slip. "I've said too much, haven't I? Oh, dear mc. Fanning the flames! It's not my intention, but I *am* proud. Our families will be united."

In wide-eyed mortification, Genevieve turned to her father. It was inevitable he would spread word but… *now*?

A warm hand cupped her elbow. Nearly spinning on her heels with a gasp, she was, at first, confused, and then angry, and finally relieved, all in the span of a few seconds, to see Mr. Rafe Fitz-Stephens standing at her side, his expression amused and his demeanor at ease.

For her ears only, he said, "We've been found out, Miss Slade. Our love affair is public knowledge." Before she could protest, he lightly squeezed her elbow. "Two choices. I introduce you to all and sundry as my betrothed, here and now, or I escort you home, the clandestine lovers wishing a rare moment of privacy."

"I wish you wouldn't say that word." She wanted to hide, but instead she slid a shy smile on her lips for the benefit of onlookers.

He glanced at her with a humored brow. "To Devington Priory?"

Genevieve nodded.

With a fingertip to the brim of his beaver hat, and a wink to their families, he wished a good day to everyone loitering in the churchyard, more than one woman blushing from the simple gesture.

"We're saved," he began as they walked down the narrow lane towards the center of Grant Lindis, "from answering probing questions. At least this round. Should we face confrontation of well-meaning but nosy neighbors, I recommend a diplomatic approach. Regardless of the question, the answers should be variations of," the next said in a high-pitched voice, "'I thought him handsome at first sight.'"

She wanted to laugh at his imitation of her, as well as his arrogance, but instead she said, "If we're betrothed, there's no point in avoiding the question."

"Are we?"

Her brow wrinkled. Subtly, she slipped her elbow free of his hand and allowed space between them.

Ignoring the scent of his perfume, that same irresistible combination she had tried to forget—citrus, rose water, and mint—she said, "I wish Papa had not said anything. If he had remained silent, we might have ended this silliness without fuss. I wrote to Mr. Thorpe, you should know. I'm certain, as soon as he receives it, he'll travel here to set all to rights." *How* he would do so remained to be seen.

Mr. Fitz-Stephens did not immediately respond. They walked in silence, interrupted only by a wave here and there from churchgoers returning home. She tried to catch a glimpse of his expression but could not see his face past her bonnet, not unless she fully turned, which would ruin her attempts to spy unnoticed.

"You care for him deeply?" he asked at last.

Now was her turn to hesitate. Nothing she could say would sound satisfactory, and she did not wish to lie.

Instead, she side-stepped his question. "You can't possibly want this betrothal. I do not grant you permission to protest or feign insult, for we both see the same side of the situation because we both know what happened. It was a misunderstanding, and Papa took advantage to trap us both, using our gentility against us. You *must* resent me. If not for participating in his machinations, then simply for being in an unlikely location at an unlikely moment."

Had all of that spilled past her lips at once? Too late to withdraw it. Not that she had said anything he did not already think or *should* think, but did she have to mention *resentment*?

With a voice too airy, too whimsical for this conversation, he said, "We are in the perfect position for friendship, then."

This time, she did laugh. "Friendship? Based on what, exactly?"

Dipping his head low, his voice dangerously close to the edge of her bonnet, he said, "I have the advantage of being the only gentleman to have seen you in curlers."

Genevieve covered her mouth to muffle a cry. Her limbs trembled and her cheeks warmed with outrage. And he called himself a gentleman!

Pretending he had not said what he had, Mr. Fitz-Stephens asked, "Your Mr. Thorpe is not going to 'demand satisfaction,' is he?"

Huffing, still hot with anger, she snapped, "Would serve you right to have a glove meet your cheek."

He chuckled. "It doesn't work quite like that these days."

She rushed to speak before he could insult her further or ask more questions about Mr. Thorpe. "Once he arrives, you need only step aside. I thank you for your gentlemanly offer, but your kindness will no longer be needed. You may return to your plans to become a London barrister and stay there hereafter."

"So, you *were* listening."

With a scoff, she turned away so he could enjoy a view of the back of her bonnet, her view the narrow lane that would take them up the drive to Devington Priory.

"Miss Slade, I believe you are an intelligent enough woman to realize the situation is not as easy as Mr. Thorpe arriving and my stepping aside, not if your father is set on this match, and not now that he has ensured word is spreading."

He paused long enough to allow her to agree or disagree if she wished. She pursed her lips.

"If extrication from this betrothal is what you wish," he continued, "I will make it my mission to see you united with your Mr. Thorpe, namely with your parents' happy approval."

"Of course, I wish this sham of a betrothal to end. Neither of us wants this. We were both coerced." Softer, less confident, she asked, "Don't you agree?"

He hesitated long enough for her to turn to face him. Whatever expression she had expected was not the one she saw.

His lips had curled into a wolfish grin, and his eyelids had drooped in admiration. "The more I recall those curlers, the more enticed I am to marry you."

Genevieve's jaw slackened. "How… how… *oof*!" She crossed her arms over her chest and quickened her steps, the house now in sight.

Behind her, Mr. Rafe Fitz-Stephens laughed heartily.

Morning twilight illuminated the world around Rafe, his legs pumping forward, his lungs expanding with the crisp country air.

Ex nihilo nihil fit. Nothing comes from nothing. Work is required to succeed. Selwyn had taught him this, never letting him forget it, all part of the training within the Vitruvian Society. It would be good to see Selwyn again once Rafe and Rupert Headley decided on the best day to call on him.

Despite the Fitz-Stephens family's penchant for late nights, Rafe rose before dawn every morning for his jog, rain or shine, the time his own. Awaiting him at the dower house would be a warm bath. While he missed having ready access to his gymnasium in London, he was hard pressed not to prefer the country air to London's soot, so much so, he spent nearly every morning questioning his future. He had always preferred the country. London offered ample conveniences, but it was not home.

The country air was not the only element to prompt him to envisage his future. For so long, he had single-mindedly barreled in one direction, at no point stopping to think about the sacrifices he would need to make. With his goal clear, he had never concerned himself with sacrifices.

Given Miss Slade had Mr. Thorpe, and this mis-understanding would be resolved before long, he need not concern himself with sacrifices even now.

The betrothal was temporary. Rafe did not wish to marry someone whose heart lay elsewhere. Thus, he would do all in his power to convince the Slades that Mr. Thorpe was the better choice for their daughter, and once that occurred, he could recuse himself from the understanding, and in doing so, reunite Miss Slade with her true love. A happy ending for everyone.

It was not the betrothal or Miss Slade that had him questioning his future, rather it was the *idea* of the betrothal and, yes, even of Miss Slade. Where should his priorities lie? Family or profession? He could have both. He need not sacrifice one for the other. But choosing the specific path he had originally planned complicated the time and attention he could devote to a family, not to mention location. He did *not* wish to raise children in or near London.

As he rounded back towards the dower house, he reconsidered his priorities. For now, his priorities were a bath, breakfast, and then a ride with Alfgar to meet Headley, all thoughts of marriage and obstinate women with grey eyes muted in anticipation of a hearty meal.

Several hours later, Rafe sat across from Headley in the tea garden.

"This is novel," Headley said, taking in the cozy surroundings.

"A new extension of the tavern. Between this, the curate, and the Slades letting my family home, I'm a stranger in my own village."

The tea garden was small, a far cry from any pleasure garden one could enjoy in London. In fact, there
was little to it aside from al fresco tables amongst a
young but burgeoning flower garden with narrow
paths and a small pond with an idyllic but rather
pointless little bridge. Why The Dragon's Breath
tavern had wanted to expand with *this*, Rafe could
only guess, but he imagined it was popular with the
ladies. Had Miss Slade enjoyed a meal here yet?

Headley dug into his mutton. "How's it living
with Mrs. Edwina? She always had a soft spot for me,
but I can't imagine living under the same roof as her."

"Gran's as high in the instep as ever, but I'm enjoying her doting, I admit. With Giles not here at present,
I'm receiving his princely treatment."

"Any word from the golden boy?"

Rafe shook his head before savoring the port.
"Not since Father invested in the latest expedition,
whatever it is."

"And you don't suspect him of pilfering?"

"Couldn't say. Gran does. She's never understood
Giles's fascination with exploration or travel. If it had
been a younger son, I don't think she would question
it, but a Fitz-Stephens heir? Insupportable."

"Always refreshing to know your grandmama
wouldn't mind you being lost at sea or thrown overboard by pirates, so long as you weren't the heir to
Devington."

Rafe laughed.

"You've said little about the Slades. Vulgar mer-
chants? Respectable but ungenteel?"

Rafe had intentionally been avoiding talk of the
Slades. He did not want to deceive his friend by not

mentioning the betrothal, but neither did he wish what should have been a happy occasion be explained as a mistake of circumstance. No matter how he worded the explanation, it did not show Miss Slade to any advantage, much less him. A betrothal should not be pitied. Ah, but dash if there was not a good explanation. Could he fake happiness and pretend it was real? All the worse when she chose to marry Mr. Thorpe. He could not keep the betrothal secret for long, but a little more time would offer him a chance to think of a believable explanation that would not humiliate him or Miss Slade.

He opted for vagueness this round. "Mr. Slade, from what I understand, is an old Oxford friend of Father's, although I've never met the family before. They, apparently, maintained correspondence throughout the years."

What else to say that would not sound negative? He refused to besmirch Miss Slade's family, regardless of the betrothal conditions.

Turning his glass one way then another, Rafe continued, "My impression of Mr. Slade is he enjoys a life of leisure, i.e., responsibility and he would not be caught in the same room. A life to be envied by many, I should think."

"I see." Headley leaned back in his chair after plying his napkin. "Lord of the manor without strings attached. A grand way to live, although there's no pride in it, but what of his family?"

Hesitantly, Rafe admitted, "Three daughters." With a chuckle to ease the constriction of his cravat, he added, "And before you raise your eyebrows, two are too young."

"Two?"

"The eldest is a pretty painting, yes, but not for you."

Rafe could only guess what Headley must be thinking—an undesirable woman? Already spoken for? Rafe marking his territory?

Whatever the case, Headley nodded. "Understood."

Rafe spotted the gleam in Headley's eyes. Changing subjects before more could slip, he asked, "Have you decided to compete?"

"You know I have. I've already rounded up our rowers for the regatta, which is more than you've done, and you live here."

Grimacing, Rafe knew what Headley was implying—he was distracted by something or *someone*. "You'll stay at the dower house for the week?"

"Unless the Slades wouldn't mind a handsome and unattached gentleman staying in his usual suite." The gleam sparkled.

"I'll ensure a room is prepared at the dower house, then," Rafe said with a wink. Easier said than done. The house was already full to bursting. The room they had set aside for Giles would have to do.

"Diana wants to join this year. Room for her, as well? *She* could stay at Devington."

She could. But that would irritate his family. "Gran will welcome her with open arms." Although where Headley's sister would room would be left for Gran to decide. "Any other plots to worm your way into the big house, or is my hospitality acceptable?"

"There are the dogs, as well, to consider…. No, I concede. For now." Headley's smirk said he would get to the bottom of why the eldest daughter was not for him. "The rowers hope to spend tomorrow practicing. Are you game, Fitz-Stephens?"

"Without hesitation. We'll want to scour the lake for Eurwendin spies first. Last year, they aimed for every advantage."

"*Spies*? Only the Fracas Frolic could turn neighboring villagers into spies." Headley shook his head. "Speaking of *spies*, I was tossing around the possibility of visiting Selwyn on Wednesday."

"I'm in. Meet at the fort? Oh, and I don't know where you got the idea Selwyn is a former spy. He was a privateer."

"I beg to differ. A spy who wants you to *think* he was a privateer. All part of his disguise. Now, unless you plan to romance me amongst the blooms," Headley said with a waggle of his eyebrows, "I propose you make good on that race you promised. Hercules is eager to show Alfgar what a horse can do." He rose and nodded for Rafe to follow.

Tossing back the remaining port, Rafe did as he was bid, eager for a stimulating ride. Alfie had shown no signs of injury since the light bruising on the journey from London and had been champing his bit to do more than ginger walks and trots about the estate grounds. Alfie was restless. As was Rafe. Who was Rafe to deny them both the pleasure of a good ride?

Chapter 11

The next day, late afternoon, the Fitz-Stephenses piled into the carriage, Noel being magnanimous enough to sit with his mother and grandmother so everyone would fit, however much of a squeeze.

Marion Fitz-Stephens whinged the whole ride from the dower house to the big house. "To have *our* carriage sent for us from *our* stables to take us to *our* house… it's outrageous."

"Hear hear," seconded Edwina Fitz-Stephens with a blaming glare to her son Anthony.

Rafe, shifting sideways so his father and Otis had more room, said, "My challenge to you is to be *kind*. *Noblesse oblige*, remember? We had this discussion."

Gran sniffed. "I'll be so sweet, your teeth will ache by the end of dinner."

Father voiced, "I think it's a kindness they invite us to dine. I wish you would come to like the Slades. Roland is the best of men, once you get to know him, and now that Rafe and Miss Slade—"

"Hush!" crowed Mother. "I'll hear no more of the *entrapment*. Rafe, darling, how have you not shaken the barnacle free yet?"

"Mother, please."

"I give you permission *not* to be a gentleman. Anthony—who taught our sons to be gentlemen rather than rogues? I blame you."

Otis and Noel exchanged glances before Otis said, "Your wish is our command, Mummy dearest."

"Don't you dare—"

"We've arrived," Rafe trumpeted, relieved to interrupt.

He had said nothing to his family about Mr. Thorpe or that the betrothal was, in all likelihood, temporary, for he saw no benefit in doing so, least of all because he could not say with any honesty that it *was* temporary. Judging from the initial reaction of the Slades to Mr. Alan Thorpe's name, it would be a forlorn hope to convince them Thorpe was the man for Miss Slade. If the mission did not succeed... It would be best for all parties to grow accustomed to each other.

The Fitz-Stephenses were shown into the drawing room—by their *own* butler into their *own* drawing room, Mother pointed out to all in hearing, but thankfully before they were within earshot of the drawing room itself. The Slades were assembled, each of the ladies looking lovelier than usual, including Mrs. Slade, who had gone above and beyond with her jewelry this evening, the sparkles nearly blinding. Beside him, his mother harrumphed.

"Anthony," Mr. Slade said in greeting, rising to shake his friend's hand and welcome the family.

Seating had been arranged, Rafe saw, to encourage he share a settee with Miss Slade, the brothers to sit on either side of Miss Slade's sisters, and his mother and grandmother to enjoy Mrs. Slade's exclusive company while Mr. Slade sequestered his father for conversation before dinner. At everyone's expressions, he was unsure who should receive his pity. He rather thought the sisters had the worst of it. His brothers were not known for their genteel charms. They would soon discover the sisters' mettle if the girls could survive before dinner without crying, losing their appetite, or demanding apologies after insult. Silently, he wished the girls luck.

He accepted the seat next to Miss Slade and flashed her a smile. "I have the best seat in the house, I'm to understand."

She cast him a sidelong glance then began fidgeting with one of her curls. Her celestial blue gown darkened the shade of grey of her eyes, awarding her an alluring air. A matching bandeau tamed her hair, but several curls had been allowed to tumble loose to tease her neck, tendrils that invited more than fidgeting fingers.

Rafe shook his head. No good could come of an attraction to her, not when the intent was to send her into someone else's arms.

Miss Slade broached conversation first. "Are your brothers here for the competition, then returning to school after, or perhaps not until Michaelmas term? Winchester, Eton, or…?"

He eyed the troublemakers, neither of whom had engaged the sisters in conversation yet, although Rafe could not say if it was the sisters ignoring them or the other way around. He suspected the former. Wise young ladies.

"A tutor from Hartminster comes three days per week. We've all been privately tutored, my older brother, as well. And you? Your sisters? No, don't tell me, there is a governess hiding behind a jib door, keeping a stern eye on her wards at all times."

Miss Slade caught herself before the dimples at the corners of her lips tugged a smile, or worse, a laugh. "No, I'm responsible for Cecilia's education, and then Cecilia's responsible for Theia's. We *did* have a governess for ages. She traveled with us happily wherever we moved. But then, quite unexpectedly, two moves ago, she married the local curate, and soon after moved with him when the bishop offered him a vicar's living. Since then, we've carried on without her except the occasional dance master, music instructor, or whoever."

"Dance master, you say." Rafe grinned. "So, you *dance*?"

"Only once. At a village assembly in our previous residence."

"Mmm." He let his gaze sweep appreciatively down to where the toes of her slippers peeked out from beneath the embroidered hem of her gown. "I wager you made a lasting impression, danced figures around the other ladies."

Her cheeks rouged pink, and she tugged at the loose curl with ferocity.

Before he could tell her about the celebratory assembly at the end of the frolic, dinner was announced.

Rafe looked about to his family to judge the expressions of dissatisfaction. Thankfully, no one seemed put out by having to interact. In fact, Mrs. Slade was flushed from the attention she had received from the Mmes. Fitz-Stephens. He doubted his mother and grandmother were anything more than civil, but despite their vocal opinions behind closed doors, they knew how to play a crowd. The fathers were too busy sharing a glass of brandy and guffawing to realize dinner was served. His brothers and her sisters still ignored each other. At least no one had been put through a window. Yet.

Throughout dinner, Rafe fought the urge to ask a dozen more questions about where she had lived previously, how long she typically lived in each location, what dances were her favorite, and so many more, but he did not wish to dominate her attention or sound like a doting betrothed. He was merely curious. It had nothing whatsoever to do with the three new curls that had fallen unbidden from the bandeau or Miss Slade's steely gaze that challenged him with each glance. Never mind she looked fine as a fivepence. It was singularly his curiosity.

As dinner wound to a close, the ladies about to return to the drawing room or the garden room, whichever of the two Mrs. Slade chose, and Mr. Slade about to invite the gentlemen to stay for port — including Otis and Noel, who were ecstatic to be included and not relegated to nursery-sitting the sisters, as they so eloquently said within hearing of said sisters — Mr. Slade turned his attention to Miss Slade.

"Genevieve, dear, could you find that book from the library? I wish to show my good friend Anthony."

She stared blankly at him. "Book?"

"You know, the book we discussed earlier today. I told you then I wanted to show him."

She shook her head, her expression pure perplexion.

"Gah. Hopeless. You'll remember as soon as you step into the library. Mr. Rafe Fitz-Stephens should escort you. Wouldn't want you getting lost."

Mother eyed Mr. Slade down her nose. "Does she often lose her way?"

Miss Slade made to protest but Miss Cecilia spoke first. "I can accompany them. Theia, as well. We want to show him the books by Trowbridge. Oh, and by —"

Mrs. Slade shrieked. "I'll not have the *g* word spoken in my hearing again! How *do* you handle wayward children, Mrs. Fitz-Stephens? My nerves are…"

As she continued to explain the state of her nerves, Rafe nodded towards the door for Miss Slade to follow before anyone was the wiser.

Genevieve followed Mr. Rafe Fitz-Stephens out of the dining room and into the garden room. She turned left towards the library, but he turned right towards the parlor.

Halting mid step, she watched him slip into the parlor, leaving her behind. She was as befuddled now as when her father had instructed her to find a book. There had been no conversation earlier that day or any time this week about a book, much less a book he wished to show his friend. It had been a ploy to give her time alone with her supposed betrothed, time she did not desire. Still, time with him sounded rather innocuous compared to the judging glances of the Mmes. Fitz-Stephens or the vapors of her mother.

She shrugged off being abandoned by her peculiar companion — what did she expect from a gentleman who favored climbing into upper story windows after midnight? — and made for the library in the west wing.

"*Psst*," came a whisper from behind her.

A glance over her shoulder met with the slow wink of Mr. Rafe Fitz-Stephens. He *come hither*-ed with his forefinger, then slipped back into the parlor.

Lips pursed, she followed.

The parlor was… empty.

She narrowed her gaze at the far door to the Great Hall, the only direction he could have gone. Why was he going in the opposite direction of the library? Traipsing around this monstrosity of a manor was not her idea of after-dinner entertainment.

A soft *scrap* followed by a softer *thud* sounded somewhere in the room. When she turned to look, he had reappeared in the far corner next to the fireplace.

Genevieve gasped.

With a darting look to the Great Hall door then back to Mr. Fitz-Stephens, she asked, "How did you appear *there* when you were not in the room upon my entry?"

He hooked an arm over the mantel, a smug grin playing at one corner of his lips. "Wouldn't you like to know."

"Well, yes, I would. And I assume *you* want me to know, or you would not have disappeared, then reappeared, for my benefit."

Wearing a full grin, he nodded for her to follow him. Again. This time, she went to him directly, loath to lose him. Once was quite enough for one day.

As casual as a lady in a millinery shop, he walked to the little bookshelf next to the hearth. Caressing his chin between his thumb and forefinger, he eyed her, then eyed the bookshelf, then eyed her again, still sporting that ridiculous grin.

"If you think to convince me *that* is the library," she began, "you can stop this tomfoolery right here, right now. I'm *not* as daft as Papa depicts me. I'm *not*—"

Whatever she was about to say—she had quite forgotten already—went unsaid, for he tapped the base of the bookshelf with the tip of his shoe, and the bookcase *clicked*. Before her disbelieving eyes, the *entire case* sighed away from the wall. Genevieve stared, mouth agape.

With another wink, he slid the corner of the case forward, and leaned just enough for him to dip behind it. She inched forward, eyeing it cautiously, as though it might bite her. When she stood where he had been standing, she could see the opening, not a full door size, only a short, pocket-sized opening. Beyond were stone stairs leading up. The stairs were narrow, the center of each step worn into a trough-shaped slope.

Tugging at her curls, one in each hand, she hesitated to step into the darkness.

A hand shot out towards her. She covered her mouth to silence her cry of alarm. It was his hand. In the dark. Reaching out for her. He curled his forefinger again then held his palm open for her to take. She gawped, strangely exhilarated. Slipping her fingers into his firm, warm palm, she allowed him to hand her gently up the stairs.

Two steps up, her slippers nestling into the worn divots, the bookshelf *clicked* back into place, shutting them into pitch black. Genevieve squeezed his hand, her pulse quickening. Next to her, he chuckled. She could not see him, but she could sense him. He was the warmth beside her, an aromatic citrusy delight that tickled her all the way to her stomach.

"There's light ahead," he promised, before guiding her further into the unknown.

They climbed one story before he paused, his hand still firmly clasping hers — for safety, of course. A squeak, as soft as a mouse, came first, and then a shaft of light shone onto the stairs. She fluttered her eyelids. He had opened a door, one of ancient oak and iron studs. When he guided her through it, she could see they were in a narrow corridor, stone floor, stone walls, only a slender crack high on the wall behind them gave way to light, the afternoon sun streaming in. The crack, she could see, was quite intentional, not the wearing of stone, but what looked almost like a spyhole, too narrow for an arrow but too finite for a fissure.

Rather than proceed forward, Mr. Fitz-Stephens released her hand and leaned against a wall to face her. "The west wing is the only remaining part of the old monastery. Passages, such as this, snake through the whole of the wing. Only a few rooms have access, and each of those with a hidden entrance. Made for great fun in a house of boys. I can tell you which doors squeak, which steps crumble beneath foot, and which areas have light. You're not afraid of spiders, are you?"

Wide-eyed, fascinated, envious of having been brought up in a house with secrets, more so to have lived in a house long enough to know its idiosyncrasies, she almost missed his question. When it dawned what he asked, she laughed aloud, a giddy sound, one full of the glee she only felt when riding.

"I *like* spiders, I'll have you know. If it can be found in nature, it has a special place in my heart, spiders included." She raised her chin, proud not to be missish.

He cocked his head. "Be careful how you use that laugh. A weapon not unlike cupid's bow."

Without explaining himself, he proceeded forward.

Fiddling with her fallen curls, she followed once more. The corridor was relatively short before turning a sharp left, then it dipped three steps down to a landing, a small wicket to the right—she assumed leading to either another room or another set of stairs—and then three steps up again for the remaining length of the hallway. This stretch was unlit, but the glow from the previous bend illuminated it just enough that she did not stumble into him. At the end of the corridor were two doors, one to the left and one to the right. It was to the right, he opened. The door was little more than half height, so Genevieve ducked to pass through it.

As soon as she stood up, she bumped into him. His laugh rumbled in the small room. He felt along the wall until she heard a *click*. In front of him, the wood paneling shifted forward, flooding the little room with sunlight. He angled the panel and stepped through the opening.

How surprised was Genevieve to realize they were in the upper gallery of the library. To either side was the mezzanine, overlooking the ground floor.

He shut the bookcase behind her until its molding *thunked* flush against the wall. "A longer route than had we entered from the garden room," he said affably, "but far more fun. I thought you might enjoy a bit of fun."

Fun? She could not hide her smile of sheer pleasure.

Leaving her behind, he circled the mezzanine, then down the spiral stairs to the ground floor. "While you find whatever book your father wishes to show mine, I'm going to grab a few works I've been sorely missing." His voice faded as he roamed the stacks below. "I hope you don't mind my raiding your library."

Under her breath, she said, "Technically, it's *your* library."

"What was that?" he called up to her.

Clearing her throat, she said with more volume, "Nothing. Carry on."

For how long did she stand there, mulling over what she had just experienced and staring at her palm in memory of it being held by his? Long enough that Mr. Fitz-Stephens caught her attention by waving a book in the air.

"Do you like poetry?" he asked.

With a flick to one of her curls, she shook herself out of her stupor and joined him on the ground floor.

She accepted the book he offered but did not have the wherewithal to comprehend the writing along the spine. It might as well have been written in Arabic. What had come over her?

A nod to the book, he said, "One of my favorites. Give it a read?" Without waiting for an answer, he turned to sift through a few more books he had stacked on a table. "Does Mr. Thorpe enjoy reading anything in particular?"

"Who?" The word sounded far breathier than she expected. She cleared her throat again. "You like poetry?"

"Do I not strike you as the poetry type?" His question was full of amusement, as though they were sharing a joke.

He took a seat at the table and thumbed through one of the volumes.

Still trapped in the peculiar daze she could not explain, she sat across from him and flipped, unseeing, through the pages of the book he had given her. For each page she turned, he turned two.

All laughter gone from his voice, he said after a stretch of silence, "I beg your pardon for upending your life. It was never my intent to distress you. Imagine my horror coming home and finding a stranger in my room. More horror still to realize the situation I inadvertently forced on you, first to fear me as a burglar, and then to be... stuck with me."

Genevieve's heart pounded as she studied his sober expression. His apology weighed heavily on her shoulders. She felt, oddly, guilty. Not about the situation so much as for blaming him, resenting him, judging him, oh, so many ill feelings towards him when she *knew* he was not to blame. It was easier to blame a stranger than her own father.

"It's I who should be apologizing, Mr. Fitz-Stephens. I must for my abominable behavior. We are, I believe, in this together, and I've been so worried you would resent me for being in the wrong place at the wrong time, I've been... defensive. I certainly must apologize for my father." She stared down at the book in her lap before asking, "Why did you not laugh at my father and leave? Why did you allow him to bully you into making a declaration when we *all* knew it was a misunderstanding and nothing nefarious?"

"Because I'm a gentleman, Miss Slade."

"Being a gentleman means marrying a stranger you'll dislike more each day since she's a barrier to your dreams?"

"Choosing to become a circuit barrister, you mean," he said, rather than asked. "Being a gentleman means sacrificing for someone else's honor. Doing so honors the gentleman in return. His sense of pleasure at exacting honor should increase exponentially each day. A gentleman, a *true* gentleman, would never harbor resentment or otherwise, rather he would make it his mission to see the lady happy with the match, more so since it was not of her choosing. As to circuit versus Old Bailey, who is to say my dream *isn't* to become a country barrister? People change. Choices change."

Genevieve compelled her attention on the book in her lap to disguise the tears stinging her eyes. Why his words caused such an emotional response, she would not admit, could not admit — she did not *know* why.

"May I call on you tomorrow afternoon?" he asked when she showed no signs of responding.

Blinking to clear her vision, and hopefully any signs of distress, she raised her chin. His expression had changed from serious to teasing, one corner lifting into the almost-familiar smirk he favored.

On her lips was a quip that he need not worry about calling on her, not with Mr. Thorpe soon to arrive, but she stopped herself before the words slipped free. She had already made that excuse before; she did not know if Mr. Thorpe really was coming; and after what he had just said…. Genevieve refused to be snotty. The reaction too often flicked like a whip in her defense, but *he* did not deserve the licks. *He* was a true gentleman. And that scared her a little.

She nodded her assent when she could not find her voice to reply.

"Splendid. I now consider it my duty to acquaint you with all Grant Lindis has to offer, which is, I regret to say, only this one-week festival." His smile deepened. "If you promise to wear your hair tomorrow as you have it now, I'll reveal what the ladies' event is going to be, and then, do my best to convince you to participate."

Brows knitting, she echoed hoarsely, "My hair?"

That deepening smile twisted with a frisson of mischief. He nodded to one of the unlit sconces hanging against a pillar, a mirrored sconce. Setting aside the book in her hands, she stepped to the mirror.

Aghast, she covered her face at the sight. She had fidgeted with her curls so much that her bandeau had been tugged to one side, the hairpins loose, and several great masses of frizzy curls hung unbound around her shoulders. What a fright, she looked! Positively indecent.

When she turned back to spy him between her fingers, still covering the shame flaming her cheeks, she growled — he was leaning back in his chair, hands folded behind his head, howling with laughter.

Uncouth man!

Genevieve did not know if she wanted to laugh or cry. So, she did a little of both.

Chapter 12

Alfgar whickered as they approached the ruins of the Rhydderch Fort in Lynntreow.

"Good memory, Alfie." Rafe slowed their pace.

While he could not yet see anyone, the clash of swords was unmistakable. Ah, yes, today was fencing day. One did not soon forget the Vitruvian Society weekly agenda. Were the new recruits disciplined disciples? Which lessons did they favor? Were any from elsewhere in Devonshire, or all from within the Hartminster deanery? He had more questions than he had time to ask.

As he and Alfgar drew closer, the open arches to the cloisters teased to the inhabitants. Rafe thought he caught sight of Headley and Selwyn, but he could not be sure. A small gathering of young men circled two fencers. Further afield, several pairs were engaged in assault.

After spending so long on the cricket pitch at Gray's Inn, the clang of swords was a welcome sound indeed. Rafe dismounted and walked Alfgar the remaining distance until he reached where the other horses grazed or dozed. Before joining the Vitruvians, he took a moment to settle Alfie and prepare himself. Chin scratches, treats, and water for his horse.

For him, he removed his outercoat, riding coat, and beaver hat. Hefting his sword from the front of his saddle, he unwrapped the leather belt from the scabbard and wrapped and tightened it around his waist.

Calling on Selwyn was never a drawing room affair with polite conversation over tea and sandwiches.

Despite it being early enough in the morning that the earthy aroma of dew filled the air, and the sun had not risen high enough to warm one's shoulders, Rafe could already feel a bead of sweat trailing down his spine. He would need to wash well before calling on Miss Slade that afternoon.

As Rafe turned to join the group, Headley waved from beneath the arcades, jogging towards Rafe.

"Selwyn is in good spirits," Headley said, dabbing his forehead with a handkerchief. "I've already gone three bouts. Nothing makes you feel old like combating youth with endless stamina."

"You're one year older than I am, hardly infirm."

"Just wait. You'll see."

"Promises, promises." Rafe surveyed the crowd as they entered the inner sanctum of the Society.

There were more attendees present than had ever been in his day. Nevertheless, the group was exclusive. For membership, one had to be recommended, attend a one-week trial, and then be voted in unanimously. One black ball, and membership was barred. This was a gentleman's club, but nothing of the likes seen in London.

Walking towards them was Baronet Lyttleparva's steward, Selwyn Relish.

He was a distinguished man with salt and pepper hair, sun-kissed complexion, laugh lines crowing the

corners of his eyes, boulders for shoulders, and tree
trunks for legs — a fierce opponent in both physical and
mental battles. No one knew his age. No one knew *him*.

Selwyn had lived in Lynntreow as the baronet's
steward and the founder of the Vitruvian Society for
a little over a decade, but where he hailed was a mystery. He had proven fluency in more languages than
the Society members knew existed and demonstrated
unbeaten combat acumen. Former pirate? Spy for the
Crown? Privateer? Runaway aristocrat? Younger son
of a peer in hiding? Former King's Counsel? Military
officer? French émigré? To the young men he trained,
he was Herculean, God-like in his knowledge, experience, and prowess.

Rafe was older now, more experienced, more
knowledgeable, both an Oxford education and legal
training in his arsenal, and yet all he saw as Selwyn
approached was the same man who had awed him
all those many years ago when he attended his first
meeting of the Society.

Headley said, as Selwyn offered his hand to Rafe,
"Look who I found — the Crown's newest barrister."

"Not quite yet," Rafe said with a flush of embarrassment. "Am awaiting the Call, so don't bewitch
me by speaking too soon."

Clasping Rafe's shoulder, Selwyn congratulated
him, welcomed him to join them for the day, and then
said, "Are you worthy to approach the Bar, Fitz-Stephens? Prove yourself in the ring. *Barba non facit
philosophum.*"

This was a challenge Rafe could not resist. A
beard does not make a philosopher, Selwyn had said
in Latin.

On the other side of Selwyn, Headley cast Rafe an "I warned you" expression.

It was another hour, at least, before Rafe would engage in battle. During the hour, he met the new members, as well as shook hands with those who had only just joined when he was leaving for Oxford but were now the mature members. With each discussion and story exchanged, the spoken language shifted, all part of the training, all part of the Society life. Of all the languages, he slipped most easily into Latin. A pity the court did not still use Law Latin. Rafe bemoaned being born half a century too late.

At last, the moment Rafe had been anticipating arrived. Selwyn chose his opponent, a freckle-faced boy of about eighteen whose focus could sharpen a blade. The Society members gathered *en masse* to watch.

Before facing off on the piste, Rafe squeezed the boy's hand, each wishing the other luck. His parting words were, *"Gladiator in arena consilium capit."*

The gladiator forms his plan in the arena. The fighter has trained until what challenges him is easy. He now adapts on the spot. Or, more appropriately understood by Rafe's opponent, the arse kicking was about to begin.

The day could not possibly improve any further, not when Genevieve had spent the morning in the village helping prepare for the frolic. The reception of the villagers had surprised her. Since moving to Grant Lindis, she had mostly been ignored except for the few curious callers who came to the house to meet the family, but now that word had spread there was an understanding between the eldest daughter and Mr. Rafe Fitz-Stephens, everyone wished to know her. From the welcoming responses, she knew them to think it was a desired match, nothing in the way of the true circumstances. Gone was her fear they would think she had trapped him.

Did it make her a bad person to wish to take advantage of the situation, to accept their kindness and play along as though this was a match between two friendly families? It seemed deceptive. And yet she could not help but relish in the reception. For the first time in her life, she was *part* of something, a recognized face in the village, an invited neighbor, everyone wanting her to take part.

On top of that, she had been with the group marking the path for the forest run. A morning in the forest? Nothing could be more divine!

The day had not begun so dreamily. On the way into the village, her mother had insisted Genevieve, Cecilia, and Theia accompany her to call on Mmes. Fitz-Stephens. Her mother had dominated the conversation, and much to Genevieve's chagrin, made the Slades sound like roaming gypsies. Mmes. Fitz-Stephens already disliked them, Genevieve suspected. But to describe the family's traipsing about the countryside, hither and yon, from one house to the next—it was insupportable.

To her relief, both Mrs. Marion Fitz-Stephens and Mrs. Edwina Fitz-Stephens were superb hostesses, never sneering. That did not stop Genevieve from feeling the eyes of judgment upon her. She wanted to reassure them the betrothal was temporary. To say so would require an explanation, and it would not do to announce Mr. Thorpe was coming, assuming he was. Besides, she did not *want* to say aloud that the betrothal would end. It must, of course. Despite Mr. Rafe Fitz-Stephens' talk of being a gentleman, nothing would change the circumstances. He had been forced. That was not a solid foundation for marriage. And yet she did not want to say the words, for saying them would make them real, and a plague upon her, but she could not stop thinking about his promise to call later this afternoon. Would he remember?

Just thinking about it had her touching a hand to her hair. She had already learned what the ladies' event in the competition would be, but she would not reveal that to him. She wanted him to tell her, just as he had promised.

And so, as the Slade ladies made their way from the village up the long drive to Devington Priory, Genevieve had a skip in her step. She had an hour before he called. Perfect. Long enough to visit the washbasin after trampling through the forest most of the morning and to change from her walking gown into her visiting gown. However foolish it was to be excited to see a man she detested — a lady *must* detest a gentleman for tumbling into her room and compromising her — she could not convince the flutter in her stomach of that fact.

If only she had not written Mr. Thorpe…

Beside her, Mama chattered, scarcely drawing breath. Cecilia responded louder than necessary to be heard over Mama. Theia ignored both, her attention fixed on a book as she walked and read simultane-ously with impressive skill. Genevieve, too, ignored them, busy skipping to the beat of her anticipation.

As the stone arches of the entry screen came into view, she put extra pep in her steps. Ahead, she saw the silhouette of a figure leaning against one of the columns—how unusual for Papa to greet them. But oh, he must have seen them coming up the drive. How kind!

It took exactly twenty-five seconds for her to real-ize the figure was not Papa.

Her heart skipped a beat as the man swaggered towards them. But *no!*—she had not yet washed and changed! Her hand touched her hair again, worried about loose curls and frizz, or worse, leaves and forest debris.

"Good afternoon," called the sultry voice of Mr. Rafe Fitz-Stephens.

In one hand, he carried a fashionable walking stick, and in the other, his beaver hat. His flaxen hair shimmered in the sunlight, never mind the sky was overcast, his teeth gleamed when he smiled, and his blue eyes sparkled, although Genevieve was too far away to see any such things or the pernickety fact that eyes did not *sparkle*. Even from this distance, his per-fume was heavenly, or so she imagined. Genevieve inhaled deeply, then exhaled her sanity.

It was the only explanation for her reaction—she had parted with sanity somewhere between the stone corridor of a forgotten monastery and the driveway.

Mama's triumphant greeting made Genevieve's ears ring. "Mr. Fitz-Stephens! Have you come to call on us? Here we are!"

"I was out for a ramble about the grounds," he said, his walking stick tapping against the gravel as he approached. "What a coincidence to bump into the most beautiful ladies at Devington Priory during my aimlessly leisure stroll."

Genevieve bit her lip to keep from laughing. Her initial reaction was to say something acerbic like, *we're the* only *ladies at Devington Priory,* but knowing him, he would spin things to include the servants or emphasize he meant the estate, not just the house, some pithy retort that would deepen his compliment rather than expostulate his silliness.

Mama insisted, "Do come inside. You must be parched."

"Ah, how you lure me, madam. You ply your charm to tempt me with sweets."

"Yes, yes, I shall have cake be brought with tea."

"I wasn't referring to cake, Mrs. Slade." He let the words linger before leaning forward as though to share a secret. "Before me stand the four most honeyed confections I've had the pleasure to know."

Mama flicked open her fan. Cecilia cooed. Theia peered over her book with batting eyelashes.

Genevieve harrumphed. What a rogue! All her excitement ebbed away.

"Alas," he continued, "I must reserve my affections for my betrothed. If she would do me the honor of accompanying me on my walk home, I would be the happiest of men." He turned the full force of his smile on her, eyebrows raised in invitation.

Chin tipped, she ignored the extra beats in her pulse. "I'm afraid I—"

"Of *course* she'll accompany you!" trumpeted Mama. "Come, girls. With me."

Cecilia and Theia muttered protests about wanting to extend their walk, but Mama dragged them with her.

Genevieve scowled at the rogue. *Honeyed confections.* Of all the asinine… Without a word, she turned towards the dower house and began walking.

"This way, Miss Slade," he said.

Slowing her gait, she glanced over her shoulder. He nodded towards the west wing of the house.

Baffled, Genevieve said, "I thought you wished me to accompany you home."

"Technically, *this* is my home." With a slow wink, he moved his hat to the hand carrying the walking stick and offered her the crook of his elbow.

She eyed his elbow. She eyed him. She eyed the direction of the dower house. Curiosity got the better of her.

Sighing, she slipped her hand around his arm and fell in step with him as they walked past the front of the house, around the west wing garden wall, past the library, and then…. He brought them directly in front of a line of yew along the north wall of the house.

Parting the branches, he revealed a camouflaged servant's entrance, a few stone steps down to a door. She did not know where the servant entrances were or were not, but did find it peculiar that the entrance was concealed. More peculiar still was their *using* a servant's entrance. Not that she was a snot, but this was highly unusual. When he realized her hesitancy, he stepped past her, down the stairs, and through the door. She was left staring at the branches.

"Psst," came his whisper.

Oh, very well. She nudged the branches out of her way so she could duck past and follow him. So help her, if he was going to promenade her through the staff quarters or the kitchens or... He stood just inside the doorway on a landing, the only option forward being stone stairs leading up.

Her heart pounded. Another secret? Forgetting herself, she tucked her hand beneath his elbow again and held firmly, caught between anticipation and the renewal of her earlier excitement.

He led her up three flights of short stairs before they came to a door. It opened with the merest suggestion.

A sharp gasp of surprise escaped her lips as she stepped inside a room, little more than a snug. It was a much-used room by the look of it. Much loved, as well. Floral paper hangings of damask green, a well-worn rug, the smallest fireplace she had ever seen, a winged chair before the hearth, two high backed chairs against the wall, short bookcases lining two of the walls, and one large window framed by damask curtains.

"It's a reading nook," he explained. "Then, I suppose it can be whatever you make of it, but we always used it as a reading nook."

"Is the only entrance the one we used?"

"Not quite." He walked to the far wall and tapped a panel in the wainscoting. A hollow report was his response. "This panel opens into the billiard room. If you stand outside the house looking up, you'll see the window here matches perfectly with those of the billiard room, seamless. The only clue you would have is if you counted the number of windows in the billiard room to realize you were one short."

She turned slowly, taking in the snug. First a secret corridor and now a hidden room. Would she ever learn all the secrets of the house? What must it have been like to grow up here? Why was he showing her all these things?

"You would think we got away with murder as children," he was saying as she continued her exploration. "We spent more time hiding and escaping in secret routes than using the main thoroughfares. Our parents knew all the hidden ways, though, and would chase us down. No sneaking to our rooms to avoid being caught with mud on our breeches."

He laughed at the memories. Genevieve struggled to imagine either Mrs. Fitz-Stephens or the Squire chasing anyone, least of all down narrow, forgotten corridors. For her part, she had never been mischievous or done anything to warrant hiding or sneaking, always the biddable daughter. She did not fight the grin teasing the corners of her lips. This was her secret now.

After she turned three full circles to gawk at the room, she realized he had set aside his stick and hat and moved one of the high-backed chairs next to the winged one.

How naughty of them, hidden in a room together when her family thought they were walking the grounds in open view, she doing little more than accompanying him to the dower house. The sheer impropriety of it all thrilled her.

Accepting the winged chair, she waved for him to join her. He did, his expression caught between irritatingly smug and disarmingly honest.

"I owe you an answer," he said cryptically.

Genevieve smoothed her gown, then folded her hands in her lap, the epitome of calm reservation, thankful her feet were tucked beneath her hem so he could not see her toes curl as she braced herself for this "answer."

"Archery." He watched her, as though waiting for a reaction. "The ladies' event. It's archery."

"Oh!" She blinked in surprise. What else had she expected him to say? "I thought your information was conditional. I recall something about my hair." Not that she wanted to remind him of her tousled curls, but since she was confident her coiffure was in perfect semblance, a little teasing seemed in order.

That cursed smirk looked back at her. "May I?" He leaned forward before she could respond and plucked something from her tresses. Held between his fingers as a trophy, and twirled to torment her, was a spindly twig.

"You tricked me, planted it there to tease me."

"*Planted* it?" He chuckled. "Appropriate choice of words."

"How is it you always see me at my worst?"

"I beg to differ, Miss Slade."

She scoffed but could feel her cheeks heating in a blush.

"Will you participate in the archery competition?" He continued to roll the twig between his fingers.

"I'm afraid I'm out of practice."

"All the more reason to join the fun. It *is* fun. No one really cares who misses or hits, who scores for the team or doesn't. If you're nervous, my mother would take pleasure in coaching you before the event. It's the last event of the frolic, so ample time to practice."

"Your mother?" She gave a soft *ha* of incredulity.

"She's a marksman with a bow, archer extraordinaire."

"I wasn't questioning her skill so much as her wishing to help me. I'm not so naïve to believe she hasn't spoken ill of me behind closed doors. I tricked you into proposing, am brandished with the guilt of keeping you from your London plans, never — "

"About my mother," he began, dismissing whatever excuse she was about to use, "…she's not only the wife of a magistrate, she's the mother of four boys, four rambunctious and troublemaking boys. If she acts like a sergeant, it's because she's had to assume the role or risk being trampled. She's not as frightening as she seems. You can win her over. Easily."

Dubious, Genevieve fidgeted, lacing and unlacing her fingers. "Pardon my doubts."

"Would you be surprised to know there was a time when my grandmother and mother disliked each other? Thick as thieves now, but it was open war once. My grandmother is a proud woman, cannot abide weakness in a Fitz-Stephens. One must bear the name with strength and condescension. Only when my mother found her voice and built a will of iron did she earn my grandmother's respect. She had to prove herself capable of heralding Fitz-Stephens men into the world, something a delicate and vaporish woman could never do, at least not according to my gran."

"So… your family values rude, outspoken, and obstinate women?"

He barked a laugh. "Nothing so vulgar. What's valued is assertiveness and knowing one's own mind. One needn't speak their mind, at least not outside the family, that would be ungenteel, but one must *know* their own mind." He studied her before adding, "Be yourself."

"I'm always myself. That's silly advice. I can't do anything to dissuade your mother from thinking — "

He held a staying hand. "When you're with your family, you're… different. You're… amiable." He cleared his throat but did not explain what he meant by *amiable*, which sounded complimentary to Genevieve, not a shortcoming. "When you're with me, you're…" He circled his hand. "Assertive."

"Obstinate, you mean. Rude. Ungenteel. Uncultured…"

"Unbowed."

She let that sink in rather than respond.

"While my mother," he continued, "may *seem* to hold you responsible for our situation — something along the lines of if you had not been party to the trap or had in any way objected to the match, you would have protested, refused my offer, etc. — it's hot air. She *knows* you're at the whim of your father's will. Every unmarried lady is. She was once an unmarried lady herself, you'll want to recall."

"She has said this?"

"No. But she's a shrewd woman. Don't let her intimidate you with the I-rule-a-house-of-boys attitude. She's syllabub inside."

At the thought, at the choice of description, even at the reminder of honeyed confections, Genevieve laughed. Once she started, she could not stop. How was she to face Mrs. Fitz-Stephens now? All she would think of was syllabub. With the tips of her fingers, she swatted at the tears in the corner of her eyes — she had not laughed quite this hard in a long time.

"Will you call me Rafe?" he asked when her laugh had softened.

The question sobered her. "Is that appropriate?"

"As appropriate as our sitting here together." His smile was sweet, gentle, only a tiny hint wicked.

She looked away, her tummy fluttering again. Not meeting his eyes, she gave a curt nod.

"And do I have permission to use your Christian name in return? Or is this to be a one-sided informality?"

With a playful sneer, she said, "You may."

She stopped herself from adding, *don't become too accustomed to it. Mr. Thorpe is coming.* The thought was so fleeting, she gave it no credence. She could scarcely remember Mr. Thorpe. Why had she written to him? With a swat at a drooping curl on her temple, she dismissed those thoughts.

Chapter 13

Rafe watched her toying with her ringlets, a trifle smitten. How the devil was he going to match-make her with Mr. Thorpe? He was unconvinced he wanted to. He *could* seduce her into falling for him, instead, steal her heart from her old love, move forward with the betrothal. But was it wise? And how arrogant of him to believe hearts were easily swayed. If she were so inconstant, that would say more about her than his acumen with the fairer sex.

Yet he could not tear his eyes from her. Etiquette had the right of it to ensure couples were chaperoned at all times. This solitude, the intimacy of it, the ability to say whatever one wished without being overheard or observed, it was dangerously intoxicating, quite heady.

Breaking his thoughts, he asked, "How are you liking Grant Lindis?"

"It's humorous you ask me today of all days because today has been the first day, I believe, of my entire life, I've felt like I was welcomed, really welcomed as a village member. I helped mark the path for the forest run."

He held up the twig. "I gathered."

She narrowed her gaze, but a becoming blush blossomed on her cheeks. "I've lived all over the

British Isles, yet never met with so warm a welcome. For a brief time, I also lived in Wales and Scotland. The longest we've lived anywhere was five years. After five years, you would think I would have been part of something, made friends, known my neighbors. Not a whit, I tell you. Most places, we only stayed for three, but that has shortened each year. We've had back-to-back one-year leases for the past four years. One year never seems long enough to try to make friends. I simply don't bother. Yet today... today proved me wrong."

Miss Slade gazed into the distance, a faint smile giving him the impression she was remembering her romp in the forest. He was only disappointed he had not been there to witness it.

"Papa loves to meet new people," she continued. "Loves entertaining and socializing. He's restless, though, and querulous if he's stuck anywhere too long. Seeing the *same* people is never as enjoyable for him as meeting new people. I think the longer he stays somewhere, the more responsibility he feels, from the care of the estate to the maintenance of existing friendships, and if there's one quality he does not like, it's responsibility. If he could see his daughters settled, I believe he would take Mama traveling abroad, although he has never said as much."

Rafe fiddled with the twig, wondering what it would be like to be brought up without a home, without consistency. He could not imagine a life without his neighbors. Every happy memory was wound around Grant Lindis or neighboring villages and towns. If pressed, he could sketch the placement of every tree in the nearby woods, mark all the best places to retreat for solitude or cause mischief with one's mates. Regardless of how their situation ended, he felt it his duty to ensure she could consider this a home, a place of friendly refuge no matter where in the world she moved next — with or without Mr. Thorpe.

"I wonder," she continued, "what stories my previous houses had to tell. I never knew to listen. Think of the hidden rooms I must have missed."

"Or, instead of thinking what's been missed, we could think of what's now been found."

He was referring to her feelings of belonging in Grant Lindis, perhaps also to this room, a haven away from troubles, but as their eyes met and held, he wondered if the words had not implied something more. Her eyes darkened to an almost smokey shade of slate. One corner of Rafe's lips quivered. In future, he may reconsider being alone with her. She was dangerous, more so because she had no awareness of the beauty she wielded, and he was not thinking only of her figure, face, and disheveled curls.

She disturbed the direction of his thoughts, but only as a ripple on the water's surface. "Were you really out walking the grounds, or was that an excuse to avoid the inevitable tray in the drawing room?"

Trying not to watch her lips form the words, he stayed focused on her eyes, not that it helped cool the skin beneath his cravat. "You said it, not me. My arrival was innocent, a gentleman caller for the Slade family, but when I was informed all were from home, impishness got the best of me. Mr. Norton hinted to everyone's whereabouts, so I decided to linger, suspecting you would return soon. Why am

I giving away my secrets? You've put a spell on me, Miss Slade."

"Genevieve," she nudged.

"*Ita vero*," he agreed. "While you were foraging in the forest, I spent the morning with old friends. Made a few new ones in the process."

She arched her brows. "Oh? Will you tell me about it, or only tease me?"

"I might have to tease you. It involves a secret society."

Her brows rose higher.

"Only jesting. It *is* a society, but not in any way secret. It's the Vitruvian Society. I've been a member since I was... oh, I'm not certain, actually... fourteen, perhaps? It's not unlike the gentlemen clubs in London, but more in the way of a sportsman club."

"As I've not been to London and have no brothers, I can honestly say I don't know anything about the gentlemen clubs in London." The admonishment was gentle, said with a breathy laugh.

"Ah, yes. There's that. Incidentally, I'm not a member of any of the London clubs, but I hear they mostly involve gambling, coffee, and gossip, although I'm sure there's more to them than that. At least, I hope so. Allow me to approach my club's introduction differently. I engaged in a duel today. How is that for an opening?"

His words had the desired effect.

She gasped and gripped the arms of her chair. "I... suppose you won?"

"By the skin of my teeth. It wasn't a duel at dawn, I should clarify, although that removes much of the drama. It was a fencing bout with one of the newer members of the Society. More than once, I thought my goose was cooked. I *did* win, but it was humbling to be so out of practice."

"*Why* were you fighting?"

"We weren't. We were engaged in conversation."

She tilted her head, the brows now furrowing.

"A fencing jest, yes? A conversation of blades?" He chuckled to himself. "Never mind my attempt at humor. In truth, we *were* engaged in conversation, more than one, in point of fact. See, a fencing bout among Society members isn't *just* about fencing. We must debate while crossing blades, the topic being the standing champion's choice. A test for both mind and body."

"I don't mean to sound ignorant, but what sort of club is this?"

It gave him pause that someone would not know about the Vitruvian Society. He should have realized she would not be familiar with it. After all, none of the barristers at Gray's Inn knew about it, nor had anyone he had met in London. But now that he was home, in his old stomping ground, it was unusual for someone not to know about the Society, even if only by reputation of its exclusivity of membership. All his brothers were members. Giles was one of the founding members.

"My apologies, Genevieve." He admired the flush along her neck at his use of her name. "I don't mean to shroud with secrecy. The society is based, in part, on the Vitruvian Man, but more specifically on the Renaissance ideologies modernized according to Descartes' treatise on man, i.e. an *enlightened* man, who embodies the tenets of reason. Such a man exemplifies athleticism, self-improvement and development, self-government, education, discussion and debate, critical thought, questioning and reasoning, just to name a few."

Her mouth formed an *oh*, but she said nothing at first. Rafe sat up a little straighter, feeling more like a bounder than an enlightened gentleman for all his flirting. He hardly exemplified any of these traits at the moment.

Instead of pointing out his flaws, she asked, "You joined to become this Vitruvian person?"

He restrained his mirth. "It's not a matter of joining. One must earn their place. An existing member must first recommend you, and then you face a one-week trial before the members vote if you're to join the ranks."

"That doesn't sound too terrible. Anyone can join if they're recommended and voted, then. And the training of all those things is after the trial?"

"Not exactly. One must already be those things, instinctively, and that must be demonstrated. The trial isn't where we attend meetings to get to know fellow members. It's a true trial, a test, one of strength, endurance, and intelligence. Trials are held twice per year, and the tests endured change each time, so there's no way to prepare. Candidates must perform mental and physical tasks under duress, such as swimming in an icy lake in the dead of winter and, upon surfacing, have to solve a complex riddle, all while half frozen and trying to build a fire using only nature's tools. Or engaging in a thirty to sixty-mile roundtrip race only to be given, immediately upon return, an ancient language to decipher rather than sustenance or rest."

"For *fun*? Who would do any of that to join a club? You're teasing me." She laughed with abandon. "To think, I believed you."

Straight faced, he said, "But it is true."

"If you were in the Army, perhaps. I don't believe you. And any matter, who would pass so fool-hardy trial?"

"It's all true. Those were off the hip examples, not necessarily real trials, but they capture the heart of the trials." He rubbed his chin in thought, feeling rather defensive of his Society and his idea of what was *fun*, while trying to understand why someone might view the whole of it as half-hinged. "It's not about passing the trial. Candidates don't know that, of course. They believe it *is* about passing, but it's not. There is no 'pass' or 'fail.' It's a personal journey, this trial. You learn your limits, as well as what you're capable of. You learn your breaking point. In this way, when you become a member of the Society, you have a fixed mark of your limit and can then train to become unbreakable. The trial is about *you*, not about the Society."

"Oh, I see. That makes much more sense. Everyone 'passes' in the end and becomes a member, everyone who wishes to, that is."

"On the contrary. Less than a quarter of the candidates who begin trial week finish. Most quit." He recalled his own trial and the myriad times he had wanted to quit. Knowing his brother was watching, and wanting to make Giles proud, he had persevered. "Once in the Society, true training begins, as members craft themselves into the ultimate polymath. We learn and practice every subject. Philosophy, poetry, music, science, mathematics, history, politics, languages, geology, biology, humanism, physics, architecture… I could go on, yes? Riding, fencing, pugilism, rowing… I could continue there, as well, you see. We become limitless. *Vincit qui se vincit*, Genevieve. He conquers who conquers himself."

He said the last with a hypocritical air that he hoped she did not notice. A man who conquers himself would be master of temptations, able to control himself and his urges, and yet he sat here in a room with a beautiful woman, alone, unguarded, a woman he inexplicably desired to kiss. That her eyes roamed over him, as though determining how well he had succeeded at becoming a polymath, did nothing more than fan the flames. Although he sat, perfectly respectable in a visiting suit, he suspected his athleticism was on display. At least he did not wear padding. And if it was not arrogant to boast, he thought his calves looked rather fetching in the clocked stockings he had chosen. No riding boots today to hide the musculature, not when making formal calls.

He flashed her a smile when her gaze returned to meet his. "Do I meet with your approval?"

"I… I don't know what you mean." A blush of deep crimson crept from the fichu tucked into her bodice, up her neck, and into her cheeks.

Satisfied, he leaned back in his chair, crossed his ankles, and folded his hands over his middle, still thumbing the twig—the last, only to antagonize her. "And that, my dear, was what I was doing this morning. Enjoying the company of other crazed individuals who take pleasure in debating while fencing, playing a piano blindfolded, or perhaps retelling Plato's allegory in ten languages. Backwards. While balancing a pineapple on one's head." When she did not laugh, he said, "That was a jest, by the way."

Her silence was discouraging. Was he boasting? He was. He must be. She thought him vain.

Sitting up again, now self-conscious, he moved the topic back to her. "Will you compete in the archery event?"

Genevieve's eyes widened, obviously surprised to have the tables turned. "I... I'm out of practice, as I said."

"All the more reason to devote this week to familiarizing yourself with the bow again. I'll speak to Mother as soon as I return to the dower house. We can arrange for the two of you to meet as early as tomorrow."

She looked down at her hands and laced her fingers. "I'm undecided. I was never good at it."

"This is an opportunity to improve yourself. Be the best you can be? Mother will be delighted to help, although she may not admit it."

Shifting in her chair, she averted her gaze. "Let me think on it. I need time to consider. I... I don't want to humiliate myself."

"Come, there's no reason not to. I won't take no for an answer," he insisted jovially. "No one will judge you. It's about having fun, practicing a skill, improving oneself, improving one's village. You can't say no."

He could not understand the hesitation. Why would she not want to hone a craft, any craft? Why would she not want to join in the fun? Rafe had no bean in this battle. It did not matter to him if she participated or not. But he could not understand why she would say no.

"I'll think about it," she repeated.

"Genevieve. Come. Why the reluctance?"

"Stop being combative," she snapped at him.

He inched further back in his chair, surprised by the harshness. "'Pon my honor, that's not my intention. I only wish to encourage you to want more for yourself. Why settle with 'out of practice'? Why settle for anything? We should always ask more of ourselves."

Rising from her chair, she said, "Not all of us are interested in swimming across icy lakes to see if we can solve a riddle or build a fire with frostbitten fingers while freezing to death."

Rafe swept a hand over his face. Where had he gone wrong? Why was she so emotional?

Tossing the twig in the empty hearth, he said, "Please, Genevieve. Sit down. Accept my apologies." He could not say *what* his apologies were, for he could not see what he had said wrong, but experience had taught him women responded well to prostration. "*Mea culpa*, Genevieve." He held out his hand palm up as a peace offering.

She stared down at it, her expression stony. At length, she took his palm in hers and allowed him to guide her back to her chair.

"We can watch the archery from the sidelines. Together." His smile was tentative.

With a sigh, she said, "No, I'll participate. I *want* to participate. But I want to because *I* want to, not because you're browbeating me into it."

Had he? He did not believe he had. Recalling his words, he was positive he was encouraging, thoughtful, rational with his explanations. It was only the silly archery event at the festival, after all. *She* was the one being defensive and emotional, beating the old brow, as it were. Rafe knew better than to say anything further. That he was frustrated by her reaction, he also kept to himself.

Instead, he adapted his approach. "If I were a betting man, I would wager you're goddess-like with a bow, although I'm certain you are as fetching without one as with, but with a bow, you would inspire Artemis herself in your majesty."

Her reply was a scowl.

He smiled a toothy grin, hoping to diffuse her ire. Hoping, as well, she would not screech *rogue* and storm out.

Inch by blessed inch, her scowl softened until she parted those cherubin lips and laughed. Rafe would *not* wager she laughed at the flirtation so much as laughed at him. He could accept that. At least he had won a laugh. Of all the opponents he had faced in the Society and in his training at Gray's Inn, he had to admit Miss Genevieve Slade was proving to be his most formidable.

Chapter 14

Rain delayed Rupert Headley's arrival by a day and a half. Saturday afternoon, the carriage pulled in front of the dower house to receive a warm welcome from the Fitz-Stephens family, all gathered at the front door.

Rafe had the honor of opening the carriage door. Headley stepped out first, and then handed down his sister, who, thankfully, had left her dog at home, as had Headley. Two manservants began unloading enough luggage for a month's stay, at least.

Nodding to the trunks, which were more than Rafe's entire family had needed for the move to the dower house, Rafe quirked a brow.

Headley leaned in to say, "They're *all* Diana's."

"Ah. Thought as much." He watched as Diana simpered from the attention of his family. "I hope you didn't think the welcoming committee was for you."

"I knew better."

The two gentlemen stood aside as the Fitz-Stephenses clamored over Diana, who they had not seen in several years, not since her debut ball. Now, she was a grown woman, her majority fast approaching. That fact had Rafe almost laughing aloud — in his eyes, she had always been, still was, and always would be

Headley's baby sister. Try as he might to see her as a grown woman, to see her as his family now saw her… no, indeed. All he saw was the petulant girl, still in the schoolroom, sweet one minute and tattle-telling the next if not allowed to join her brother and his friend in their fun.

Mother, at last, noticed Headley standing by the carriage. "Rupert, darling, come and kiss me. I can't apologize enough about the room. You'll be disappointed not to have your usual suite. We've put you in Giles's room, not that Giles knows he has a room since he's not here to use it. It must do for now."

Diana was non-stop excitement as everyone headed inside. "I've heard there's archery. I simply must compete. They won't mind if I don't live here, will they? Think we can fool them? Pretend I'm a cousin who has been living here all along, only am so terribly shy I've never left the house? Which room will be my room? It's a pity we can't stay at the Priory, but I do understand. Don't think I don't understand. I understand perfectly." She rambled on, including her despair about leaving her puppy behind at her brother's insistence.

The family was enamored, as they always had been. They hung on her every word as they guided her through the entrance hall and into the drawing room.

Headley and Rafe lingered in the entrance hall. "A welcome reprieve," said Headley. "Only Diana can turn an hour carriage drive into five hours, or so it felt to me."

"You're in good company now. My mother will keep her occupied. Mark my words."

They stepped into the drawing room to join the others at the same moment Rafe's father said to Diana, "You're about her same age, if I'm not mistaken. I think the two of you will get along famously. We'll have to arrange a call."

"When will we find the time?" Mother asked through gritted teeth.

Taking a seat, Headley accepted the teacup from Gran, then turned to Diana. "With whom will you be getting along famously?"

Diana pinched her brother's arm. "Rafe's betrothed, of course."

Headley choked on his tea.

"I can't believe you didn't tell me," Diana rebuked. "Naughty of you! I can't wait to meet her. We'll be the best of friends."

Setting his teacup and saucer aside, Headley exchanged glances with Rafe, who could do little more than shrug sheepishly. "Di," Headley enquired, "is she, by chance, the eldest of the Slade sisters?"

"You're a tease, Rupert! He would never marry a younger sister, would he?" Diana dissolved into laughter, which proved contagious, for however sore of a subject the betrothal was with the family, everyone joined her in laughing, even Otis and Noel.

Rafe rubbed the back of his neck and avoided Headley's questioning brow.

If he thought he would have a chance to explain, offer a reasonable excuse why he had not said something sooner, Rafe was mistaken. After they polished the tea, everyone dispersed to allow Diana and Headley a chance to see their rooms and settle in for the week's stay. Rafe attempted to divert Headley towards the alcove below the stairs.

Rather than be led, Headley paused long enough to say in a low voice, "Love at first sight, old boy? I suspected as much when you tried to put me off the scent. And before you deny it or muster some unlikely excuse, know I'm onto you — only the deepest infatuation would induce *you* to matrimony."

All Rafe was allowed was a second sheepish shrug before Headley was off to explore his accommodations.

Rafe was acutely aware of Headley's side-long glances to Miss Genevieve Slade during church service on Sunday. Introductions had been made before entering the church, but they had been brief and formal, except where Diana was concerned, who slipped her hand in the crook of Genevieve's elbow and declared they were instant friends.

Fortunately, Rafe's family was too well mannered to have said ought between Headley's arrival and now about the betrothal being anything except the normal outcome between two friendly families with similarly aged children. Keeping a secret from Headley was not his intention, but nothing good came from bandying talk of compromises and forced betrothals. If Headley wished to think it true love, so be it. Rafe would worry later about what to do when the betrothal ended, specifically since it would end with Mr. Thorpe stealing the bride.

After church, they lingered briefly in the churchyard. Rafe stood beside Genevieve, playing the besotted betrothed, although her attention was on whatever Diana was saying.

Mr. Slade asked, looking between Rafe and his father, "Tea? Dinner? Supper? With what can I tempt you? We're hoping to become better acquainted with your guests."

With a quick glance to his mother and grand-mother, Rafe said, "I believe my family is otherwise engaged, Mr. Slade, but I would be honored to call this afternoon with Mr. Headley and Miss Headley. We're for The Dragon's Breath at present."

"Splendid! We'll look forward to this afternoon, then." Mr. Slade turned to gather his wife and daughters.

The looks of relief on the faces of Rafe's family were comical. All except his father, that was, who looked disappointed not to be included. Rafe would make it up to him later with more cases to study.

A short time later, Rafe and Headley sat in the tap room.

"I admire your fortitude," Headley said. "No fawning, no drooling, not a single simper. I had expected you to ply her fan in lovesick obedience."

"So besotted you thought I would lose my head? Never! She may have stolen my heart but not my sense." Rafe affected a self-conscious laugh, think-ing he would not have been half bad in the theatre.

"She was composed, as well. Only stole a few glances. The essence of propriety. I admit, I'm dis-appointed. I was certain I would catch the two of you behind the church, stealing kisses rather than glances."

"And give you ammunition for jests? I'm cleverer than you take me." Rafe joked but could not soon lose the thought of kissing her behind the church, or anywhere, really. In the forest by the tower seemed appropriate. Or in the monastic corridor. Or...

A hand waved before his face. Rafe blinked.

"Besotted indeed." Headley laughed. "I retract my compliment about your fortitude. One mention of her, and you're already woolgathering. Would you like my handkerchief to wipe the drool?"

Rafe har-hared before drowning the thoughts of kissing Genevieve with a gulp or five of his beverage. As he set the glass on the table, his lips parted to discuss the first event of the competition tomorrow morning, a disagreement between a patron and the publican caught his attention.

The publican, Mr. Snawdune, had crossed his arms and was looking down his nose at the patron, who stood just out of Rafe's view. "'Tis Sunday, innit. No traveling on Sunday. Not 'round here. Besides, the frolic is tomorrow, innit. No rooms available. Full up from here to Hartminster."

"I can only apologize," said the man. "My travel hasn't been smooth. I had hoped to rely on the mail, but everything that could go wrong has gone wrong. I've arrived far later than planned, and I haven't a place to stay. I beg of you — "

Mr. Snawdune snorted. "You're going ter beg me? That's rich. As I said, full up from here to Hartminster, Mr. Thorpe. 'Tis a fine walk from here to there so best start troddin'."

Mr. *Thorpe*?

Rafe rose from his chair, holding a staying hand before Headley could question Rafe's motives.

The Mr. Thorpe?

Curiosity beat a tattoo in his chest. He could hardly believe his luck to be in The Dragon's Breath at the moment *the* Mr. Thorpe arrived. It could be none other than *him*.

As he approached, his smile broadened.

In one fell swoop, Rafe clapped a hand on Mr. Thorpe's shoulder and said to the back of the man's head, all while Mr. Snawdune observed with furrowed brows, "*Alan* Thorpe? Is that you? I almost didn't recognize you after all these years."

Mr. Thorpe turned around to face Rafe with a look of sheer bafflement.

Rafe took the man's measure in a single glance. *Soft* was the first word that came to mind. Not necessarily a milksop, at least not that he could ascertain from his quick perusal, but certainly *soft*. A gentle face that looked far younger than the man's age, a slight stature, perhaps a head shorter than Rafe, slim but not necessarily weak, modestly attired, but that could be excused by travel. And *this* was the love of Genevieve's life? Rafe tried to reserve judgment. For now.

Mr. Thorpe opened his mouth to reply, but before he could utter something ridiculous like asking who Rafe was, Rafe wrapped his arm around the man's shoulders and drew him against his side.

"Mr. Snawdune. What a great pleasure it is that you are here to witness this reunion. I've not seen Mr. Alan Thorpe since… Oxford. Yes, those were the days, were they not, *Alan*?"

The ice on Mr. Snawdune's brows thawed, and his furrow softened. "Why didn't ye' say you was a friend of Mr. Fitz-Stephens?" The question chided more than enquired. Eyes on Rafe, he began to ask something, but hesitated, thought for a moment, and then tapped the side of his nose. "You'd be offering him a room, Mr. Fitz-Stephens, if it weren't for... *the situation*, am I right?"

"'Pon rep, you've the right of it." Rafe coughed a laugh. "The *situation* is tricky. The dower house is full, and, well, you know how things are with the Priory."

Mr. Snawdune nodded. "Would ye' look here, Mr. Thorpe! A room just come available. An't the best, but it'll do in a pinch."

"That is too kind," Rafe said. "I'll take care of everything," he added with a knowing nod. "You're competing in the frolic, after all, aren't you, Alan?"

Mr. Thorpe mouthed like a fish out of water but said nothing.

Mr. Snawdune said, "Upstairs. Third door to the left. We'll have it ready shortly."

Rafe shook the publican's hand and, arm still draped over Mr. Thorpe's shoulders, steered him towards the table where Headley waited patiently, one brow arched in amused curiosity. A private word with the new guest of Grant Lindis was of the utmost importance, but it would have to wait.

Nudging Mr. Thorpe into a chair at the table, Rafe nodded to one of the barmaids to bring another round, namely one for the newcomer.

"Headley, allow me to introduce a good friend of Miss Slade's, Mr. Thorpe. This, my good man, is Mr. Headley, and I," he began, then paused to share in a laugh at the absurdity of the situation, although Mr. Thorpe was too perplexed to share anything, "am Mr. Fitz-Stephens, Miss Slade's betrothed. I'm *positive* she's written to you about me."

He was not positive about any such thing. Rafe had no way of knowing what Genevieve had written.

To his relief, understanding flickered across Mr. Thorpe's face as he shook first Headley's hand and then Rafe's. "She sent you here to welcome me? How thoughtful. But then, she could not possibly know I would arrive today. I am grateful, nonetheless."

Headley looked from Mr. Thorpe to Rafe, the curious brow still arched. "Fitz-Stephens, tell me you're not planning a wedding by license, Mr. Thorpe and I invited to serve as witnesses. Besotted though you may be, I should hope I deserve enough courtesy to be forewarned. Then, you've been full of surprises since I stepped out of the carriage."

"Nothing of the sort!" Rafe answered briskly before Mr. Thorpe could answer for him. "Our good friend here has arrived to, uh, join us in the competition. Miss Slade would not take no for an answer. Isn't that right, Mr. Thorpe?"

"The—the *competition*?" repeated Mr. Thorpe with a slight stammer and audible gulp.

"If I recall correctly," Rafe said, "Miss Slade mentioned your interest in the relay swim on Wednesday. Yes? I'm positive that was it." Slapping his thigh, he continued, "Headley and I are calling on the Slades in a few. You must join us. Miss Slade will want to know you've arrived."

The naysayer in him warned this could turn out poorly since Mr. and Mrs. Slade had expressed opposition to Mr. Thorpe, but with Headley and his sister present, they would surely be decorous. In fact, their presence may be the saving grace needed.

Headley asked, "If this is the plan, shall I collect Diana and meet you at the Priory?"

Nodding, Rafe said, "I'll show Thorpe to his room first. Half an hour?"

All agreed, Mr. Thorpe looked quite bowled over by Rafe and Headley's aggressive decision making on his behalf.

Once Headley departed, Rafe did as promised and escorted the gentleman to the room upstairs. The Dragon's Breath was a tavern, not a coaching inn, but it was a large enough tavern to have assembly rooms on the second floor and a handful of guest quarters on the first floor above the tap room, reserved almost exclusively for the annual Fracas Frolic. What Mr. Snawdune did with the rooms for the rest of the year was anyone's guess.

The room was ready for Mr. Thorpe, including the trunk he had brought and a washbasin with fresh water in the pitcher.

When the door closed behind Rafe, Thorpe said, "I can't thank you enough, Mr. Fitz-Stephens. Without your intervention, I would have faced a week sleeping in a barn, I fear."

"It's the least I could do for Miss Slade's intended." Bold words, but Rafe believed in a direct approach and wanted the man to know all was understood, no misconceptions, no enmity.

Thorpe spun around and stuttered, "In-in-intended? Whatever do you mean? Are *you* not her betrothed?"

"No need to dissemble with pretense in private. Miss Slade has explained everything to me regarding the affection between the two of you. I promise I will not stand in the way. This betrothal is a matter of convenience until the two of you can be reunited."

One hand against the wall, as though he may faint, and one hand over his heart, Thorpe said, "There's — there's been a misunderstanding. There's no aff-affection between Miss Slade and myself."

Rafe cocked his head. What the devil was this man saying? "If there's no affection, then… why have you come to Grant Lindis?"

"Miss Slade bade me come to her aid with a… a… *difficult* situation."

"Speak plainly, please. I've held nothing back, nor should you."

Thorpe swallowed. "An… *undesirable* arrangement." He flushed red when he said this, the word *undesirable* little more than a whisper. "She's a friend. Nothing more. After she spent so much time offering companionship to my grandmother, I promised my eternal devotion… as a friend. Should she need aught, she need only write. I'm a man of my word, Mr. Fitz-Stephens."

Rafe frowned. A *friend*? A friend with a needy grandmother? How was Rafe supposed to convince the Slades that Thorpe was the better match if Thorpe himself denied being a match at all? Thorpe was supposed to be their salvation.

"Having met you," Thorpe continued, "I don't understand what's undesirable. Women are peculiar. Is this not… desirable for you?" He continued to blush every time he said *desirable*.

Rafe did not answer. Instead, he slipped a hand into his pocket to reach for his little box. Flicking open the lid, he pinched an herb inside. "Mint?" he offered Thorpe.

Well, there was nothing for it. Rafe would have to convince Thorpe to fall in love with Genevieve. That was the only answer. That was the only way out.

Chapter 15

T he only sound to be heard in the drawing room at Devington Priory was the sighs of Mrs. Slade as she attempted to embroider, a skill she did not possess nor wish to possess, but a skill she insisted she feign when expecting callers. For callers to see her working a needle and thread was enough. Mr. Slade was pacing before the window. Genevieve slumped in a chair, drumming her fingers on the arm and wondering if Philomena would be interested in a ride to the tower. Neither Cecilia nor Theia were present, however much they wished to see Mr. Headley again. Mrs. Slade had banished them from the room. A good thing, too, as Genevieve did not think Mr. Headley would wish to be overwhelmed by the doe-eyed stares of two schoolroom-aged girls.

Mr. Headley was certainly handsome enough to tempt any woman, but now that she tried to recall his features, she could not. The only face that signified was Rafe's. This would not do. She was trying to *end* the betrothal, not begin a romance. Peculiar — she could not immediately recall why she wished to end it.

The front door knocker echoed in the distance.

Mrs. Slade dropped her needle. Mr. Slade cleared his throat and snatched a book as a prop. Genevieve sat up straight, eyes fixed on the drawing room door.

Good heavens. What was wrong with her? It might not be him. It could be anyone. Just because he had promised to call did not mean he was doing so presently. Nevertheless, she was flustered. Her cheeks warmed; her hands fidgeted; her stomach somersaulted.

The door opened. Rather than the butler announcing the guests, Rafe stepped in with a flourishing bow. Her parents eagerly welcomed him, forgetting they were trying to look busy and important and not at all as though they had been waiting for him to call. Rafe, in turn, made a grand show of his arrival by kissing both Mrs. Slade's cheeks, pumping Mr. Slade's hand, and then kissing the air above Genevieve's knuckles.

"My second family," he said, mirth in his voice. "I have brought you the surprise of good company. But wait, where is Miss Cecilia and Miss Theia?"

Mrs. Slade waved her embroidery absently. "I've sent them away. No one wants children in the drawing room."

"They shall be missed, but I understand." Turning to the doorway, he said a little louder. "Now, for your surprise."

Miss Headley stepped into the room first. Before Rafe could announce her or say ought about her, she rustled into the room to take Genevieve's hands between hers and sit next to her new friend, already launching into animation.

"You *must* join us for archery practice tomorrow afternoon," she said, flashing a quick smile to Mama and Papa before turning back to Genevieve. "It is all arranged, and you cannot say no, but if you do say no, I will not accept it and find a way to lure you away from the house, although I know you will accept because you would not wish to disappoint your new friend."

So rapidly she talked, and with such earnestness, Genevieve missed Mr. Headley's entrance.

Only when she heard the deep tones of male voices did she realize he had already walked across the room, greeted her parents, and was in discussion with her father and Rafe, alongside Mr. Thorpe, her mother rising from her chair to join their conversation, not to be left out.

Genevieve turned back to Miss Headley.

"This will be my first ever frolic," said Miss Headley. "I've wished to participate for years, but first I was too young, or so said Rupert, which is complete nonsense because children of all ages participate, although I grant you, not in archery, which did not apply last year when they had lawn bowls for the ladies, but then I was not allowed because Rafe was at university and Rupert could not be certain he would return for the frolic, which of course he did because Rafe never misses a frolic, and then…"

Genevieve jerked her head to stare at her parents, missing whatever else Miss Headley said.

Mr. Thorpe?

Her jaw dropped.

Her eyes widened.

Mr. Thorpe?

She could not immediately understand how he had arrived in the drawing room. But then—elation! He had come! He had come in response to her request!

Then panic. But *no*—he had come.

Why was he here with Rafe? Oh, dear heavens. Had he already spoken to Rafe? How was this possible? *Oh, please, please, do not let the two of them have spoken yet.* This would ruin Rafe's opinion of her! She needed to speak to him first, to explain the situation and what she needed from him. Without her guidance, Mr. Thorpe would not know what to say and could undo all her hopes by saying all the things he ought not say. Then, *what* were her hopes? Her gaze shifted between Rafe and Mr. Thorpe.

She strained over Miss Headley's chatter to hear what was being said. Something about Rafe inviting his dear friend to the competition only to discover his dear friend already knew the Slades — what a coincidence! Genevieve's eyes narrowed. So convincing he was, she questioned if he really *did* know Mr. Thorpe and had not said before because he did not realize it was the *same* Mr. Thorpe.

Oh, this was dreadful. Their one hope of salvation from this mockery of a betrothal, and Rafe had already claimed him as *his* friend. Then, did Rafe not want to end the betrothal, as well? Did *she*?

"Miss Slade!" interrupted a voice.

Genevieve shook the thoughts from her head and looked back at Miss Headley, whose attention was now fixed across the room at the figure walking towards them. *Mr. Thorpe.*

Trying not to look too eager, too pleased, too panicked, too *everything* she was feeling, Genevieve rose and extended her hand. "Mr. Thorpe. What brings you to Grant Lindis?"

This was not how she had envisioned their reunion, not when they both knew what brought him here.

"You've not heard, then," said Mr. Thorpe. "Mr. Fitz-Stephens is an excellent secret keeper. He's invited me to the competition. I'm to… to swim. When he discovered *his* Alan Thorpe was the same as *your* Alan Thorpe, he… he insisted I join him to… to call on you. Imagine our mutual surprise!"

Yes, imagine indeed.

Her heart went out to poor Mr. Thorpe, who, despite his brave words, was not a convincing actor. His *surprise* sounded forced, his volume a trifle too loud, and his voice stilted, the weight of the tale carried by a too-broad smile. She glanced at her parents. So enraptured by whatever Rafe and Mr. Headley were saying, they did not appear to mind Mr. Thorpe's presence nor show signs of suspecting he was here by *her* request. How could it not be obvious to them?

She shook Mr. Thorpe's hand and said, "An unexpected surprise, I agree. I hope we will have the opportunity to exchange our adventures, discover what each has been doing since last we met. As you can see, I've moved again. Oh! But how rude of me." She turned to Miss Headley. "You've both been introduced, I presume? Seeing that you've arrived together?"

Miss Headley tittered and shook Mr. Thorpe's hand just as he was saying that yes, they had met on the way here. Ignoring what he was saying, she pressed, "It's good to meet you *again*! I never dreamed it would be so soon."

Mr. Thorpe chortled at the silliness, as did Genevieve. The latter exhaled her relief. She had not yet devised a plan for how to get him into the house or convince her parents of a pre-existing understanding, short of eloping, that was, which she knew Mr. Thorpe would never agree to, no matter how kindhearted he was or how much he wished to help her. Yet here he was.

In her periphery, she caught Rafe winking at her.

Chapter 16

All night, Genevieve tossed and turned, listening to the rain pelt the windows and the thunder rumble. It was not the storm that kept her awake but worry that the morning's race would be canceled either because it continued to rain or because the path was too muddy. The first race of the competition was the forest run through Stonebriar Woods. She had helped mark the racepath with pennant-waving stakes and decorate the trees with streamers. Would all that work be ruined? A streak of lightning, followed by a clap of thunder, sent her burrowing beneath her covers with a groan over the ill-timed weather.

She need not have fretted. Morning arrived to clear, albeit cloudy, skies. In the distance, she swore she could hear the rhythmic beat of drums, the pre-race festivities already in full swing, the drums marking the heartbeat of Grant Lindis. By the time she joined her family to set off for the first day of the Fracas Frolic, she was positively giddy. Neither she nor her sisters could stand still. They fidgeted. They squealed. They skipped. None knew what to expect, which intensified the anticipation.

As they entered the village and fell into step with others heading for Stonebriar Woods, Genevieve searched the crowd for Rafe. Was he already at the starting line? Of course, he would be racing today. That was why he had returned to Grant Lindis — to race. An oversight they had not planned to meet at the Priory and walk together.

There was no place for decorum today. Unruly children darted unchecked through the streets, brandishing handmade flags and dragging suspiciously familiar streamers behind them. Everyone, it seemed, was singing, only no one was singing in unison, each group of friends or family in harmony with no one except themselves, the tunes discordant with other passersby, the lyrics disjointed, yet every broken refrain or croaked chord was music to Genevieve's ears. She did not know any songs about racing, but not to be outdone, she cleared her throat and began bellowing a nonsense tune of her own. And why should she not?

Cecilia and Theia stared at her as though she had sprouted two extra heads, but not for long. Establishing a simple enough melody and a rather silly chorus, Genevieve goaded them into joining her.

The air was muggy, but no one cared. Only a mild trace of a breeze whispered from the east. Had she thought ahead, she could have painted a fan to match the race day flags. Next year. She could paint one each for her sisters and — next year? But she would not be here next year. Not unless…

As a sharp pain squeezed her heart, she spotted Rafe waving over the crowd.

His face lit with a smile to have spied his quarry. He stood at the edge of the copse, the crowd dispersing every which way, some heading into the woods, some heading south along the forest edge, others northwest. Beside him stood Mr. Headley and Mr. Thorpe. As Genevieve's family approached the group, Miss Headley appeared from behind two burly men, effortlessly coiffed and as giddy as Genevieve.

"Miss Slade!" She reached Genevieve before anyone else. With a quick nod and smile to Cecilia, Theia, and Papa and Mama, she said to Genevieve, "You must join us. I won't accept no for an answer! Rafe has chosen a perfect location for us to view the race." Without waiting for a response, she turned to Genevieve's parents. "Mrs. Fitz-Stephens insists you join her at the finish line. May I steal Miss Slade to have to myself? I promise not to allow her out of my sight."

With a laugh, she dragged Genevieve towards Rafe before anyone could answer. There was little else Genevieve could do except laugh with her, although she had a few more reasons to laugh, such as Mrs. Fitz-Stephens inviting her parents to join her—now *that* was as likely as pigs flying over Grant Lindis.

Genevieve's first words to Rafe were, "I worried all night rain would cancel the race."

She promptly blushed to have implied she had done anything at night, least of all because anything she had done at night would have been done in *his* bedchamber, in *his* bed, and while she was fashioned in her nightrail and curlers, just as he had seen her that first night.

Unfazed, Rafe looked to his companions, then said, "*Nothing* cancels the Fracas Frolic."

Messrs. Headley and Thorpe took the opportunity to shake her hand. She felt ever so guilty about

Mr. Thorpe. He seemed in good spirits at least. But he had come all this way for her, and she had not once had the chance to speak with him. To see him now, she would never guess him lamenting his journey or regretting his decision, for he was smartly, if not a trifle modestly, dressed, a friendly curl to his thin lips, and an eagerness about his person, as though he, like her, was caught up in the gaiety of the day.

"Follow me," Rafe said, exchanging places with Miss Headley so smoothly, it was as though Rafe had been beside her the whole time.

Without a by-your-leave, Rafe led her into the woods, leaving everyone else behind. She glanced back as the trees closed in to block her view.

"I've chosen the best vantage point." When he saw her glancing back again, he added, "They'll join us soon."

"Where are we going?" She asked, but so delighted by the pre-festival excitement, she would not have minded if the best view were from the inside of a barn.

He did not immediately answer, but that was not avoidance on his part, she realized, rather because he was choosing their path with care. The forest bed was far drier than she would have expected after the evening's storm, but there were muddy patches that would not have done her half-boots a kindness. How thoughtful of him to ensure her hem did not catch on underbrush or soak in an inch of mud.

At length, he said, "Many believe the finish line is the best position, but where's the fun in that? The best part is watching the racers. There's a bird's eye view ahead. We won't be able to see the full path, of course, but since it turns back on itself, we'll be able to see at least three of the obstacles the racers must traverse."

"You'll need to hurry if you're to make it to the starting line in time," Genevieve said as they reached a curious collection of tree stumps overlooking where the forest's terrain sloped steeply towards the valley.

When she turned, she squealed to see the flags she had positioned, or at least some of them. The race path went past the stumps, down the slope, and then circled back up before dipping again to continue around and out of view. Oh! This was a perfect position! One of the obstacles she would be able to see in action was the log climb.

Ignoring her comment about the starting line, he said, "Behold. The best vista for the race. I wager I'm not the only one with the idea. Wait and see. Before the race begins, others will gather *en masse*." Even as he said it, voices from elsewhere in the woods called to each other. "The racers for Grant Lindis will wear red armbands, the Eurwendins yellow."

"Where's your armband?"

He grimaced a grin. "Not racing today. Instead, I'm your escort."

"You're not racing? But... but pray, I thought that was the whole point of returning from London. To race."

"And scuff my boots?"

"What happened to you marching across Devonshire in the dead of winter and all that claptrap?"

He barked a laugh. "I'm saving my strength for tomorrow's regatta."

She harrumphed and eyed the stumps.

Rafe tugged a handkerchief from his waistcoat pocket and spread it across the stump. "For you, my lady."

Accepting the offer, however small the linen square, she sat, thankful not to have a repeat of the damp derriere, one of the many memories that plagued her — all of which involved Rafe.

He joined her. "My brothers are racing. This run is most enjoyed by the younger men, namely those under twenty."

"Are you saying you're *too old* to race?"

"I'm saying I wouldn't want my experience to dampen their fun, seeing as how I would all too easily win."

Genevieve laughed so jovially, she had tears in the corners of her eyes, not so much because of what he said but how he said it, with tongue-in-cheek arrogance so sardonic as to beggar belief. He smirked at her response.

"I suppose," Genevieve began, fluttering her eyelashes with angelic innocence, "that means neither Mr. Headley nor Mr. Thorpe will be racing this week. We wouldn't want them to be disheartened by your superhuman athleticism."

"I promise to curb my skills, moderate my epic strength, and curtail my stamina, all to provide them a chance at saving face." Rafe raised his beaver hat to comb a hand through his hair, slowing the movement to casually flex for her.

"You, sir, are incorrigible," she chided.

The rustle of branches being brushed aside and the murmur of voices proved Rafe correct — their privacy was soon to be interrupted by others who wished for a bird's eye view of the race path.

Rafe said, "As it happens, Headley will be joining in several of the races, but I could only convince Mr. Thorpe to swim. We'll see how well he paddles on Wednesday."

Genevieve looked in the direction of the voices, trying to appear nonchalant at the mention of Mr. Thorpe. She did not wish to discuss him until she had spoken to him herself. They needed a game plan, she and Mr. Thorpe.

If Rafe noticed her reticence, he gave no indication. On the contrary, he pressed the issue. "Speaking of the noble Mr. Thorpe, who traveled a great distance to appear at the side of his ladylove and rescue her from the dastardly deeds of this roguish scoundrel, I was under the impression the two of you were deeply in love, a love never to be torn asunder, by bumbling lotharios or otherwise."

His words jested, his tone light and airy.

Genevieve, however, went still, her eyes dragging from the depths of the forest to her folded hands. *How. Utterly. Mortifying.*

In her defense, she said, "I never led you to believe anything of the sort."

"Hmm. So this... 'understanding,'" he said, waving a hand as if to emphasize the word, "was of... convenience... or... *contrivance*?"

"I resent that remark!" She shot off the stump and drew herself up, shoulders back.

When she looked upon him with a quelling glare, he looked back with raised brows and nothing short of amusement. He did not rise from his makeshift chair, as would have been appropriate, rather he crossed one ankle over his opposite knee and grinned.

"I mean no offense, my darling betrothed. I merely wish to understand the nature of your relationship with Mr. Thorpe. Such would aid me in... er... aiding you."

Genevieve continued to glare at him. Her mind whirled. She did not know what Mr. Thorpe had said, but in all likelihood, he had expressed the truth, which was not what he needed to have said to Mr. Rafe Fitz-Stephens, who would now comprehend her trifling faradiddle.

She heaved a sigh and slumped back onto the stump with a none-too-gentle flop. "He's a *friend*. A *good* friend. I have moved too frequently in my life to make friends, lasting ones anyway, but he is a *good* man who offers nothing but *goodness* to every-one he knows and comes from a *good* family, and we established a remarkably *good* friendship in our brief acquaintance."

"*Good* enough that you believe he would marry you to save you from marrying me?"

"Yes. Possibly. Wait. No. I mean..."

"Mmm hmm. And... you believe all a *good* mar-riage needs is a *good* friend, nothing more?"

"It's a start!" She spoke so brusquely, the group passing nearby in search of a stump of their own looked over at her. Lowering her voice, she said, "I didn't know you, as you'll recall. You were a burglar who stole into my room in the middle of the night, and suddenly Papa saw it as the match of the century, which made no logical sense — you could have been a highwayman for all we knew, never mind your lineage. *Obviously*, friendship sounded a better basis for marriage than a stranger prone to tumbling into rooms and invading one's privacy."

"And now?"

She glanced up. He stared at her in earnest, all visible signs of jesting gone from his expression. She returned her gaze to her hands.

"You're not a stranger anymore, I'll admit. But I don't want to be bullied into marriage any more than you do."

"No one will bully you. We're in this together, remember?" He reached over and rubbed a knuckle against the back of her hand.

So simple of a movement, so light of a touch, but tears welled in her eyes, thankfully not falling, for she would simply die if he saw them.

Had they not been talking about Mr. Thorpe? How had *their* betrothal come into conversation? What she could not understand was the sensation that it was becoming her choice to accept or deny him rather than their mutual mission to end the betrothal no matter what. He could not wish to marry her. All his teasing and flirting aside, he could not wish to continue with this. No, he must be gauging her feelings for Mr. Thorpe to better plan how to make *that* match viable. Yes, that was it. She had misunderstood his tone, his questions, and his *everything* in her muddled state.

The mellifluous voice of an angel interrupted her thoughts.

"There you both are!" Miss Headley led her brother and Mr. Thorpe towards Rafe and Genevieve. "Sneaky of you to steal a moment alone."

Rafe intimated an affront to his gentlemanly manners. "Oh, I say. 'Pon my honor, I would never!"

Miss Headley shared a knowing look with Genevieve, one that offered all the conspiratorial plotting of a young lady who suspected her friend wanted *alone* time with her betrothed. Genevieve could feel her cheeks burning.

Mr. Thorpe accepted the seat next to Genevieve just as a bugle trumpeted in the distance.

"The race has begun," Rafe said. "It'll be a few moments before the racers make it this far. Headley, sit. I can't see anything with your shoulders blocking my view."

Mr. Headley turned to choose a stump. In a sweep, his gaze caught Mr. Thorpe.

Mr. Thorpe looked back at him, questioning.

Mr. Headley's eyes narrowed.

Mr. Thorpe shifted on his stump.

Genevieve looked from one to the other, unsure what sort of exchange was occurring.

Rafe waved a hand. "Sit already."

Whatever silent communication occurred, Genevieve was unsure — then it could have been her imagination after the awkward exchange with Rafe. In the work of a moment, Miss Headley reached out for Mr. Thorpe's hands and tugged him to stand before stealing his stump, sitting next to Genevieve in his place. She then patted the stump next to her. Mr. Thorpe accepted. Mr. Headley then sat on the opposite side, boxing in Mr. Thorpe. It was the most absurd game of musical chairs Genevieve had witnessed.

She did not linger on the peculiarity for long. Cheers filled the woods, echoing off the trees. The sounds of a stampede came barreling towards them. Miss Headley clapped her hands. Mr. Headley whistled. Rafe stood and cheered just as the first set of racers crested the hill and began to descend the slope, their red and yellow armbands bright against the green foliage and brown tree trunks.

A handful of racers passed, a couple slipping in the mud, the rest clamoring to climb the logs blocking the path. Shortly following was another set, close on the heels of the first racers. Genevieve forgot to make note of what color the armband was of the racer in the lead. It was all too thrilling to care who won. The racers were, as Rafe had said, young, but the ages were varied, from young boys to a few men who were surely older than Rafe and Mr. Headley, and certainly Mr. Thorpe.

Before she realized Rafe had moved, he clasped her hand in invitation to join him. "Move closer?" he asked, nodding his head towards the path.

She joined him at the edge of the flags, nearly within arm's reach of the racers, just as his brothers came into view. So pleased, she waved and cheered them on.

"Is that Mr. Fitz-Stephens?" she asked, incredulous to see Rafe's father not only keeping pace with his sons but about to take the lead before them.

"Ha! I hadn't expected that."

"Oh, can we please meet them at the finish line? I want to see them cross it! But we can't possibly beat them there, can we?"

"*Au contraire, mademoiselle*. We'll take the direct route, if you'd like, while they're still traversing the obstacles and doubling back for more."

The Headleys and Mr. Thorpe brooked no argument as they left the stumps for the finish line.

Around the finish was the most populated, but not many people were standing, as tables and chairs had been scattered for comfort, the chairs having been hauled from people's homes, the tavern, the tea garden, and every which place, as far as Genevieve could tell. She caught sight of Rafe's mother and grandmother before she saw her family seated with them. Nudging Rafe in that direction, they joined them but remained standing.

Behind her, she could hear Miss Headley talking a mile a minute to Mr. Thorpe and her brother. Before her, Rafe's mother was chittering almost as animatedly to Genevieve's mother, a sight she never thought to witness. The snippets she could hear were about Mr. Fitz-Stephens' determination to beat his sons' race time. A pity Papa had not joined the race. Maybe she could convince him yet, even if the foot race was not an option.

A great cheer roared through the crowd as a young man with a red armband came loping out of the woods to cross the finish line with a win for Grant Lindis.

Genevieve gave a little jump and hugged Rafe's arm. "We won! We won!"

Rafe, wearing a humored smile, said, "Only this race. We need a majority this week to pocket the competition."

She paid him little mind, too delighted over the win and the whole of the event to care about details. Repeating, "We won!" a few more times than necessary, she forgot to release his arm.

Chapter 17

Following the forest run, participants and spectators alike joined together on the village green for a different kind of racing, a series of sack and three-legged races.

"These don't count towards the competition points," Rafe explained as he escorted Genevieve, their families ahead of them, and the Headleys and Mr. Thorpe behind. "After every competition event, we celebrate before returning home to recover for the next day, when we do it all over again."

Today had already offered Genevieve enough excitement to last a lifetime. There was a full week of this ahead? She may well expire from overstimulation.

By the time they reached the green, the first set of racers for the three-legged race were already preparing. She laughed to herself to see Papa trying to convince Mama. The Fitz-Stephens had no such hesitations. Mr. Fitz-Stephens was tying his leg to Mrs. Fitz-Stephens', while Mr. Otis Fitz-Stephens was collecting rope to race with his grandmother.

Mr. Thorpe sidled next to Genevieve and Rafe. "You'll be wanting to join in the fun together. I've brought extra rope." He handed a piece to Rafe, who stared at it rather than take it.

"Nonsense, Thorpe. We've reserved this race for *you* and Miss Slade. Don't you recall us agreeing to that earlier? You were wishing for a chance to talk about your previous acquaintance."

"Was I?" Mr. Thorpe looked between them with a blank expression, as though trying to remember a discussion Genevieve suspected never happened.

"Undoubtedly!" Rafe slipped Genevieve's hand from his arm to Mr. Thorpe's forearm.

Behind Genevieve came a squeak. They turned to find Mr. Headley and Miss Headley, the latter wearing the most heart-wrenched, crestfallen expression, worthy of a stage actress.

"You promised the three-legged race to *me*, Mr. Thorpe," Miss Headley insisted. "Am I to compete with my dearest friend for your favor? She has her betrothed, and I have…." She choked a sob when she looked over at her brother.

"Now, now, Miss Headley," Mr. Thorpe reassured, dropping Genevieve's hand to take Miss Headley's instead. "I've not given away your race. Have I, Miss Slade?"

"Mr. Thorpe was only now saying how much he looked forward to racing with you," Genevieve confirmed.

As soon as Mr. Thorpe turned his gaze, Miss Headley winked at Genevieve with the same knowing look from earlier, as though to say she had come to save the day from this trouble-making interloper who meant to come between the betrothed couple.

Rafe hummed in thought as Mr. Thorpe and Miss Headley joined the starting line to tie their rope and as Mr. Headley sought her sisters, presumably to ask one or both to race. "My efforts are being undermined," he said.

"Try harder," she teased.

"Yes, well, when the world is determined to match *us*, it's an uphill battle, isn't it?" He squatted on his haunches to secure their rope, never mind they were ages away from the starting line and still had to reach it before the race began.

"I should think a member of your Vitruvian Society would only accept uphill challenges, otherwise, what's the point? It would be too *easy*."

He tightened the rope with a tug of his hand.

Out of the corner of her eyes she saw Cecilia storming in the opposite direction, Mr. Headley escorting Theia to the starting line instead. Genevieve was about to suggest they hobble to her until she spotted Mr. Noel Fitz-Stephens block Cecilia's path, a rope in his open palm.

Rafe rose and swept a hand before them. "Shall we practice with a sedate walk to the starting line?"

The race was ridiculous fun, beyond Genevieve's imagination, more cause for laughter than competition. Bodies tripped and fell around them, couples clung to each other, some marched with a steady rhythm, counting aloud their steps, while others could not match gait or speed. Unabashedly, Genevieve clung to Rafe, his strong arm holding her steady as he counted off their steps with a one-two, one-two. Even after they returned to the starting line, she could not say who had won or how they ranked—she was far too busy enjoying the whole affair.

By the time Genevieve exhausted herself, she had participated in four more three-legged races—one with her father, one with Rafe's father, one with Mr. Otis Fitz-Stephens, and one with a village boy who blushed when he asked her — and one sack race — which she vowed never to do again since the hopping had quite jarred her senses. The festivities remained in full swing even after the races had ended. Children flew kites, a few families picnicked along the perimeter, and the tea garden opened for business.

A world away from genteel society, from the decorous expectations of the beau monde and those fashionable members of Society with a capital S. This was, she decided, the best day of her life, better still than the day she helped stake the race path through the woods. Would she feel this way about every day this week? She thought she might. No one treated her as an outsider. Although she did not know many names or faces, and certainly none of the villagers from Eurwendin, they all accepted her as a part of Grant Lindis, as though she had lived there for years. Everything felt *right*. This was the beginning. Of what, she did not know. But it was a beginning. A beginning of belonging? Of securing lasting friendships? Of making happy memories to take with her wherever she went next? Throughout it all, she found her gaze wandering back to Rafe.

"We're returning to the house, love," Mama said, interrupting the direction of Genevieve's gaze, which predictably was on Rafe once more as he laughed over whatever Miss Headley had said to him. "Are you joining us, or is Mr. Fitz-Stephens to escort you?" The *or* portion of her question was emphasized to the point of encouraging that choice.

"Actually, I'm supposed to accompany Mrs. Fitz-Stephens and Miss Headley to the dower house for the archery lesson."

"Oh! Oh yes. I had quite forgotten." Mama tried to appear nonchalant but could not hide the playful hop at recalling this tidbit. "A remarkable woman is your prospective mother-in-law. To devote her time to instruct you — it shows how dedicated she is to ensure you're the perfect wife for her son."

Genevieve cringed but said nothing.

"Do you think Mr. Headley will take to Cecilia? What a perfect match that would be. I regret sending her from the drawing room when he called. I shan't make that mistake twice."

"Mama! You will *not* matchmake Cecilia. She's only a child."

"It's time she's out in society. I've coddled her too long." Pointing her fan towards Mr. Thorpe, Mama said, "I'll *not*, however, have her in the drawing room with *that* useless article. I am surprised someone of Mr. Fitz-Stephens' consequence is on friendly terms with the man. I wanted to be angry when Mr. Thorpe came to the house — the audacity to call uninvited! But to discover he's a friend of Mr. Fitz-Stephens… well, I'll be a gracious hostess, but only so long as Mr. Fitz-Stephens is present."

Genevieve's saving grace from hearing more complaints was Rafe heading in their direction, bearing the gait of a knight to the rescue of his fair maiden. Mama was not so terrible, but at present, Genevieve was all too happy to be rescued.

"Mrs. Slade, Miss Slade," he greeted. "Would you grant me permission to — "

"Yes, yes," Mama said with a wave of her fan. "Accompany her to the dower house for archery. I insist."

Rafe offered his arm, which Genevieve accepted.

Once they were out of earshot, Rafe said, "If we go now, we'll be too far ahead for a certain pair of siblings to interfere."

She first caught sight of Mr. Thorpe waiting ahead of them, and then spied the Headleys on the other side of the green, talking with Mr. and Mrs. Fitz-Stephens. Ah. Rafe was quite determined, then. She had underestimated him. As relieved as she ought to be that he did, indeed, want to find a way out of the betrothal with Mr. Thorpe's help, she felt anything but relieved. Her chest weighed curiously heavy. Was it the pang of rejection? So silly of her.

They joined Mr. Thorpe, and all three fell into step towards the estate. From the green until they reached the edge of the village, they held light conversation, remarking on the luck of the weather, the amusement of the forest run, even a squabble over who had been the muddiest racer crossing the finish line.

Once they passed the village, Rafe halted. "Blast and double blast!"

Genevieve and Mr. Thorpe slowed to look back in surprise.

"I forgot my handkerchief in the forest! I can't leave it." Hands held palms out in helpless surrender, Rafe pleaded with his eyes that they understand the enormity of the problem — *his handkerchief!*

Genevieve frowned. She recalled with perfect clarity his sweeping the handkerchief from the stump and folding it into his pocket before they moved closer to the race path.

"Mr. Thorpe," Rafe said, "*Alan*, can I beg you to look after her? Keep her safe in my absence? Guard her with your life? I shan't be more than a moment. A quick jog. I'll race the wind. But I can't leave my handkerchief, you understand."

"Of course, Mr. Fitz-Stephens. Never doubt my loyalty, not for a minute." Mr. Thorpe stood straight. "I am your man."

And with that, Rafe turned from whence they came and jogged away.

It was a kindness, she decided. Ensuring she and Mr. Thorpe had the much-needed time to speak. Long at last, they could formulate a plan, she and Mr. Thorpe. They could justify his traveling all the way to Devonshire to aid her. Every ill thought she had entertained about Rafe Fitz-Stephens was replaced with the recognition of his unselfish kindness. In his pursuit of the handkerchief she knew was safely tucked in his pocket, he thought only of her.

"Shall I speak first?" she asked. "Yes, I shall. Let me express how grateful I am you have answered my letter with your presence. I had hoped, but I was not disillusioned, you would. There were your grandparents to consider, the travel itself, the aid you could offer—everything! But here you are, my loyal friend." Overcome, Genevieve hiccupped and struggled not to cry.

Why was she becoming a watering pot over *Mr. Thorpe*? Her only relief was Rafe was not here to witness this.

Mr. Thorpe shuffled his feet, looking altogether uncomfortable. At length, he said, "I couldn't *not* come, Miss Slade. Your letter communicated your desperation perfectly. I could never allow a friend to be so aggrieved."

"Now that you're here, you see my predicament."

He rubbed the back of his neck and looked down at his boots. "Not... precisely. Your letter implied... that is to say... I had expected to find the gentleman in question... oh, how to say.... Could you explain why you are against the match? Having met him, I don't see—"

"My father *forced* this against our will, threatening to ruin one or both of us over what he knew was not true," Genevieve pressed, her tone begging to be understood. "He used Mr. Fitz-Stephens' gentility against him and my reputation against me. It was the worst sort of manipulation, so unlike Papa. I don't know what came over him. But there stood a complete stranger that Papa insisted I marry. I can't possibly marry a complete stranger. Don't you see? And he'll come to resent me, even if he convinces himself this is for the best. He has plans to become a barrister in London."

As her excuses tumbled forth, pleading for Mr. Thorpe's wrinkled brow to understand the seriousness of her plight, the desperation to rid herself of this betrothal, Genevieve wondered if anything she had said was true. It *had* been true. They *had* been strangers. He *had* wanted to practice law in London, criminal rather than civil, which was all the circuit could offer. Resentment *was* a real possibility. But now? Was any of it true now? They were no longer strangers. They were almost friends.

Mr. Thorpe began to pace. "Don't take offense, Miss Slade, when I admit I... I find him to be the very best of men. Our acquaintance has been short, granted, but he is a gentleman. I struggle to see the problem. Have you tried to make him *not* a stranger?" When she did not respond other than to wring her handkerchief, he said, "I don't see Mr. Fitz-Stephens resenting you. He is far too sensible."

"We have become acquainted," she admitted. "But only because we've been forced to. With this betrothal hanging overhead, how are we to develop any sort of friendship? Consider yours and mine. We have a *true* friendship. I could never have that with Mr. Fitz-Stephens, not with us both knowing we're *forced* to marry, all because my father had a bee in his bonnet one day and threatened us over a misunderstanding."

He stopped pacing and leaned against the fencing along the road. "I'm here to help, Miss Slade. I'm not clear what it is you wish me to do, however. If it's within my power and within reason, I will do what I can to keep you from marrying into unhappiness."

Genevieve twisted her handkerchief one way then another. She did not know what he could do. She had hoped he would arrive and… and *what*? Convince her parents *they* had an understanding and demand she make good on the promise so they could marry instead? That this was exactly what she had hoped when she wrote the letter was not something she wished to admit, not with him standing a few feet away. How had she ever thought she could marry Mr. Thorpe? He was such a *good* man. His being here proved that. She cared for his grandparents, with whom he resided, and that offered a promising start to a marriage—family one liked. But…

She tried to imagine him taking seven strides towards her, wrapping his arms around her, and dipping her into a dramatic kiss. Not only could she *not* imagine it, she was a little ill at the thought. It would not be unlike kissing one's sibling. She felt peaky.

Nothing against him, of course. He was the most amiable man she had ever known.

Mr. Thorpe studied her with his soulful brown eyes, reminding her of a faithful hound.

What a dreadful person she was. First, she thought of him as a brother. Then, she equated him to a hound! Poor Mr. Thorpe. And why should she not fancy him? He was handsome in his own way, predictable and devoted. She *should* fancy him. She *could* fancy him.

Pulling her shoulders back, she took one step towards him, her mind made up to *try* to kiss him and see if they could muster feelings for each other, enough attraction to fuel them both to think of a dozen ways and two dozen reasons to break this contrived betrothal.

"I have it!" he said, punching his fist into his open palm.

Her foot had not risen an inch from the ground for her second step. She relaxed, leaning a little away from him.

"I'll convince your parents that Mr. Fitz-Stephens isn't the *best* choice. I could never besmirch his name. Never that. But if I could help them consider *other* matches that would be better, more desirable, they might think twice about forcing the betrothal. If they could give you the *choice*, then you could walk away freely without repercussions. What might Mr. Slade think of an *aristocrat*, hmm?"

Genevieve blinked. "You don't know any aristocrats."

"Well, no, but that hardly matters. What matters is enticing Mr. Slade to a *different* type of match, set his eyes elsewhere in hopes of freeing you from this obligation."

She frowned.

His expression had lit with the genius of his idea, but seeing her lackluster reaction, it dimmed again. "It's all I know to offer, Miss Slade. Unless…"

"Unless?" She shifted her stance, hope rising.

"Unless I can convince *you* and *Mr. Fitz-Stephens* that the betrothal is precisely what you both want."

"Arg!" Genevieve threw her hands up and resumed her walk in the direction of the estate.

Mr. Thorpe followed behind her but said nothing, the *thunk* of earth beneath his boots signaling to her he remained present, guarding her with his life, as he had promised Rafe. Thankfully, that task was not long at hand, for before they had walked a tenth of a mile, Rafe returned, jogging to them with a wave of his handkerchief and a jolly, "Success!"

Assuming his place by her side, Rafe secured her hand over his forearm. "Miss me?"

In answer to his smirk, she added with a sly smirk of her own, "I hardly noticed your absence, not with Mr. Thorpe to keep me company."

"If you hope to make me jealous, it's working." Rafe lifted her hand and kissed the air above her knuckles.

Mr. Thorpe tugged at his forelock. "Now, now, I've no wish to cause jealousy. I merely did as I was bid, Mr. Fitz-Stephens. And since you've returned to your lady's side, I best excuse myself to the tavern. Not that I don't mind the exercise but, you see, I... er—"

Walking backwards as he talked, Mr. Thorpe shrugged, pivoted, and returned in the direction they had come.

Chapter 18

The mirror's reflection never lied. It flirted. It winked. It complimented. Rafe angled to admire how expertly the cut of the coat framed his breeches. Best dressed gentleman of the evening? Yes, he believed he would be. The reflection agreed.

Someone knocked on the dressing room door.

"Come."

Rafe tousled his hair for the finale.

Headley stepped in with a sweeping gaze over Rafe's preening. Rather than tease or expostulate, he nodded his approval.

Fingers combing through the unruly locks at his crown, Rafe's hands stilled to spy Headley's coat in his reflection — the shade of Headley's superfine was *perfection*. Blast. Was it too late to change his own attire? His jeweled blue could not compete.

With a flick to his tails, Headley took a seat. "Ready? Or are you going to change two more times?"

Grunting, Rafe gave his waistcoat a firm tug before turning to his table to gather his handkerchief and little gold box. On second thought… Opening a drawer, he selected two different fobs, then spun around to face Headley.

"Left fob," Headley said without hesitation.

Rafe nodded. Excellent choice. He made quick work of adding the fob.

As he slipped the other back into the drawer, he hesitated, rubbing a finger over the gemstone.

"You don't need both, Fitz-Stephens, not this evening. Close the drawer."

He closed it. Should he bring his card case? A flask? Quizzing glass? What about—

"No," answered Headley to Rafe's unvoiced questions. "Whatever it is, you don't need it. Supper with tea, a card game if we're fortunate, and ample opportunities to steal kisses from Miss Slade behind the curtains—what more does one need for so simple an evening?"

"More mint." Rafe retrieved his gold box from his pocket to refill.

"Ah, now you've mentioned, I've been meaning to ask. Any chance I could beg more of your toothpowder? I can't replicate the recipe to save my life, and my valet is threatening to quit if he catches me mixing herbs again."

As Rafe secured a jar for Headley, the pounding of feet could be heard on the stairs, his brothers descending with the grace of hippos. "You saw one of the new Vitruvian members at the run, yes? Pity he only observed. Could have made an impressive performance of the forest obstacles, I'd wager."

Headley chuckled before saying, "I didn't think you noticed. You were too busy disappearing into the woods with Miss Slade." He waggled his eyebrows. "Do you need a chaperone? I'm not altogether certain you can be trusted with a beautiful lady."

"And give you the chance to work your charms? It's bad enough your coat this evening makes you look taller. I can't compete with your charms *and* your coat."

"It's not *me* you have to worry about."

Rafe arched a brow.

"Tell me about this Thorpe character. A friend of Miss Slade, you had said."

"That's right. She had written to him about the betrothal. He's here to… approve the match."

Headley's pursed lips told Rafe he did not believe that for a second. "If so, why did you introduce him to *her* parents as *your* friend?"

"Because he is. Any friend of hers is a friend of mine."

Eyes narrowed over the pursed lips. "Whatever your motives, Fitz-Stephens, I'm not convinced Thorpe isn't a fox in the hen house. The more innocent the face, the less I trust it. Di and I were talking—"

"Woah now. No need for you or Diana to worry about Mr. Thorpe. For that matter, *if* Miss Slade decided she preferred Mr. Thorpe to me, I would give them my blessing, for he is a *good* man, and I wish for nothing except her happiness."

Of all the reactions Rafe least expected, laughter was the one.

Headley threw back his head with a laugh. "What a tale of cock and bull. You win this round, Fitz-Stephens."

They left the dressing room with Headley still laughing and Rafe feeling smugly victorious at side-stepping, although he doubted he would have a better excuse next round.

The Fitz-Stephenses, as well as the Headleys and Mr. Thorpe, assembled in front of the dower house as several manservants readied the lanterns. The evening was dark, the stars hidden behind cloud cover, and the air was warm, but that did not deter anyone from the brisk walk from the dower house to the main house. The Slades, in their defense, had offered to send the carriage. With spirits elevated from the first day of the frolic and three additional guests in tow, no one wished to cram inside a carriage for such a short journey.

And so, in all their finery, they walked, enjoying their own company.

The only word of complaint came from Gran. "It's *our* village's competition and *our* right to celebrate," she said. "The Fitz-Stephenses should be hosting in their own home, not attending as *guests*."

To Rafe's surprise, his mother did not echo Gran's sentiment, as she usually did, rather she said, "I'm attending for the sake of Miss Slade. She has far more sense than I've heretofore given her credit. In truth, I believe she won my favor at first loosed arrow."

Rafe prepared to remark, but Diana touched his elbow and said in a low voice, "The archery lesson went exceedingly well. Miss Slade is not exactly the most talented archer, but she is an apt pupil. We've another lesson planned tomorrow." Lowering to nearly a whisper, she asked, "Are you going to confess to me why your mother thought her insensible? I'm all ears."

"Genevieve declined lessons at first. Mother dislikes being told no," was all Rafe said, his tone serious but his wink teasing.

Diana tittered but said no more on the subject.

Rather than meet in the drawing room, the Fitz-Stephenses and guests joined the Slades in the games room. Along with the card tables, ready for play, was a sideboard of various foods, from cheeses to fricassee. Congenial company, oysters, cards, a beautiful lady — what more could a gentleman wish from his evening?

As everyone chose their table, Rafe nudged Mr. Thorpe to partner with Genevieve. The disapproving gaze of Mrs. Slade was not disguised as she joined their table, partnering Rafe.

With another nudge for Mr. Thorpe to shuffle the cards, Rafe said, "Have I mentioned, Mrs. Slade, my friend Mr. Thorpe will be competing in the swim relay the day after tomorrow? I hope you'll join me in cheering him as he takes on the Eurwendin team. If I'm not mistaken, Mr. Thorpe will surprise us with his swimming prowess."

Mrs. Slade eyed the man doubtfully.

Mr. Thorpe dealt the cards. "I will represent Grant Lindis to the best of my abilities, Mr. Fitz-Stephens, but I could never hope to gain the praise of persons of *quality*. Only a true athlete could do that, like... like an aristocrat." He nodded sagely to Mrs. Slade, then looked to his companions around the table.

Mrs. Slade stared, perplexed.

Rafe scratched his chin and quirked a brow at Genevieve.

"What are you on about?" Headley asked from one table over.

"It's not polite to eavesdrop," Rafe said, leaning back in his bergère chair to see Headley past Diana's ostrich feather. "Pay attention to your own game before your sister wins your inheritance."

Mrs. Slade chortled before turning her attention to Mr. Thorpe. "What *are* you on about?"

"The allure of aristocrats. They're superior in all ways to us humble gentlemen. They've the leisure to pursue athletic endeavors, thus winning the approval of parents and young ladies alike."

Headley interjected again from his table, "Are you saying aristocrats are attractive suitors because they enjoy foxhunting?"

A smattering of laughter circled the room.

Rafe had no idea what Thorpe was trying to say or accomplish, but a rescue was in order before Thorpe made himself even less attractive in Mr. and Mrs. Slade's eyes.

"I see your point," Rafe said, "and I raise you your own athleticism. How much more impressive is it to compete in a swim race than to pursue those activities popular amongst aristocrats, which are rarely challenging, nothing akin to a race? Between caring for your grandparents and calling on your friends, you expertly navigate the waters. What woman could resist you?" Turning to Mrs. Slade, he added, "More to the point, what wise guardian could deny their daughter so fine a gentleman? Is this not what every parent wishes, Mrs. Slade? An able-bodied man with strong familial ties and a competitive spirit. Why, I would go so far as to say there is an ambitious streak in him."

Mrs. Slade opened her mouth to reply, but Mr. Thorpe spoke over her. "No need to deflect, Mr. Fitz-Stephens. You've described the sort of aristocratic bachelor I had in mind. There are no stronger famil- ial ties than those of bluebloods. Ambitious socially, competitive politically. Am I right?"

"You unnecessarily cast yourself in the shade, Thorpe," Rafe countered. "I see before me the best of men. I could only wish to be half the man you are, seizing the noble qualities every aristocrat strives for — you have them in abundance! A man of virtue, loyalty, admirable connections with friends in multi- ple counties, humor and wit — why, you're willing to aid friends on a moment's notice — you, Thorpe, are the man to have by one's side. If I had a daughter, I would be fortunate to invite you as a suitor."

"Me? Oh no, Mr. Fitz-Stephens. You should aspire for a far greater match for your daughter, a viscount at least."

Intercepting the volley, Diana said from the table she shared with her brother, "Too lofty, Mr. Thorpe! I would never wish to seek the attentions of a nob. I grant you, there are some who would, but not all women are so singularly minded. I ask you, what are the advantages? Some of us wish only for a gen- tleman who will think the world revolves around *us*. Praise and the occasional new bonnet are what some of us dream."

"Someone *tall*," said Miss Cecilia, who had been invited to join for the evening. Eyeing Headley across from her, she fluttered eyelashes, "I prefer tall and handsome. Who cares if he bears a title?"

Poor Headley stared at his cards and cleared his throat.

Rafe drew the attention away from Cecilia's child- ish flirtation. "Stability is of the utmost importance, never mind height. London, for instance, is hardly the place to bring a bride or raise a family, rather within the family home in the rural countryside, now there is perfection on a tray. Is that not something you can offer, Mr. Thorpe? You live in the family home, do you not, caring for your grandparents? The noblest task I could imagine of any gentleman."

Gran raised her voice from the sideboard. "That eliminates you as a desirable suitor, Rafe. Mr. Thorpe, you have my permission to move into the dower house and wait on me hand and foot. You'll be the catch of Devonshire."

The room filled with laughter, and to Rafe's relief, the subject changed without any effort on his part.

His attempt to sing the praises of Mr. Thorpe could only be described as a failure. Was Thorpe not on his side? Were they not working together to convince the Slades to free Genevieve of the betrothal? Granted, Rafe's plan was to convince them Thorpe was the best replacement for Rafe, and Thorpe had confessed he was not romantically interested in Genevieve, but it seemed so easy to help them fall for each other while also convincing her parents. Or at least it *had* seemed easy. Not so easy when Thorpe was undermining him.

He glanced at Genevieve. She was watching him. Was it the stuffiness of the room, or were her cheeks rosy? Ah, it must be a residual glow from the frolic. Her eyes were bright, her cheeks pink, her lips curved in a playful smile. Even he could not deny it had been an enjoyable day, more so with her by his side, but that was simply explained — he had experienced the frolic anew, seeing it vicariously from her perspective.

It took at least an hour to steal her away from the others for a semi-private discussion. Nothing was private with so many eyes watching them but grazing at the sideboard with voices lowered was as secluded as Rafe could achieve. His invitation for a game of billiards had resulted in Miss Cecilia harassing poor Headley again, so he had abandoned that avenue. His gaze flicked to the curtains over Genevieve's shoulder. Curse Headley's teasing. On second thought, he was tempted to allow Miss Cecilia to pursue the man out of revenge for slipping into Rafe's head the thought of kissing Genevieve behind the curtains. Temptation to lead her that direction had him reaching for the sweetbread instead.

Between bites, Rafe asked, his voice as low as possible, "Your conversation with you-know-who—successful?"

She grimaced, inching her fingers towards a glass of Madeira, then pretending to change her mind, only to return for the Madeira, anything to extend their time at the sideboard without raising suspicion. "Mostly. His idea of helping is to convince them a better match could be had."

"A better match than me? That's unlikely." Rafe snorted.

Genevieve pinched his arm. "It's more help than you're offering. What was all that about *him* being so great?"

"I was under the impression we were trying to swap beaux. Him instead of me? Yes? Is that not the goal?"

She looked down at her glass, failing to meet his eyes. "Past tense."

"Ah." He took a few more bites to mull that over.

He still thought it the most likely of their options. A ready gentleman? What more could the Slades want? And if he could entice the two to fall in love, as he had once thought they already were, all the better. Alas, if Thorpe would not have her, and if she only saw in him friendship, there was not much Rafe could do.

Dusting his hands with his handkerchief, he said, "All we need to happen is for them to give you a choice. There doesn't *need* to be another suitor."

Rafe knew her parents would do nothing publicly if he recused himself from the betrothal, but he had not known that upon first meeting, and at this point, he could not do so without damaging Genevieve's reputation. He had given his word and would not retract that or risk casting a shadow on Genevieve — everyone would wonder why she had been rejected by a suitor, never believing the break was amicable. No, if this betrothal was to end, she would need to end it, and the only way that would happen is for her parents to offer the option.

Convincing her the threats made by her father were all for show was unlikely. She believed them enough never to risk uttering the emphatic *no*. Was this not how young ladies were brought up? To obey their parents without question? The concept was foreign to Rafe, having not only been brought up in a house of boys but also taught to question everything, namely authority. Unquestioning obedience was a lady's plight and one he abhorred and did not comprehend.

"What if…" she began, eyes remaining downcast. "What if we could tease them with a different suitor, someone who would play along since Mr. Thorpe will not?"

Hmm. That had been the purpose of Thorpe. Did the man have to be so difficult? Why had he bothered coming all this way if he was not going to sacrifice himself for the cause? Hmm. Whoever would play along would need to be able to tempt her parents away from Rafe while simultaneously avoiding parson's mousetrap. Rafe did not trust Mr. Slade not to trap a second suitor. The only person —

"No." Rafe stared at Genevieve's unruly curls. "*No.*"

"He wouldn't agree?"

"No, I — " Rafe stopped and reached for a glass of wine, his gaze falling on Headley faking a losing hand so his sister would win.

There was nothing Rafe could say that would not make him sound a jealous fool. The thought of Headley flirting with Genevieve, even as a playact, had Rafe's fingers biting into his palm. Rationalizing the reaction was beyond his faculties at present.

If he was jealous over the *thought* of Headley flirting, how the devil was he going to feel when they succeeded in convincing her parents to offer her the choice… and she rejected him as a result? The betrothal would be severed. She would move with her parents at the end of the lease. Or marry someone else.

He shuddered, pushing from his mind what *could* be and focusing on how relieved he *would* be not to be tied to someone who did not want him.

Genevieve said, "I only thought of him because he's your friend and would be discreet, as well as more convincing than Mr. Thorpe without the risk of him taking advantage of the situation. Our goal, after all, is for us both to be free, not compromised twice over."

"You needn't explain. I understand. He *is* a good choice, except for one snag." That Rafe was on the verge of jealous outrage. Instead of admitting that aloud, he said, "He believes the betrothal is real. Love at first sight and all that."

She looked up in surprise. "But... I thought..."

He raised his glass. "A gentleman through and through."

Genevieve mouthed *oh* and flushed pink in the candlelight. He watched her as she thought through what that meant, not least of which was the devotion of his family by proxy. If he did not know better, he would assume she was accustomed to the London crowd and their tireless need for gossip and drama. *No, dear Genevieve, you are witnessing centuries of good breeding, gentility at its finest.*

She bit her bottom lip, then questioned, "How will you explain the split?"

"Ah, he'll have to nurse my broken heart. He and Diana both. Worry not, my darling. I will never paint you as the villain. Irreparable differences? We did not suit despite undying attraction?" Hooding his eyes with a sultry gaze, he whispered, "Confusing lust for love."

With an *oof*, Genevieve turned to face the side-board. "You're *insufferable*. A gentleman—my left foot." Setting her glass on the discard tray, she abandoned him to stand behind Diana.

Rafe chuckled, feeling the green-eyed monster slip back into hiding and his jovial self returning.

Chapter 19

The riverbank had never been so colorful, the crowd cheering in fancy dress, counting down for the event after the regatta when they would have their turn at participating in a race of their own.

Rafe positioned his feet in the six-oared boat and readied for action.

Headley, sitting in front of Rafe, tossed his voice over his shoulder, "Remind you of Oxford?"

"Indubitably." Rafe's gaze combed the bank in search of Genevieve. When he did not see her, her family, or his family, he concluded they were further downstream, closer to the finish line.

"We need a name for our team. Bad luck without it."

"Is it? I've never heard that. You made it up." Rafe adjusted his robe so it would not tangle with his legs during the race.

As with the crowd, he and the team wore fancy dress. There would be no time to change between the regatta and the festival. A *toga virilis* was, perhaps, not the best choice for rowing. The entire team wore matching togas. In the boat next to theirs were the Eurwendin racers, dressed as pirates. One of the rowers Rafe knew from the Society, Mr. Gavin Proudie. They nodded in recognition. With luck, they could chat after the race.

Within Rafe's boat, the fellow closest to the coxswain—this being the first year Giles Fitz-Stephens was not serving in the role—said, "An't it tradition to name the team after the best tavern? I propose The Dragon's Breath."

All in the boat assented. Rafe chuckled. They would not sport the name for more than ten minutes, but if having a name boosted their morale, so be it. Pity they had not adopted the name earlier to enjoy it longer. Keep it for next year? Sure, why not? They had practiced together in preparation for today, all already experienced rowers, but they could hardly be considered a rowing club, not when they only rowed together each summer for the frolic. Regardless, the rowers celebrated their new team name in honor of the best tavern in Grant Lindis—never mind it was the only tavern in Grant Lindis.

Mr. Burgess, the coxswain, shouted something unintelligible. Between the crowd, the Eurwendin rowers, and the choppy waters, Rafe could not hear him.

Headley called over his shoulder again, his voice also nearly drowned out by the din, "Two minutes. Look lively."

The crowd's cheers increased in a deafening crescendo as both teams took their oars in hand, straightened their posture, and readied for the bugle. Rafe's heart pounded with anticipation. His breathing deepened, steadied. His focus funneled.

At one minute, Rafe's war cry reached all the way to the coxswain, "*Non ducor, duco!*"

He knew his words reached them all, because the team echoed in unison, "I am not led, I lead!"

The bugle trumpeted.

The crowd disappeared. The cheers muffled. All Rafe heard was the rhythm of the row. His fingers cradled the oar. The blade dipped into the water cleanly, quickly, effortlessly. His back muscles contracted as he drove through his legs, swinging his body in an arc. His pull of the oar accelerated at the finish for a clean extraction of the blade from the water. He relaxed into the recovery as he leaned forward, controlling his body's swing with a pivot from his hips, readying to repeat the whole process again.

His body synchronized, arms, back, and legs responding to his cues: catch, drive, release, recover. He worked in tandem with his teammates, each person contributing uniquely with strength, technique, or rhythm. It was not a professional crew, not by any stretch, but they worked well together and knew their business.

But so did the Eurwendin crew.

After forty strokes, Rafe felt the tension building, his muscles burning from the effort, an uncomfortable sensation that he craved. His body screamed for a reprieve, but his mind begged for more.

Their position in the competition informed the power behind his drive. He breathed through the cycle, counting his strokes.

The boats were neck and neck.

Rafe pushed through the drive.

His crew pulled into the lead.

He recovered for two strokes.

The Eurwendins nosed ahead.

Rafe pushed harder, matching the power of his crew.

Somewhere in the recesses of his mind, he wondered if Genevieve could see him, if she was impressed, if she was proud, if she liked what she saw. Vain thoughts, but they fueled him to dig deeper into the pockets of his reserves to row harder, row faster.

Irrationally, he wanted to impress her.

Catch, drive, release, recover.

The bugle sounded. The finish line had been crossed. Rafe leveraged the oar out of the water and relaxed, then looked around to gain his bearings. Mr. Burgess, balancing at the stern, stood and released a chest thumping roar. Headley twisted in his seat just enough to show a profiled smile of victory. They had won.

Smiling so broadly his cheeks hurt as much as the rest of him, Rafe searched the banks until... Genevieve waved to him, looking quite fetching as Aphrodite. In truth, he had no idea what her costume was meant to resemble, but she looked like Aphrodite to him. He waved back, his smile more for her than for the win. Later, he could convince himself it was the heat of the moment, the excitement of the victory, but for now, he relished sharing a moment of affection with her, her radiance the only attribute he acknowledged.

Genevieve helped her sisters and Miss Headley climb aboard the makeshift longship, their vessel looking more in keeping with a miniature Viking craft than a chariot fit for goddesses, which was how they were all dressed, Genevieve as Artemis, which had been

Mrs. Fitz-Stephens' idea. All along the river, villagers prepared to race in the capture-the-boat event. Rafts, fishing boats, sculls, and unidentified vessels not fit to stay afloat littered the shallows of the river.

From what Genevieve understood, the misnamed capture-the-boat event originated from an older tradition when the regatta used rowboats rather than single-seated sculls. Once the regatta racers crossed the finish line, the villagers would literally capture the boats from the rowers, tossing them overboard and commandeering the crafts. Now, however, not-quite-safe-for-water crafts were prepared in advance of the frolic, decorated with flags, household items, handcrafted sundries, anything to make the boat unique and entertaining, be it themed or not. The boat next to Genevieve's was decorated in kitchenware, old pots and ladles adorning the sides.

The challenge of this race was first to stay afloat and second to paddle using anything except an oar. The owners of the kitchen boat, she noticed, wielded pans for paddles.

"Look! There's Rafe," said Miss Headley, pointing to a raft further downstream.

Genevieve, holding a tea tray as her oar, searched the river. With so much chaos, she could not find him. She would have to paddle swiftly to beat the boats around her if she wanted to catch up to him. So quickly had the event changed from the official race to this silly fancy dress race that she had lost sight of him on the water and not yet been able to congratulate him on his team's win. She thought it best not to mention how magnificent he had performed. He was vain enough as it was. And she certainly did not wish for him to think she had been the least besotted with him.

Somewhere, a fiddler struck up a lively tune. Picnic linen perched on grassy knolls as those not participating set about to be entertained. A few groups danced together to the music. As with yesterday, kites rode high in the breeze. Genevieve did not deceive herself into believing life in Grant Lindis was like this year-round. It had been quiet before this week, after all. Nevertheless, she was enamored by life here. Could they not stay? Could this not be their permanent home? They could not live in Devington Priory, of course, past the lease, but what of another house nearby? This was the first time in her life she felt she *belonged*.

Before Genevieve was ready, the bugle sounded to begin the race. She braced herself for the boat to lurch forward. Instead, hardly any boat around her moved an inch. Grabbing her tray, she positioned herself near the edge and began paddling, laughing more than progressing. Her sisters, using umbrellas for oars, splashed each other more than moved the boat. Miss Headley, also using a tray, made better headway. Genevieve mimicked her method of paddling, and the boat drifted forward.

There was more laughter than movement, but surprisingly, their trays were more effective than some of the other tools around them. They passed a rowboat decorated as a dragon, the oars of choice being boots worn over hands like gloves. The owners of the dragon boat were having far too good a time to notice they were mostly moored and were being passed by a longship of goddesses with umbrellas and trays. The first boat to pass Genevieve was adorned by garlands, the tools of choice being shovels. The captain of the vessel waved as they passed.

"Paddle faster, Miss Slade! We'll never catch Rupert and Rafe at this speed!"

Genevieve was tempted to abandon hope in favor of joining her sisters' water fight. Alas, she could not disappoint Miss Headley.

Dipping her tray in with vigor, she looked up and shrieked, "Wait! Stop paddling!" They were heading towards two boats at war.

The sailors of one were bucketing water into the other, while the sinking crew were trying to board the other vessel before theirs went under. Genevieve's crew watched in one part horror and one part amusement. Before their eyes, the crew of the sinking boat leapt aboard the other vessel, shifting the balance and capsizing it, the lot tipping overboard into the water.

Well, the saboteurs deserved it.

What she expected to discover, as the goddesses' boat drifted past, was a few Grant Lindis villagers dunking and squabbling with Eurwendin villagers. Instead, the boat swept past a band of brothers engaged in a water brawl, in no hurry to swim ashore, all good humor without malice.

Was it possible to fall a little in love with a man from his parish of residence?

Just as she thought this irrational bit of silliness, she spied Rafe on a simple raft. He and Mr. Headley held cricket bats for oars. He had not yet seen her approaching. His raft floated without progress, bobbing in place so he could chat with the people in the punt a little further ahead, the people being Mr.

Fitz-Stephens, Rafe's two younger brothers, and — oh!
And her father! How delightful to see him enjoying
the event. The Fitz-Stephenses were dressed as a king
with his two court jesters, while her father was dis-
appointingly plainly attired.

"Rupert!" called Miss Headley, waving her dripping tray with triumph to have caught up with the raft.

Mr. Headley prepared for their approach. As his
sister's bow knocked into Mr. Anthony Fitz-Stephens'
stern, Mr. Headley leapt aboard the longship, which
was an impressive feat of its own merit, but more so
since his flying lunge was accomplished in a toga.
Cecilia and Theia watched with mouths agape as he
defied gravity, then dissolved into giggles and sighs
when he arched a brow in their direction.

Rafe balked at being abandoned.

Before Genevieve realized what was happening,
Mr. Headley apologized profusely, then hoisted
her overboard with an unceremonious grunt. She
screeched, her fate too horrific to fathom. Squeezing her eyes closed and gulping air, she prepared for
the splash. Rather than caught by the murky water,
strong hands embraced her.

"Welcome aboard," Rafe said, his face shadowed
by the sunlight behind him.

He steadied her on her feet. Orienting herself
took more than a moment. Her boat nudged past Mr.
Fitz-Stephens' crew and left her behind on Rafe's raft.
Oh! Her tray. She must have dropped her tray. A
quick glance down showed she was still in one piece,
had not so much as lost a shoe, only the tray.

Rafe handed her a cricket bat. "Shall we show
them how it's done?" He pushed his bat against

the riverbank to propel them forward and regain momentum.

"What a heathen!" Genevieve said with a huff and nod towards Mr. Headley. Her outrage was unconvincing, considering she was grinning, a laugh on her lips.

"Pity Diana. She's had to tolerate him her entire life."

"I formally retract my idea regarding him — you know to what I refer. How could anyone with sense prefer him to you?"

He said nothing, merely cast her a curious glance before returning to his paddling.

They were not far from the finish line. Was she disappointed? Yes, undeniably. They had no time to exchange more than pleasantries. She had not yet congratulated him on the regatta. As their raft sidled with the shore, a gentleman she did not know approached to help them disembark.

Rafe accepted the man's help first so he could be the one to bring Genevieve ashore. "May I introduce an old friend of mine? This is Mr. Proudie." In a teasing whisper, loud enough for Mr. Proudie to hear, he added, "A Eurwendin, if you don't mind fraternizing with the enemy."

"How do you do?" Genevieve extended a hand.

"This is Miss Slade," Rafe said.

He was on the cusp of saying more as she shook Mr. Proudie's hand, but she did not learn if he was to introduce her as his betrothed, a member of the family letting his house, or otherwise, for Miss Headley interrupted to slip her hand into the crook of Genevieve's elbow and steal her away. With a lingering glance over her shoulder, Genevieve cast an apologetic look at Rafe and his companion.

Beneath a stately yew, Mrs. Fitz-Stephens, Mr. Thorpe, and Mama were arranging picnic treats.

Genevieve quizzed Miss Headley, "Where are my sisters?"

"Rupert volunteered for the clean-up crew to help remove the boats from the river." Miss Headley tittered.

"Ah, and so they volunteered, as well. How magnanimous of them."

Her heart bled for poor Mr. Headley. She would have thought Theia, at least, would have more sense than to ogle the gentleman, least of all since her age did not predispose her to romance, but Cecilia had a curious way of influencing Theia until an onlooker would be challenged to tell them apart in ages.

"Look. Mr. Thorpe is wearing the garland I made." Miss Headley tittered anew, not that she had stopped since her report about Rupert's whereabouts.

Mr. Thorpe was as plainly dressed as Papa but wore a garland over his brow and a wreath about his neck. He greeted them both with a hearty welcome, then struck a pose. "I'm Dionysus. Did you guess?"

Miss Headley fussed over his wreath while Genevieve shook her head, all astonishment. Staid Mr. Thorpe was the antithesis of Dionysus.

Mrs. Fitz-Stephens patted next to her for Genevieve to join but Miss Headley turned away from Mr. Thorpe's wreath long enough to say, "Oh no! We aren't joining yet. I wish to take a turn with Miss Slade first. May we?"

Mama whined to delay the picnic.

Mrs. Fitz-Stephens, however, obliged. "Yes, of course, dear. You'll want to find your land legs after the race. Will you both want to proceed from here to the dower house for the archery lesson, or will you want to rest first?"

Genevieve offered, "I venture we have the lesson first. It would save a great deal of walking back and forth between houses, and once I lie down, I might not rise again until dinner."

"Splendid. It is as I had hoped," Mrs. Fitz-Stephens said, but then added with a mock scold, "You misled me, Miss Slade. You and my son. I was led to believe you had little skill with a bow. How surprised was I to learn otherwise."

"Oh! Not a whit! You flatter me. I can count on two hands the number of times I've hit the target."

Chortling, Mrs. Fitz-Stephens said, "I'll not fall for your false modesty twice." Crooking a finger for Genevieve to come closer, she said in a low voice, "After the frolic ends, you should try fencing."

"*You fence*?" Genevieve could not disguise the awe in her voice.

"Avidly. And I would be delighted to teach someone with an aptitude to learn."

Whispering, she asked, "But isn't it inappropriate for women to fence?"

"It wouldn't be half as much fun otherwise." Mrs. Fitz-Stephens winked at Miss Headley, who had been listening to every word.

Genevieve looked from one to the other. Was it possible to admire others over *fencing*?

With a tug, Miss Headley guided her away from the picnic and through the maze of the crowd until they found open ground to walk.

"Let's not beat about the bush," Miss Headley said. "The direct approach is always best. Rather than dancing around what we wish to say, saying all the meaningless things we don't truly want to say, all to avoid saying what it is we intend to say, it is far superior to have out with the main intent, then we've said what we desired, have our reply, and needn't be left wondering what it would have been had we not danced about saying all the things and—"

"Miss Headley, please, say whatever it is you have to say." Genevieve was more amused than curious. Knowing Miss Headley, all the young lady wished to say was *that* which she had just said, a treatise on direct speaking.

"Diana, if you please. We're good friends now, aren't we? So good we're nearly sisters. And being as close to sisters as we could be—I've always thought it would be lovely to have a sister—we should vow to tell each other everything."

Telling her sisters anything was usually a recipe for disaster, but she held her peace.

"Now, *Genevieve*, dear sister. Tell me about Mr. Thorpe."

So surprised at the turn in conversation, Genevieve slowed her pace. "Mr. Thorpe?"

"Yes, Mr. Thorpe. You see, Rupert and I have been talking. Rupert says he's a friend of yours, but Rafe introduced him as a friend of *his*, and since neither of you has known the other for terribly long, we find it difficult to believe he can be a friend to you both, although I suppose he could be if we believe in coincidences, which I don't, and that has led us to wonder—us being Rupert and I, of course—*who is Mr. Thorpe*, and why is he ingratiating himself with both families?"

Caught off guard, Genevieve hesitated to reply. She did not wish for whatever she said to contradict whatever Rafe might say, or Mr. Thorpe, for that matter. It was fortuitous this question had not been posed sooner, though, for had she thought Mr. Thorpe meant to win her from Rafe, she would have an altogether different answer.

"He's my friend, but since learning of the betrothal, he's done his best to befriend Rafe, as well. It's his way of approving the match."

Diana thought for a moment, then said, "Let me understand you. He's your *friend*, and he wishes to *approve* the betrothal between you and Rafe."

"Yes."

"He disclosed traveling from Gloucestershire. He traveled all this way to approve the betrothal? I'll be the first to admit I wish I had friends so devoted. Take the two of us—would you travel all the way to, let's say, Oxfordshire to set eyes on my betrothed if I hinted to you about a love interest?"

With confidence, Genevieve confessed, "Yes, I would. It *is* unusual for a gentleman to do so for a lady, I grant you, but here he is, nonetheless." Squeezing Diana's arm, she said, "I can't say this is what friends do because I've never had any friends. Mr. Thorpe was the first friend I made, which sounds pitiful when it was only a couple of years ago that we first met, when Papa had secured a lease in Gloucestershire, next door to the Thorpe family, as it happened. Mr. Thorpe is like no one I've ever met, Diana. He *cares*. He puts friends and family first. He's genuine."

"This is all reassuring. You see, and don't laugh, but Rupert and I feared he meant ill. That, perhaps without your realizing it, he had fallen a little in love with you and came to cause mischief. We sound so unchristian for our worries, don't we? Only, Rupert thought it strange, Mr. Thorpe being an unmarried gentleman, that he would come running at the first mention of your betrothal. Who does that unless they mean mischief?"

"A *friend* does that." Genevieve did not feel so much as the tiniest stab of guilt, for everything she said was true. It was *she* who had meant mischief in thinking she could convince Mr. Thorpe to take Rafe's place. Mr. Thorpe had been doing exactly what he was characterized as doing in Genevieve's pretty defense of him — being a friend.

Diana laughed gleefully. "I'm so happy we're the best of friends. And how lucky you are to be marrying Rafe! Everyone envies you, you must realize. Rafe has been much sought after but he's too much in his own head, I think, to notice."

Turning to see the dreamy gaze in Diana's expression, Genevieve ventured, "And you? Did you ever… consider Rafe?"

"As soon as I would Rupert! Good heavens no. He's like an older brother, an obnoxious older brother to boot, but don't consider that a reflection of him, merely how I know him. And before you think he's thrown his eye at his friend's little sister, rest assured he would never consider someone as silly as me. He needs someone sensible. He would never waste his time with silliness, and I'm the first to admit I am very silly indeed. And now that I've had my say, and you've had yours, and we've not beat any bushes, I'll race you back to the picnic."

Hiking the hem of her goddess robe, Diana skipped away from Genevieve before darting in the direction they had come.

Chapter 20

Feet propped, fingers laced behind his head, Rafe drifted in and out of consciousness, light snores waking him long enough to shift his position on the settee before he began the whole process of nodding off again. To say he was exhausted was an understatement. A little rain would not be remiss, anything to cool the air, which was stuffier and more oppressive by the hour, aiding his exhaustion. Elsewhere in the house, his family's voices drifted into the parlor. The rhythm of their muffled words lulled Rafe back to sleep.

In that strange realm between wakefulness and dream, he relished the feel of Genevieve's fingers massaging his scalp. He should not encourage this sort of behavior. Was he not trying to convince her parents to consider a better match, anything to tempt them away from forcing the betrothal, to give her the choice to walk away without damage to either of their reputations? If he was trying to extricate them both from the situation, why was he allowing her to run her hands through his hair? Mmm. Those soft hands traced the curve of his neck, pure velvet against his skin, and then across his shoulders, kneading the sore muscles. *Keep doing that*, he mumbled, *and I'll have no choice but to keep you.*

The parlor door opened to a thunder of voices, his family talking over each other as they entered. Rafe jerked awake. With a swift glance around, he reassured himself he was in the room alone. Only a dream.

"Up, Fitz-Stephens. Dinner at the tea garden." Headley swaggered to the settee and knocked Rafe's feet to the floor so he could sit down.

Gran sat in a chair by the window. Reaching into a nearby basket, she retrieved her embroidery. "Good choice. I've given the cook the day off."

"The day off?" exclaimed Rafe's father. "What will we eat? I don't fancy dinner at a tavern, garden or no garden."

Mother smirked. "All part of your plan. Now we must ingratiate ourselves with the Slades."

"That's likely," said Otis. "You only want Cook's frolic menu."

"Can I be blamed if she's spoiled me over the years?"

Gran grumbled about allowing strangers to eat their own food in their own house.

Rafe looked around. "Where's Diana?"

"With your one true love," Headley said, "pretending she has a sister rather than an *odious* brother — her words."

Noel and Otis snickered, but Rafe suspected it was to the first part of Headley's reply rather than the last.

"Right." Rafe sat up. "If I want food, my choices are dinner with the Slades or dinner at the tea garden. My my, what delectable choices you offer." Standing, he nodded to the door. "To The Dragon's Breath we're bound."

His stomach grumbled in agreement. Manly company over meat and ale was what he needed. That would cleanse his daydreams of sultry fingers. Grunting and monosyllabic conversation awaited.

Half an hour later, they were seated around a table in the tea garden, speaking only of manly pursuits. Thorpe tried to keep pace but was out of his element. Rafe suspected the poor man did not have much in the way of male companions. Outings like this would do him good.

Thorpe dabbed at the corners of his mouth with the linen. "You're saying he was a spy who became a privateer, or a privateer who became a spy?"

In contrast, Rafe made a show of wiping his mouth with the back of his hand. This was a man's dinner! Did Thorpe not see that? No women or thoughts of women allowed, and most definitely no hair fondling or shoulder kneading. To make his point, Rafe took a hearty mouthful of his mutton before answering, his words muffled.

Thorpe watched him with curiosity.

So did Headley.

Swallowing, Rafe tried again. "Or he's the son of a duke in hiding. Perhaps a former circus performer. Could be a foreign prince. No one knows." He elbowed the table and took another bite much too big to chew with any grace, willing juice to dribble down his chin—that would surely mark the end to tantalizing daydreams!

"And he leads this band of merry polymaths?" Thorpe stared in disbelief. "How can he be trusted if you don't know his past?"

Headley leaned back to cradle his mug. "He's proven himself. I'd trust him over my own mother if it came to it, and I would never doubt her, so consider that."

Pushing his plate away after another curious glance to Rafe's manhandling of the mutton, Thorpe asked, "Why do the Society members not dominate the Fracas Frolic? Would that not ensure easy wins for the competitions?"

"The Society isn't *just* about physical training," Headley said. "We spend as much time debating, philosophizing, reading, studying. It's not all fencing bouts."

"Yes, but—"

Rafe interrupted, "Members are from all over, not solely Grant Lindis or Eurwendin, as it happens. Don't think many members even know about the frolic or care. As to the frolic, it isn't about winning or competing. It's fun. To come together and pretend for one week that life isn't knocking at the door. For one week, there are no scandals, there is no poverty, there is simple village fun. I think the history is darker, a feud between the two villages, but no one knows the origin beyond hyperbolic fairytales. More to the point, no one wishes to remember. We only want to have fun."

"Too right," Headley agreed. "Not that long ago, it was exceedingly competitive. Participants would train for weeks, forming winning teams. Now, people can volunteer the day of the event if they wish. No skill required."

Rafe raised a finger to his mouth, about to lick the grease. Blast. His pursuits into manliness were not working. The back of his hand felt gritty from using it as a napkin. Admitting defeat, he dipped his fingers into the provided water bowl and used his linen like the gentleman he was. If he could not drown his desires in grease, how else was he to free his memory of those roaming fingers? She would laugh him out of the tea garden if she knew he had been *dreaming* about her.

"What we need, Headley, is a day of mischief." Rafe ignored the niggling recollection that the last time he thought a little mischief would be fun, he had ended up in a woman's bedchamber being challenged to a duel or the altar, in whichever order necessary.

Headley's brow furrowed. "Not to be insensitive, Fitz-Stephens, but did I miss an important turn of events? The last I heard, you had forsworn mischief making. I believe the rationale was you needing to be a good boy to meet the Inns of Court's moral conduct requirements. 'Nothing reprehensible for old Fitz-Stephens, not any longer,' you had said, and I quote."

"Yes, well, I don't mean anything nefarious. Something simple. A jest amongst friends. Eggs on Proudie's carriage seat — that sort of thing. *You* have nothing holding you back."

"Correct. I can be as naughty as I like. Are you certain you should be associating with a rogue?" Headley bowed his head to hide a grin.

Thorpe looked from one to the other, concern etched in his features. "You're both having me on. Neither of you are… *rogues*." Fidgeting, he glanced to ensure no one was overhearing them.

Rafe leaned closer. "Ask Headley about the time he was almost caught sneaking out of Lady Pennyworth's private parlor."

"I'm fortunate the bushes were below the window to catch my fall."

"Her *husband* almost caught them *in flagrante delicto*," Rafe added.

Shrugging a shoulder, Headley said, "Nothing so sordid. She had agreed to teach me to waltz so I would not make a cake of myself at the assembly. If memory hasn't failed me, that was when I was hoping to make a good impression on Miss Jocelyn."

With a slow wink, Rafe said, "There's a euphemism if ever I heard one. Teach you to 'waltz.'"

Thorpe's face resembled a ruby. "What's... what's a waltz?"

Simultaneously, Rafe said, "A euphemism," while Headley said, "A dance."

Headley said to Thorpe, eyes trained on Rafe, "*Risus abundant in ore stultorum.* Laughter is abundant in the mouth of fools."

Rueful, Rafe raised his cup and said to Thorpe, returning Headley's gaze, "*Castigat ridendo mores.* Laughter corrects morals."

"Touché, Fitz-Stephens. Now, what about you, Mr. Thorpe? Are you Sir Galahad or Sir Bors?"

Thorpe's eyes widened. "I beg your pardon."

Rafe signaled for Thorpe to have another round. His tankard was looking far too dry. "What Headley The Waltzer is asking is if you're a good boy or bad boy, chaste or a little saucy."

"I gathered." Thorpe nodded thanks to the barmaid, then waited for her to leave before answering. "I believe a man's best quality is loyalty. I flatter myself by saying I am, above all things, loyal."

Rafe and Headley exchanged glances.

"I've been informed by a somewhat reliable source," Headley began, "that your being in Grant Lindis for the frolic is a display of loyalty. Is that so?"

Sitting up straighter, Rafe reached for his tankard.

Without a single stutter, Thorpe said with confidence, "It is just so. Miss Slade informed me of her betrothal, and I arrived in short order to assess for myself the gentleman in question."

Grimacing, Rafe tucked his expression behind the brim. How had everything seemed so easy at first? Have Genevieve's true love arrive and claim there had been an understanding already established, so Rafe could slip away into the night a free man, Genevieve to wed her rightful beloved. How had it all come to this? A *friend* arriving to support the betrothal rather than contradict it. Rafe dreaming of Genevieve's tender fingers. Conversations over ale about *loyalty*. At this rate, he might as well have the banns read. The noose was tightening a little more every day.

"And?" Headley probed. "What is your assessment?"

"A finer gentleman I've not met. Er, that is, until I met you, Mr. Headley. *Two* of the finest gentlemen I've met. I dare say Miss Slade is fortunate. As is Mr. Fitz-Stephens, of course, I hasten to add. Yes, fortunate, as well, for Miss Slade is a fine woman, a finer woman I've not—er, until meeting Miss Headley, who happens *also* to be a fine woman."

Headley waved away whatever obsequiousness Thorpe was going to say next.

"Look who we have here," rang a feminine voice from behind Rafe.

He froze, his tankard held midway between mouth and table. Headley and Thorpe eyed over his shoulder.

Only Thorpe reacted, his face returning to a normal shade of pale, and his expression one of both relief and welcome. "Miss Headley, Miss Slade," Thorpe said, rising from his chair.

Rafe mumbled an oath under his breath, then whispered to Headley, "*Lupus in fabula.*"

"Speak of the devil, indeed." Headley rose in greeting.

Try as he might to appear nonchalant, Rafe could not meet Genevieve's gaze when he rose and turned around. His scalp remembered all too well her gentle caress.

"Come to join us?" Thorpe asked, digging Rafe's hole deeper.

Diana blushed. "We had planned a far cleverer way to steal a seat at your table, one to emphasize the sheer coincidence of us bumping into the three of you, but now that you've called out our true intentions, I suppose we can't hide behind subterfuge. Yes, we've come to join you. Do you mind?"

She nodded for two chairs to be added to the garden table before anyone could answer one way or the other.

"We *were* expecting dinner at the Priory," Diana continued, "but Mrs. Slade dragged away a certain gentleman's mother and grandmother to gossip in her apartments over a tray. Enter the perfect excuse on a silver platter for the Misters to have a fathers-with-out-hovering-wives dinner in the billiard room. The last we saw of the pair of gigglers—Genevieve's sisters, not the fathers—was when they slumped away in utter devastation that Rupert was not joining for dinner. And so, here we are! Now, is someone going to offer me a tankard of ale and leg of mutton, or will I have to order for myself?" She tittered as she tugged off her gloves.

Chapter 21

T he next morning saw everyone returning to
the riverbank for the relay swim. Well, almost
everyone. The steady rain kept many spectators
at home, but none of the racers backed down, not
even Mr. Thorpe.

"We're with you, Mr. Thorpe! You're almost there!"
Genevieve cheered him on as he swam.

Ahead, Rafe's brothers treaded water, waiting for
Thorpe to pass the baton so they could have their turn
to swim the distance for the team. Mr. Thorpe was not
a half bad swimmer, as it turned out. With practice,
he could gain speed, but Genevieve was relieved by
his performance, considering there was little doubt
Rafe had volunteered him — he could not have known
if Mr. Thorpe could swim!

Rafe shadowed her. "Thorpe, Thorpe, Thorpe!"

His chanting matched the drumming of her pulse.
Since their arrival at the riverbank, she could not meet
his eyes, not after spending much of her evening in
the hidden snug he had shown her.

Something unnamable had compelled her to go
there last night. Rather than take the route he had
shown her, she made a mission to discover the hidden
panel in the billiard room. Giddiness had been her
reward when she realized mission success. With her,

she had brought a book and a candelabra. The snug had seemed the perfect place to hide from her sisters and enjoy a moment's peace. The trouble was rather than read, her mind had wandered, recalling when she had shared the room with him, seeing him in the chair, feeling his presence. It was ludicrous. Yet she could not get him out of her head.

He brushed against her when he raised his hands to clap in time with his chanting.

So innocent of a touch, his forearm grazing her elbow, but her breathing shallowed. Giving her umbrella a twirl, water droplets flying around her and undoubtedly onto Rafe's sleeve, she stared ahead, refusing to look over.

She blamed the Headleys. It was easy to despise Rafe when her family pressed the match, her father forever hanging over her head the words "compromise" and "ruination," amongst other less savory ones, her mother gushing about it being the match of the year, and Cecilia elbowing her about evening assignations. The more they pressed, the more she resisted, blaming Rafe for trapping *her* in this situation, while feeling guilty for trapping *him*. But then, there were the Headleys.

Both Mr. Headley and Diana believed it a love match. Their every word, their every action strengthened that belief, to the point that when talking to Diana, Genevieve was almost convinced of it herself. Preposterous to think Rafe would fall for her.

If they had not been forced by her father, *would* they have considered each other? She did not think so. Oh, she could not convince herself she would not have noticed him, for she was positive she would have, but he was a man in demand, a man with a never-a-dull-moment life, surrounded by friends and family; he would not have looked twice at her.

Genevieve glanced in his direction. He caught her gaze and winked. Her heart fluttered. How had it come to this? She was in trouble. The worst kind: *infatuated*. It was unfair! If he found a way, as he had said, to prompt her parents to offer her a choice, how could she choose *against* the betrothal if she were besotted with him and knew the heartbreak that would follow? In good conscience, she could not choose *for* the betrothal. He needed to be a free man to make his own choices.

She had done him a disservice when they first met, thinking him reckless, a libertine even, for climbing into a window, and then assuming him weak to allow her father to subject them to this unwanted match. Rafe was none of these things. He was what he said he was—a gentleman. Gentleman or not, she could not disillusion herself that if she chose to maintain the betrothal, they would rub well together. Likely, they would realize too late how different they were.

Braving a glance from beneath her umbrella, she narrowed her eyes at his profile. If she focused on all his pesky traits, all the things she disliked, she could remind herself they would never suit.

"Noel has the baton," Rafe said. "The team will make good time while he has it. Once he passes it to Otis, however, all wagers are off."

Searching the river, she spotted them a good distance away. Poor Mr. Thorpe. So lost in thought, she had forgotten to watch his swimming efforts.

"Care for a walk?"

She jerked her attention to Rafe. "A walk?" She almost added *in the rain*, but she was more shocked to be invited for a walk, never mind the weather.

Clasping his hands behind his back, he looked around at the crowd. "Unless you'd rather see the end of the race. I thought after yesterday's excitement, it might be a welcome retreat to… walk. Steal a rare moment alone. A ramble to the woods' edge and back?"

"Oh. Um. Yes. That would be lovely."

The pitter-patter overhead mocked her choice of descriptors.

As she took his proffered arm, she rebuked herself. *Pull yourself together, Genevieve, or he'll know you're having second thoughts, then he'll feel more trapped and more manipulated than he already must feel. Pull. Yourself. Together.* Standing a little straighter, a little more rigid, she bore her stodgiest expression.

He guided her around the mud puddles and through the crowd, which was nowhere as dense as yesterday's. "Are you ready for the archery event?"

A safe topic. Good. It was difficult to concentrate with the sweet aroma of his perfume and the warmth of his arm beneath her glove.

"I have no preconceived expectations of hitting the target, but it will be the most fun I've had in an age, I believe. I'm curious to see who competes. I might learn a trick or two from watching them. Oh! Oh no. The weather. Will we not have lessons today? I wonder."

"Considering it could rain during the event, I doubt my mother will cancel the lesson if you're willing to attend. She'll think it good practice. I suggest the widest-brimmed bonnet you own."

She glanced at him from beneath her umbrella and laughed. Rain dripped from the brim of his beaver hat, soaking the shoulders of his caped greatcoat. "Would you like to share my umbrella?"

"And admit defeat?"

Genevieve raised it to tempt him.

He looked from it to her, pensive. "A gentleman is never afraid of rain; thus, he need not seek shelter beneath a lady's parasol. However, I believe this one time we may make an exception."

Covering her hand with his to clasp hers more firmly on his forearm, he tugged her closer, pressing her against his side. She gasped at the sudden contact, only distantly aware his damp coat wet the side of her gown.

"Ah yes, much better," he said, ducking his head under the umbrella. "Far more intimate, don't you think? I can whisper roguish sentiments into your ear and admire your blush from a more advantageous angle."

"Rafe!" Genevieve tugged her hand to free herself only to knock the umbrella akilter, sending a river of cold water over the oiled silk and down her neck, where it promptly trailed along her back.

She shrieked.

Pulling her closer, he said, "My greatest pleasure this week will be seeing you handle a bow."

The way he emphasized *pleasure* and *bow* had her blushing, predictably, no doubt, more so than what he likely intended considering she replaced *bow* with *beau* in her mind, namely the gentleman caller kind whose name rhymes with chafe, which was precisely what same-said gentleman was doing to her state of mind.

Breathing deeply to steady her nerves, she said, "If you're fortunate, you'll see me handling a sword with more finesse."

Rafe coughed a tremulous laugh. Now was his turn to flush pink, although she could not understand what she had said to embarrass him.

Continuing, she added, "Your mother is going to teach me how to fence."

"Ah. Yes. I understand now. For a moment I thought *you* were whispering roguish sentiments into my ear. Yes, fencing. Mmm."

Genevieve eyed him askance. It was unconventional for her to learn to fence, being a woman, but she would hardly call it roguish.

Rafe guided her towards the woods, then turned so they could walk alongside the tree line. "I could teach you."

"Would that be appropriate?"

"If it's our secret."

"My sister has teased me relentlessly about our trysts, disbelieving you accidentally chose my window to tumble into. After all my claims of innocence, here you are proposing a tryst. How would I ever face her in the morning room?" Genevieve teased but only to disguise her desire to accept his offer, assuming he was serious and not teasing her himself.

"Better not risk it then. Miss Cecilia — I assume she's your accuser — seems relentless. Let's not give her any ammunition. At least not yet. My mother can train you, and then I can challenge you. At least then you'll be a worthy adversary."

"Oof!" Genevieve tipped her umbrella to shower him with rain. "I'll show you a worthy adversary, Rafe Fitz-Stephens."

"I surrender!" He lifted her hand to kiss her gloved knuckles. "Have mercy. I'm already drenched."

"Good." She raised a defiant chin.

"Now, to my more pressing question of the day. Are you so in love you're ready to stay here forever?"

Taken off her guard, Genevieve stumbled. Rafe clasped her arm, steadying her.

"I—I beg your pardon," was all she could muster.

"The Fracas Frolic. Has it won you over? Are you in love with Grant Lindis?"

"Oh!" To cover her misunderstanding, she laughed gaily. "Grant Lindis. Yes, quite. I was thinking only the other day how pleasant it would be for Papa to settle somewhere nearby and for us to make this our home, permanently. I don't see Papa ever settling, but a girl can dream."

"Not to disappoint you, but the frolic is only one week. For the rest of the year, all is quiet. It could be perceived as dull by some, although I've always found ample to occupy my time."

Relaxing against him, she asked, "What is life like in London? I've been to York and Birmingham, but after all these years, I've never been to London. I expect it's one entertainment after another, easier to make friends than in the countryside."

"On the contrary, or perhaps because it's so crowded, a city that never sleeps, one finds more strangers than friends and no real entertainment, at least not the kind I enjoy. The entertainment in London is where someone or something humors you while you remain passive. The theatre, the opera, the pleasure gardens, the horse races, the park—there's no end to what you can do to *be* entertained. I prefer to be the doer. I would rather be the chap on the horse, not watching someone else race. Or be the pugilist in the ring rather than cheering on another gentleman. All I enjoy is in the countryside."

"And yet you wish to be in London for your profession?"

Rafe shrugged. "It's an option."

She waited for him to say more. When he did not, she said, "I, too, find the countryside more pleasurable. I don't, however, understand how someone befriends anyone when there are so few choices. Let us suppose my family has just moved to a new village. We cannot call on anyone to introduce ourselves, rather we must wait until neighbors call on us, and then amongst them, there are only a few who offer desirable companionship. One neighbor may be too high in the instep, another too chatty…. You see what I mean."

He took his time in answering. When he did, he had to speak a little louder to be heard over the rain, which had worsened from a steady drizzle to a determined patter, soon, she feared, to become a deluge from which an umbrella could not save them.

"Have you *tried* to make friends?" he questioned.

Taken aback, she stammered, "I—of course I have!"

"What I mean is previously, as you've done here. Did you join committees? Did you initiate calls after introductions? Did you offer the neighbor too high in the instep a chance to reveal the warmth beneath the frost or the chatty neighbor the opportunity to be heard?"

Genevieve huffed. "If you're insinuating I'm at fault for not making friends, you are mistaken. I consider myself quite friendly."

"Mmm. Case in point."

"I *do* beg your pardon, sir." She removed her hand from his arm and raised her chin a fraction higher.

"In my experience, life gives what you offer. *Si vis amari ama.* If you want to be loved, love. No matter the location or the neighbors, it's my choices that determine how enjoyable the experience. If company is unpleasant, it's on my shoulders to turn it into a pleasant encounter."

Genevieve heard the wisdom but felt the sting of accusation — was it she who interpreted it that way or he who meant it? It stung because it was true. "Am I to understand you're attempting to make the best of *this* unpleasant companion, or that I should be making a more concentrated effort to find *you* more pleasant?"

Her words were harsh. She had intended to tease, to turn her inner outrage into something they could laugh about, goad him into a roguish reply, but her tone did not cooperate. Her tone snapped with steely teeth.

Rafe leaned away, studying her with his soulful blue eyes, the rain drumming against his hat as he moved from the refuge of the umbrella. Rather than reply, he smiled. The smile, however, did not envelop her with warmth. It chilled her. A cold shroud.

"I…" Genevieve began, wanting to grab his arm and pull him back beneath the umbrella. "I did not mean that how it sounded."

The brittle smile remained. "You'll be wet through if we don't find shelter. To the tavern? Mr. Snawdune, the publican, has promised the first twenty patrons a round on the house. A glass of cider is perfect for this weather, don't you agree?"

She wanted to protest, to stomp her foot and demand they stand in the rain until he smiled again, a genuine smile, not this diminutive, melancholic smile that set her teeth on edge. In the end, she walked alongside him to the tavern.

Chapter 22

The tavern teemed with frolic attendees. Diana spotted Genevieve shortly after arrival and stole her from Rafe, escorting her to the table her family had secured. By the time they reached the table, Rafe had slipped into the crowd. Genevieve craned to find him, but he was nowhere to be seen.

"Where is he? Will he be able to find us?" she asked Diana.

"He's probably already left for the dower house. The Fitz-Stephenses made for home, Rupert along with them. I'm only the teensiest pouty that Mr. Thorpe isn't here, not that I don't find your sisters congenial company, but I wanted to ask Mr. Thorpe about the race, namely what it's like to compete, for this is his first competition, as well as mine, and yours for that matter, so perhaps he has suggestions for how to overcome nervousness. Are you as nervous as I am? Mrs. Fitz-Stephens says it is anticipation not nervousness, but how does one discern the difference?" With a glance to the stairs in the far corner, she added, "I hope Mr. Thorpe will join us after he's refreshed. If you thought Rafe looked like a drowned rat, you can imagine Mr. Thorpe's state after swimming!"

"Did we win?" Genevieve nodded to her parents and made a face at her sisters, all of whom were absorbed in their own conversations.

"Eurwendin took this win, sadly. I only hope the egg and spoon race isn't canceled. Will it ever stop raining? More importantly, will you partner me for the race? Oh, but then who will partner Mr. Thorpe? Oh dear."

Genevieve let Diana rattle on, her attention on the crowd. Had Rafe returned home? That gave her no opportunity to tease him back to a real smile. Part of her wanted to explain to him her defensiveness, how what he said, even in jest, was true, and that it was her own doing for not making each residence her home. But what would be the point? All excuses. Excuses for snapping at him when he had not deserved it.

She could tell him the truth, if she were brave: she had snapped because she feared her feelings for him. By that same token, she could not admit the truth, for she feared more his rejection.

"When did you know?" Diana asked.

Blinking, Genevieve stared at Diana, at a loss as to what Diana had been saying or to what she now referred.

"I hope you don't think me impolite," Diana continued, unperturbed by Genevieve's blank stare, "but I simply must know. Was it love at first sight? Rupert says it must have been for Rafe. What about you? What was it about him that struck you?"

"I... He..." Genevieve looked down at her hands, at a loss for how to answer. "Must it be sudden? Like a lightning strike? Or for some does it take more time?"

Diana tapped her mouth with her forefinger. "I don't suppose it's the same for everyone, no. For some, it's sudden, yes. I'm not one to know, but from what I've observed, some are slower about it, a gradual realization. Was it that way with you? Oh my, that means Rafe fell first! Head over teakettle at first meeting! It must be so. I wish I had been here for your courtship. A whirlwind romance, was it? It would have to be. How did he charm you?"

Blushing, Genevieve thought, *He did fall first, head over heels in the literal sense, directly over my windowsill.* She gurgled a laugh aloud. Diana mistook the laughter for Genevieve recalling her first swell of love and joined with tittering and hand squeezing, as though they both recalled in unison that magical moment. It all made Genevieve laugh that much harder.

"I can't pinpoint a moment," she confessed at last. "Somewhere between him knocking over the washbasin and revealing the box of mint in his pocket. Must it be one aspect? Like a smile? Or can it be a combination, innocent flirtation complemented by Latin ramblings?" She did not bother to hide her blush, not from Diana.

With a sigh, Diana said, "That's the best way to fall in love. Then you know it's real. You've not been taken in by a handsome face. Oh, I'm so happy he's found you!" She squeezed Genevieve's hand again, this time with a little bounce.

As far as Genevieve was concerned, the day's festivities had come to an end. She was ready to return home, change, and find an excuse to make her way to the dower house. What she would say or do remained to be seen, but she wanted to smooth over her ill-mannered behavior and ensure all was right between them, regardless to what end that led.

Alas, the day was not over. The rain lightened enough for the egg and spoon race to be held as planned, the muddy green making it all the more fun, at least for some. Genevieve did not participate. As the race began, she cheered Diana and Mr. Thorpe, along with her sisters, and her parents, who were having the most fun she had seen them have, and then while everyone shuffled their way to and fro, she slipped away, her final destination the dower house.

The walk was long and lonely, more so because of the rain, which at least had softened to a mist. She wanted to reach the dower house before her family returned home, so she would only have long enough to change into dry clothes and attempt to tame her hair, which she suspected had become a country unto itself with the rain and humidity. For the walk, she tried to plot an excuse for calling on the Fitz-Stephenses. She could not call on Rafe, betrothed or not. The best plan was to say she had arrived for the archery lesson exceedingly early to take advantage of the mist in case the rain returned. A silly excuse. She did not want to start the lesson early, nor did she wish to have it without Diana. But what else could she say? Then, regardless of what she said, Rafe may not join to greet her, much less find an excuse of his own to sequester her.

A foolish plan. She should have stayed for the race.

Defeated and soggy, she reached the Priory. When she stepped into the entrance hall, she started.

Through the drawing room doors, filtered by way of the Great Hall, then filling the entrance hall, resounded the majesty of the pianoforte. A sonata. She racked her brain. Haydn. Yes, his sonata in C minor. Or was it… no, that was the piece. She had never played it, but Theia had an impressive repertoire. How had Theia returned home before Genevieve? Her sister had been hobbling across a muddy field the last Genevieve saw her.

Rather than proceed upstairs to change, she followed the music. It compelled her forward. Muddy footprints across the floor, she could not stop her progress through the entrance hall and into the Great Hall. The drawing room doors stood open. They invited her to creep closer. The music swelled, echoing through the hall, impassioned. No plodding fingers, only a graceful cadence of expression. Genevieve's steps slowed until she stood, dripping on the floor, too overcome to proceed. She did not recall the sonata being so exquisite.

Who was turning the pages? She did not hear the rustle of paper. Mesmerized, she willed herself to move.

Inching past the drawing room doors, she leaned to spy the piano while remaining unseen, not wanting Theia's concentration broken. When she glimpsed the player, she gasped aloud. The music stopped.

Rafe turned from the keyboard to see her half hidden behind the door. "My apologies. I thought you were in the village."

She parted lips to speak, but he rose and raised a staying hand.

"That's a lie," he said. "Yes, I thought you were in the village, but that implies I had sneaked in for my own amusement. In truth, I had hoped to time my arrival with your return. I would have waited outside except…. I am unforgivably rude, explaining myself when you're dripping on the rug."

Genevieve knew by the warmth of her face she was flushed. What a terrible state she must be in!

"Stay. I won't be more than a moment." She spun around, ready to rush upstairs, only to turn around again. "I didn't know you played."

Only now did she notice there was no sheet music. He had played from memory. As if his skill with ivory and ebony was not extraordinary enough.

"*Dulce est desipere in loco,*" he said. "It is sweet on occasion to play the fool."

With a lift of her mud splashed hem, she darted in the direction she had come. Rafe watched her depart, disappointed she would change.

Sodden and frizzy. Her disheveled imperfection was most becoming, reminiscent of when he had first come upon her in the woods after riding. In this state, she seemed more herself, less constrained. While he had little on which to base the theory, he suspected she was more at home in nature than a drawing room, someone who preferred to ride like the wind or walk barefoot in a beck.

Looking about him, he tried to recall what he had been doing moments prior. Ah, the piano. He returned to the chair, his fingers stroking the keys.

What had he been playing? Depressing a chord, he let his hands choose a tune.

So lost in thought, he could not say what he played now, much less prior. This daze had held him captive for the past couple hours. To win her or to release her. His hesitation centered on whether winning her was the best for them both, or if this sudden attraction was from proximity alone, no substance beyond convenience. She did not love someone else. That had been his original catalyst for disentangling them from the web her father had weaved. She still blamed him, he believed, but he could remedy that. He was confident he could. But *should* he? That question circled and circled and circled.

"I hope you'll forgive me. It was the best I could do in a hurry."

Removing fingers from piano, he turned to see Genevieve standing in the doorway again, this time in a simple muslin gown the color of daffodils, a modest fichu tucked into her bodice. Her curls had been hastily wrapped with a turban. Rafe tried to swallow, his throat dry, his tongue heavy.

They began speaking simultaneously, her with, "I had hoped to see…" and him with, "Will you save me a dance?"

They waited, then tried again, her with, "What dance?" and him with, "To see what?"

Genevieve bit her bottom lip, then waved a hand to one of the chairs. "Will you join me? I could ring for a tray."

Rafe shook his head. "I only called to ask you the one question. I won't linger."

"There's no rush. Everyone is at the race. No one is here to catch us alone."

A slow smirk lifted the fog of his daze. "No one to compromise us? Force me to declare myself?"

A smirk of her own reflected his. Whatever she had been wanting to say, she kept to herself, waiting for him to speak next. He did not hesitate.

"There will be an assembly Friday. The winner of the frolic hosts it, so I cannot say if it'll be in Eurwendin or here, but there *will* be an assembly. Will you save me a dance?"

If she was surprised to hear of the dance, she did not show it. Instead, her smirk became a teasing grin. "Only one dance?"

Pulling his shoulders back, he said, "As your devoted bridegroom, I would expect two."

"Staking your property?"

"Precisely."

"And if an aristocratic bachelor begs for my hand? Am I to favor you over him for a *second* dance?"

"Unless you wish to be tossed over my shoulder."

"Why, Rafe Fitz-Stephens, I never knew you were possessive. Only two dances? Not a third?"

Rafe crossed to her in seven strides, stopping inches away. He did not miss the frisson of surprise in her expression, one mingled with anticipation and uncertainty.

Capturing her hand, he brought it to his lips. "With you, I claim every dance."

Before she could answer, he kissed the air above her knuckles, then swept from the room in what he hoped was an air of intrigue and irresistible masculinity.

With one leg stretched on the settee and one knee bent, shoes abandoned on the parlor rug, Rafe beheld an Old Bailey transcript. Early evening was settling in, but the curtains remained open, and the setting sun provided enough light without the aid of candles — yet.

He scribbled along the corner of the transcript with a piece of twine-wrapped graphite. A little more shading, perhaps. Yes, that would improve his annotation.

His father was due to join him to discuss the case and offer his insight as a magistrate. A perfect time for the two to put their heads together. Everyone except Gran had plans elsewhere. Gran embraced the chance for much needed privacy, having grumbled most of the afternoon about the overcrowding in her house. Headley and Diana had agreed to celebrate with Mr. Thorpe after his first competition. Rafe ought to be with them. He felt a trifle guilty. Perhaps, if he and his father did not while away the hours, he would join them at the tavern. Or perhaps not. He would decide later.

Shading finished, he darkened the finer lines.

From behind him, his father asked, "Are we discussing the court case or your ode to Miss Slade?"

Rafe blanched at having been caught. "Do you think *A Beauty Beneath the Oak* will make me the next da Vinci?" Rafe admired his handiwork. The corner of the transcript had never looked so good.

"Heaven help us if you doodle Miss Slade's likeness while in court." Taking the chair across from the settee, his father crossed one leg over the other.

"Shall we discuss the tactics used by the barristers in the case, or would you prefer to playact a case of my choosing instead?"

Her hair was not right. Not enough volume. Rafe added a few more curls, exaggerating the ones escaping the jeweled hairpins. Much better.

"Rafe?" His father waited before clearing his throat loudly.

Rafe raised his gaze. Father's eyebrows were arched, a humored lift at the corners of his mouth. Feeling his face warming, Rafe tossed the pencil on the table.

"Do you think," he began, not meeting his father's eyes, "Mother would be disappointed if I pursued the circuit rather than the Old Bailey?"

A flick of his gaze spied the surprise in his father's expression before he returned his concentration to the settee cushion.

With care, Father said, "She only wishes for your happiness. I believe her concern would lie in the challenge. In the circuit court, you will not find the level of challenge that would normally stimulate you. As an alternative, you could begin in London, and then request to work the Assizes, which allow for more time in the countryside while still seeing criminal cases. It would mean more travel, but it could offer the option for what I think you're really asking."

Rafe did not respond. Instead, he tucked the hand not holding the transcript beneath him to resist chewing on his nails, an old habit he had not acted on in years.

"Would *you* be disappointed," Father continued when the silence was not filled, "not to reach the King's Counsel? It was your hope for the distant future. The circuit courts are little more than misdemeanors. Would you not grow bored?"

Haltingly, Rafe said, "If I were concentrated on a different kind of challenge, the familial kind, how could I possibly grow bored?"

"Am I to assume Miss Slade would not wish to live in or around London?"

With a flinch to have her name brought into the conversation, his father essentially calling Rafe's hand, he said, "*I* do not wish to raise a family in or around London." He paused to consider his next words, then said, "I have regarded my chosen profession as a means to happiness. It's not, though, is it? A profession is never intended to be the means to happiness. If anything, it's a way to fill time until one discovers the true meaning of happiness."

Father released a low whistle. "Am I to take it that Miss Slade has turned from undesirable to a means of happiness?"

Was she? Rafe could not readily answer. All he knew at this juncture was he was more interested in winning her affection than losing her. He had not yet satisfied his question of if they would suit, nor if she could think of him beyond the catalyst for all her woes. And then there was the question of how to turn sardonic flirtation into genuine adoration without appearing disingenuous. *Acta, non verba.* Deeds, not words, or as John Pym and others preferred, actions speak louder than words.

His father again filled the silence. "I've noticed your mother is beginning to favor Miss Slade. She *is* an amiable girl. It has always been my hope that, with time, everyone would realize this to be the brilliant match it is. Roland had thought Giles would suit, but I warned him against the match, and that was before I knew Giles would leave for another harebrained expedition, which proved my point, I dare say. Took me long enough to convince Roland you were the man for Miss Slade. I'm relieved he saw reason, because here you both are, young love burgeoning."

Turning to face his father, Rafe's brows puckered. "You foresaw our match?"

"What's there not to foresee? Your dispositions align well, something Roland led me to believe before I met her, and now something I see for myself since meeting her."

"How... fortuitous." Rafe said nothing further, not wanting his father to realize the slip and give up the game.

Although he shifted the conversation to the case in hand, Rafe's mind whirred with the implications of his father's words.

They had intended to matchmake their children.

Rafe's appearance that fateful evening had played agreeably into Mr. Slade's hand, then, for it had already been decided the two would be matched once he arrived, or so his father's confidence led him to believe. Much like the lease, Mother was not privy to Father's matchmaking plans. How would it have gone had Rafe not tumbled heels over head into her bedchamber? Would they have ensured the two partnered for games? Sat together at the dinner table? Accompanied each other hither and yon? Or was it to be more direct, the two of them sitting in the study with their fathers waving the marriage settlement?

As embittered as Rafe thought he ought to be at this newfound tidbit, the shackle tightening about his ankle, he was relieved, relieved and amused. Retrieving the pencil from the table, he returned to his sketch while his father offered the magistrate's perspective on the case.

Chapter 23

A rrow nocked, stance set, back of hand flat, Genevieve anchored the string against her cheek. Concentrating on the tip to aim, she braced, then loosed the arrow.

The clock ticked, counting down.

She had eleven more arrows in her quiver and less than four minutes to release them, which for Mrs. Fitz-Stephens was enough time to hit the target twelve times and rest for a spot of tea, but for Genevieve, time mocked her inexperience. Twenty seconds per arrow. It sounded like an eternity; it felt like a blink of an eye. There was no time to search the crowd for Rafe or wonder if he was watching, cheering her on, and possibly — hopefully — admiring her courage rather than her skill, or lack thereof.

She reached for the next arrow. Nock, anchor, brace, aim, loose. However nervous, her hands held steady. The acceleration of her pulse was excitement, not fear. Another arrow. Another hit.

At least there was only one target. During the lessons, Mrs. Fitz-Stephens had set up several, each at a different distance.

Behind her, the next archer on the team awaited her turn. Next to her, with ample space between, were three queues, each with their own target, two teams per village. Another arrow. Another hit. None of the hits proved exceptional, no bullseyes, but that they all penetrated the target was ecstasy to Genevieve.

She reached for the last arrow, grasping empty air. Oh! She was out. She had lost count. With a quick curtsy, she handed her gear to the young lady behind her, then moved to the sidelines. Diana was two people away from a turn. Genevieve saluted for luck.

Mama greeted her with an air kiss. "Masterfully done, I dare say. Cecilia will be disappointed if she doesn't do half as well." The last teammate in their queue was Cecilia, who had decided to join only minutes before the start of the event. "Theia, love, why did you not join?"

Genevieve turned to find Theia hiding behind her.

"What if the string were to snap?" Theia whined. "I couldn't bear it!"

Too late to reassure her sister the string would not snap, Genevieve left it, turning her attention back to the competition. The team next to theirs, also representing Grant Lindis, was mostly composed of the young girls from Lindstow Manor, or a handful of them, anyway, those few who were not of the same mind as Theia in fearing the bow.

"Hush!" Genevieve commanded with a wave of her hand. "Diana is stepping into position."

They collectively held their breath. The first arrow hit only an inch below the bullseye. The second hit dead center. The third paired it as a mate. Genevieve cheered. A few people away, Mr. Thorpe and Mr. Headley cheered louder. By the time Diana finished, the center of the target was littered with arrows, proving her prowess with a bow. With Diana on their team, this would surely be a win for Grant Lindis. Assistants rushed to remove the arrows as the next young lady prepared.

Diana first joined Genevieve with a squeal, then squeezed the hands of both Theia and Mama, before skipping over to her brother and Mr. Thorpe. Mr. Thorpe, that fortunate gentleman, received a kiss on the cheek in Diana's exuberance.

Where was Rafe? Genevieve searched the crowd. He had wished her luck before the event began, but he was nowhere — oh, there he was. Tucked behind a gaggle of noncompeting Lindstow Manor girls, Rafe stood talking with Genevieve's Papa, the two laughing.

By the time she turned around, Cecilia had finished her turn — all her arrows flinging far and above the target to destinations uncharted — and the points were being tallied for a Grant Lindis victory. Even while hugging her sisters, Genevieve's attention remained riveted on Rafe and Papa — whatever could be so amusing?

Slipping away before her mother and sisters noticed, she marched towards the two gentlemen, her path unimpeded as the crowd dispersed in preparation for the afternoon fête. Her father, turned away from her, did not see her approaching. Rafe caught sight of her in his peripheral — she knew the moment he did because his lips curved into a smirk. Once within earshot, she sharpened her attention to distinguish their voices from the others around her, hoping to eavesdrop a little before announcing her presence to her father.

"I'll introduce you to Sir Courtney," Rafe was promising as she drew closer.

"Oh, I say, a capital idea." Hooking his fingers around the front edges of his superfine coat, Papa added, "Not that I'm one to ramble."

Genevieve slowed her pace, befuddled, but wanting to hear more.

Rafe offered no such allowances. "Ah, Miss Slade, our archer extraordinaire. Join us."

However facetious the compliment, she flushed.

"I'm a man with a mission, Miss Slade. I aim to encourage your father to join the Eurwendin Ramblers. Opportunities in abundance to make those all-important connections, but above all else, the chance to explore. The group turns a simple ramble into an adventure."

Stifling a giggle to think of her father hiking, she nodded with her most earnest expression. "Just what you've hoped for, Papa. A way to meet neighbors."

"Precisely my point," Papa agreed, chin raised with an air of importance to be soon hobnobbing with the likes of Sir Courtney, whoever he was.

To further his point, Rafe said, "With such a group, you needn't relocate to travel. A pity you did not find the group earlier. It would have saved you from moving to seek adventure."

Genevieve remained silent. Papa was not exactly a seeker of adventure so much as an escapee from responsibility, namely that which came with ownership. Still, if anyone could convince her father to set roots, it would be Rafe.

But then, since when was Rafe solicitous of her family's future? Was he playacting the devoted betrothed? She questioned him with a quizzing gaze.

"It is, undoubtedly, in my favor," Rafe continued, "you did *not* find such a group sooner. Had you done so, you may never have come to Grant Lindis, and then I would not have met the lovely Miss Slade."

Papa frowned. "Nonsense. Of course you would have met her. How else would I have convinced you she's the perfect bride?"

Rafe laughed heartily. "*Ita vero*. Yes, indeed."

Genevieve looked from Rafe to her father and back. What a peculiar comment. Eyes crinkled at the corners, Rafe did not appear the least perturbed by it. She could be overtired, but what her father said did not make sense. He had not tried to convince either of them of anything, only forced them together over a misunderstanding. Had he intended them to meet? He could not have. They had all known the two eldest sons were indisposed, the eldest on an expedition of some sort and the second in London with no plans to return this year. Shaking her head, she turned her attention back to her father.

"Eh, puss? What do you say?" Papa waited for her reply.

When she stared at him, befuddled, Rafe saved her with, "As exciting as the fête is sure to be, if you feel in any way as I did after the regatta, you are ready to sleep for twenty-four hours straight."

Genevieve mouthed a *thank you* before saying, "You understand too well. The excitement of the event has taxed me to exhaustion. I wonder if Diana might consider accompanying me back to the Priory for tea and quiet."

Papa nodded towards the Headleys. "Looks to me she's coping fine without you. Take Theia."

Turning, Genevieve saw Mr. Headley talking with Diana, and…. Diana's arm was threaded with Mr. Thorpe's. With a raise of her eyebrows, Genevieve glanced at Rafe, who replied with a nearly imperceptible shrug of his shoulders. A hand on a gentleman's forearm for balance when walking was one thing, but one should never tuck a hand in the crook of a gentleman's arm unless the relationship was quite serious. Genevieve hoped Diana's friendly nature was not going to be misinterpreted as something more.

Chapter 24

Ball in hand, Rafe pivoted, then threw it to Johnny Smith, the blacksmith's son. Smith arched his arm towards the wickets, but the ball missed and rolled away. Rafe groaned with a tug at his sweaty hair.

The final cricket match of the Fracas Frolic had begun early that Friday morning. It was now well past noon. Rafe's stomach grumbled. They were so close. So were the Eurwendins. The second inning, eleventh batman on the pitch, Rafe's team fielding, Grant Lindis held the lead, barely. Two runs and the Eurwendin team would win, but one out, and Grant Lindis had the trophy.

When Noel tossed the ball to Headley, Rafe shouted the final war cry, "*Carthago delenta est!*"

Headley cradled the ball.

The crowd held a collective breath.

Rafe eyed the two umpires—Father and the rector of Eurwendin. He eyed the two batsmen on the pitch. He eyed the sideliners and caught a glimpse of Genevieve, her hands pressed to her bosom. His attention returned to Headley.

With finesse, Headley bowled to the batsman.

A *crack* shattered the air, and the ball arched in flight. As Rafe's gaze followed it, the Eurwendin crowd erupted in celebration, realizing, along with the fielding side, this was an easy four run win. Dropping his chin to his chest, he accepted the loss.

Just as he expected the crowd to storm the pitch with congratulations for their sons, husbands, brothers, fathers, and so forth, a deafening silence descended. He looked around. All eyes were on his father. Mr. Anthony Fitz-Stephens had lifted his forefinger. Rafe's jaw slackened, his mouth hanging agape—the batman was *out*? But—then he saw the reason. Running towards the pitch, hand raised high, was Smith. The boy had caught the ball midair.

The shift, as everyone realized the implication, was palpable. Rafe whooped and jogged to Headley for a hearty handshake. With the last batman out, the four runs were forfeited, and the Grant Lindis team won by the skin of their teeth.

While the crowd did not exactly storm the pitch, an impressive number walked purposefully to their loved ones with congratulations or commiserations, as appropriate. Genevieve was no exception. She hurried to Rafe. For a brief heel to toe lean, he thought she was going to embrace him. Pity she changed her mind.

"Our first win in three years," he admitted.

His shirt clung in damp discomfort, his waistcoat dusty, his boots and buckskins conspicuously muddy—even the hair at the nape of his neck dripped with shudder-inducing perspiration—yet he willed her to step one foot closer, close enough for him to grab her and pull her to him in what he could excuse as a celebratory embrace. Within the next twenty seconds, he wagered he could acquit his impropriety with the excuse of the win. Rafe inched closer in invitation.

"Three years? Oh my!" Genevieve's nervous laugh accompanied a hasty step backwards — away from him.

Twenty seconds elapsed while he pleaded with her grey eyes to be daring.

"Will you join us?" she asked, taking another step back. "Diana and Mr. Thorpe were lucky enough to secure a table for the game. Diana will want to tell you in detail that we stayed for the entirety. I can't say the same for my family, I'm afraid, as they left after the first inning to enjoy nuncheon at the tavern. I hope they returned in time for the win, but I've not seen them."

She rambled. She rambled as she took yet another step away. Rafe had not moved, hopeful that his disappointment was not written in the exhaustion of his face. He had not wanted her to wrap her arms around him, not until she had come close to doing so. Now he could think of little else. Had they won? Had they been playing a game? For all he could remember, he had been standing in this same position for the whole of the morning, waiting for her, waiting to know the sensation of her cheek against his, her sigh near his ear.

Audentes fortuna iuvat, he thought. Fortune favors the bold.

"Headley will listen to Diana's myriad observations. Thorpe will compliment them. I wish only to listen to you. Walk with me *andante* to The Dragon's Breath?"

More's the pity the fête had been yesterday, otherwise he could have walked her about the green at leisure. Now, the cricket pitch was fast emptying, some still milling, most returning home to prepare for the assembly that evening. With an indecisive glance at the sidelines, presumably where Diana and Mr. Thorpe, and likely now Headley, as well, were sitting, Genevieve looked at Rafe with her bottom lip tucked between her teeth.

And he wanted to be a barrister? Not only could he not read the meaning behind her expressions or guess her thoughts, he could not think of a single witty word to say. Where had his confidence gone? Had he not but a few days earlier boasted to himself about how easy it would be to win her over? Now, he was an inexperienced boy kicking the dirt, bashful in the presence of a beautiful lady.

The longer he stood, waiting for her reply, the more aware of his shabbiness he became. He ran a hand through his damp locks, grimacing with regret before his fingertips reached the ends of his hair.

"Perhaps we'll see my family," was her long-awaited answer.

Yes, perhaps. His shoulders rounded.

Rather than offer a sweat-soaked arm, Rafe clasped his hands behind his back and proceeded towards the tavern, his pace slow, his steps measured. He wished he had his walking stick, something to busy his hands and give him an air of importance, at least a slight appeal to vanity.

"I plan to introduce your father to Sir Courtney at the assembly this evening," he said, in want of conversation.

"You can't possibly think Papa will be induced to purchase a house if he joins this rambling group," she said with a playful tut. "At least, I assume that's your goal. Papa will not be so incentivized."

"He wishes to be introduced to society — or as he thinks of it, society with a capital S, *Society* — and that is precisely what I plan to do, starting this evening. Lord Karras never misses an assembly — he being Eurwendin's resident blueblood. Ample opportunity to make introductions."

"You're so well connected? I hadn't realized." Her expression was hidden by the brim of her bonnet, not that he could have read it had he seen it, but her tone was surprised, if not a little in awe. But then with a contradictory laugh, as though to call out his jest, she asked, "You actually *know* aristocrats?"

"Only enough to make an introduction. My father could, instead, but my understanding is your father wishes for *me* to introduce him. An opening, I suspect, for him to present me as his intended son-in-law, or merely *an opening*, full stop."

"Since when have you become so accommodating? You must recall, Rafe, Papa is the villain in our tale. You really should not encourage him. The more he thinks you have something to offer him, the stronger his hold on this situation." Hesitantly, turning her head to look askance at him, but not enough for him to see past the dreaded edge of the bonnet, she added, "We *are* trying to find a way out, are we not?"

Rubbing the back of his neck with his handkerchief, he ignored her question and said, "I have a theory."

It had not been his intention to mention this. However much the theory amused him, it held no bearing on his increasing attraction. The conversation's direction was outpacing him. He looked around to ensure no one was in eavesdropping range and that they still had enough distance to the tavern to make espousing his theory possible. Dash it. He had *not* planned on confessing this. What would it achieve? Alas. *Alcea iacta est.* The die was cast.

"I suspect our fathers had planned all along to introduce us, and I don't mean for the purpose of family dinners."

It took ten slow steps for Genevieve to react. At first, she remained silent, pensive, but finally, she laughed a sharp *ha*. "Don't be silly. Papa could never have guessed he would find you... um... where he found you."

"That's not quite what I mean. I think *that* particular incident was a matter of convenience, too perfect for him not to take advantage of. It's my theory that our fathers had wished to match us, marriage on their mind, but in a more subtle way, beginning with an introduction, followed by contrived seating at dinners, encouraged pairing during cards — you know this game as well as I do — all with the hope we would... suit. My theory further posits that with the disappointment at my not returning to Grant Lindis, your father grasped at the presented opportunity when I suddenly did arrive, however unexpected the manner."

And the further he thought about this, the more Mr. Slade's initial reaction made sense. He had *demanded satisfaction*, not knowing Rafe was Rafe, rather thinking Rafe either a burglar, as Genevieve had, or thinking exactly what he had claimed to be thinking — Rafe was a rogue caught in a clandestine tryst with the sweet Miss Slade, who Mr. Slade had already quasi promised to the second son of Anthony Fitz-Stephens. The *demand* changed from a duel to declaration only after Rafe's identity was made known. Yes, Rafe was positive of his assertion.

Genevieve's pace stalled. "It was planned from the start? Whether or not you played the burglar? They were going to force us no matter what?"

"Er, I wouldn't say *force*, no. I believe, had I not 'played the burglar,' the match would have been more… how to say… organic."

"But if they had already decided, then we had no choice. Partnering at games or otherwise, they would have forced us."

Rafe twisted his handkerchief one way then the other. Not only had he not planned to broach this, it was not going in any way how he would have expected had he indeed planned to broach this. Her tone was caught somewhere between defensive and accusatory, not in the least seeing the humor as he did or, to a greater extent, the relief.

"I think you're looking at this from the wrong perspective, Genevieve. Or I'm explaining my theory poorly."

"I do beg your pardon." Her tone, affronted, bit the air. "I'm *looking at this incorrectly*? It's *my* view, is it not?"

"That's not what I mean. Dash it. Hear me out?" He swiped his brow with his handkerchief. "First, this is only a *theory*. My belief does not make it true. Second, *if* true, it offers a logical explanation for your father's behavior and choices, legitimizing them, really."

"That does not make what he did any more acceptable!" She caught herself as her voice rose, lowering when she said, "We should have the choice, not be tossed together, two strangers with different plans. Did they consult us? Did they ask us our wishes?"

"I believe they would have. I believe, if they had been given the chance, their intention had been to see if we suited, to *hope* we suited, and if nothing came of it, no reason to mention their matchmaking."

Her laugh cut at his esteem. "Oh no, if my father set out to match us, we would have been matched. Just as he ensured when circumstances changed."

"I think he deserves the benefit of our doubt, Genevieve. When he caught me in your — er — in the compromising situation, he spoke out of turn, not knowing it was *me* to whom he was speaking, and only when he realized — oh dash it; why am I explaining this? Does it matter? I ask you, pray, would it have been so terrible for them to match us, had I not blundered through the window?"

She stared at him as though a second head sprouted from his neck. "What are you asking, exactly?"

"Do you suppose their matchmaking would have worked, had I arrived in respectable fashion, as they had hoped and planned? Introduction. Dinners. Cards. No direct interference from them." His words edged with desperation, or so they sounded to him. Could she hear the pounding of his pulse?

"I — I — this is silly. It did not happen that way. We can only face how it *did* happen and handle accordingly with the situation as it is now."

He considered his options. The outlook was not promising if he chose to continue the conversation. Rather than seeing the situation from his perspective, she was stuck in the rut of her father's manipulating a single incident. Or she was pretending to be. He could not say. To continue was futile, and he had no wish to dig himself a deeper hole. What should have been a lark, them both laughing at the possibility and how it could have gone, had become a row.

With a faint smile, he said, "You're right. Shall we part ways here? Miss Cecilia has been trying to capture your attention from the tea garden, and I suspect my brothers need supervision if they're to find their way safely back to the dower house — and I refer to everyone else's safety from the pair of mischief makers."

When she glanced around to see her sister waving some distance away, she nodded. She seemed on the cusp of saying something, but he did not wait to hear it.

Rafe had the last word. "Remember you've promised me a dance this evening." Then, with a gallant bow, he took his leave of her, biting his tongue when he wanted to add, *actually, three dances.* The levity, he feared, would have been unappreciated.

Chapter 25

The gentle sway of lanterns cast a prismatic glow over the flowers, the dance held not in the assembly rooms of the tavern but in the new tea garden. Ah, the perfect ambiance: a soft breeze and a cloudless summer sky, light despite the sun having set.

Diana tugged at Rafe's sleeve, eager to see everything and everyone. The hand not dragging Rafe was tucked under Genevieve's arm.

"When does the dancing begin?" Diana prodded for the fifth time since they had arrived. "I vow to dance every dance, and if no gentleman asks me, I will ask you, Genevieve, so I do not miss a single step this evening. I would ask you, dear Rafe, but that would not be at all the thing, as I daren't make your ladylove jealous." She said the last with a shrill, tickling laugh. "Would it be a terrible faux pas to dance with Rupert? I know husbands should never dance with their wives, but what of siblings? I'm unfamiliar with Society rules, and what a shame to waste a dance when, in a pinch, I could press Rupert to dance with me. That would be superior to missing a dance, don't you think?"

Sharing a wink with Genevieve as Diana rattled, Rafe tried to guide them towards Headley and

Thorpe, who were talking near the nasturtiums. No luck. Diana ignored his nudge and tugged again at his sleeve as she threaded the garden paths.

When Diana took a breath to say more, Genevieve asked, "If Eurwendin had won, would we have been in the assembly rooms of their tavern instead?"

Both ladies looked at Rafe.

"Possibly. The Winsome Wyvern is a coaching inn. Much larger than our humble tavern."

"Oooh, so we would have had a grand ball, then?" Diana interposed.

"Not quite," he said, his shoulders shaking with a chuckle. "Last year, rather than an assembly, they hosted an afternoon fête to outdo ours—and succeeded. Their Punch and Judy Show is first rate, I admit. There was a medieval tournament for our amusement, as well. They do love their reenactments. And to end the fête, country dancing. As you see, we do things a little differently from them in Grant Lindis."

As they took a turn about the golden blossoms of the calendulas, a commotion on the outdoor dance floor drew their attention and stilled their steps. The dean of Hartminster was beginning his presentation of the winning cup, which, much to Rafe's companions' amusement, was a wassail bowl.

Rafe lowered his voice to say, "It'll be passed around for everyone to sip, and then displayed in the tavern for the year."

Genevieve wrinkled her nose. "Must we?"

"Of course, we must!" expostulated Diana, aghast. "I've been waiting at least ten years to attend the frolic. I refuse to miss any part of it."

Leaning behind Diana, he caught Genevieve's attention with an expression he hoped conveyed the answer she had wanted to hear.

"We should move closer," Diana urged. "I can't hear anything he's saying."

Rafe rooted his stance when she tried to tug again. "He gives the same speech every year, and since he doesn't attend the frolic, just the celebration, he only knows who won based on which village he's in. 'Good people of… er… *let me eyeball my notes*… Grant Windis… er… Lindis, rather, I present to thee a bowl of gold… er… wood….' yadda yadda."

"How do I tolerate you, Rafe Fitz-Stephens?" Diana asked with a disdainful sniff. "You're odious. The dean's words must be wise. And I'm missing them."

As she pouted and Genevieve stifled a laugh, Rafe continued in his nasal imitation of the dean's voice, "'Imbibe, my good people of Brant Gindis, to restore vitality and share glory. May your drunken steps prove you as foolish as your brethren in Dimwiener, er, Eurwendingy, uh –'"

Diana punched him in the arm.

"Ow." He rubbed his embroidered sleeve with a playful wince.

The speech, thankfully, was not long. They waited for the crowd to mill again before making their way to Rafe's parents, who were standing with Genevieve's parents, something they never would have done voluntarily before the frolic, or at least his mother would not have. As they drew near, Rafe slowed his steps to linger behind Diana so he could slip closer to Genevieve. If he did not say something now, he may lose the chance. Seeing his intention, she, too, stalled, allowing Diana to proceed ahead of them. Genevieve raised inquisitive eyebrows.

"I'm hoping for the supper dance," he said. "Before the queue of lovestruck swain forms, all pleading a dance, I want to express my hope you'll save the supper dance for me."

"We'll see," was all she said before skipping ahead to join Diana.

Had it not been for the gleam in her eyes, he would have been tugging at his cravat.

For the first dance, Rafe was safe from envy. His father escorted Genevieve to the floor, just as Rafe did with Mrs. Slade, in turn. The Fracas Frolic Assembly was a gay affair, lively country dances the score, clapping and whistling not uncommon, a lifetime away from London ballrooms, stately balls, and courtly dances. Reels ruled the realm. Figures were simple, no complicated steps requiring dance masters. The dress of the evening was Sunday best.

Rafe had not noticed what Diana was wearing, nor his mother, nor Mrs. Slade, never mind the latter partnered with him for the dance. He could, however, recite without another glance what Genevieve wore: Silk. Lavender. Embroidered hem. Plumes.

Her eyes reflected the hue of her gown, giving the illusion they, too, were lavender. The cut of the gown schooled Rafe's gaze on those lovely lavender hues so reflected because he could not bring himself to make the same mistake twice, i.e. allowing his gaze to travel below her chin. He was a hot-blooded man, after all, and knew his weaknesses. Her figure in the gown being one. The lavender waterfalled, form perfect, a flow of silken grace. Likewise, the neckline dipped far too low for the tightness of his cravat to bear. Rafe kept his eyes forward, still oblivious to what Mrs. Slade wore but aware of the owner of the dancing plumes at the top of the set.

When the dance ended, he escorted Mrs. Slade to the perimeter — near an herbaceous parterre improved by a swaying stained-glass lantern — his attention riveted across the garden on a young Eurwendin who was asking Genevieve for the next set before she had left the floor from the first. Given how much she wanted to be part of village life, this boded well for her having a full evening of dancing. Only a pity it could not be Rafe soliciting every dance.

As a distraction, he turned to Mr. Slade. Over the man's shoulder, Rafe spotted Sir Courtney, arriving fashionably late. Perfect timing! He could make the introductions — and distract himself further.

The best description of Sir Courtney was convivial. He held no objection to being introduced to Mr. Slade and devoted more than half the next dance doing his poor best to recruit Mr. Slade for his rambling group. Caught in his own sycophantic trap, Slade had no choice but to accept, at least until he could think of an excuse to share a brandy regularly with Sir Courtney without the need for adventure, or so Rafe surmised from the trapped-rabbit expression Slade bore.

As they talked, Rafe watched Genevieve from the corner of his eyes.

He almost missed Sir Courtney's departure, the man having spied Rafe's mother and wishing to request the next dance. No sooner had he departed than Lord Karras stepped in, blocking Rafe's view of the dancers.

Quizzing glass raised to one eye, Karras spared Rafe a cursory glance, looking away as he asked in his supercilious voice, "Sir Courtney?"

"Missed him by mere seconds. I shall benefit from his misfortune, as I wish to introduce someone to you."

Slade sucked in his paunch and straightened his shoulders, recognizing an aristocrat without a word from Rafe.

Karras turned languidly to study the man standing beside Rafe. "Must you?" Dropping the glass by its ribbon, he sighed with boredom.

Rafe chose to take that as a yes, namely because Karras waited for the introduction rather than walking away.

The two men did not move in the same circles, but Rafe believed they respected each other, if for different reasons, Rafe admiring Karras' exquisite raiment, a dandy of the first water, this evening being no exception — the intricate weave of the cravat, the diamonds in the folds, oh, how superbly the linen wreathed the man's neck in a trone d'amour knot — and Karras admiring Rafe's reputation for being one of the best whips — a curiosity, Rafe had always thought, because he believed it was his reputation admired, not the skill itself.

"May I introduce Mr. Roland Slade? New to the area, but with a salver topped daily with cards, including that of Sir Courtney." A slight exaggeration given the introduction had only now been made to the latter.

Karras sighed again, swinging his glass as a pendulum. "Slade, you say? Of the Somerset Slades?"

Mr. Slade's forehead wrinkled a smile. "Why, yes."

"Mmm." With the noncommittal sound, Karras graced Slade with a slight nod.

As Slade doubled over in an obsequious bow, Rafe completed the introductions with a simple, "Viscount Karras."

Before more could be said, the dance ended, and Genevieve's partner escorted her to her father's side before taking his leave. Her eyes met Rafe's first, then moved with interest to the stranger.

The quizzing glass stopped swinging. The frown pinching Karras' brow softened as he swept his gaze over Genevieve.

Rafe's fingers involuntarily curled into his palm.

Without missing a beat, Slade waved a hand to his lordship. "If I may, my new acquaintance is Viscount Karras. Your lordship, this lovely dove is my daughter, Miss Slade."

Rafe cleared his throat, waiting for Mr. Slade to add the all-important *on dit* about his daughter being Rafe's betrothed.

Instead, Karras bowed, a hand over his heart as though struck by Cupid's arrow. "I will not allow you to dance the next with anyone except me."

Slipping her hand in his, Genevieve allowed him to escort her to the dance floor.

Rafe flexed and folded his fingers.

His memory recalled Thorpe's once-upon-a-time praise singing of aristocrats in his efforts to tempt the Slades to angle for a larger fish by freeing Genevieve of the betrothal. They had not listened at the time, not when they already had Rafe, but had Thorpe's words made an impression, nevertheless? Surely not. It would negate his theory of their fathers' matchmaking. It would turn Mr. Slade into a far more unscrupulous character. It would…

He shivered. It chilled him to see Slade so dazzled. Was Genevieve dazzled?

Chapter 26

A s the sky darkened and the lamplight shone brighter, the evening breeze sharpened, crisp and cool. Or Rafe's heart had frozen. He could not be sure which. Too desolate for conversation, he watched the couple dance a merry jig. Her feathery curls jounced with her rhythmic steps. Each time she laughed, the pit of Rafe's stomach lurched and fell somewhere at his feet.

If only Karras were a sloppy dresser. Not only did the man have a finer cravat than Rafe this evening, he now also had the lady. Lord Karras made love to her with half-lidded eyes. A lump lodged in Rafe's throat. At least neither Genevieve nor Mr. Slade yet knew Lord Karras sported a courtesy title, his father being the Earl of Silverton, the ancestral estate situated in northwest Devonshire, while Karras spent most of his time in one of the family's holdings, Teasleigh Park, on the outskirts of Eurwendin. Someone else could divulge that information, perhaps Karras himself. Rafe refused to contribute to the dazzle.

"She's even more beautiful when she's happy," observed a voice behind him. "Not that she's ever unhappy. At least, not that I've known. But she's a greater degree happier than usual, I'd say."

Startled out of his spycraft, Rafe turned to see not Mr. Slade standing at his side but Alan Thorpe. A quick glance showed Slade had pursued Sir Courtney while Rafe was preoccupied with the dancers.

"She's always beautiful," Rafe replied, "but please don't say she's happier than usual. A cut to the esteem, that."

Thorpe's brows met. "I only wish for Di—Miss Headley, I mean, to be at her happiest. How is this a cut?"

Rafe looked askance at Thorpe. "Ah, right. Diana. Yes. I thought you meant Genevieve."

"Ooh, I see." He looked from the dancers to Rafe, studying them both at length before saying, "That explains it."

"Ugly sight to witness," Rafe admitted.

"Your complexion, you mean? Positively peaky. Green with envy, as they say?"

"That too. I was referring to them dancing."

"Ooh." After a few false starts and *hmms*, Thorpe asked, "Does this not work in your favor? He's the very sort to tempt Mr. Slade from holding to the betrothal agreement."

"You took the words from my lips."

When Rafe offered nothing more, Thorpe again looked from the dancers to Rafe, *hmmed* to himself a few more times, then asked, "Have you told her your sentiments have changed?"

Rafe scoffed, which sounded almost like a snarl. "Don't be daft. She resents being forced into this. If I align myself with her father, she'll feel that much more trapped, that much more manipulated. My only hope is for her to find me so droll she forgets I was to blame and becomes fond of me."

"I'm the last person to offer advice." Thorpe stuttered a laugh. "But I do have the advantage of knowing Miss Slade longer. If I were in your shoes—and what exquisite satin they are, I might add—I would be bold in speech, plainspoken. Without your honesty, I fear she'll think you're being kind from obligation, not from the stirrings of your heart."

"Poetic," grunted Rafe.

Karras took advantage of one of the turns to whisper something into Genevieve's ear. Pink dotted her cheeks, but she laughed heartily. Rafe swallowed.

Under his breath, Rafe said, "*Flectere si nequeo superos, Acheronta movebo.* If I cannot bend the will of Heaven, I shall move Hell."

"The way I see it," Thorpe continued, "if her head is so easily turned, she's not for you. But I never took Miss Slade for one such." He rocked heel to toe. "Plain speak is best, I say. Tell her your devotion is genuine."

Easy for him to say. It was not his heart on display.

"I would offer my services in whatever way they may be useful, Mr. Fitz-Stephens, except I leave on the morrow."

Startled, Rafe tore his eyes from the dancers to take in the sheepish expression of Mr. Thorpe. "Tomorrow? Leaving? Whatever for?"

Flushing scarlet, he looked down at the buckles of his pumps. "I have some, er, traveling to do. That is, rather, I must confer with my grandparents on a matter of some importance before returning for an interview."

"An interview? Would it not be more prudent to conduct this interview first, while in the area, before proceeding home?"

"Yes, well, that it would, except, well, you see, it's a matter of some delicacy. This is not a task one undertakes without full familial support. You see, I intend to offer my hand."

So stunned, Rafe stumbled one step back. "*Your hand*? In *marriage*? To whom?"

It struck him before Thorpe answered. Diana Headley. By Jupiter! Rafe blanched. Had Thorpe misconstrued Diana's friendly nature and planned to pursue her unbidden? What a disaster. His mind whirring like a timepiece, he tried to find the right words to dissuade Thorpe before he not only found his heart broken but likely also his nose, and once Headley had his way, possibly an arm or leg. Rafe could not allow poor Alan Thorpe to face this fate without at least an attempt at intervention.

Before Thorpe admitted the name, Rafe lobbed his arm around the man's shoulders and guided him down one of the garden paths. "Say no more. I'm more observant than I seem and have seen the two of you much in each other's company of late. The thing is…" now was his turn to *hmm*. "The thing is, Alan, I feel it's my duty as your friend to recommend not acting in haste, not when the feelings of the other party could be… um… otherwise engaged."

Thorpe listened, nodding, but then slowed his pace to look sidelong at Rafe. "There's no reason to wait. When a gentleman knows himself to be in love, *he knows*. I have no reason to doubt, second guess, or wait."

"Yes, but women are complicated creatures, and although they may be friendly, even flirty, this behavior can be deceiving to us more simple gents, who then fancy the lady in question, and thus ourselves, infatuated, when—"

"But she's already accepted my offer."

Rafe stopped dead in his tracks. "Diana? *Accepted*?"

The situation was worse than he feared. Diana was toying with Thorpe, and Headley was going to rip the man limb from limb.

"Before you say it's only been a week," Thorpe protested, "I repeat that when a gentleman knows, he knows."

"I must urge caution. Her brother is a force to be reckoned with on the best of days, and if he—"

"He's already given his approval, Mr. Fitz-Stephens."

Rafe gaped. What the devil had he missed this week?

"We'll not proceed until my grandparents meet her. And I still must ask permission from her father before I can officially offer marriage. But I don't foresee any difficulties. Only the usual nervousness I've come to understand accompanies being a prospective bridegroom." While Rafe continued to gape, Thorpe clasped his hand and pumped it. "I have you to thank. You and Miss Slade. I'll always be of service to you both. Say the word, and I'm by your side. Without the two of you, Diana and I never would have met."

As though arriving on cue, Diana flounced towards them. "Has the wassail bowl made its way this direction? I've been searching between dances but can never find it. I refuse to miss my turn. Oh! Rafe! Your expression!" She tittered giddily. "Naughty, Alan! You must have told him. I insisted I wanted to tell him. I can see I'll have to take you in hand if you're going to ignore my requests and spill all my best secrets the moment my back is turned." Tucking her hand into the crook of Thorpe's arm, she probed Rafe with, "Why have you not danced with Genevieve? What must she think to have her own betrothed neglect her?"

"I'll collect her for the supper dance."

With a doubtful frown, Diana warned, "I hope she knows that. More to the point, why are you *only* wanting the supper dance? A lady is likely to think you don't care."

"Uh, the dictates of good etiquette make the rules, my dearest. A gentleman ought not dance more than—"

"Fiddlesticks. Come, Alan. Let us show him how wrong he is. You're mine for the next three dances." With that, she pulled him behind her towards the dance floor.

Rafe had little time to consider the conversation or search the crowd for Genevieve and Karras. Headley swaggered down the garden path, nodding to his sister and Thorpe as he passed, then headed for the bench a few paces behind Rafe.

"Di insists we return home tomorrow. Impetuous chit."

Rafe joined him on the bench, the wood cool enough to be felt through his satin breeches. "More to the point, *Thorpe*? How the devil did I miss this? How is he not displayed on the pillory, tarred and feathered? I like the man, but this is Diana we're talking about."

"I'm amusing her while offering him the opportunity to prove himself. Don't be fooled, Fitz-Stephens.

You won't be attending a wedding any time soon. At least not until I've closely supervised a strict courtship." He laced his fingers behind his head. "I've encouraged him to return home first, give them both time to cool their heads, give me time to speak with Father and Mam so they don't feel blindsided or think some rogue has been philandering under my watch."

"You're serious? He'll return, you know he will, and he'll court her. Then what?"

"Then... fancy a stay in Glanvale to attend my sister's wedding?"

Rafe laughed incredulously. "I never thought I would see the day. You're turning soft in your dotage."

"Speaking of weddings — and I ask not because I'm interested but because talking about my sister at an assembly is not top of my list — when's yours? Spoken with that doddering fool of a vicar yet about the banns?"

"About that." Rafe tugged at the ends of his hair, fighting the urge to comb his fingers through his locks in fear of disassembling the careful styling he had spent nearly an hour perfecting.

"Trouble in paradise? Already? 'Fess, Fitz-Stephens. What have you said to upset her? Does Di need to play mediator? She's fluent in 'woman,' you know."

"Oh, it's not that. Not exactly. I..." He pulled at the tips of his gloves, instead, to avoid disheveling his hair. A tug to each finger, and then a flex for a tighter fit, then a tug, repeating the whole again, a nervous delay tactic if he was honest with himself. "I'm smitten, truth be told. Couldn't say how or when or why, but a bug bit me when I wasn't looking, and now I'm good and truly smitten. Only, she's... not as taken with me as I am with her, I fear."

He wanted to scan the gardens for her — was she sitting out the next dance to spend more time with Karras? He resisted, not wanting to look quite so lovesick in front of Headley. A man did have his pride.

"Thorpe shared pearls of wisdom with me," Rafe divulged.

Beside him, Headley's shoulders shook with laughter. "I never dreamt I would say this, Fitz-Stephens, but whatever he said might be worth heeding. In one week, he came, he met, and he wooed. What a woman sees in him that we don't is beyond my comprehension, but the fact remains, his success speaks for itself."

"That's depressing."

"My pleasure."

He hesitated to admit this, but if he could not to Headley, who else? "She danced with Karras. Seemed taken with him. So was Mr. Slade."

"*Mmm*, I see."

"That was Thorpe's reaction, more or less."

Headley slapped Rafe on the back none-too-gently. "You *are* smitten, my good man, to allow the green-eyed monster to rear its head over that pompous popinjay. If you of a few months ago could hear yourself talking now..." Standing, he added, "Stop moping and go dance with your lady. What would the Rafe Fitz-Stephens of old have done? My guess is *l' étreinte* by moonlight — that would solve most of your problems." He waggled his eyebrows before leaving Rafe to consider this sage advice.

Chapter 27

M r. Proudie, a gentleman from Eurwendin, and from what Genevieve recalled from their brief introduction earlier in the week, an acquaintance of Rafe's, led her to one of the benches following their dance. He promised to return with a glass of Madeira while she rested her feet. She never dreamt she would dance every set at an assembly. During her one and only previous assembly, she had sat with the spinsters and wallflowers and, alternately, hid behind her mother. It was not that gentlemen did not wish to dance with her, she did not believe, rather the Slades did not know enough people to make the appropriate introductions.

Tonight, she had danced every dance so far. Her feet ached. Not that she would complain. She did not care if she ever walked again—let her feet throb! Curling her toes in her shoes, she searched the crowd for Rafe. Was the supper dance soon?

Mr. Proudie weaved his way to her, two glasses in his hand and a tall figure in his shadow. Her heart skipped a beat. She smiled as she accepted the wine from Mr. Proudie with a word of gratitude.

The shadow emerged from behind him. "Miss Slade," greeted Mr. Headley.

However crestfallen that he was not Rafe, she held her smile, hoping her disappointment did not show. "How are you enjoying the evening, Mr. Headley?"

"Not as well as Proudie. He's had the honor of taking you for a twirl."

Exaggerating the batting of her eyelashes, she offered, "If that's a solicitation for the next dance, you're in luck."

Before she lost her opportunity to quench her thirst after so many turns about the floor, she took a few generous but not unladylike sips.

Proudie bowed to them both. "I believe that's my cue. Miss Slade. Headley." He offered to take her glass as he departed.

"You know each other," she observed.

"Since our youth. He's a member of the Vitruvian Society."

Had Rafe not mentioned that during the frolic? She recalled meeting Proudie, but all the faces and names blurred after so eventful a week. She flexed her feet with a wince.

"Not too sore, I hope?" Headley enquired, nodding to her shoes. "We could sit this out if you'd prefer. Gossip like old maids instead."

She shook her head. "I would not miss dancing with you for the world."

As they joined the dancers, Diana and Mr. Thorpe squeezed in beside them.

Diana, holding tight to Mr. Thorpe's hand, squealed her delight. "We'll all be able to dance together!"

Just as the music struck, a pair of latecomers darted in at the bottom of the set. Genevieve's breath caught. Rafe. She could not catch a glimpse of his partner but wished they could have joined the quartet of her and Mr. Headley, and Diana and Mr. Thorpe.

They waited for the dance to reach them, the top of the set enjoying lively figures first. Conversation kicked off around them.

"Di and I leave tomorrow," Mr. Headley said.

"So soon?" Before he could answer, she realized the rush given they could not travel on Sunday and would be too exhausted after the assembly to travel tomorrow. "Oh, I understand. If you wait, it will not be until Monday before you can depart. I wish we all had more time together. You're not so very far away, are you?"

"Not at all. The northernmost village in the deanery. At most an hour, but that's only if taking a leisurely pace and going through Sidonia."

That Diana would be leaving was disheartening, but there had never been the expectation the Headleys would stay long once the frolic ended.

"While I have the chance," Mr. Headley ventured, "I want to express my relief you'll be marrying Fitz-Stephens."

"Relief?" Genevieve echoed with an unrepressed laugh.

"I feared he would die a bachelor, most certainly in a mad-cap, reckless scheme, either from his misguided sense of adventure or to prove himself."

"You're provoking me, Mr. Headley, and I shan't listen to a word of this slander!" She laughed harder still at his long face, the twinkling in his eyes belying his mischief.

"Oh, but it's true, Miss Slade. I was certain no woman would agree to marry him. Women have far more sense."

"Are you implying I've lost my senses?"

The dance made its way down the line to them, their conversation delayed.

Genevieve knew Mr. Headley jested. Rafe could have any woman he wanted, and yet he was, presently, trapped with her, the last woman he could desire, for even if she were the prettiest and wittiest girl of his acquaintance, no man wanted to be forced into marriage. She felt one part proud to be his temporary betrothed, one part defensive at any insinuation, jest or not, that a woman could reject him, and two parts melancholy to think of the betrothal dissolving once they convinced her father to give her a choice.

When the dance provided them with the next opportunity to speak, she chided Mr. Headley. "As his closest friend, you should praise him to me, convince me I've made the best match, not tell me I've taken leave of my senses."

"Must I convince you?"

"No, I'm perfectly aware of how remarkable he is."

Mr. Headley cracked a sly smile. "You should tell him rather than me."

"Don't be absurd! He's perfectly aware of that fact already."

"I don't disagree, but is he aware *you* think so?"

Genevieve's smile faltered at the edges. "That point does not signify, sir."

"Wouldn't want him to become too conceited? To have won the lady's hand *and* her affection. Could go to his head. We'd never hear the end of it."

"You're still teasing me, confounded man."

The dance swept them away again, the conversation left to simmer. By the time they could exchange words once more, the dance was at an end.

Before Mr. Headley parted ways, he leaned closely with a whisper. "Tell him how you feel. Even a love-struck fool needs reassurances now and again."

She smiled but said nothing, thinking that if Mr. Headley knew the truth of the situation, he would not call Rafe a lovestruck fool nor would he recommend she share her feelings one way or another. Mr. Headley still thought them a love match. A knot tightened in Genevieve's stomach that it could not be further from the truth.

Diana clasped Genevieve's hand, Mr. Thorpe by her side. "You're going to dance with Alan next. I insist. He has something *wonderful* to tell you. And so you know, we have *you* to thank, you and Rafe. Love at first sight agrees with you both. Who could not fall in love, as well, seeing the two of you together? You inspire the muses!" Placing Genevieve's hand into Mr. Thorpe's, Diana squeezed his fingers around his new dance partner. "Now you can't be jealous if I steal a dance with Rafe." With a giggle, she disappeared between people, presumably to find Rafe.

Genevieve looked wide-eyed at Mr. Thorpe. "What on earth was that about?"

Her companion's cheeks flushed. He did not immediately answer the question, rather he slipped his hand free of hers and asked instead, "May I have the next dance, Miss Slade?"

"It would be my pleasure. Besides, if we chose not to dance, I daren't face Diana's disapproval."

"Nor I," he said, the flush creeping along his neck.

Their dance was more sedate, ample opportunity to talk, although neither were overly eager to do so, not because they did not wish to, but because there did not seem an immediate need to. Genevieve enjoyed dancing with a trusted friend. His presence was calming. She recalled why she had entrusted him with her unusual situation to begin with — he was the most level-headed, trustworthy, and stalwart person she had met. With him, there was no need for nervousness or worry, no confusion about what he was thinking or might do or say next. With him, she could simply *be*.

At length, Mr. Thorpe said softly, "I must offer my apologies, Miss Slade. I fear I've failed you. You asked for my aid, and I've been unable to help your parents see things differently."

"Oh, good heavens. You have not failed me! You have been the dearest friend I could wish for."

"If that were so, I would have been able to succeed in either convincing your parents as you had wished or convincing you."

Her steps fumbled. "Me? Whatever do you mean?"

"It's my opinion you and Mr. Fitz-Stephens are well suited. I approve of him, Miss Slade, wholeheartedly, and think you would both regret not taking advantage of the situation, if for no other reason than to see if I'm correct."

"No! You're quite mistaken! We do not suit at all. And if we did, which we do not, we cannot simply forget the situation. No gentleman wishes to be forced into marriage. There are far too many complications."

Mr. Thorpe shrugged his shoulders. "The situation, as I see it, is an opportunity. Rather than ask why you're being punished, you should ask what you're meant to accomplish. It's not my place to say, but it is my humble opinion that the good Lord does not present trials to punish rather to strengthen, even to reward. Take my traveling here to aid you, Miss Slade. The situation presented an opportunity of a lifetime — the chance to meet Diana Headley."

Genevieve stumbled again, making quite the cake of herself in the dance, thankful it was sedate enough no one appeared to notice her missteps. "What about Diana?"

"She's asked me to be the one to tell you, seeing we've known each other longer. We have an understanding. More than that. I must remember I'm speaking with *you*, and thus, I may be honest to the point of vulgarity — we're in love, Miss Slade!"

Had Genevieve been taking a sip of wine, she would have choked. Thankfully, she was on a dance floor, which meant her only sin was another stumble, this time right into Mr. Thorpe, who gallantly caught her and righted her, the sole witness being Diana — and, oh dear, Rafe, as well, who eyed her with a quizzical lift of his brow. What a clumsy oaf! But... *Diana*? And *Mr. Thorpe*? In love? Preposterous!

"It's been but a week!" she protested.

His smile was full of guilty pleasure. "When a gentleman knows, he knows."

"But... but..." she stuttered, not knowing how to respond to the news.

Diana and Mr. Thorpe were so different. How had Genevieve not realized they had been making eyes at each other all this week?

After struggling to understand, she finally said, "It is my turn to apologize. You've announced the happiest news I could possibly hear, and all I've done is sputter in shock. What a terrible friend I am! I am so happy for you and certainly for her, although she must already know what a gem you are, the luckiest of ladies, to be sure. When is the wedding? Oh, I couldn't be happier, truly."

"Not for four to six months, I would assume. If I could marry her tomorrow, I would. The families must meet, and I wish to court her properly, nothing so havey-cavey as a week's romance to make her parents think ill of me. Once I have her father's permission, there will be the banns."

"If we weren't in the middle of the dance floor, I would hug you!"

"I might know someone more deserving of that embrace."

"Yes, I shall wrap my arms around Diana's neck the second the dance ends." Her gaze sought Diana and Rafe as they skipped in a merry circle with the other dancers of their set.

"Oh no, you mistake me, Miss Slade. It was not to Diana I referred." Mr. Thorpe's mouth contorted into an expression Genevieve had never witnessed him bear before — a roguish grin.

Realizing he had meant Rafe, she tried for a sulky huff but could achieve no such reaction, not in the presence of that roguish grin, so out of character for Mr. Thorpe. Instead, she pulled a face before breaking out into a grin of her own.

Following his bow, Mr. Thorpe rose, his eyes trained over Genevieve's shoulder. Her breath caught. Rafe must be approaching.

Heart in her throat, she pivoted.

A burly fellow drew near the edge of the dance floor, the wassail bowl in his hands. Genevieve squeaked, darting for an escape path. Only vaguely was she aware of Mr. Thorpe laughing at her and Diana's mellifluous voice, elated to have found the bowl at last.

Slipping between two would-be dancers, she halted face to chest with a silken waistcoat. A lift of her chin proved what she anticipated most. Rafe.

Smiling coyly, he urged, "This way." His gloved hand palmed her elbow, and he guided her to the other side of the dance floor. "Safe from the bowl. For now."

Eyes level with his neckcloth, she said sardonically, "My hero."

"No need to shower me with gratitude. Rescuing damsels in distress is a pastime of mine, you know."

So languidly and so prosaically were his words spoken, Genevieve could not disguise her gurgle of laughter. "Do you often meet damsels pursued by wassail bowls?"

"You would be surprised. Left unchecked, they've grown brazen—the bowls, not the damsels."

"Fortunately for me, then, the mighty bowl hunter is afoot."

"Impeccable timing, as always." Winking, he clarified, "The supper dance is next."

"Oh," was all she could muster, gooseflesh kissing her arms. Was it overly warm? The breeze chilled her feverish skin.

As an excuse to avert her eyes from his regard, she turned back to watch the bowl's progress, Diana and Mr. Thorpe having a sip before passing it on.

His voice closer than it had been before she turned, he said in low tones, "*Nemo saltat sobrius*. Nobody dances sober."

"The wassail?"

When she risked a glance, he shook his head, a secretive smile playing his lips. "I wasn't referring to wine." Leaving her to decipher the meaning, he reached for her hand and laced his fingers with hers. "I have a different dance in mind for us."

A trifle distressed, but mostly piqued, she allowed him to lead her away from the dancers and into the garden. Down a narrow path, they passed two benches but did not stop at either, then slipped beneath the thatched eave of the tavern to follow the side of the building until the lantern light gave way to quarter moonlight. Only then did he stop, their location secluded from the garden.

Her emotions warred between scandalized and tantalized. "What game are you playing, Rafe?"

"No game. I wish to waltz with you. The music doesn't matter."

"But… I don't know how to waltz." She knew *of* this dance, at least, but that did not assuage her of his intentions. "This is all too irregular. We should join the others."

Shocking her to the tips of her stockinged feet, he drew her against him, their bodies only separated by their intertwined hands. In a sultry voice he said, "*Nitimur in vetitum*. We strive for the forbidden," then stepped back just enough to guide for a turn under his arm.

She gasped a laugh at the turn only to have her breath stolen when he drew her once more against him.

"A variation of the Duke of Kent's waltz," he said. "I hope it's saucy enough to embolden but not to insult. How is it so far?"

With a breathy chuckle, she was swept into another turn. It did not matter that she did not know the steps, for he guided her with expertise, nor did it matter that the music had not begun to play in the tea garden. She felt the music rather than heard it. In only a few turns, she forgot their friendship was conditional, forgot their relationship was temporary, forgot their betrothal was manipulated, and above all else, forgot her attraction was unrequited. Sinking into his embrace, she followed his lead, intoxicated by the intimacy of the dance.

Oh. *Nemo saltat sobrius. Oh!* She understood what Rafe had meant now.

"You've taken my breath away this evening, Genevieve. To say you're the handsomest woman present would be an understatement."

She wanted to laugh at his silliness, call him out for being roguish, scold him for teasing her, but his expression was earnest, and she could not bring herself to break the spell. For a moment, she relished the sensation of sincerity. Lie or truth, she wanted his words to be ardent. Desperately.

"Have I mentioned how masterful you wielded the bow?" he continued, kindling the fire with every word. "Your arrow pierced my heart, dearest. I'm quite undone, besotted, truth be told."

He did not appear perturbed she had not responded to his lavish praise. He drew her to him for lengthier embraces before relaxing and turning her again. As the music in the tea garden struck its first chord, at last, he drew her to him one last time, his breathing deep and steady, his eyes trained on hers, bright in the moonlight. She leaned into him, lightheaded by the heady sweetness of his perfume.

Rafe leaned closer, lowering until she caught the scent of mint. She felt his breath on her cheek. Her heart pounded erratically. Her eyelids fluttered.

Then he lifted her hand between them, and with his eyes still locked with hers, he kissed the knuckles of her lavender, kid gloves.

When he stepped back, a chill swept over Genevieve, sending a shiver from head to toe, her lips aching for what they had been deprived. Why had he not kissed her? She was certain he meant to. But then, she had never been kissed before—had she read too much into the moment? Her heart sank to realize he had only been playing the role of besotted betrothed. She blinked rapidly and turned away, not wanting him to see how much the moment had affected her— how foolish he would think her!

"I have a confession," he said.

She swallowed the lump in her throat. Without turning around, she nodded for him to continue. All she wanted to do was return to the assembly.

"I…" he began, his voice hitching. "I'll understand if you object." He cleared his throat, but his words came out hoarsely. "I want to court you."

She spun around. "I beg your pardon — you *what*?"

"It's ridiculous, I know. We're *technically* betrothed already, and I'm supposed to be finding a way to extricate us from the betrothal so you can choose, even if that choice is someone else. You'll think me a traitor now. If so, I completely understand and will do as you bid." He fumbled with his fob, fidgeting. "But… since we've become better acquainted, I believe we rub well together. I believe our fathers knew what they were about, if my theory rings true, and I think we would be better served to accept the situation than object. I speak for myself, in full disclosure, when I admit that I don't want you to choose someone else. However unusual our circumstances began, I think it time we embrace this chance. If I could court you with full intention towards matrimony, not this betrothal game we've been playing, we might discover… we… suit."

The spell he had cast with his waltz disintegrated. Pretending to brush an errant hair from her face, which in turn wet her gloves with fresh tears, she chortled mirthlessly. From seductor by moonlight to her father's stooge in a single confession. And she had thought he had fallen for her! She had thought he wished to kiss her! A veriest understatement should her acceptance cross her lips, leastways while she was still tempted to fling herself into his arms. But his words… his sentiments… These were not words of affection, adoration, *love*, not of a man wishing to kiss a woman by moonlight. These were words of acquiescence. He was giving into her father's manipulation because he did not know how to end the betrothal without the man's wrath and threats to ruin reputations. She should be flattered, she supposed, just as she should have been flattered when he had been the consummate gentleman and proposed — he was willing to make the best of the situation, enough to say they *rubbed well together*.

Hardening her heart, she took a step closer and reached for his hand to squeeze it. "No." She let his hand fall back to his side as she stepped further away, putting distance between them. "I want my freedom. You do, as well — I know you do — although you've convinced yourself otherwise to make this situation tolerable. We have each played our part, but it's time one of us defended ourselves. If it must be me, then so be it. I will request an interview with my father tomorrow and tell him to do his worst."

Rafe stared at her in abject horror. "I misspoke. I chose the wrong words. Please, let me try again. Let me tell you how infatuated I am. Just as you *think* you know I want freedom, I *know* you harbor feelings for me, beyond playacting. If I did not believe so, I wouldn't fight, but I *know* you feel what I do. I saw it now. I saw it in your eyes. I felt it in my arms when we danced."

Genevieve backstepped, shaking her head. "It doesn't *matter*. Do you not understand? Whatever you're feeling, it's an illusion. You've convinced yourself because you're a gentleman. Once free of me, you'll have time to reflect and see it's not real. You'll thank me. You'll be able to go to London and be a barrister at the Old Bailey like you planned. All your dreams will come true without this millstone about your neck."

He strode towards her, arms outstretched to embrace her, but she sidestepped him. "Genevieve.

Please. Let me explain myself better. Dash the circumstances that brought us together."

"But they're *everything*. I cannot disremember them. I will not. I will not be *forced*, no matter what our feelings may be, and I know your feelings are as forced as the betrothal. Give yourself time to meditate on them, and you'll see I'm right. Let me go, Rafe. Oh, just let me go."

Breaking free from his emotional hold, she tripped around the side of the tavern to return to the tea garden.

Chapter 28

D awn's rays stretched across the desk in the study. Rafe watched the light's inching progress as the clock on the mantelpiece ticked. He had been waiting for Mr. Slade for the better part of half an hour. Understandable given both the early hour and the late evening, but it was imperative Rafe speak to him before Genevieve requested an audience.

If he had followed his intuition rather than open his big mouth, he would not be in this sticky wicket.

His only hope was Slade's sympathy—which he did not hold in high esteem—for if what Rafe had to say met with an unsympathetic ear, Mr. Slade was more apt to demand the banns be read immediately than offer the aid Rafe needed to ensure Genevieve had the freedom of choice. If Genevieve spoke to her father first, the demand for banns was certain. The responsibility weighed on Rafe's shoulders to help her win her freedom of choice so he may then win her heart without reservations.

The study door opened, then closed. So anxious, Rafe jerked in surprise. Without acknowledging the guest, Mr. Slade grumbled his way to the desk. Eyes averted, he lowered into the chair, shifting his weight to find comfort, then drummed his fingers on the desktop. Rafe waited, still standing, invisible to his host. The clock continued to tick.

At length, the door opened again, this time to the butler carrying a tray. On it perched one steaming coffee cup.

Once the butler bowed his way back out the door, Mr. Slade took three healthy pulls of coffee, then turned his attention to a gilded snuff box. A flick of the lid. A pinch of snuff. A sniff with each nostril. A flick of the lid.

The only muscle on Rafe that moved was a tick in his cheek as he clenched his jaw.

Without looking up or inviting his guest to sit, Mr. Slade murmured into his coffee cup, "No."

Rafe waited for more. The clock ticked.

When nothing further was forthcoming, Rafe cleared his throat and asked, "Begging your pardon, sir, but to what do I owe this answer?"

The man's eyes met Rafe's over the brim of the cup. Another swig.

Setting down the coffee, Mr. Slade laced his hands over his paunch, twiddling a button on his waistcoat. "I'll tell you what I told my daughter last night: *no*. I will not release either of you from the betrothal. You gave me your word as a gentleman to honor the match. She gave me her word as my daughter to obey. Seems to me the calling of the banns is overdue. Allowed too much time for her to ruminate."

Rafe let the words sink in rather than jump to respond. He had not anticipated her to seek an audience following the assembly. Later this morning after a proper lie in, yes. Last night, or rather in the wee hours, no. This changed everything Rafe had planned to say. A new plan... he needed a new plan. *Think*.

"You're exactly right, sir, except for your assumption of why I've requested an audience."

Mr. Slade knit his brows.

"I assure you I'm a man of my word. I've no wish to be released from the betrothal. On the contrary. As to why I'm here, I... I arrived early to invite you for a ride. Sir Courtney is an early riser, as am I, and I thought you might care to call on him with me." Rafe grimaced inwardly at the impromptu invitation.

The crease between the brows softened as they rose, wrinkling Mr. Slade's broad forehead instead. "Is this so?" He rubbed his chin, either pondering if he wished to ride or if Rafe was honest. "Chose a dashed, poor day for it, boy. Sleepless night, what with the assembly, and now this nonsense with my daughter. You'd no notion she came to me, fit to be tied?"

"I did not, sir. If I may be so bold to admit, I'm only partially surprised. I may have overstepped at the assembly. I never expected her to cry off, but in hindsight I can better understand my error. *Ubi amor, ibi dolor,* as they say. Where there is love, there is pain."

"Is that so? Pull the rope, if you please." Mr. Slade waved a hand to the bellrope behind Rafe.

Obediently, Rafe turned to give it a tug, then accepted the chair Mr. Slade offered, thinking this bode well for the conversation. He was improvising and uncertain of Slade's reactions. If his improvisation failed, he and Genevieve would be heading for the altar with bared teeth rather than fluttering eyelashes.

When the butler peeked in, Mr. Slade asked for a cup of coffee for Mr. Fitz-Stephens. They waited for the deed to be done before ought else was said.

Fueled with a cup of coffee he did not particularly want but was obliged to drink, Rafe initiated, "About that ride…"

"Yes, yes, inconvenient timing but I'll have the horses readied in a few — dash it, I should have said something when he brought the coffee. Could you pull the — ah, never mind. We can see to it shortly. I'll need time to prepare, as well. Now. I have a bone to pick with you if you're to blame for my daughter's tantrum. Tell me why she hurled herself at me like a feral cat, hissing and spitting."

Rafe outwardly flushed but internally chuckled, not so much at the visual but knowing Genevieve did no such thing. More accurately, she would have been the submissive daughter he recalled when he first proposed, begging her father for pity with downcast eyes. The only person he suspected she would unsheathe her claws for was himself.

"I tried to kiss her," he confessed with a boyish grin, even if that was not how it had happened. If he judged Mr. Slade correctly…

Slade frowned for fifteen seconds before guffawing. "My daughter's missish, is she? Now I see. Oh yes, now I see all too clearly. Next time, don't *try*, if you take my meaning. Women need firmness."

"Yes, sir. I take your meaning." Schooling his expression to be one of a devoted pupil, he leaned forward with interest and nursed the cup of bitter. "She's not likely to be receptive now. I wish I had enticed in her the desire to embrace me rather than enforce my will. You know how she is."

It was not lost on Rafe they were discussing the intimacy of a first kiss when the betrothal itself had been manipulated from the accusation of there being far more intimacy than kisses, but such appeared to be lost on Mr. Slade.

"Nonsense. Take her in hand, boy. She'll learn her place quick enough."

"Indeed, sir, I suspect she would. But with all due respect, I'd favor a more delicate approach after seeing her reaction. Don't fancy being set upon by a hissing puss. You know how headstrong she can be. Take her request as evidence. *Res ipsa loquitur.* The evidence speaks for itself. So opposed to having a kiss forced on her, she was compelled to cry off. I'm not of a mind to try again for fear I'll meet the feral side you mentioned." He affected a fearful shudder.

Mr. Slade's mood had shifted from gruff to amused, the corners of his mouth quirking as he chuckled. "We'll speak with the vicar. The sooner the banns are read, the sooner she'll be a pliable bride. The two of you are well matched; I saw to that. She will realize it, too, in time."

"However uncustomary, I'd favor her choosing me rather than being forced. Don't fancy dragging an unwilling bride to the altar any more than I fancy sharp claws. Force is what has her reacting violently. She wants the choice, I gather." Gazing at his cup, forlorn, he said dejectedly, "Drat if I know how to give her *choice.*"

"To choose you, eh? Most asinine idea I've ever heard."

"I rather think I cut a dashing figure, not that she's noticed with her heels dug into the ground. If she could see me as a friend rather than foe, I could woo her into falling head over heels for me. I'm afraid

I'm forever a foe now. I'm the man who trapped her into marriage. She'll never forgive me, not with the trappings cinched."

Mr. Slade tipped his cup towards him with a grunt, confirming it was empty. "You've had time enough to woo her."

"I've had time enough to fall for *her*. I'm at a loss for how to remove her veil of resentment. If she could but see me without the bindings of the betrothal…" Rafe affected his best lost boy impression, followed swiftly by a wistful, wide-eyed plea. "Do you have any suggestions, sir? Some way to convince her to choose me rather than forcing my attentions?"

Slade harrumphed. More to himself than to Rafe, he mumbled, "Don't much care what she wants when I know what's best for her. The sooner she recognizes that, the better, but she's stubborn to a fault. Didn't know you were a green lad. More's the pity." Harrumphing again, he stared into his empty cup, lost in thought, making inarticulate murmurs before muttering, "Hard lot in life, she proclaimed. Painted me a right villain. *My* fault she never took in society, befriending no one 'cept that milksop Thorpe. *My* fault she's dragged here, forced there." His next words were grumbled with such unintelligible ferocity Rafe could not make them out. Then louder, he said, "S'pose I could grant her request."

With all the alarm his words could muster, Rafe exclaimed, "To sever the betrothal? No, sir, I'll not have it. Gave you my word."

"No, no, you're not following me, daft article. If I granted her request *in theory*, you could have, let's say, two weeks to win her favor. If you can't do that in two weeks, I'm having the banns called, and that's that."

"An illusion?" Rafe asked dumbly. Tricky business, this. If he failed to win her affection…

"Genius of me, if I do say so myself. Frankly tired of her playing me the villain. I sympathize with you there, young Fitz-Stephens. Don't mistake my meaning—the betrothal is rock solid. Only my daughter will *think* otherwise." Grumbling, Slade added under his breath, "Chance to choose. Daftest notion I've ever heard." Then aloud, "Two weeks. If you can't win her favor by then, you're dimmer than I thought. Point of fact, if you're that dimwitted, I may change my mind altogether and call on Lord Karras."

Taken by surprise yet again, Rafe gulped the coffee.

Before he could reply, Mr. Slade trumpeted a laugh. "Only jesting. I wouldn't have that dandy for all the titles in England. Prissy tulip, that one. Now, about this ride to call on Sir Courtney."

The walk back to the dower house was overlong, his feet taking him a circuitous route to give him more time to think. As it was, this was the only time to himself he would have now that he had promised to ride with Mr. Slade to Eurwendin. He had half an hour to change into his riding raiment.

With only a sleepless night to fuel his day, his focus waned. After the assembly ended, he had devoted much of the night hours to preparing his request to Mr. Slade, which had been a fruitless waste of time, as it turned out. Then he had risen early, and despite the light drizzle glazing the windows, he had attended to a morning jog to clear his thoughts, the mist carrying the earthy tang of wet grass. Throughout his jog, he had oscillated between brokenhearted and confident he could mend this. All he had to do was convince Mr. Slade to offer her the freedom of choice, and then Rafe could prove to her he loved her with sincerity, not reluctance, and hopefully vice versa. He had seen infatuation in her eyes. He was confident she felt, at the very least, romantically inclined towards him. Now, he needed a new plan. If he had misjudged her, the noose would tighten at the end of two weeks. *Amor et melle et felle est fecundissimus.* Love is rich with both honey and venom.

He returned to the dower house in perfect time to bid Headley and Diana farewell, along with his expressed hope that Thorpe liked dogs—which awarded him a playful punch in the arm.

The house was quiet when Genevieve returned after a morning in the village. Had she known the evening would run so unexpected of a course, she would not have promised her sisters to help with the postfrolic cleanup, not that either of her sisters had been of much service, Cecilia spending the time whinging with new friends and Theia wandering off to pluck tree leaves for her journal.

What Genevieve wanted now was to wash, change, and rest.

The evening had gone from bad to worse. A moment of romance, *the* moment of romance when she was positive Rafe would confess his love for her, had turned sour, his confession being of resignation rather than words of affection to match her own heart's desires. Then the disaster of begging her father for sympathy. She should have waited until morning. The memory of his flared nostrils, his heavy eyebrows, his flinging accusations of her being a disloyal daughter, all rushed back with a heavy weight to her chest.

With hand over heart, she slumped up the stairs to her bedchamber.

Genevieve had not been disloyal. Was pleading for a reprieve so that she might know Rafe's true affections evidence of disloyalty? What did he care if there was genuine affection or not, he had put to her. It was the match that was important, and besides, if he did not do his duty by affiancing her to Fitz-Stephens, the two maids who had witnessed a gentleman in the bedchamber would be all too happy to wag tongues about Miss Slade's loose morals. With spilled tears, Genevieve had spit back at him that her reputation did not matter when they would move again to yet another village with nameless faces.

She had meant the last, and yet she had not. She *wanted* to marry Rafe. But not by force. Not if it meant marrying a man *resigned* to like her, never to love her genuinely.

Genevieve sighed.

Papa was right. She was disloyal. Her saving grace was that Rafe did not know the depth of her affection nor did he know she had gone to her father. He need never know. With this advantage, she could turn the tables, pretend her reaction at the assembly had been but a trifle. Now, they could move forward with *resignation*. In time, she could hope his love would grow, not because he forced it but because she would be the best wife, the most obedient wife, and he would become fond of her, more so over the years. Yes, this was the right course. Was this not the way of most marriages? At least she had the advantage of being a little in love with her bridegroom.

A knock on her bedchamber door disrupted her woolgathering.

"Yes?" She had not washed yet, not changed, only made it from the door to the bedside, where she now sat, staring at the wall opposite.

The door parted, and a maid's cap appeared. "Mr. Slade's sent for you, miss. In his study."

Her pulse thumped erratically. *The banns.* Now that he had thought over her pleas, he would demand the banns.

Voice cracking, she mustered, "I'll be there promptly."

Chapter 29

R afe read the brief missive more than a dozen times. With each read, his grin broadened.

Mr. Fitz-Stephens,

I hope you'll excuse this breach of decorum, for it is improper to correspond with a man not one's betrothed. Read that again, and you'll understand the reason I am writing. My father has agreed to dissolve the betrothal. We have succeeded! I cannot speak to what changed his mind, but I believe my willingness to face him and share my sentiments has moved his sympathies. We are free! I thank you for being a consummate gentleman.

Your friend,
Miss Slade

She did not shoo him to London, mention choosing someone more suited, or any other possible point that might have persuaded him away from her. This was not a dismissive letter. On its face was a notice to quit, her official cry off. But Rafe read much more into the letter, and what he read pleased him.

He had a plan. A dashing plan. A plan to have her swooning into his arms by the end of two weeks. Whatever apprehension he had after the interview with Slade relaxed. Now to put his plan into action. Oh, what a devilishly splendid plan!

Monday morning, Genevieve tripped down the stairs with gay abandon. Well, the descent was far more sedate to observant eyes, but from Genevieve's perspective, she held a distinct pep in her step. Freedom felt glorious! Like a hot brick on a cold day or the sun on one's cheeks after a swim. For the first time in her life, she could *choose*. If she did not wish to marry a stranger, she was not obliged. If she wished to marry for love, she could do so, and now she would *know* it was love, true rather than manufactured.

And so, down the stairs she flew, a cageless bird, on the romp to the lake. Hand on the banister, she pivoted towards the entrance hall, bumping headlong into Cecilia.

"Where are you bound, and may I join?" Cecilia asked, looping her arm around Genevieve's.

"If you wish. I'm for the lake." Flashing a mischievous grin, she added, "If I don't return with a fresh row of freckles, I'll have failed my mission."

"The *lake*! But that's nearly five miles away!" Slipping her hand free, Cecilia tutted. She turned towards the stairs only to spin around to face Genevieve, her lips curling into a smirk. "If I wish? Think you're *so* clever. You knew I would say no but invited me to divert suspicion. You're meeting Mr. Fitz-Stephens! A lover's tryst! I should have known. No one has the right to look so provokingly happy *unless* they're bound for a lover's tryst. I'm right, aren't I?"

Returning her sister's smirk, Genevieve corrected, "You are *not*. For, you see, dearest sister mine, Papa has absolved me. I'm *free* to do as I wish."

With narrowed gaze, Cecilia eyed Genevieve queerly. "What are you saying?"

"I'm no longer *forced* to marry Mr. Fitz-Stephens. Granted, I *can*, if I wish, but Papa will not force me."

"Piffle. Papa did no such thing. If he did, he's fooling! And what daft cow would cry off with Mr. Fitz-Stephens as the bridegroom?"

"No fooling. I am *free*." She took two steps towards the entrance hall before Cecilia caught her arm.

"You mean *Mr. Fitz-Stephens* is free. Free to look about him? Is he really?" Cecilia's eyes twinkled. "*You* may walk to the lake, but *I'm* walking to the dower house. And don't you dare say I can't, or I'll call your bluff about Papa."

Lifting her hem, Cecilia skipped past Genevieve, her destination, presumably, the dower house. Genevieve shrugged. She waited a few minutes to avoid bumping into her sister again, using the time to don her bonnet and tie the ribbons beneath her chin.

When she stepped out of the house, none other than Cecilia caught up to her, having stalked the front door to pounce.

"Why?" Cecilia questioned. "Why would Papa break the betrothal?"

"Because I begged him to. It was a farce from the beginning, and I finally had the courage to stand up to him and tell him that very thing. He listened because he knows I'm right."

"Right? About *what*? It was a brilliant match!"

"But it wasn't *my* choice," Genevieve defended. "I think we should all have the courage to stand up to him. We always do what he wants. We obey his every order. How many more times is he going to drag us across England because *he* wants it? We've been his marionettes too long. I consider my defiance in your favor and Theia's because he's not likely to compromise either of you into a match now."

A frown tugged at Cecilia's expression of curiosity. "You're the most selfish person I know."

Genevieve's mouth fell agape. "I'm *what*?"

"Selfish. Do you ever listen to yourself? 'Oh, woe is me, forced to tour the countryside, forced to live a life of luxury, forced to see England from one end to the other, forced into an understanding with a Nonpareil, forced—'"

"Stop," she interrupted with a quelling glance. "You paint our life in watercolor, Cecilia, and that is not how it has been. We move into houses not our own, living like veritable gypsies, never staying long enough to befriend—"

"No, that's *you*. You never bother. You're too busy pouting to befriend anyone. I, on the other hand, have the pleasure of not one or two friends but dozens. I *love* living like a gypsy, as you say. And if Papa's choice for you, regardless of his reasons, is an Incomparable Nonesuch of Quality, then I shall beg him to compromise me into a match by whatever means necessary."

"You wouldn't say that if you were *forced* to marry a stranger."

"I suppose you're right," Cecilia conceded. "I would most assuredly feel persecuted, then I would pout about it, blame Papa, and cry off."

Bristling, Genevieve retorted, her voice tremulous, "I'm sorry you think me so horrid a person."

Cecilia sighed. "I don't. You know I don't. I simply don't understand you. If the sun were shining, you would portend rain. From my purview, we should enjoy the sun until it rains, and when it does, we may dance in Heaven's waterfall." With a look of pitying condescension, she offered, "I'm happy for you if you're happy. After all, now I can hope your loss is my gain."

On that, Cecilia turned away and headed for the dower house, leaving Genevieve to her thoughts.

Genevieve did not begin her journey back to the house for some hours later. The lake water had been cool to her bare feet, the perfect juxtaposition to the warm sun on her skin. The bonnet had been tossed aside, along with her fichu, stockings, and shoes. Her only regret was not bringing a linen sheet on which to lie, for the grass had been damp from Sunday's rain. It did not matter a whit, though. She expected no callers and would not see a soul on the walk home.

Her intention had been to celebrate her freedom. The actuality of the outing, however, had been meditative. Cecilia often spouted silliness, and if that silliness antagonized her sisters, all the better, and so nothing Cecilia had said should have troubled Genevieve. Spoken, then forgotten.

Except one trifling fact.

What Cecilia said recalled something Rafe had said. At the time, she had thought him blaming her for her unhappiness and friendless state, but now, she did not believe that was what he meant, not at all. He had tried to prevail upon her a different kind of choice, the choice of clarity, propitiousness, the ability to see in every moment an auspicious opportunity.

After a morning's meditation, she understood, or thought she did.

Understanding and accepting were different beasts, however. Knowing she must make the best of undesirable situations did not make them any more desirable, but there was so little in life of which she held control. Thus was the lot of the female sex, she supposed. But did that lack of control dictate her sensibility? Must it? She had thought herself fighting the control, the warrior who refused to be cowed, but on reflection, she saw it quite the opposite — she allowed herself to be stripped of happiness. And who cared if she was happy or unhappy? No one except herself. Hitherto, *that* thought had always contributed more unhappiness. If she and she alone could allay unhappiness, why not *do it*?

Had she drawn this conclusion earlier, she would not have gone to her father. She would have accepted Rafe's offer. At this moment, they could have been riding together across estate grounds, him courting her favor. What a fool she had been! There was no use boohooing over her decision now, nor of all the friends she had missed meeting over the years by not exerting herself. The way forward was what mattered.

She had broken the betrothal not to split from Rafe, only to give them the choice to fall in love, or not, and she had hoped he might wish to pursue her with genuine adoration. Cecilia's words haunted her, though. Her actions might have unintended consequences. With his freedom, he could look about him. Who could blame him if he did? *She* had not made herself appealing. She had made a point to do quite the opposite to repel him. Who wished to pursue a prudish and combative woman? *Oh, Genevieve, you fool!* Not once had she given him a reason to love *her*.

Well, she had a plan now. The cool waters of the lake had set her right. She had a plan. A dashing plan. A plan to have him swooning in her arms! She need only put the plan into action. Oh, what a splendid plan!

With these happy aspirations, she set off back to the manor.

She would need to sneak through the hidden passage Rafe had shown her to avoid Mama's censure. In one hand, she carried her shoes, stockings, and fichu, in her other, her bonnet. Her walking gown was hopefully not beyond repair, however noticeable the grass stains and mud-coated hem. It was all so *freeing*. How glorious was life! How bountiful nature! The earth squelched between her bare toes, downy soft.

Ahead, the Priory came into view over the brow of the hill. Blithely, she ascended the gentle slope, invigorated by the walk, not all of which had been traversed barefooted, but here on the well-scythed lawn, indubitably. Her thoughts turned to Mr. Thorpe and Diana.

Just so, the silhouette of a horse and rider crested, approaching from the Priory.

Papa would lecture her for traipsing the countryside as she was, but not even accusations of being an urchin could ruin her mood. In anticipation of his mortified expression, she swung her bonnet with glee and quickened her pace to greet him. Only when it was too late to divert her path did she realize the rider was not Papa.

The expression she had expected Papa to wear overcame her features instead: sheer horror tainted her brow. *Rafe Fitz-Stephens* trotted towards her.

In all his majesty glory, he slowed his horse, came to a prancing stop, and doffed his beaver hat in greeting. "You're looking in rude health, Miss Slade, in fine fettle."

Genevieve mouthed a silent reply, her jaw working as a fish out of water. *Good Lord in Heaven!* What had happened since Friday? Had she been this blind, or...

Mounted on his trusted steed was an Adonis. Never in her life had she beheld such magnificence, nor buckskins quite so snug. Her eyes bulged. His buff buckskins hugged his thighs like a second skin, leaving no doubt to the strength and musculature beneath. His top boots shone with a reflective gleam, so well fitted about his calves, one knew with certainty the gentleman would never require padding for evening attire. His waistcoat and coat were molded to his frame, accentuating powerful shoulders and a broad chest, the ensemble quite *point-de-vice*, especially the meticulously knotted cravat. She knew little of cravat tying, but she knew enough to recognize a superior neckcloth and the expert hands to have wielded it.

His golden curls were windswept into luxurious temptation, seducing one's fingers to feel their silken texture. And while she admired those locks, they were tucked away beneath the curved brim of the hat as he returned hat to head.

Genevieve's eyes met Rafe's. His Nordic blues flashed mischief. Patiently, he awaited her response, a deepening smirk drawing ample attention to the naughty cleft in his chin.

Mortification of all mortifications! She had not replied! Like a tongue-tied green girl, she stood gaping at him. Her cheeks warmed.

His horse blew a snort, impatient, unlike his rider.

"What are you doing here?" she demanded querulously.

With a flash of pearly whites, he said, "I live here."

"Well, yes, but that doesn't signify." Her cheeks emblazoned from warm to inferno.

"I rather think it does." His voice trembled with a repressed laugh.

"Oh! You are an insufferable man. You know perfectly well what I mean. What are you doing *here*?"

"Riding, my good neighbor. Alfgar fancied a stretch of his legs, as did I."

Her pulse raced at the attention he drew to his legs, the muscles flexing as he kept Alfgar steady.

"Tetchy today, Miss Slade?"

"I—well—I—of course not! I'm perfectly content, I'll have you know. More than content. Deliriously happy. I am merely caught by surprise."

"Mmm. Yes, so I gathered." The playful arch of a brow spoke volumes as his gaze swept over her. "You've been kissed by more than the sun today, I see. How envious must be Helios." With that cryptic comment, he tipped his hat, bid her a good day, then waltzed off.

In high dudgeon to be caught so unawares, she marched to the house and up to her bedchamber by way of the front door, entrance hall, and main stairs, not caring if she met Mama on the way. With a toss of her limp bonnet and fichu onto a chair and her shoes and stockings onto the floor, she plopped into the chair before her dressing table.

One look in the mirror sent her shrieking into her dressing room and tugging at the bellrope. A thick streak of mud marred her cheek from one corner of her lips up to her temple, disappearing into her hairline where a rogue leaf burrowed into her curls as ostentatiously as an ostrich plume.

Burying her face in her hands, she laughed herself silly.

Chapter 30

Tuesday brought no occasion to enact her plan. The rain showers did little to help. Now it was Wednesday, and already her splendidly dashing plan was failing—how could it be otherwise when her first encounter with Rafe had been so disastrous? She must, must, must initiate the next meeting to gain advantage.

A fine declaration but not so easily seen to fruition.

Genevieve glanced sidelong at Viscount Karras and exhaled her boredom.

"And then, Miss Slade, I said to him, 'My good man, that is *not* the Karras Fold. To master this delicate work of art takes subtle nuance which you do not possess.'" Karras chortled with a flounce of his hand to invite Genevieve to share his laugh.

"A witty rejoinder, my lord, to be sure," she said flatly.

When Papa granted her freedom, she had not expected him to invite a suitor in replacement. Sneaky of him. Then, she should have known better. This *was* Papa, after all. He had cleverly disguised his scheme by entertaining Lord Karras. But who should he ask to join them in the garden room before *inconveniently* being called away? Genevieve. Of course. *Show him the garden*, Papa had prompted, promising to return post-haste.

Right. This was a coup if ever Genevieve witnessed.

His Lordship's voice drifted into her thoughts. "Are you aware if Mr. Fitz-Stephens — second son, not Squire — is due to the Priory soon?"

Jerking her attention to her companion, she stuttered, "I... I... pardon?"

A flick of the wrist towards the garden room windows. "Mr. Fitz-Stephens. I had hoped to discuss with him the procurement of a horse."

"I'm not privy to the gentleman's plans, I'm afraid."

He croaked a laugh. "I should hope not. How droll you are, Miss Slade! His card, rather. Has he expressed his intention to call?"

"Papa would know better than I."

"I should not have troubled you. The anticipation has me forgetting my attentions to *you*. You, and only you, should receive my undivided conversation. You'll forgive that I'm excessively diverted by a horse? It's a deliciously handsome beast, I'm led to believe — strong bones, smooth lines, flawless flesh."

Ignoring whatever the dip in his voice insinuated, Genevieve turned her attention back to the garden as she assured, "There is nothing to forgive, my lord."

The sad truth was she would love nothing more than to talk about horses, but not with Lord Karras.

"Ah, too right, but I dare say it is in poor taste to divulge my lust for horseflesh to a young lady who must know nothing of sport or animal. Now, let us speak of more personal matters. I fear I only have the pleasure of your company for a short breadth. Tell me, do you paint?"

His tone implied *paint* was something more suggestive than watercolors. Genevieve bared her teeth in a grimaced smile. Where, oh where, was her father? And for that matter, where was Mama or Cecilia or Theia or *anyone*? She would trade places in a heartbeat.

As she thought this, relief was in reach—one of the garden room doors opened.

Papa stepped out, followed by Rafe. Her heart skipped a beat.

He was as majestic as he had been during their previous encounter, dressed for riding again, not for a social call, the ensemble different, the buckskins a slightly darker shade, but the effect was no less startling. She knew her face was flushed. Thankfully, she could blame the garden sun.

Next to her, Lord Karras whisked a vial from one of his pockets and nudged it towards her. Perplexed, she stared at the vial in his hand.

"The sun, Miss Slade. I dare say I've been remiss. I've kept you overlong out of doors. Have a whiff to restore your nerves before you swoon. I shall see you into the garden room."

Had he not been so earnest, she would have cracked a laugh. He offered smelling salts to revive her from the heat-induced blush. Oh, for heaven's sake! It was too much. Genevieve bit her bottom lip to keep from cackling.

Oh… Oh! Oh, but wait. *Oh, Genevieve, where is your head!* Her plan! Her splendidly devilish plan!

She seized the moment. Clawing at the air, she clasped Lord Karras' arm with one hand and flung the other to her forehead—knocking her bonnet askew. "Lord Karras. I fear I shall faint! Will you catch me if I —" She softened her knees into a carefully maneuvered swoon — directly into his arms.

With her eyelids fluttering closed, she could not see what happened around her, but she could hear all too clearly the voices of Papa and Rafe closing in. Lord Karras held her so awkwardly, she suspected he might drop her. She clung to him.

A jocular voice jested, "Hands full already, Karras? Vigorous business, the petticoat-line."

"A little help, please," Lord Karras supplicated. "I've readied the hartshorn, but I can't shift her. She's fainted dead away."

A chuckle drew near her before supple arms encircled her waist, replacing those of Lord Karras. Minty breath tickled her ear. So arousing was the caress, she nearly forgot herself and leapt away. By sheer will, she held fast to her charade. Nevertheless, the minty breath was not fooled.

As Lord Karras fumbled to open the vial, the breath whispered, "If your intent is to seduce with feminine wiles, it's working."

Just as the vial inched towards her nose, she swatted at the hands holding her and jumped to safety, ready to swing at the coxcomb that called himself a *gentleman*.

"Hurrah," Lord Karras said, relieved. "Never leave home without hartshorn. A lady's dearest friend, my mother always says."

Genevieve reoriented herself. Her plan. Must stick to the plan. *Do not allow him to knock you akilter, Genevieve!*

One hand to heart, she reached the other to touch Lord Karras' coat sleeve. "Oh, Lord Karras. How can I ever thank you? You are kindness itself, the best of men! The heat, as you said…. I was quite overcome. May I take your arm? For safety."

Tucking away his vial and looking inordinately pleased with himself, he sneaked a smug smile before offering his arm to Genevieve.

Papa frowned his disapproval—curious since Genevieve thought he ought to be pleased with the turn of events. Rafe, that foul man, waggled his eyebrows. Oof! If she could punch his arm, she would!

"Lord Karras and I have been admiring the gardens," she bragged. "So *wonderful* of a time we've shared together. Before I was overcome by the sun, you were saying something so witty I could not keep from laughing." She laughed in demonstration. "What was it you were saying, *my* lord? You had me *swooning* from your wit."

Chest puffed, the viscount said, "I was remarking my lust for Mr. Fitz-Stephens' arrival."

Genevieve spluttered a laugh and gripped the arm tighter. "Oh, there's that humor of yours. Oh my. Yes, your interest in *horses*. And *then*, you shared with me how pleasurable was my company."

"I dare say, I was thinking to myself I must invite the Slades, those same-said Slades related to the oh-so-respectable Slades of Somerset, to dinner—my parents are due in a sennight. My family has expectations, you must understand, and I would find the antithesis of those expectations the most diverting of all should we dine together with my father, in particular."

Gritting her teeth, she eyed him. The antithesis? The *antithesis*!

Rafe cleared his throat and said, "I believe what our illustrious viscount means to say is he favors a spirited lady."

"Too right," agreed the viscount, raising his quizzing glass.

Papa tutted. "Too much sun affects the senses. If you'll excuse us, Genevieve, Mr. Fitz-Stephens and I will escort Lord Karras to the stableyard. There's a horse needing our attention."

Her companion extracted himself from her grasp, then bowed. "A pleasure, Miss Slade. I hope to call again soon, should my company be welcome."

With a darting glance to Rafe, she said to the viscount, "*Always*, my lord."

Rafe flipped his hat on his head and winked before setting off to follow the other two gentlemen.

Before they had reached the edge of the garden, she fled — with ladylike leisure until she reached the garden room — upstairs to her bedchamber to spy into her mirror.

Ah HA! About time!

She preened before the glass. Oh, she looked *divine*. He must have noticed. He could not have missed noticing. Her cheeks were rouged by a natural flush, her hair coiffed without a pin out of place, her bonnet angled just so — only teasingly askew from her faux faint — and her figure showing quite to advantage in her afternoon gown. No mud on her cheek today. No, sir. Today, she looked irresistible! She blew a kiss to her reflection.

One ankle crossed over the other, shoes tucked beneath the sofa, Rafe lounged in languor in Gran's parlor. In his hands was a case transcript. In his mind was a vision of loveliness.

His grand plan had been set into motion, but it would take the full two weeks to see the effect. What he needed was more contact. Attraction was one thing, love another. Initiating encounters that were not overtly contrived was the challenge, but somehow, he needed to pick up the pace. One encounter every other day would not accomplish his goal, not within two weeks. Already Thursday, his time was running short.

If he was not mistaken, his prospective bride had hatched a plan of her own, although he was unsure of her intentions — induce jealousy? Unnecessary since Rafe was already invested. It was *he* who was trying to win *her*, after all. Still, her behavior had proved not only amusing but heartening. The show had been for his benefit, of that he was certain. Then, could he be so certain? Truly? She thought herself free to make a choice. Did it follow her choice would be Rafe? All his smug certainty dipped into doubt. He needed more encounters, and that was that.

Pencil in hand, he added to the sketch in the corner of the transcript — a leaf tangled in her curls. The parlor door clicked open. Rafe flipped the document over with a start. When he turned to see his visitor, he dropped the pencil.

Genevieve swept into the room.

The temperature beneath his cravat increased to volcanic, and his heart pounded.

A vision of loveliness.

Think straight, Rafe. Don't be distracted.

Tucking the document beneath his glass of claret, he retrieved his shoes with languid movement, arranging his features as he did so to affect blithe confidence. Pity he was not attired smartly. Nothing he owned lacked quality, but he could not be sure a lamentable wrinkle or two had not pressed into the back of his coat from his lazy lounging, nor was his at-home raiment the first stare of fashion. This did *not* aid his plan. But what could he do?

Shoes returned to feet, he rose with a flourishing bow before flashing his guest a roguish grin.

Whatever he had just been thinking vanished with a *poof.*

His eyes widened.

His lips parted.

With supercilious ennui, she looked about the room, chin raised, mouth pouting in a moue. "Am I early?"

He waved for her to join him in the adjacent chair, then resumed his seat. "To quicken my pulse?" Leaning back, Rafe stretched his arm across the top of the sofa, taking her measure with a stroll of his half-lidded gaze. "I'd say you're right on time."

"You'll not provoke me, Mr. Fitz-Stephens, not today. I'm quite impervious." Curling her lips into a sardonic smile, she added, "Today is my fencing lesson."

"Already *en garde* with a silver tongue. And if I should feint my advances?"

"No need to be coy, or you'll find yourself outmatched with my parries."

Tongue in cheek, he leered wantonly. "Am *I* to be your fencing instructor, then?"

"Don't flatter yourself. Mrs. Fitz-Stephens is to teach me. You're merely my rehearsal match."

"A practice engagement? How appropriate."

"Touché, Mr. Fitz-Stephens."

If she thought him in command of the situation, she gave no indication, nothing like when he took her by surprise on her return from a ramble, perfectly in control of the occasion, and she had known it. No prudish airs today, no gaping stares, no wandering eyes, not even vexation or exasperation; on the contrary, she met his gaze with challenging invitation, a knowing smile dimpling her cheeks.

He was undone, her obedient servant.

Even the prim miss he had met yesterday at the Priory, the delicate wisp in lilac muslin and lace who depended on a gentleman and his salts for revival was nowhere to be seen. In her place, perched on the edge of the chair was a vivacious nymph, her wild curls bound by a wide bandeau — the escape artists tantalizing and teasing as they traced the curve of her face in cunning coils — and her ensemble sumptuously sporting.

The gown itself was nothing unusual, peach with a high waist, punctuated by half-boots, but the spencer drew his attention and admiration. The worsted jacket hugged her figure, the sleeves trimmed short, just below her shoulders, with peach undersleeves reaching to her wrists in a loose, breezy gauze. The perfect spencer for a sportswoman to allow for freedom of movement while maintaining modesty.

A lump rose in Rafe's throat at the word *modesty* when her curves tormented him. He rather thought that was the point. She had dressed in sporting provocation for him. But how selfish of a presumption. Naturally, she would wear sporting attire for a fencing lesson, nothing to do with him.

If, and this was a considerable *if*, teasing him was the point — wishful thinking — she may be disappointed to learn it was not the curves that most tempted him, at least not entirely. It was *she* who tempted him. She looked more herself than he had seen her yet. A woman ready to spar. *That* had him feverish beneath his cravat.

Under his breath, he said, "*Timeo Danaos et dona ferentes.*"

"What was that? You should not mumble in the presence of a lady, sir."

"I fear Greeks, even if they bring gifts."

Chortling, she said, "No need to fear, then, for I am neither Greek nor have I brought a gift."

"Oh, I rather think you have."

Her eyes flashed, but she did not give away her reaction. "Did Lord Karras purchase the horse?"

"I see what you did there," he said with a chuckle. "*Ito vero.* Yes, indeed, he did. My father was pleased. Another feather in *your* father's cap for arranging the deal."

"I gathered Papa was arranging a different bargain in the process." One corner of her mouth dimpled at her cleverness.

"Bargaining in hearts or reputations?" He nibbled at her bait.

"As elegant a dresser as he is a dancer," she said suggestively. "Lord Karras, that is, not Papa."

"A shame he's not as skilled a rider."

"That is a bare-knuckled blow, Mr. Fitz-Stephens. Not everyone can have as fine a seat as yours." With a little gasp at her slip, she pursed her lips and blushed.

Rafe assumed the memory of their mounted encounter was fresh in her mind. Although he wore linen pantaloons rather than his buckskins, he chose that moment to cross one leg over the other, satisfied when she stole a glance in her periphery.

"Should we search for your mother?" She looked towards the open door of the parlor. "I can't think I was quite so early."

"Early enough to apprise me of your presence," he teased. "Now I'll know you're on the grounds wielding a sword. You expect me not to peek? If I'm to score a touch, I must learn when to recognize my adversary's feints."

"You are *not* a gentleman." Two rosy circles rouged her cheeks.

He feigned an innocent look. "No parry? I'm disappointed."

"To peek would be the height of impertinence. It is my first lesson, you understand." With a bashful look beneath her lashes, she quipped, "A worthy adversary need not peek, for he would know to anticipate all advances."

Chapter 31

G enevieve tugged the shawl around her shoulders to stave off the chill. The hidden snug was an inexplicably drafty room. Despite the curtains drawn open, no friendly moonlight shone, the dark room lit by a single candelabra. It was sufficient. She burrowed into the fireside chair, her knees drawn up, a book open for her reading pleasure.

From time to time, voices drifted into the snug, distant but inebriated enough to be heard two rooms over. Papa was entertaining. A gentleman's evening, he called it. Thankfully, they were at the card table in the games room rather than in the billiard room, which in this monstrosity of a mansion were two distinct rooms, as were the stag saloon and smoking parlor, not to mention the anteroom with its private entrance to the library mezzanine.

As interruptive as the voices were to her reading, they brought a smile. Papa was enjoying himself. He loved nothing more than the company of fellow gentlemen, more so with a festive spirit and wagers laid bare. Despite being a goer, he struggled to make alliances. Unlike Genevieve, he tried. He put himself about as much as he could, but neighbors were either wary of a stranger or, she suspected, found him too obsequious. Simply put, he tried too hard. That Lord Karras had called said more for the aristocrat's desire for a horse than his interest in forming an alliance with Mr. Roland Slade. Sir Courtney appeared to like him, though. And then there was Mr. Anthony Fitz-Stephens.

The party this evening consisted of those two men, as well as the Fitz-Stephens boys, Rafe included.

The ladies were not invited. Gentlemen only, Papa had huffed. Once Cecilia got wind that Mr. Rafe Fitz-Stephens would be present, Genevieve knew not a moment's peace.

One of Cecilia's arguments being, "I could pretend to have left something in the games room—an excuse to enter uninvited. And how breathtaking I'll look in your lace and satin!"

Another being, "We could fancy a game of billiards, and so enraptured by the sound of the balls, they'll wish to join us, or at least Rafe Fitz-Stephens and his brothers will, not Papa and his friends," the last said with a wrinkle of her pert nose.

With a new scheme every quarter hour, Genevieve had taken to hiding, first the garden room, then the parlor, after that the library, then her bedchamber…. Cecilia found her every time. Until now. Cecilia did not know about the snug. Genevieve wished Cecilia likewise did not know about the betrothal's end. As relieving as it was to be free of Papa's force, Genevieve regretted telling Cecilia. By that token, she had decided not to tell anyone else yet, or at least not fan about the fact.

"Do you think I could compromise a betrothal if I sneaked into his bedchamber as he did yours?" Cecilia had asked with all the impertinence and indelicacy of a girl of fifteen.

A pity there were no nunneries to which she could send her sister.

She turned a page in her book, read the first line, then realized she had not paid attention to the previous page. Flipping back, she began reading again with more attention.

The spirit of Miss Margland was as haughty as her intellects were weak; and her disposition was so querulous, that, in her constant suspicion of humiliation, she seemed always looking for an affront, and ready primed for a contest.

Genevieve huffed. "In my defense, at least my intellect is not weak," she said aloud to the empty room. "I sympathize with the inequitable characterization, Miss Margland. You've been unfairly maligned. Querulous and looking for an affront, indeed. Fanny Burney has done you a grave injustice." With a harrumph, she continued to read from *Camilla*.

Mid-way through the next page, a *thump* and *scrape* drew her attention. A quick look about the room confirmed she was alone. She strained to listen. *Shuffle, scuffle, scrape.* Rats? She shuddered, drawing the shawl tighter. In the distance, the guffaws of the gentlemen could still be heard. Closer, just behind her, were the softer sounds.

Unfurling from her folded comfort, she stole a glance behind the chair.

She shrieked, then clasped a hand over her mouth.

Rafe leaned against the paneled wall, taking in her dishabille.

"How... what... *why*?" she stammered.

"Hidden panel," he said with a hollow tap against the wall's recess, "should answer the *how*—which should not surprise you, but I'm simply delighted it did. *What* is more difficult to answer. To which *what* do you refer? *Why* is easier. I came to retrieve a book."

"A book," she echoed, struggling to gain her bearings.

How did he always manage to catch her at the most inopportune moments?

"Indeed. A book. Why else should I sneak in here?" His eyes twinkled mischief in the candlelight.

"I thought you were gaming. What could you possibly want with a book?" She narrowed her gaze. "Are you foxed?"

"Not I, fair maiden. I cannot say the same for Otis, who is acting quite the young buck this evening, and I suspect will have a head for his troubles in the morning. In his cups already and nowhere near midnight. Noel, at least, is behaving with a modicum more respectability, but I suspect that'll only last for one or two more games before he, too, succumbs to Dionysus' seduction. I'll say this much for them—they'll only do it once."

Ignoring everything else he had said, she probed, "What book?"

"You question my intention?" The face of innocence stared back at her with large, round eyes. Then, with impish transformation, his features sparked into a devilish grin. "Would you be flattered or affronted if I used the excuse as a ruse to seek you out?"

She tossed her gaze to the ceiling. "Now I know you truly are seeking a book. Carry on, sir." Cozying back into her chair, she stared at the next page as though enthralled.

The chuckle behind her was so close, she squeaked a *meep*.

Rafe leaned over her, his arm cradling the top of the chair. "Alone in a secret room. Think of the sundry ways I could take advantage of the opportunity."

She inhaled sharply, then wished she had not, for her nostrils filled with the romance of his rose and citrus perfume.

Closing her book, she rose and set it in the chair. "Don't be a numpty. We both know you are too much of a gentleman to do anything untoward."

"If I recall correctly, the last we spoke, you informed me I was *not* a gentleman. An invitation if ever I heard one." Arm still draped over the top of the chair, he stepped around and closer to her.

She sidestepped to one of the bookshelves. "Now, let me see. Have you come for *The Sorrows of Young Werther*? Or perhaps *Candide*? Oh, here's one by Tyndale on equitation, which you ought to read if you expect to keep pace with me on horseback. No, no, this is more your style." She retrieved from the shelf a leather-bound book and waved it. "*Thomas Shandy*, am I right?"

"Successful fencing lesson, I take it?" His eyes danced with laughter. "I've come for Thomas Bewick's *History of British Birds*."

"Birds? What a Banbury tale!"

"Not in the least. I've recently taken up ornithology."

"Identify any rare birds lately?"

He waggled his eyebrows. "One fine lady bird."

Pursing her lips, she shelved Shandy, searched for the Bewick book, then shoved it at him with a quelling stare.

When he tried to take it, she held fast. "Do you not mean a *bird of prey*?"

He tugged the book free. "That's my girl."

After a sharp bark of laughter, she quipped, "I am, emphatically, *not* — "

A toss of the book onto the chair atop *Camilla*, he lunged forward with the grace of a seasoned swordsman and pulled her against him with a single sweep of his arm about her waist.

She gasped, her hands instinctively pressing against his waistcoat. Beneath her palms, she could feel the beat of his heart.

He leaned closer until the whisper of his words caressed her cheek. "Aren't you?"

His smirk lingered, but his eyes searched hers, the blue of his irises dark in the dimly lit room, his pupils hard and penetrating. Rafe dipped his gaze to her lips and lingered. As she relaxed against him, her heart in her throat and her pulse racing, he inched away, releasing his hold with lingering allure.

In one fell movement, he snatched the book and strode to the hidden panel. Just before he ducked through the passage, he turned back to admire her so openly, her knees nearly caved. Then, with a wink, he was gone.

Chapter 32

Rafe surveyed the lay before him. A veritable feast, really. Fit for a fairy queen. Cook had done right by him today. Propped on his elbow, one leg stretched, one knee bent, he lounged on the picnic linen and waited, poised in his second finest riding attire. A few yards away, Alfgar grazed at the edge of the woods. There was no way to know how soon she would happen by, especially if she extended her ride, but he was certain of her destination. To occupy himself, he flipped through the bird book.

Less than half an hour later, he heard the unmistakable thunder of hooves. Alfgar's ears perked, as aware of their prospective company as his companion.

After snatching a biscuit, Rafe trained his attention on the book. Just on the edge of where clearing met forest, the new arrival snorted and shook her mane — the horse that was, although Rafe would not be surprised if the rider's reaction was similar. He nibbled the biscuit and turned a page.

"You can't be here!" exclaimed his guest.

Shifting his eyes forward, he nodded in greeting. "You'll find, upon further enquiry, this is my family's estate, and thus, I can be here."

Genevieve, mounted side saddle atop Philomena and looking most fetching in a rose riding habit, scoffed. "Impossible man. I meant this particular location. This is *my* place. Find your own spot to sprawl."

Stretching an arm across his bent knee, he said, "I claimed it first. Before you were born, I'd wager. Therefore, dibs." He popped the remainder of the biscuit in his mouth and returned his attention to the book.

Philomena pranced, indicative of her impatience for her rider to dismount or resume the ride.

"My father has let the entire estate," Genevieve said. "By that legality, this spot is *mine* until the lease ends."

Casting a wounded frown, he asked, "Would you so callously have me abandon my picnic?" Before she replied, he sat up and slipped a hand into the picnic basket with a gasp of surprise. "Oh my! We're in luck." Out he drew a second glass, into which he poured the sherry.

Genevieve harrumphed but did him the honor of preparing to dismount. He rose to offer his aid, but she was grounded and gathering her habit's train over her arm before he was halfway to her. She eyed the feast and him dubiously. With a nod, she accepted his hand to help her sit. At least she allowed him a few courtesies, he thought ruefully.

"One might suspect you of spying, Mr. Fitz-Stephens. How else would you know I was coming here? Hoping to antagonize me, I'm sure."

"Need I point out the obvious?" Returning to his side with a raised elbow and bent knee, he invited repose. "I was already here. It is you who have interrupted my picnic. By that token, you're the spy come to harass me." He saluted her with his sherry before taking a sip.

"You should be so fortunate."

"Your recalcitrant tone tells me you think my head is turned by… *spirited* women."

She huffed. "Why should I care what sort of woman turns your head? We're no longer betrothed; in case you need to be reminded."

"The more you protest, my darling girl, the more convinced I am you're here to charm me, however unorthodox your methods."

The blush on her cheeks belied her intentions. In brisk tones, she snapped, "You mistake my motive with your own. Why you think *my* head should be turned by sandwiches, cake, and biscuits is a mystery, for do you not know young ladies are far more swayed by aristocratic titles?"

"Just as gentlemen are most moved by demure young ladies. We love to be fawned over, complimented, plied with fans and batting eyelashes, the more simpering the better."

"And there I know you are wrong. I offer Diana as an example. She would never fawn or simper, and yet she secured her match in under a week."

"By that same token, *you* are wrong, for Mr. Thorpe has no aristocratic title."

"Yes, well, there are always exceptions, I suppose. *She* can be the exemption to the rule." Her cheeks still reflecting the shade of her riding habit, Genevieve tried one of the sandwiches.

Rolling onto his back, he stretched out both legs to cross his ankles with a creak of his calfskin boots, and then laced his fingers behind his head. Above him, a bright but cloud-covered sky speckled light through the canopy of leaves. He dared not glance her way. He need not even if he dared. That her gaze swept over him beneath her sooty lashes was a certainty. Her silence confirmed this.

Rafe questioned, "Which of us was more shocked about that pairing, do you think?"

"Most certainly I was. I concede I don't know Diana well. Perhaps I should not have been surprised had I known her better? But Mr. Thorpe took me quite by surprise. He's not an assertive gentleman, meek, really, so I can only assume it was Diana who pressed her attentions."

From the corner of his eye, he saw her sampling the sherry. "Headley and Diana were convinced Thorpe was here to steal you from me," he said. "They tried to intervene, the interesting consequence being Diana thrown together with Thorpe, all under our nose. Headley mistrusted Thorpe so deeply, I'm shocked he accepted the man's suit for his sister. But we can't know what was or was not said when our attentions were… otherwise engaged."

Genevieve tittered. "They thought Thorpe was trying to steal me?" Her titter increased to a bold laugh.

"Hardly a laughing matter. He *was*."

"Well, not quite. I was trying to convince him to steal me. He was less than cooperative."

"Ah, see? Proves my point." He waited for her curiosity to build. "Gentlemen prefer batting eyelashes to insolence."

A gurgle of anger bubbled across the picnic linen from him. Rafe held his composure for precisely twenty seconds before he lost it to mirth, tears welling from his laughter. Although she pouted and grumbled, she soon joined his laughter.

"It's for the best," she said. "I don't think I could ever marry someone like Thorpe. He is the kindest of men, but…."

Intrigued, he rolled back onto his side, resting his temple on his open palm. "You desire someone more assertive? More…"

"More skilled with a whip."

He choked as he swallowed and had to thump his chest to recover. Eyes watering, he coughed hoarsely, "Begging pardon?"

"You know, a good horseman. Handy with the ribbons and that."

"Ah. Mmm." With a grin, he said, "You should have fallen for Headley, then. I'm no slouch with the ribbons, but Headley could beat me in a race blindfolded. Exceptional rider and driver."

"But it is not Headley's seat I have been admiring."

Rafe's eyebrows shot up at this flirty admission. His grin deepened into vain smugness as he met her gaze and held it.

Although her gaze did not waver, she began to giggle. At first he thought it a shy affectation, part of her flirtation, a mock simper, in fact, but the more she giggled, the more self-conscious he became. His smugness shifted into a half-hearted chuckle before dipping into a frown. She soon covered her face with her hands and began laughing with far more hilarity than he thought reference to his seat warranted.

And then he felt it.

A nip at his hair. A soft tug. At first a coquettish bit of friskiness, but after a couple of caresses, the tug stung his scalp. Ducking with a swat of his hand, he turned to see what the devil was behind him. Genevieve's hearty laughter did nothing to help.

Standing over him, her muzzle nudging towards his hair for another go, was Philomena.

He dodged the nip and tried to shoo her away. She ignored him, enamored by his golden locks.

"Help?" Rafe rose to kneeling.

"Here's your chance," Genevieve said between hysterics. "You can prove to me what a dashing horseman you are." She squealed with laughter.

"Against this she-devil? I'd as soon pit my skills against an angry bull." He dodged the muzzle again. "Next time, I'll convince Lord Karras that Philly's the one for him. Would serve him right."

"She heard that. If you don't wish for a bald patch, you should apologize."

"I'm not apologizing to—" He tried to move the nibbling muzzle away with a gentle caress, but she shook him off and snapped at his hand. "My humble apologies, fair goddess. How fortunate am I to have my hair mistaken for fresh hay. You have done me the greatest honor."

Still enjoying the show, Genevieve clucked her tongue. The mare responded immediately, walking over to Genevieve to nuzzle her neck.

Rafe clasped his hands in a sign of gratitude before trying to comb his hair with his fingers. Genevieve spoke quietly to the horse. Whatever she said, Philomena appeared to understand, as the horse made her way to stand near Alfgar. With his picnic not turning out as he had planned, he settled back onto the linen and hid his chagrin behind the glass of sherry.

"How did your brothers fare?"

A change in subject. Good. He had little doubt *his* face now reflected the rose of her riding habit.

"I left Otis with a vial of smelling salts and Noel with a chamber pot. Young fools. If they're anything like their older brothers, yours truly included, they'll only do it once and learn their lesson. I'm thankful their *once* was in the company of Father rather than young lads who might make merry of the experience."

"I'm sorry they're suffering today."

"I'm not." Rafe tipped back his glass. "They'll know their limits now."

"Oh, but I thought Vitruvians preferred to be limitless." The coyness of her words had him barking a laugh, forgetting his embarrassment with the horse.

"Ho ho! You remembered my waffle." Wiping his glass clean, he tucked it back into the basket. "What would impress you most?"

She knit her brows. "What exactly are you asking? Between limitless and self-imposed limits?"

He shook his head, then with as playful a tone as he could muster, despite the gravity of the question—he still had a game to play, after all—he questioned, "More to the point, when are you going to admit you're in love with me?"

Her face expressed a myriad of emotions as she studied him, as if searching for his intention. Jest? Earnest? Tease? Provocation? Admission? Her expression questioned all possibilities.

After a brief interval of silence, her features smoothed, and she dimpled a smirk. "When you can prove your worthiness."

"Have I something more to prove?" He eyed the horses skeptically. "Handling temperamental mares aside, I'm quite the catch, you know. Wouldn't want me to get away. Would you?"

Genevieve batted her eyelashes. "On the contrary. I rather think *I'm* the catch." Rising from the sheet, she gathered her habit's train over her arm and challenged, "The question is, can you catch me?"

She darted towards Philomena.

Rafe was slow to comprehend. When it hit him, he scrambled up and leapt from the blanket, rushing forward, only to turn back and try to throw everything into the basket, not wanting to leave it, then cursed his folly and raced towards Alfie, leaving the picnic behind. By the time he mounted Alfie, she had already cantered off. He gave Alfie a squeeze with his legs and a word of encouragement. Alfie took off in pursuit.

Over her shoulder, she laughed, leading him a merry chase.

Then, as adroit a rider as she was, it was no chase for Alfie. Rafe held back, enjoying himself too much to catch her, keeping the distance enough to be convincing. As she circled back towards the woods, her bonnet flew free, and her hair unbound from its confines, flowing freely behind her in a whipping array of glorious curls. He had nothing of the sort to worry about. His hat remained behind with the picnic. The moment she realized she had lost her bonnet was the moment he seized. She slowed to glance at it, dancing, caught on the wind. Indecisive, she eyed the bonnet, then Rafe. Quick in the saddle, she urged Philomena to escape, leaving the bonnet behind. Rafe bolted forward.

Alfgar sidled Philomena, then slowed her with a cutting maneuver before moving ahead to block her path. Genevieve turned her mare one way then another, trying to pass. Rafe blocked each attempt. When she settled back with a toss of her curls, conceding his win, he guided his horse next to hers, then shimmied until his calf brushed her legs.

Philomena shied sideways away from him. Alfgar moved closer.

Rafe leaned to capture Genevieve's hands. "Gotcha'."

Arching her brows, she said, "I beg to differ. You've caught my horse, sir, but not me."

Freeing herself from his grasp, she urged her mare once more, leaving him in a cloud of her unruly laughter.

"That's what we get, Alfie, for being gentlemen. I think it's time we won this silly game, don't you?"

Alfie snorted.

Rafe counted to ten to give her ample headway. At zero, he bellowed a war cry and launched his Andalusian forward.

Leaning into the chase, Genevieve sped into a gallop, leaving kicked up clumps of earth in her wake as she laughed into the wind, gleeful to be in the lead.

Her glee did not linger long. Behind her came no friendly hoofbeats. She glanced back. No one pursued her. Slowing Philly, she looked furtively around and strained to listen. Only nature met her ears. Where was Rafe?

Hardly a chase if he was not on her heels. Had he stopped to retrieve her bonnet? Surely not. Or… No, he could not know her destination was a return to the picnic by the tower. A gamble if he assumed so and chose a shorter route, for she could easily ride elsewhere. She had half a mind to leave him behind for presuming her actions, but…

"We can beat him there, Philly. If he's taking a shortcut, it means he'll go through the woods. That'll slow his pace. Come on, girl!"

With a triumphant cry, she urged Philly forward in haste.

Not in a million years would she admit to Rafe this was the most fun she had ever had in her life, second only to their flirtatious quarrels.

By the time she reached the edge of the woods, she was breathing heavily, a bit sore in the rump, and grinning like a banshee — that was, until she saw Alfgar grazing and Rafe leaning against a tree, ankles crossed, eyes trained on his pocket watch.

"You are a foul cheat!" she accused. "How did you manage it? You couldn't have possibly beaten us!"

He pushed off the tree and offered to help her dismount, crinkles framing his eyes as he expressed his smugness.

"I most assuredly do not need your aid," she protested. "Now, confess. How did you arrive first?"

Ignoring her swatting hands, he wrapped his arms around her waist to pull her from Philomena. "Alfie is Pegasus in disguise. Did I never mention?"

She continued to swat at him, trying to free herself from his grasp. "Libertine! Lothario! Remove your hands at once!"

"You've not complained before," he teased as he tugged her off the saddle and into his arms.

Genevieve had no choice except to drape her arms around his neck as she slid down his torso, his chest vibrating with a deep chuckle. He made no moves to release her nor to deepen the intimacy. She wriggled for freedom.

"You cannot deny," he began, "I've caught you this time."

Trapped between him and Philly was certainly one way to define caught. "By cheating! That doesn't count. We'll need a second trial."

"Mmm. I'll grant you a second trial if you admit you're in love with me."

"Oh! That is unfair. You're trying to trick me." She struggled in vain.

Philomena, curse the beast, did not move, pinning Genevieve against Rafe. His chest rumbled again with another chuckle.

"And if I've fallen deeply in love with someone else in the past few days?" she pressed, however tremulous her voice.

"Jealousy won't work, I'm afraid. Not when your eyes tell me a different story."

His gaze was so intense, so close, she feared she may well swoon this time, no feint needed. He leaned in and kissed the tip of her nose.

Genevieve squeaked. "You're free to choose anyone, Rafe. Haven't you wanted to look about you?"

He inched back, releasing his embrace by slow measure. A crease formed between his brows, accompanied by a rueful squint.

Silently, he backed away. Then, steadily, he began packing everything into the basket. Genevieve tried to control her breathing, still flushed from their embrace, feeling like a fool for taking her tease too far, for pushing rather than accepting. Walking past him, her train gathered over her arm, she sat on the boulder and watched him. The trouble was knowing when enough was enough, for she liked their sparring and knew he did, as well, or so it had become clear to her over the course of the week. When was it playful sparring versus rejection?

As languid as his movements, he made short work of packing the basket, then secured it to Alfgar's saddle. Retrieving a few horse treats of some sort or another, he offered first to Alfgar, and then with that task complete, he approached Philomena and scratched her chin to offer her treats, as well. Genevieve wanted to break the silence but did not know what to say. No, that was not entirely true. She knew what she *could* say but feared the words more than anything. His actions spoke volumes, but could *he* not say the words first? So she could be sure? So she could know he was serious and not teasing? She had broken the betrothal so she could be certain, and yet he still could not say the words to her.

When she rose and made her way to him, searching for something to say, anything to break the silence, he looked up at her with bright, watering eyes, his arm slung over Philomena with affected sensibility. So moved by his emotions, so angry with herself for causing him to weep, she went to him, her own eyes burning with unshed tears.

With a hand on his sleeve, she said, "Oh, Rafe. I'm so sorry for ruining every tender moment. I—"

Rafe interrupted her, wheezing between gritted teeth, "I appreciate the sentiment but… your horse is standing on my foot."

Genevieve looked down. Philly's hoof rested proudly on Rafe's boot. Caught between laughing at the situation, chastising him for misleading her with his unshed tears, and berating herself for being a silly goose about *everything*, she swallowed her embarrassment and coaxed Philly to move. As soon as his boot was free, he sobbed a laughing note of gratitude and limped to the rock to sit.

Hands clasped in prayer and fingers pressed to her lips, Genevieve said, "I should send for help. Is your foot broken? Can you feel your toes?"

He dabbed his eyes with his handkerchief. "I can feel them well enough. No need to send for help. Aside from an inevitable hoof-sized bruise, I'm more worried about the damage to my boot."

"You would be. Insufferable man."

Joining him, she stood next to the boulder and studied the top of his head. Her hand trembled, but she reached over and ruffled his hair. She drew back her hand and waited for a response. When he did not immediately react, she combed her fingers through his hair, marveling at the silken texture.

"I'll need help standing," he said.

"Yes, yes, of course. Anything." She bent down to offer assistance.

Gingerly, he wrapped an arm across her shoulders and leaned his weight onto one foot to stand, hobbling as he righted himself.

"Let me help you to the horses," she suggested, then, "Does it hurt terribly?"

With a groan, he said, "Immeasurably. In fact, I think you'll have to kiss it and make it better."

Retreating, she began to say, "I beg your—"

But before the words left her lips, he captured her in his arms, dipped her, and kissed her.

Her world turned topsy-turvy. The hard press of his lips softened against hers in a tantalizing whirl of sensation. Her fingers dug into the musculature of his shoulders as he brushed his lips against hers before deepening the kiss. So intimate, so intoxicating, her toes curled. She clung tighter, wanting more, puckering to extend the kiss when he made to retreat. He obliged with a low chuckle that tickled her senses.

Sooner than she wished, he softened his hold and leaned back to help her regain her balance. He did not break the embrace quickly. With tender eyes, he studied her, his hand caressing the small of her back.

When he finally released her, he brought both hands up and cradled her face. Sinking his fingers into her bed of loose curls, he sighed. With a lingering look, he walked over to Philomena, then laced his hands to help Genevieve mount.

Foggy and tongue tied, she managed to say, "It worked."

He arched a brow as she stepped into his hands and was boosted onto the side saddle.

Adjusting her train to cover her ankles, she said, "You're not limping. I kissed it and made it better."

Before mounting Alfgar, Rafe tossed his head back with a laugh.

"Wait," she prompted as he readied his reins. "Aren't we going to talk about this?"

Donning his beaver hat, he winked at her and guided his horse towards the Priory. Over his shoulder he said as his parting words, "Only when you admit you're head over heels in love with me."

Chapter 33

Two days passed without incident. Rafe was champing at the bit to make an excuse to see her, but he wanted her to stew a little. She should wonder by of her own accord for her next fencing lesson. From there, Rafe would find a reason to venture to the Priory and make his presence known, complete with the continuation and further enaction of his plan, the *coup de grâce* for the final week.

A good plan. Until he received the letter.

Not the letter from Giles, which arrived the same day and had the family gathered in the drawing room to read and reread the correspondence, each family member having a turn to read aloud. Giles wrote of success in his expedition, a return within the next six months or sooner, and a surprise he would wait to share in person. A guessing game ensued for the best answer to this "surprise." So enraptured by Giles's letter, the well-worn and crumpled note for Rafe went unnoticed for some time.

Only as the Fitz-Stephenses dispersed to their own devices and Rafe went about his day, did he spy the letter on the salver in the entrance hall, buried beneath sundry ignored missives of less import.

Addressed to him, he took it into the parlor for privacy. The letter's deplorable condition told a story of misdirection and misadventure before finding its way to the correct personage. He flipped it over to eye the seal. Staring back at him was a griffin encircled by the too tiny and unreadable motto *Integra Lex Aequi Custos Rectique Magistra Non Habet Affectus Sed Causas Gubernat*. He need not be able to decipher the wax imprint to know what the words said. He knew them by heart. "Impartial justice, guardian of equity, mistress of the law, without fear or favor rules men's causes aright." The seal of Gray's Inn.

Heart thumping to the beat of a team of horses, he hooked his thumb beneath the wax-sealed fold, trying not to rip the paper. Unfolding, he held his breath as he read. His eyes combed the page thrice before he refolded and sat, steadying his breath and the trembling of his hand.

He was called to the Bar to serve as barrister for England and Wales.

His application for the Trinity Call ceremony had been accepted. The letter confirmed and congratulated, inviting him to take his oath. As it sank in, the elation boiled and bubbled. He stood. He sat. He stood again. He walked towards the parlor door, walked back to the sofa, walked to the door again. And then with an almighty cry, he rejoiced with a *whoop*. The family came running.

Rafe unfolded the letter once more and waved it. "I've been called! My application has been accepted! I'm a bloody barrister!"

Otis kindly pointed out, "Not yet. Gotta' attend the ceremony and all."

Mother embraced Rafe and peppered his temple with motherly kisses. "Ignore your brother." Then to said brother, "A technicality only, Otis."

"No, itan't," Otis argued. "Don't attend the ceremony, and he an't a barrister. Am I right?" He looked around him for confirmation.

Father leaned across the sofa to box Otis's ears, drawing laughter from the lot.

But then it sank in. Otis was right.

Rafe's smile faded. "Dear Lord. I'll never make it. The ceremony is July 18th. It'll take me at least a week, and that's if I leave at first light on the morrow and the stars are aligned and our glorious English weather is cooperative."

Noel chimed in with, "Take the mail coach. You'll be there in 24 hours, easy."

"My grandson will *not* take the mail coach," Gran protested with a shake of her stick. "Fitz-Stephenses do *not* take public transport." With a decisive nod, she added, "Nor do barristers."

Mother agreed, brushing Rafe's hair out of his eyes, clearly in a maternal mood.

Noel and Otis exchanged corroborating glances and shrugged.

"Take the gig. Spring the horses," Father said, rubbing the side of his nose.

Rafe shook his head. "It won't prove helpful if I break my neck trying to arrive on time. I'll take Alfgar. If the dashed letter had arrived last week, we could have arranged for a horse exchange. I would have made excellent time. No, I'll take Alfgar. We'll need most of today to prepare. Food and water for him in the saddle bags, at least until the first stop, will save time. With only the necessary rests along the way, we can make decent time."

He tried not to think about the thrown shoe from his ride here. This journey *had* to go smoothly.

If he missed, the next Call ceremony was not until Deferred Trinity in late October or the last ceremony in November. What a kick in the shin that would be to wait so long, assuming they allowed him after missing his first Call.

Within the hour, preparations for the trip were set into motion, and a footman was sent to the Priory with a message for the stables. Thankfully, Rafe need not pack much, only the necessities for travel, since he had left his London possessions in his wardrobe at Gray's Inn. As he rummaged through his bedchamber, tempted to ring for the valet to do the work for him, and feeling anxious and excited, and thus indecisive about what to bring, what to wear, what to do, a rush of panic flooded him — *Genevieve*.

His plan was not complete. He had only just begun! One week remained, and by that fact, *only* one week remained. He could not flee to London with things unsettled. Slade would suffer from apoplexy, and Genevieve may misconstrue Rafe's actions as a dismissal. Their relationship was at a tipping point. If he left, this could ruin everything, but if he attempted to confront her now, to push her into action, she could resist and run, undoing all his work over the past week and leaving him in a sticky wicket from which he may not be able to recover. He *needed* this second week to accomplish his goal.

Sitting on the edge of his bed, he sank his fingers into his hair and cradled his head. What the devil was he going to do?

The solace to his anguish was imagining marching into the Priory, scooping Genevieve over his shoulder, slinging her over Alfgar — or more appropriate into the gig as he confiscated it — and abducted her for the ride to London. How was that for a forced betrothal? He chuckled. He wagered he could win her heart during that journey.

If he were not a gentleman, he might be inclined towards that plan — desperate times and all. If it were earlier in the day, he could head to Exeter for a word with the bishop, secure a common license, and then slap that on a table before her as proof of his affection, although he would still be leaving for London tomorrow morning before a marriage ceremony could take place. Shame. He rather liked the slapdashery of it, the dramatic flair.

Arg! His choices were limited, at least if he wanted to win her heart without her doubts or fears or reservations getting in the way. He had today and only today. More problematic, today needed to be devoted to preparing for the journey and an early evening's sleep.

Groaning, he rose, gave his cravat a straighten in the mirror, and headed out for the Priory.

It was one thing to propose to a woman and reassure the father that the situation was in hand, and quite another to do so before one had completed the wooing process. Rafe could not be certain in any way she would accept. There had not been enough time. His plan was lacking a full week. Either those two days for her to mull over their picnic needed to do the trick — and if he had known, he would not have wasted those two days, desirous of her stewing or not — or Slade needed to be considerate and give him more time. His hope was on Slade more than Genevieve being receptive to his proposal. He would need to see Slade first to determine if he was going to put on the most romantic show of his life, complete with bended knee, or more simply, promise her romance upon his return.

While he was at the Priory, he could visit the stables.

He reached the front door and used the knocker without sparing the iron. A footman answered, saw it was Rafe, and opened the door wide without question.

The butler peeked into the entrance hall. "Master Fitz-Stephens. How may I be of service?"

"I'm here to see Mr. Slade. If you could press this is a matter of urgency, as well as delicacy, I'd be appreciative."

"I'm afraid, sir, Mr. Slade is from home, as is the family."

Rafe exhaled with a puff of his cheeks. "Do you know how long they'll be away? I can wait in the drawing room. Or, if you think it'll be longer than a wait would permit, you could send word to the dower house when they return."

"If you'll forgive me, sir, for being the bearer of ill-tidings, they'll be away the remainder of the day. Sir Courtney has invited them for dinner."

"For dinner. Then.... they could return before dusk." Under his breath he added, "Not if I know Sir Courtney." A little louder he vented his frustration, "This will not do. This simply will not do."

"A note, sir? I'll see he receives it." Then with a knowing glint in his eyes, he said, "A discreet message for the young mistress would, also, be sure to reach her."

With a nod, Rafe conceded, "That will have to do. I can only hope for understanding."

The butler led Rafe into the study so he could dash off whatever note he wished. "May I be permitted to offer congratulations, sir?"

"Word travels fast. Naturally it does. The stables are probably in chaos preparing for my departure. Yes, you may offer felicitations, and I will receive them with a smile and a jig — as soon as your back is turned, of course," he added with a wink.

"Very good, sir."

The butler ducked out of the study long enough for Rafe to compose a letter to Slade explaining the situation, assuring him of his faithfulness, and begging for a brief reprieve, whereupon he would make good on his promise as soon as he returned. He folded this, then started a new note for Genevieve. With this, he struggled. Confess undying devotion? Promise he would resume paying her court upon his return — which somehow sounded more like a threat when he tried to write the words?

Ah, it was no use. He did not know what to say that would not give up the game or presume an intimacy she would deny, not with her believing the betrothal had been dissolved.

After a few false starts, he drew a fresh slip and wrote,

I must away to London to answer my Call to the Bar. When next we meet, I hope to hear your confession. You know to what I refer. Your most devoted servant.

That should work in his favor. He admired his cleverness before folding the letter and flourishing a G on the front of the missive. Before leaving the Priory for the stables, he placed both notes in the butler's hands to ensure each party received their note in as timely a fashion as possible.

Not how he had wished to handle the situation. This left too much unresolved, too much reliance on Slade's goodwill and Genevieve's patience. More desirable would have been to settle matters himself now and tête-à-tête. If he had more time, he would ride to Eurwendin and invite himself into Sir Courtney's home for the express purpose of begging an audience with the man's guests. Alas.

Once the ceremony concluded, he would choose the Western circuit, hoping that was pleasing to the parties in question, arrange for his possessions at Gray's Inn to be sent to Devonshire, and then return post-haste so he could perfect his pursuit of his fair damsel.

Rafe had done what he could for the present. Now to see to the preparations of his departure, eat a hearty meal, and retire early.

Chapter 34

The carriage lumbered up the drive, the evening dark, Theia's snores the only sounds from within, competing against the clomp of horse hooves and the creaks and groans of the carriage. Genevieve stared out into the darkness. Next to her, Mama nodded off, her head rolling onto Genevieve's shoulder before rousing with a jerk. Papa stared out the opposite window. Cecilia was the only one still lively, nudging Genevieve's shin from the bench opposite and making faces.

It had been a long, never-ending day, and a long, never-ending evening. Midnight was surely upon them. Not that dinner with Sir Courtney had been anything other than enjoyable, simply long. The Slades were unaccustomed to late evening hours. Sir Courtney had no children and no wife to keep his guests occupied while he and Papa consorted about rambles she did not think Papa would ever take and other topics of little interest to the ladies, turning an already lingering evening into a tedious one.

Her attention had wandered, mostly in the direction of Rafe. He had not happened on her in two days. Two days! Yes, she had seen him at church, but they had not exchanged more than pleasantries. Was he waiting for her to speak first? Was he angry she had not confessed her feelings? Was it a game to him? Oh, she did not know what to think. Her fencing lesson fast approached. She could seek him out then and gauge the weather, so to speak.

Rocking to a stop — and sending Mama rolling forward until Genevieve tugged her back — the carriage pulled in front of the house. Home at last. A washbasin, a nightrail, and a pillow were top of her list of most desirable things, aside from Rafe, of course. What was it that Roman poet had said? Absence makes the heart grow fonder, she believed. Two days was hardly a period of absence. But to have left her with such a command as he had done!

Genevieve accepted the footman's hand and stepped down from the carriage. The butler waited by the open front door.

Just as she stepped over the threshold, she heard the butler saying to Papa, "…an urgent letter, sir. Promised Master Fitz-Stephens you would receive it without delay."

Cecilia elbowed Genevieve. "I wager he's decided I'm the young lady for him. Couldn't wait until morning. Lost your chance!" Smothering her humor with a hand, she padded into the stairwell, leaving Genevieve to scowl after her.

Too curious to pretend she had not overheard, she followed Papa into his study.

Without acknowledging his shadow, he retrieved the note propped in bold view on the desk. He remained silent for an agonizing stretch of time. The letter held between his hands, he stared at it, unflinching, unresponsive. The stretch allowed a million and one thoughts to dance in her head. Rafe wished an audience to offer his hand, this time by his own voli-tion. Rafe had a change of heart and wished to pursue Cecilia. Rafe thought it best that Lord Karras be per-suaded to press his suit.

So silly for her to think any of these. If any were true, Rafe would have waited until the morning and said them himself. It must be something unimport-ant, likely about the horse sale, certainly that if he expressed it in a letter rather than in person. But then… why the urgency?

"Well," Papa said at last, "it would seem your young man has decided London is the best course for his immediate future."

Genevieve flinched. "I don't understand."

Papa flicked the paper. "Says here he's off to London. By morning twilight, he'll be gone." With a sharp look at Genevieve, he said, "Must not have been given a reason to stay."

"But… I…" she stammered, feeling faint.

"Sure, sure, he'll return. At some point. Family home and that. But to what end?" Tossing the letter on the desk, he went to the cabinet and began pour-ing a glass of brandy. "A man knows when he's not wanted," he muttered.

Her vision blurred.

Before she made a silly goose of herself, she ran from the study and up to her bedchamber.

Just as she was about to fling herself onto the bed, a voice from the dressing table said, "Should have confessed."

Genevieve stumbled over her feet, clasping the bedpost in time to keep herself from falling face first onto the rug. Seated in the chair, feet propped up

with ankles crossed on the table, sat a most unladylike and smirking Cecilia, wafting an unfolded letter
in her hand.

Sniffing the paper, she said, "Smells *divine*, strik-
ingly like a gentleman we both know."

With a wipe of her wet cheeks, Genevieve lunged
forward. "Give me that," she cried, trying to snatch
the letter from her sister.

Cecilia played an infuriating game of keep away
before Genevieve managed to wrangle it from her,
crumpling the side of the letter in the process. Smooth-
ing it against the table, Genevieve read.

Confusion first. Then a single *ha* of laughter. Followed by relief. And then another swell of panic.

She did not fully understand what the letter
meant. Well, she did, but she did not know what it
meant as far as the future. When next they met? In a
year? In a month? Papa knew something she did not,
something Rafe had not written in this letter, something that gave Papa the impression Rafe had chosen
the Old Bailey rather than matrimony, something that
indicated Rafe would not return soon. *This* letter did
not deny those possibilities, but it felt more hopeful,
as though he were dashing to London on a quick
errand and might return any day.

That was not what he had written, however, nor
was that what Papa had led her to believe.

Cecilia poked her in the arm. "What confession?"

Genevieve swatted at her, rereading the letter
again, trying to understand what it meant. Had he
chosen the Old Bailey? Had he waited the two days,
and when she did not go to him, he took that as her
answer and made his choice?

Oh, she did not know!

"*What* confession?" Cecilia urged, then with suspicion, "Are you in an interesting condition?"

Jerking her attention to Cecilia, Genevieve coughed an incredulous laugh. "Am I *what*?"

"You know…." Cecilia crossed her arms and arched her eyebrows.

Genevieve was about to give her sister a firm set down when it occurred that Cecilia could not know *what* an interesting condition referred to, most likely hearing it whispered in the village. She probably thought it meant something along the lines of being in love.

"My confession is for Rafe's ears only, nosy blowsy."

"Seems to me you've lost your chance to confess to him. Off to London, he says. I wager your cerulean scarf he won't return. No reason, is there? Only a curmudgeonly spinster."

"I'm *not* a spinster, nor am I a curmudgeon. Doesn't speak well for you, either, if he has no reason to return."

Cecilia shrugged. "Now. Tell me what confession would have kept him here."

Genevieve sighed herself over to the side of the bed. What confession, indeed. What confession she did not make to him, the only words he needed to hear to help him realize there was more to life than pursuing a profession. Was it selfish for her to want him to stay? She should be celebrating—he had received his Call to the Bar! A momentous moment. His dreams were coming true. But he would not choose the Western circuit if he did not believe she loved him. He would move to London forever.

Ignoring her sister, she fought against the welling tears. She would *not* cry. There must be a way to seize the moment. If she could but think of a way, she would act. She would *not* lose him, not of her own making.

Chapter 35

Rafe awoke with a start. His eyes darted in the darkness of his bedchamber. All was quiet. Must have been a dream. Settling back into the comfort of his pillow, he closed his eyes and relaxed.

Thump.

He tensed and sat up, searching the room for movement, light, anything. Being a moonless night, he could not make out much in the room. Only the faintest of starlight shone in the sky through the open window. He strained to listen.

Creak.

The sound came from outside the window. His first thoughts were of Otis and Noel. One or both were up to no good. Should he stop them? Hushed voices could be heard; he would guess from the ground. Groaning, he tossed back the sheets. Not the best night for them to choose mischief.

The creaking increased double-time, like someone ascending the stairs, only outside his window rather than outside his bedchamber door. Then the creaking stopped. A furtive whisper hissed from below. A verbal exchange occurred, two quarrelling whispers, followed by silence. Creaking resumed.

Rafe, still in bed, stared with furrowed brows at the window. What the devil were his brothers up to?

The faint silhouette of a head appeared an inch above the windowsill. A flailing hand followed. Then a squeak. An urgent whisper from the ground pre-empted a rising mass of curls as the owner of said curls struggled to gain purchase of the windowsill.

Lacing his fingers behind his head, he leaned against the headboard and watched the theatrical, thoroughly entertained and endlessly curious about the turn of events. A *coup de théâtre* if ever he saw one.

Not long did he have to wait before an arm hooked itself over the windowsill and hauled up the body that went with it—lovingly silhouetted against the night sky; the only disappointment being the missing moonlight to highlight the assets. He held motionless when his burglar peered into the room. Satisfied by the stillness, the figure mounted the sill.

Only when one leg was solidly over with a foot planted on the rug and two hands holding steady did Rafe speak.

"What ho! Am I being burgled?"

The figure froze, lost her balance, and tumbled into the room with a screech.

Throwing his legs over the side of the bed, he rushed to the fallen shadow to offer his hand.

The shadow hissed, "You s-s-startled me! I could have fallen to my death!"

"Says the burglar creeping into my chamber window in the dead of night." He helped his mid-night caller stand. "Shall I light a candle, *mademoiselle*?"

"No!" She choked on the word.

"We're to conference in the dark?"

"You're not dressed," came the strangled words.

"I most certainly am. In my nightshirt. One moment and I'll don a banyan." As he did just this, he said, "You know, if you're taking up sneaking into gentlemen's bedchambers at night, you ought not be shocked to find them in a state of undress. Stands to reason, yes?" Returning to her side, he snaked an arm around her waist and pulled her against him. She protested but only halfheartedly. "What is it you wish to burgle? No, wait, don't tell me. My heart?"

"You are ruining my pretty speech," she protested petulently.

He nuzzled her neck, his arms tightening. "By all means, orate."

Perhaps unfair of him to disturb her concentration, but really, what did she expect after tumbling headlong into his bedchamber in the wee hours? He brushed his lips against her neck, working his way up and along the curve of her face, tracing her beauty with his amor.

"I—I—you—you can't go to London," she stammered.

"No?" he asked as he kissed the corners of her mouth.

"No! I mean, not until… not until I make my confession. And then… then…"

He smothered whatever she was trying to say with his lips.

When she melted against him, he prompted, "You were saying?"

"Mmm. That was lov—"

He returned to her lips again for a deeper kiss. Only when she was quite breathless did he ease his ardor. He did not, however, release her, merely softened his embrace.

With a nudge of his nose against her cheek, he reminded, "You were confessing something, I believe. Explaining why I shouldn't go to London."

"You should. Yes, you must, but not to stay. That is, not unless you wish to. What I have to say might change that, but… do you wish to go to London?"

"Genevieve, love, we are *in pari delicto*. Let us not equivocate, not now. I'm leaving for London in a few hours for my Call ceremony. When I return, and believe me, I will return with all the haste Alfgar will afford me, I'm going to marry you. Why? Because I'm so deeply in love with you, I would rather a lifetime of three-legged races by your side than a seat at the King's Bench. Deeply *in* love doesn't do my feelings justice, does it? I *love* you, more so when you quarrel with me and lead me a merry dance, but most especially because I know you love me, too, though you're too proud to admit it."

"Am not," she protested with a giggle as he returned to kissing the side of her neck.

"Not in love with me?" He nibbled her earlobe.

"Of *course* I love you. I meant I'm not too proud. And you're a dastardly villain to have stolen my confession from me!" She pinched his arm. "*I* was to say it first!"

"You did."

"What? No, I didn't." Her words weakened into a soft sigh as he continued his ministrations.

"Mmm. Yes, you did. When you climbed over the windowsill."

"Oh? Did I?" The words were whispered on another breathy exhale.

"*Amor vincit omnia*," he said.

As he parted his lips to translate, another head appeared over the windowsill.

A shrill squeal shattered their romance. "Genevieve! You were supposed to confess your interesting condition, not *kiss* him!"

Rafe arched a perplexed eyebrow at Miss Cecilia first, then turned back to question Genevieve. Interesting condition?

The latter pressed two fingers to his lips. This time, it was she who was interrupted. His bedchamber door swung open to Gran holding a candlestick, his parents behind her, waving various items that might be used as defense against a burglar, and both his brothers ogling at the *two* women in Rafe's bedchamber.

Rafe sighed. "Oh, dear me. It appears we've been compromised."

Genevieve said, "You'll have to marry me now." Before anyone could respond, least of all Rafe, she wrapped her arms around his neck and kissed him to seal their betrothal for all to see.

Epilogue

One year later

"What do you think?" Rafe asked Genevieve. She surveyed the modest manor with a critical eye but did not immediately reply.

He boasted, "*I* think it the perfect home. And we both know, I'm always right."

With a rueful wrinkle of her nose to Rafe, she said, "It'll do."

"It'll do? It'll do! It comes with a steward to do all the work! How are you not impressed?"

"I'll be impressed if Papa stays here a full year."

Rafe tossed his gaze to the sky. "There is no pleasing you, Mrs. Fitz-Stephens." Draping an arm around her shoulder, he tugged her close to kiss her temple. "Let us both hope he stays here indefinitely because he has already purchased it. Papers signed, hands shaken, done and dusted."

"He can always travel if he becomes restless."

"Precisely my point."

"I think he'll like living near Sir Courtney. The two are thick as thieves." She squeezed his waist. "Oh, Rafe. I don't know how you managed it, but you've truly done it. You've convinced my father to settle down at last. Now, Cecilia and Theia can have consistency and a home of their own."

"My part was far more selfish, you realize. I want our home to ourselves. Of the six months since our purchase, we've had exactly two weeks without your family, and that was five months ago. I'm ready for them to *move out*."

"But… Mama has been so helpful with the redecorating. *You* said you liked the silk paper hangings she chose for the drawing room."

He growled. "There's an important task I've been needing to see to that can't be done with them living under our roof."

"What's that?"

"Get them out of our house, and you'll find out."

"You're so insensitive! I think we should help them redecorate their new manor before they move in. They can stay with us a little longer—unless you tell me what's so important. That *might* spur me to action."

"You're not allowed to contradict *everything* I say and call it flirting. I'll accept *half* but not a contradiction more." Guiding her back to the horses for the journey from Eurwendin back to Grant Lindis, he poked, just so she would quarrel again. "Besides, as fond as I am of my in-laws, I refuse to have children until *our* home is guestless. Thus, the sooner they move, the better."

"Children? Rafe! You cannot be serious. We've only been married nine months, and you've only been an active circuit barrister for ten. We aren't possibly ready! I'm not at all ready, not for *children*. Would five years from now not sound more harmonious? Ten even?"

"Twaddle! I'm ready now. Children in the nursery, embroidery by the fire while I lounge lazily in slippers and banyan… I might invest in a pipe."

"But you don't smoke."

"No one says it has to be lit."

"A dog too?"

"Quite."

Genevieve roared with laughter. "Only yesterday you wanted to travel for the next six months."

"But that was only because you said you wanted to settle into domestic bliss."

Removing her bonnet, she swatted him with it. "Can you never be serious?"

"Contradictions work both ways, love." He winked. "You want me to be serious, eh? I can be serious." Helping her mount onto Philomena, he glanced up at her with his most somber expression, only the tilt at the corner of his lips belying his humor. "Tomorrow, your family moves into *their* house — my foot is firm. I'm more ready than I have words to describe because we have a *serious* task to attend to, beginning the moment they step over the threshold, their backs to our humble abode."

"Don't leave me in suspense."

He did just that as he mounted Alfgar and began an ambling walk down the drive. Not until they reached the gatehouse did he say, "I'm determined, by the end of our first week, to have made love to you in every room — with my poetry, of course." He added under his breath, "By the end of the first day, more like."

"Mmm. I do love poetry," she replied with a flirty smile. "Well…" she drawled, "while we're being serious, I hope you *are* ready for children because…. I might be in an interesting condition."

Rafe drew Alfgar to a stop and turned to stare at her in horror-struck fascination.

With a twinkle in her eyes, she said, "You know… the interesting condition of being *in love*." She cackled at her jest, a vexing affectation she knew ribbed him.

Rafe did not immediately flick the reins. Instead, he studied her until he was satisfied he read the mischievous twinkle accurately. "Your eyes are telling me more than you're saying."

Casting him a sly grin, she said, "If you want to know what my eyes are saying, you'll have to catch me first." With a sudden burst, she urged Philomena forward, leaving Rafe in stunned silence and a cloud of dust.

With a pat to Alfie's neck, he began, "As the Romans would say on the verge of battle…" then finished with a thunderous war cry, "'*nobiscum Deus*!'" Feeling inordinately satisfied with his life, he launched Alfgar after Genevieve, hot on her heels.

A Note from the Author

Dear Reader,

Thank you for purchasing and reading this book. If you're interested in exploring some of the research that went into this book and others, check out my research blog: https://www.paullettgolden.com/bookresearch

Supporting indie writers who brave self-publishing is important and appreciated. I hope you'll continue reading my novels, as I have many more titles to come.

I humbly request you review this book on Amazon with an honest opinion. Reviewing elsewhere is additionally much appreciated.

One way to support writers you've enjoyed reading, indie or otherwise, is to share their work with friends, family, book clubs, etc. Lend books, share books, exchange books, recommend books, and gift books. If you especially enjoyed a writer's book, lend it to someone to read in case they might find a new favorite author in the book you've shared.

Connect with me online: www.paullettgolden. com, www.facebook.com/paullettgolden, www.x.com/paullettgolden, and www.instagram. com/paullettgolden, as well as Amazon's Author Central, Goodreads, BookBub, and LibraryThing.

All the best,
Paullett Golden

About the Author

Celebrated for her complex characters, realistic conflicts, and sensual portrayal of love, Paullett Golden writes historical romance for intellectuals. Her novels, set primarily in Georgian England, challenge the genre's norm by starring characters loved for their imperfections and idiosyncrasies. The writing aims for historical immersion into the social mores and nuances of Georgian England. Her plots explore human psyche, mental and physical trauma, and personal convictions. Her stories show love overcoming adversity. Whatever our self-doubts, *love will out.*

Paullett Golden completed her post-graduate work at King's College London, studying Classic British Literature. Her Ph.D. is in Composition and Rhetoric, her M.A. in British Literature from the Enlightenment through the Victorian era, and her B.A. in English. Her specializations include creative writing and professional writing. She has served as a University Professor for nearly three decades and is a seasoned keynote speaker, commencement speaker, conference presenter, workshop facilitator, and writing retreat facilitator.

As an ovarian cancer survivor, she makes each day count, enjoying an active lifestyle of Spartan racing, powerlifting, hiking, antique car restoration, drag racing, butterfly gardening, competitive shooting, and gaming. Her greatest writing inspirations, and the reasons she chose to write in the clean historical romance genre, are Jane Austen, Charlotte Brontë, and Elizabeth Gaskell.

Connect online

paullettgolden.com
facebook.com/paullettgolden
x.com/paullettgolden
instagram.com/paullettgolden

www.ingramcontent.com/pod-product-compliance
Lightning Source LLC
Chambersburg PA
CBHW031422240626
47154CB00001B/152